Praise for
Hello from the Gillespies

"Your three young adult kids are screwups, your handsome husband's made some rotten choices, and menopause isn't your friend. Do you give up and settle in with a DVD of *The Thorn Birds*? In the face of quotidian family hell, outback wife Angela Gillespie has a different approach. With warmth, vivid characters, and a sharp eye toward observing twenty-first-century life, Monica McInerney isn't just one of my favorite writers from Down Under but from anywhere." —Sally Koslow, author of *The Widow Waltz*

Praise for
The House of Memories

"*The House of Memories* is a suspenseful, deeply emotional story of a woman's journey to save herself from drowning in grief. Its exploration of the depths of heartbreak is unblinkingly honest, yet ultimately, it's a celebration of the power of family and connection to heal and inspire hope. An unforgettable read." —*New York Times* bestselling author Susan Wiggs

"Beautifully composed of equal parts soul and wit, *The House of Memories* is a deeply affecting novel about the anguish that breaks us and the relationships that can put us back together. Monica McInerney's tale of a family struggling to move forward in the aftermath of one terrible moment in time is everything that a powerful story of healing from grief should be. Its heart is huge, its pulse palpable, and its narrators irresistible. I read it voraciously." —Erika Marks, author of *The Guest House*

"The twists and turns of modern families are explored in this warm novel, which will have you reaching for the tissue box. This will keep [McInerney's] longtime fans happy and make her many new ones." —*Woman's Day* (Australia)

"A compelling tale that is ultimately uplifting." —*Sunday Mail* (Australia)

continued . . .

MONICA McINERNEY

HELLO from the GILLESPIES

A NOVEL

 NEW AMERICAN LIBRARY

New American Library
Published by the Penguin Group
Penguin Group (USA) LLC, 375 Hudson Street,
New York, New York 10014

USA | Canada | UK | Ireland | Australia | New Zealand | India | South Africa | China
penguin.com
A Penguin Random House Company

First published by New American Library,
a division of Penguin Group (USA) LLC

First Printing, November 2014

LIBRARY OF CONGRESS CATALOGING-IN-PUBLICATION DATA:

McInerney, Monica.
Hello from the Gillespies: a novel / Monica McInerney.
pages cm
ISBN 978-0-451-46672-3 (paperback)
1. Domestic fiction.   I. Title.
PR9619.4.M385H45 2014
823'.92—dc23   2014023486

Printed in the United States of America
10 9 8 7 6 5 4 3 2 1

Set in Bell MT
Designed by Spring Hoteling

In memory of a wonderful woman,
Dympna Dolan of Tatestown, County Meath, Ireland

HELLO

from the

GILLESPIES

ONE

It was December first. Angela Gillespie did as she'd done on that date for the past thirty-three years. She sat down at her desk before dinner and prepared to write her annual Christmas letter.

After doing so many, she had the process down to a fine art. It was a matter of leafing through her diary to recall the year's main events, writing an update about each member of the family—herself, her husband and their four children—attaching a photo or two, then sending it off.

She'd written her first Christmas letter the same year she was married. Transformed from single traveler Angela Richardson of Forest Hill, London, to newlywed Mrs. Nick Gillespie of Errigal, a sheep station in outback South Australia, she couldn't have been further from her old life, in distance or lifestyle. She'd decided an annual letter was the best way of keeping in contact with her friends and relatives back home. As the years went by, she'd added Nick's relatives, their neighbors and her new Australian friends to the mailing list. It now went to more than a hundred people worldwide.

Her early letters had been in traditional form, typed on an old typewriter on their big kitchen table, then taken into Hawker, the nearest town (almost an hour's drive away), photocopied and posted. It was much easier these days, the letters sent instantly via the wonder of e-mail. Even so, she still printed out paper copies and kept them stored in the filing cabinet beside the desk.

She knew the children found the whole idea mortifying— they, and Nick, had stopped reading the letters long ago— but perhaps in years to come they might like to see them. Angela hoped so. She secretly thought of them as historical documents. All the facts of their lives were there, after all, recorded in brief dispatches. She'd read back through them all only recently.

She'd written about her first years of marriage: "Nick and I couldn't be happier! I am loving my new life on the land too. I can now name five species of native birds by their calls alone, four varieties of gum trees by their bark, and last week I drove a tractor for the first time. There's hope for this London-born city girl yet!" She wrote about the arrival of the twins less than a year after their wedding day: "We already knew it would be twins, but it was still an incredible surprise to see two of them. One is so dark; the other is so fair; both are so beautiful. We're naming them after my grandmothers, Victoria and Genevieve." Three years later, she wrote about Lindy's arrival: "A third girl! Another beautiful brunette. The twins can't wait to get their hands on their new little playmate. I get to name her too (Nick and I struck a deal on our wedding night: I name any girls; he names any boys). I've chosen my favorite name from Shakespeare—Rosalind. The twins are already calling her Lindy!" The next two decades of updates were about outback station life, family holidays, academic results, hobbies, pets and funny incidents involving the girls, each report chatty and cheery.

Eleven years ago, she'd included a piece of news that she suspected had shocked her readers as much as it had her. At the age of forty-four, she was pregnant again. She'd thought she was menopausal. She'd discovered she was almost five months pregnant when a routine visit to the doctor led to an unexpected pregnancy test and an even more unexpected result. Two days after the birth, breaking with tradition, she'd sent out a special midyear e-mail to everyone on her mailing list. *It's a boy!!! Our first son!!! Nick gets to name one at last!!!!*

She'd used far too many exclamation marks, she noticed afterward. Postbirth endorphins at work, she presumed. Either that or delayed shock at the names Nick had chosen for their son. At her hospital bedside, he'd confessed he had promised his long-deceased and sentimental grandfather that he would name any future son after the first Gillespies—two male cousins—to come from Ireland to Australia in the 1880s. Which was why their fourth (and definitely final) child was baptized Ignatius Sean Aloysius Joseph Gillespie.

One of Nick's friends had been very amused. "He'll either be the first Australian Pope or end up running a New York speakeasy."

At first Angela tried to insist everyone call him Ignatius, but it was a losing battle. She'd long realized that the shortening of names was a national pastime in Australia. He was Iggy within a day of his baptism. A week later, even that was shortened. He'd been called Ig ever since.

She could hear his voice now, floating down the hall from the kitchen. The homestead was big, with six bedrooms, two living rooms and a high-ceilinged dining room, all linked by the long hall, but sound still carried well. Ig and Lindy were playing—attempting to play—a game of Scrabble before dinner. Angela could also hear the faint strains of Irish music coming from the dining room. She knew Nick was in there working on his family research. Over the past six months, the large polished table had slowly become covered in stacks of hardback books on aspects of Australian and Irish history. Not just books, but also shipping records, hand-drawn family trees and photographs. They weren't just in the dining room either. The office too. In fact, every surface in the house had started to accumulate history journals or family tree paraphernalia of one form or another. The previous week Angela had searched for her car keys for nearly an hour before finding them beneath a pile of ancestry magazines.

Beside her, the six o'clock news jingle sounded from the radio. Angela blinked. She'd better get a move on if she was to send her letter tonight. She clicked on her template document, with its border of Christmas trees already in place, along with her traditional opening line in Christmassy red and green letters ("Hello from the Gillespies!") and equally festive farewell ("A Very Merry Christmas from Angela and all the gang!"). All she had to do now was fill in the blank middle section with her family news.

One minute passed, then another. The words just wouldn't come. Perhaps she should break with tradition and choose the photos first. She opened the folder of digital shots she'd collected over the past twelve months. She usually sent a group one, but the family hadn't all been together and in front of a camera for nearly two years. Could she just send separate and recent photos of each of them instead?

She clicked through the possibilities, starting with the twins. No, Victoria wouldn't be happy with any of those going into wide circulation. *Wide* being the operative word, unfortunately. Not that Angela would ever say it to her, but Victoria had put on a *lot* of weight since she'd moved to Sydney nearly two years earlier. Comfort eating, Angela suspected, after the stressful time she'd had in her work as a radio producer. She still looked lovely, though, Angela thought. Like a pretty, rosy-cheeked milkmaid, with her blond hair curling to her shoulders, and her blue eyes. But she might not appreciate Angela's sending out photos just at the moment.

As for Genevieve—the most recent photo she'd e-mailed from New York wasn't really suitable for public viewing either. For a hairdresser, and especially a hairdresser working in the glamorous American film and TV world, Genevieve took a very devil-may-care approach to her own hair. She looked like she was on the way to a fancy dress party in this latest shot, her newly acquired bright blue dreadlocks tied in a loose knot on top of her head, her dark eyes heavy with eyeliner, as usual, and alight with mischief, also as usual. She'd explained it all in her e-mail. A hairdresser friend had needed to practice dreadlock extensions for a film she was working on and Genevieve had volunteered as the guinea pig. *It's only temporary, promise!* she'd written. *Thank God for that!* Angela had e-mailed straight back. *Ig said to tell you that you look like a feral Smurf.* Genevieve had been very amused by that. Genevieve was very amused by most things.

There were several recent photos of Lindy, but unfortunately she looked like a prisoner on the run in most of them, wild-eyed and panicky. The camera really didn't lie, Angela thought. Poor Lindy *was* a bag of nerves these days. Her general air of disarray wasn't helped by the fact she'd taken to wearing her long brown hair in two messy bunches, like a little girl. It was the in fashion in Melbourne circles, she'd told Angela. Which circles? Angela had wondered. Kindergarten? She hadn't said it aloud. She'd learned the hard way over the years that there was no teasing Lindy about her appearance. Or about anything, really.

At least there were dozens of photos of Ig to choose from. He loved being in front of a camera. But none of them was suitable either. His dark red curls badly needed a cut and she hadn't gotten around to it yet, deciding to wait until Genevieve and her scissors were home again. In the meantime, he looked more like her fourth daughter than her only son. If she attached one of those photos to her Christmas letter, she'd receive a disapproving e-mail from Nick's aunt

Celia. Celia had very strict ideas about suitable haircuts for boys. Celia had very strict ideas about everything.

As for recent photos of herself and Nick together . . . It felt like they'd hardly been in the same room for months, let alone in front of the same camera. She turned and looked at the back wall of the office. Thirty-two photos of her and Nick looked back at her. The photos were another tradition she had started the year they were married. An annual photo of the two of them in the same position, standing in front of the homestead gate, the big stone house behind them, that huge sky above them, all space and light. Each year she'd sent one print back home to her parents in London and framed another for this wall. As the years had gone by, the children had appeared in the photos with them too. Angela stood now and looked at each of them in turn. Not at her own image, but at Nick standing to her left in every photo, six foot one to her five foot five.

He hadn't changed much over the years, as tall, lean and tanned in the most recent photo as he was in the earlier ones. She reached for the first photo, studying it closely, clearly remembering this early moment of their married lives. It had taken them eight tries to get the self-timing camera to work properly. They'd been about to give up when it clicked. She was looking straight at the camera, wearing a cornflower-blue cotton dress the same color as her eyes, her hair a mass of black curls, her smile wide, if on the verge of frozen, after so many attempts to get the shot. Beside her, Nick was dressed in dark jeans and a white shirt, the sleeves rolled up. He wasn't only smiling but laughing, completely relaxed, indulging her, gazing down at her with such amusement. Such pride. Such love.

She felt that jolt inside her again. Like a sudden pain, a pang. She still couldn't put an exact name on it. Was it sadness? Fear? Confusion? All of those and something else. It was the closest she'd felt to homesickness since she was a child. A longing for someone. The feeling of missing them, wanting them so badly that it physically hurt. It was how she had felt about Nick for months now. She couldn't understand it, no matter how much she tried. How could it be that her husband could be physically so close to her every day, beside her in bed every night, yet so far away, so distant, so—

"Ha! I win again!"

The cheer from the kitchen interrupted her anxious thoughts. They would get her nowhere; she knew that already. She also needed to concentrate on her letter. She decided to forget about sending individual photos. She'd do what she'd done with her previous letter and attach a family group shot from a few years ago. She hoped no one would notice she, Nick and the girls all looked younger and that Ig appeared to be shrinking rather than growing.

Back at the computer, a chime alerted her to an incoming e-mail. She opened it, secretly glad of another distraction. *Thank you, Angela, our Outback Angel!!!!* the subject line read. It was from an elderly couple in Chicago, just home after their once-in-a-lifetime trip to Australia, including a week staying on Errigal.

Angela had joined the outback station stay program thirteen years earlier, after the three girls had left home, and before Ig had arrived. It had initially been a financial decision. The drought had hit them hard; the wool industry had collapsed. Like all their neighbors, they had needed some extra income. While she'd often helped out with the practical side of station life, Nick had never discussed the station's finances with her, despite her frequent requests to be involved. Angela had known, though, that every extra dollar would be useful. To her own surprise, she'd discovered she didn't have a flair for just hosting visitors and tour guiding, but for promotion too. She'd joined forces with local tourism associations, advertising Errigal's isolation and beauty wherever she could. She'd done the occasional interview on the radio, in newspapers, even once on TV. "The English rose of the Australian outback," the interviewer had called her.

She'd started small, doing up the old governess's quarters that adjoined the homestead, welcoming couples and families, one or two a month, from March until November. The numbers had grown as each year passed, expanding to include school groups who were happy to sleep rough in the shearers' quarters if they weren't in use by Errigal's contract shearers. At last count, nearly five hundred people had stayed with them on Errigal, not just from all over Australia but from overseas too—Europe, Asia, America—all seeking a taste of life on an isolated outback station with Angela as their guide.

While Nick had been busy elsewhere on the station, moving stock, maintaining their property, she'd taken her guests on long drives through the empty landscape, pointing out not just Wilpena Pound and Rawnsley Bluff, two landmarks of the Flinders Ranges, but the smaller, less well-known peaks and valleys too. Everything had a name and a story attached. Over the years she had heard them all from Nick, from their Aboriginal stockmen, from their neighbors. She'd loved sharing not only the stories, but all the statistics too. Their property was 170,000 acres, 265 square miles. At its peak, before the drought, it had been home to 10,000 sheep. Huge numbers, but they still took up only a tiny part of this enormous country.

Even after Ig's surprise arrival, Angela had continued to host visitors, bringing him along in his car seat in the 4WD. She'd taken her guests to all the best lookout spots, enjoying their delight in photographing not just the vast, empty scenery around them, but also the kangaroos, emus and lizards. They were a part of day-to-day life for her now, but still a wonder to overseas visitors. She'd shared stories of the area's Aboriginal history, showing her guests rock carvings and explaining stories of the Dreaming, about the Adnyamathanha people who had first lived in this area. She'd talked about the Irish Gillespies who had settled here in the 1880s, taken her guests into the now-disused wool-shed, let them feel the wooden rails and floorboards made smooth from years of lanolin-rich fleeces. If it was the right time of the year weather-wise, sometimes they even camped out under the stars. She'd learned all the constellations over the years, the Southern Cross, the Pointers, different stars from the ones she'd known growing up in England.

Reading the comments in the visitors' books always brought back many memories. "This place is one of the world's best-kept secrets, please stop advertising!" "A once-in-a-lifetime stay, thank you so, so, so much." Ig was often mentioned too. "What a cute kid! Come visit us in the US someday, Ig!" He'd featured in many of their guests' photos over the years as well, she knew, looking the part of the wild outback kid with his mop of hair, his shorts and T-shirts no matter the weather and, more often than not, his bare and dusty feet too.

This couple from Chicago had been among her favorite guests. Everything they'd seen, from the smallest bird to the most vivid red sunset over the nearby Chace Range, had been declared "absolutely one hundred percent awesome." Their e-mail was as enthusiastic. *We miss you, Angela! Chicago is too noisy for us now. We miss Errigal and the bird sounds and that huge, huge sky, and the colors and the quiet and most of all we miss you looking after us, spoiling us every hour of every day!* She was tempted to read on, but there wasn't time now. She had work to do. A letter to write.

It did feel like work for once.

Come on, Angela, she thought. Get started. She moved her chair closer to the computer. Her fingers hesitated over the keys. Just do it, she told herself, feeling a headache start to pulse. Get it written, get it sent out, and then you can go and lie down. Even if only for a few minutes.

She finally started, summoning the usual cheery tone she used for her letters, recalling opening sentences from previous years, hoping no one would notice they'd been recycled.

Yes, it's Angela back again! Can you believe twelve months have passed since I last wrote to you? Where has the time gone? Everything is great with us, after another action-packed and fun-filled year for all the Gillespies. I hope it's been a good year for all of you too!

She stopped there and thought back over the past year. She thought of all her Christmas letters over the decades. All those bright, happy letters, putting the best possible spin on their lives, making it sound as though the Gillespies were the luckiest, loveliest, most successful, well-balanced, supportive family in all Australia, and possibly even the world. She had always skipped over any troubles. Avoided mention of any tensions. Edited out any sticky subjects. It had felt like the right thing to do, even if she knew they sometimes sounded too good to be true.

She felt her headache pulse faster and rubbed her temple automatically. It wasn't just the headaches that had kept striking with regularity lately. At the age of fifty-five, something else had started to happen. She'd talked about it with her neighbor Joan, a former nurse and also a station wife. In her mid-sixties, straight-talking and kind, Joan was her best friend in the area, the one person who had genuinely welcomed her when she'd arrived, a wide-eyed, secretly homesick English girl. They didn't often meet in person—they lived nearly seventy kilometers apart—but they spoke on the phone regularly, often daily. Angela had shared her worries with Joan several weeks earlier.

"Is it a secret symptom of life after menopause, one that no one talks about?" she'd asked.

"I'm still not sure what 'it' is, exactly. You need to be clearer with me. Have you developed blue spots? A forked tongue?"

Angela tried to summarize it. "It's like a constant urge to tell the truth."

"Oh, that!" Joan said, laughing. "That's just wisdom

setting in. You're losing patience with beating around the bush, you mean? You want to get straight to the point all the time? I always feel like that these days. Go for it, love! Let it rip! Tell the truth! It's good for you."

But how could she change overnight? Angela had thought afterward. Not after years of being the person in her family who smoothed things over, kept everyone happy, kept their family show on the road. So she'd still tried to be the good, kind, polite, well-mannered woman she'd been brought up to be. The Angela who Nick had married. The mother her children knew. The welcoming host and tour guide. The neighbor who could be relied on to help out, lend a hand . . .

But the new, peculiar sensation wouldn't go away. It truly was starting to feel as if there were another Angela inside her, struggling to get out. As if the headaches were a symptom of it, evidence of the "real" her trying to break through the "polite" her. A growing urge to be different, to go back to being the Angela she was when she first came backpacking to Australia all those years before. Adventurous Angela. Full of hope and anticipation Angela. Not the Angela she had become. Ordinary Angela.

Anxious Angela.

She turned and gazed out of the office window behind her. It was still bright outside, but the shadow cast by the deep veranda allowed her to see her reflection. Her head of black curls was now threaded with silver. Her once-pale skin had seen too much sun since she'd arrived nearly thirty-four—how could it possibly be so many?—years ago. She took off her reading glasses and leaned forward. People used to tell her she had beautiful eyes. Such an unusual blue. Nick had often told her they were the first thing he'd noticed the night they met. But after three decades of squinting into bright sunlight, even they seemed to have faded. She still noticed the strength of the light here. At home in England, the weather had been soft, misty, blurred around the edges. Here, the weather was a wild creature, fierce, untamed, with a mind of its own. *Oh, you must love all that sunshine*, English school friends had written over the years. *Aren't you the jammy thing! Weren't you in the right place at the right time when that property heir dropped in for a beer!*

She'd told the story so many times, not just to neighbors and friends, but to her station stay visitors too. They always wanted to know how an Englishwoman like her had come to live in the outback. Everyone seemed to love the whole romance of her and Nick's first meeting, the sheer chance of it. There she was, a twenty-two-year-old English backpacker filling in behind the bar for one night for a friend who'd gotten food poisoning. Nick was twenty-eight, from South Australia, in Sydney for one night to go to a big rugby game. He'd arranged to meet friends, got lost and walked into her pub to ask for directions.

She still remembered her first sight of him. Was it fate or destiny or sheer chance that she had looked up just as he came in the door? She'd been reading *Wuthering Heights* at the time, her head full of thoughts of Heathcliff. It was as if an Australian version had walked in. It wasn't his looks or his height. He wasn't conventionally handsome. It was the energy coming off him. A vitality. She'd have guessed even before he told her that his job was a physical, outdoors one.

It wasn't just his tan. He looked fit, strong too. His hair was as dark as hers, his eyes a deep brown. Irish coloring, she'd learned later. She'd helped him with the directions, even drawing a rough map on a beer coaster. On impulse, she offered him a drink on the house. He accepted, but only if he could buy her one at the same time. She was due a break. Over their drinks, they talked. And talked. And laughed. He noticed the time first. He had to go or he'd miss the match. They arranged to meet for a drink after it.

They spent more hours together that night, more talking, more laughing, the physical attraction growing between them by the minute. He wasn't like any man she'd met before, in England or Australia. He was curious. Thoughtful. Clever, but he wore it lightly. If his eyes were a window to the soul, she could tell he was kind, intelligent, amused, admiring. He walked her back to her hostel. She added good manners to his list of qualities. They didn't kiss that night. They met for lunch at his hotel the next day, kissed as they were saying good-bye and were still kissing twenty minutes later. She flew to South Australia a week later to see him again. That was when she learned he wasn't just a farmer but heir to an enormous property on the edge of the outback. "Oh, it's so romantic!" her friends said. "He's like an Australian Mr. Darcy!"

They were married within a year. She was pregnant three months later. The twins arrived a week before their first anniversary.

"A marriage written in the stars," her father said in his effusive speech after their wedding in the cathedral in Adelaide. It was a Gillespie family tradition to be married there, even though Angela had secretly hoped they might get married in the tiny chapel on the Errigal property. *But how would everyone fit?* Nick had said, smiling. After a moment she'd smiled back. She'd been joking, she said. But she hadn't. She'd loved that tiny chapel from the first time she saw it. She wasn't very religious; that wasn't what appealed to her. She'd loved it as a beautiful building filled with history. The old golden stone, the hand-carved wood, the pews polished to a high gleam by all the farmers and their families who had traveled miles over the years to meet there and pray . . .

It wasn't a chapel anymore. It had long been deconsecrated. Fifteen years earlier, an electrical storm blew off a section of its roof and knocked out a side wall. It was now little more than a ruin. Even so, she liked to walk across the paddocks to it as often as she could, even for just a few minutes of peace and quiet. She'd sit on one of the remaining pews, look up at the open sky and simply listen. She'd hear the wind slinking through the leaves of the gum trees. The galahs with their squawks, like scratches down a blackboard, a sound to make you wince but one she'd grown to love. If she sat very still, she'd hear more. Lizards skittering across the stone wall beside her. The distant rusty grind of the windmill sails. Sometimes, rarely, the sound of a car on the dirt road, tires on loose gravel. Eventually, as she became stiller, she would hear her own breathing, slow breaths in, slow breaths out . . .

Then always, before too long, a voice. Or two voices. Calling for her across the paddocks. "Mum?" *"Mum?"* She'd wait for the second call, able to tell even from this distance whether it was urgent or not, whether she could walk back slowly across the scratchy soil, or whether she should run. Only twice had she needed to run, both in recent years, to rescue Ig from physical predicaments. He'd gotten his head trapped in the rungs of a kitchen chair one day. Another time, he was up on top of the pantry cupboard and couldn't get down. It had been so different raising a boy. Her three daughters had never gotten themselves into so many physical scrapes, had they? If they had, she'd conveniently forgotten them. But having a son—her intense love for Ig—had taken her by surprise in so many ways. What was that joke? "If your mother tells you that she doesn't have a favorite child, then you're not her favorite child." That didn't apply to Angela, though. She didn't have any favorites. She loved her four children equally. Of course she did.

She stood and walked over to the window. She couldn't see much from this side of the homestead, but she knew what was out there. The lawn they tried valiantly to keep green for at least a month or two each year, using water that was always so precious. The old stone toolshed with the blue wooden door that now housed her secondhand pottery wheel and drying kiln. She'd taken up pottery as a hobby in recent months, for reasons she still didn't quite understand herself. Beside it, the rosebush that Nick had planted for her as a surprise first anniversary present, which still miraculously produced bright red blooms, despite the droughts and heat waves it had endured. All the other station buildings, the woolshed, the shearers' quarters, the machinery shed. Beyond the station itself, the vast paddocks that one day soon would sprout mining equipment, exploration vehicles . . .

Farther away again, kilometer after kilometer of long, straight dirt roads, with the curving hills of the Chace Range visible on one side, views across to the Flinders Ranges and the distinctive crater shape of Wilpena Pound on the other. Then tarred main roads, then wide highways leading to small towns and to a city, eventually. But overwhelmingly, all around their old stone homestead, there was nothing but wide-open space, for as far as—

"Don't be mean!"

The voice—Ig's—made her jump. The game of Scrabble was obviously over. An argument had begun. What was the trigger this time, Angela wondered. Lindy teasing him about his long hair, perhaps? Angela wished she wouldn't do that. At twenty-nine, she really was old enough to know better. Or was it about whose turn it was to set the table? Even at the age of ten, Ig spent more time arguing about children's rights than it would take him to do the task in question. Lindy seemed to have decided she was a guest here, not a family member with housekeeping obligations. In less than a fortnight, the twins would be back home too, arriving with their jumble of suitcases, their constant chatter, taking over the house with their two big personalities. They were powerful enough apart, unstoppable together. Genevieve had put it into words once, at just the age of five. "You can never win, Mum. It's two of us against one of you."

Not only them. Nick's aunt Celia would be here soon as well, trailing a cloud of too-strong musky perfume, her sharp eyes noting every fault in Angela's housekeeping, her over-cultivated voice airing her ever-ready opinions about the children.

And Nick? Once, they would have laughed about it all together. She'd have had his support, his listening ear. It would have been the two of them united, his wit and humor helping her cope with anything life threw at her. But now?

Her head started to throb again, just above her left ear. The headaches had started five months ago. She'd waged a quiet war against them since then. Her doctor in Port Augusta had sent her for different tests, even a brain scan. She'd been given the all clear, but the headaches had continued. Since then, she'd tried medication, massage, acupuncture, to no avail. She'd talk to her doctor about it again in the new year. There was too much else happening now. Not just the twins coming home, Aunt Celia's arrival, Christmas to organize. The Gillespies were also this year's hosts of the mid-December woolshed party. The station families took turns hosting an annual gathering, and it was the Gillespies' turn again. Angela had been planning it for weeks. Their freezer was already full of party food, and there was a delivery due the next day of all the rented tables, chairs, glasses and crockery.

No, there definitely wasn't time now to worry about a headache. It would have to wait until January. Perhaps she could combine a visit to the specialist in Adelaide with a shopping trip. She could even treat herself to a nice solo lunch afterward in one of the restaurants near the river. She could sit there with a book and a glass of wine, take as long as she liked. Perhaps she could even stay the night in Adelaide before the four-hour journey home again. Yes, that's exactly what she'd do. Have some peace and quiet. What did they call it in the magazines? Having "me time"?

But not tonight. There was no time for any of that tonight. She had a Christmas letter to write and send. She turned back to the computer, fighting that overwhelmed feeling again. She thought back over all that had happened to her family during the past twelve months, wondering how on earth she could turn it all into one of her cheery Christmas letters. Joan's voice suddenly came to her mind, as if she were standing there beside her.

Go for it, love! Let it rip! Tell the truth! It's good for you.

She actually laughed out loud. Tell the truth? How could she?

Go for it, love! It's good for you.

Angela stared at the screen for a long moment. Then she started a new letter, typing faster than she'd ever typed before.

TWO

Hello from the Gillespies!

Yes, it's Angela back again. Can you believe a
year has passed since I last wrote to you
all? I hope you've all had a great twelve
months and are now looking forward to special
family Christmas celebrations together.

It's been a terrible year for the Gillespies.
Everything seems to have gone wrong for us.

I'll start with the children.

Genevieve: I'm worried she's been away in America for too long, working in a fake TV world with fake TV people. She's always loved to gossip and I've loved hearing her stories, but it's gone beyond fun chitchat now. She's become obsessed with celebrity news and is far too indiscreet about the people she works with. I've tried to warn her, but she just laughs it off, like she laughs everything off. She's also started talking in a strange hybrid Australian-American drawl whenever she calls us (which isn't often, she sends us most of her news via Facebook or Instamatic or whatever those Internet things are called). She's such a talented hairdresser, I'm not surprised that she's found work with Hollywood film and TV stars, but I'm worried she's got too swept up in all the gossip and glitter of it, and has lost sight of who she really is.

She's coming home for Christmas, for the first time in three years, but she can only stay for ten days. It was all the time she could get off, she said. Apparently most Americans have very short holidays. But she's Australian, not American, and I wish she would come back home for good. Not necessarily to live here on the station with us, but back in the same country again. There's enough TV and film work in Australia

for her these days, isn't there? Even up here,
miles from anywhere—we're always hearing about
film and TV crews staying in Hawker, working
on this horror film or that end-of-the-world
drama. (It is very beautiful around here, but
very empty, hardly a house or a telegraph pole
for kilometers, a filmmaker's dream.) But I can't
beg Genevieve to come home, can I? I don't
want to be the kind of mother who puts pressure on her children, especially one as spir-
ited and independent as Genevieve. Even if
it's what I really want and what I think she
needs.

Angela stopped there, feeling oddly breathless but also
strangely exhilarated. Joan was right. It felt so good to let
all her troubles spill out like this. What was the word for it?
Liberating? That was it. She felt liberated. She started typing again, her fingers flying across the keyboard.

Victoria: I'm worried about her too. I'd hoped
my mother's intuition was wrong, but then Genevieve (accidentally? On purpose?) let a few
details slip and I knew for sure. Victoria and
the (very well-known) radio announcer she
worked with as a producer in Sydney have been
having an affair. That married, very well-known
radio announcer. That married, very well-
known radio announcer who was in the papers

for all the wrong reasons last month. Those of you in Australia probably heard or read about it. Victoria always used to tell me his bad behavior was just an act for the ratings, that he was a complete softie underneath, but I've wondered if she's a bit naive, especially coming from a country radio station background and not really knowing how big city media types like him operate. And the awful thing is I was right. Look at the trouble he left her in after that incident in the studio. It's so unfair, none of it was her fault. He was the one who came in to work drunk (and more than drunk, from what Victoria told me—yes, cocaine too) after a big night out on the town, ranting and raving like a lunatic, locking her out of the studio when she went to get him coffee and taking to the airwaves throwing libelous insults at everyone you can think of, our politicians, sports people, actors (even Hugh Jackman). Yet *she* ended up being blamed for it, as his producer, and her photo was splashed all over the papers and the Internet. My poor Victoria. It's been awful, especially because she's now unemployed while the whole thing has somehow done wonders for his career. I'll never understand how the media works. I just hope that now they're not working together, any relationship is over too.

I'd never tell her this, but I really wish she would come back to South Australia permanently too, maybe even get a job back in her old radio station up here. She's a country girl deep down. I've never thought big city life was for her. I actually thought that of all the children, she would be the one who would take over from Nick. She was always out working on the station with him, asking him questions, learning about the stock, the equipment. She was his shadow, even talking about going to do an agriculture course at university after she'd finished her journalism degree. But then when she and Fred Lawson broke up (the oldest son of one of our neighbors, they went out with each other for four years, until Fred went overseas) she seemed to lose heart and interest in running Errigal. Then Genevieve talked her into applying for the cadetship at the radio station in Port Pirie, and that was that. Before we knew it she was a radio producer on a big show in Sydney. And look where that's left her now. Unemployed and publicly humiliated, all alone there. I hate to think of her like that.

There was no stopping Angela now.

As for *Lindy*: My poor Lindy. She's already back here on the station, after her latest attempt at independence in Melbourne landed her in a bit of a mess. A bit of a debt-ridden mess. A lot of a debt-ridden mess, if I'm being totally honest. I really hoped she'd found her career niche with her online crafts Web site. She's tried so many jobs over the years since she finished her arts degree—nursing, child care, landscape gardening, secretarial work. This crafts Web site seemed to bring two others together—her brief foray into IT work and her summer job in a fabric store. It sounded like such a good idea too, making personalized cushions for people to mark special occasions. Of course Nick and I were happy to lend her the seed money. And perhaps it did make sense for her to put in a bulk order for her cushion material. But 16 crates of it? From dubious suppliers in China? Delivered to her tiny flat in Melbourne? The first we knew about it was when she called, in floods of tears, begging for help. Thank heavens Nick knew a local truck driver who was happy to pick up not just the crates but also Lindy and her belongings. She arrived a month ago and she's been crying pretty much since. But I know there's more to her problems than a loss of face, bad debt and an oversupply of cushion stuffing. I'm waiting for her to tell me she's pregnant. Or a drug addict. Or a pregnant drug addict. All or any of which would be fine, it really would. We'd deal with it, somehow. But we can't start fixing it if we don't know what the problem is, can we? And in the meantime, she won't leave the station, not even to go into Hawker or to visit any of our neighbors. She spends most days following me around, talking or crying. Talking and crying. Was she always so needy? Or such a drama queen?

Angela stopped for a moment to catch her breath. A moment was all she needed.

As for *Ig*: My darling Ignatius. I love my little Ig very much. Which is why I can say with certainty that he has turned into a very weird little boy. It's not just his long hair. Or the stubbornness. Or the running away from boarding school in Adelaide, three times in the last term alone. He's started talking to himself again. Not to "himself," unfortunately. He's back talking to Robbie, his imaginary friend. When it first happened a few years ago, I decided to ignore it, and sure enough, it stopped, but now it's happening again. Robbie's back full-time. Ig is ten years old. Surely he should have grown out of that kind of behavior by now? Joan tells me not to worry, that lots of kids have imaginary friends, especially youngest kids who live on a station miles from anywhere. But

I've googled imaginary friends. It isn't normal at his age, is it? It's not just funny chit-chat, either, asking us to set an extra place or leave a seat for Robbie in the car. He has entire conversations with someone (at least Ig assures me Robbie is a "someone," not a "some-thing") that only he can see or hear. But am I overreacting? Should I be glad that he seems so happy in his own company? Even if he isn't exactly on his own?

She hesitated then. It had been almost easy to share her worries about her children. But where could she possibly begin with Nick?

She called Joan's advice to mind again. *Tell the truth.* She took a deep breath and began.

Nick: I am so worried about Nick. Worried and sad and confused, about him and about us.

He's leased out half the station to a mining company. It came as a complete shock to me. To the children too. He said he had no choice, that things were still so bad after all the years of drought, after the wool industry collapsed, that he had to accept the offer they made. I knew he'd been having meetings, and had been out on the property with different groups of people in the past year but either he'd implied or I assumed they were stock agents, that

he was planning on increasing our sheep numbers again, after we'd gradually had to sell
them all off in recent years. I was wrong. It
turns out they were geologists and represen-
tatives from the mining company, running test
after test until they'd confirmed they'd found
something. The something is diamonds. It's
not that simple of course. They don't just dig
a few feet and there are diamonds everywhere.
It's a huge operation, a matter of finding
something called kimberlite pipes first. And
it's luck as much as geology if they do, apparently. But they have found enough small
diamonds to be optimistic enough to strike
this deal. I don't know the exact figures involved. All I know is that after the initial
lump sum for the lease, the money will be
paid in installments, each one dependent on
the results of the next geological test. Something like that, anyway. I've asked him to
tell me more, but the shutters come down each
time. All he will say is he had no choice but
to accept it.

I knew things had been tough, of course, even
though Nick has always insisted on taking care
of the financial side of station life. His late
father was the same, apparently. His mother,
may she rest in peace too, always told me to be
glad about it, that it was just the Gillespie

way, that I had enough on my plate with the children. But I never felt like that about station life. I thought of Nick and I as equals, both doing what we could to keep the station running through the good and bad years.

There was no discussion with me about the lease, though. By the time he told me, it was a done deal. He's signed a five-year exploration lease, with him employed in a caretaker role, to maintain the fences, windmills, floodgates etc. on their half of the property. The most we can hope for is that nothing will happen for months, or possibly even years, at the exploration stage, and that more years will be taken up with environmental studies before they start digging. But what will my station stay visitors think? What will this do to our beautiful landscape? To tourism in the area? We're more than a hundred kilometers from the Flinders Ranges National Park, and our station is so far off the highway that we're not really on the main tourist trail, and the mining company apparently assured Nick that there would be minimal environmental damage, but there will still be some impact, surely?

Only our nearest neighbors know so far. After the deal was signed, Nick visited everyone to tell them. He wouldn't tell me much about their reaction, but I could guess. Shock. Anger. Joan says there's been some jealousy too. I can't blame any of them. I'm also worried about the woolshed party. I don't know for sure if everyone will still come. Or if there'll be some kind of a protest if they do.

It's not just the mining deal Nick won't talk about. He and I don't seem to be able to talk about anything anymore. It's as if he's closed himself off from me. All he seems to care about these days is his family research. It's become an obsession. He spends hours on the computer every day, reading articles about Irish and Australian history, ordering history books online, e-mailing Gillespies in all corners of the globe, tracing his Irish ancestors as far back as he can. He even seems to be talking about organizing an international Gillespie reunion. Not here on Errigal, but in Ireland. I overheard him talking to his aunt Celia on the phone. That came as a huge shock to me too. He's never even traveled outside Australia before. I've been waiting for him to talk to me about it, but he hasn't said a word.

I just don't know what to do. I can't stop thinking that all of this is my fault, that

there is something I should have noticed,
something I should have helped him with, before it got this bad between us. He's a different man these days. I don't know him anymore.
It's not just that he won't talk to me. Everything is different with him now. He was always
so active, up at dawn, working outside all
day. Now that we're not a working station anymore, now that we don't have any stock (the
last of it was sold off five months ago), it's
as if he has lost interest in the outside
world. He does the basic maintenance work
that needs to be done, but that's it. It's
been months since he went in to Hawker to
have a beer with his friends. If it was up to
him, I'm sure he'd cancel the woolshed party
too—even though we've been waiting for our
turn again for years, and it's one of the biggest events out here. I'm worried that he
won't even join us for the party. If he can't
talk to his own wife, his own family, how will
he talk to his neighbors?

Angela had to stop there and decide whether she wanted
to put what else she believed into words. After a moment,
she started typing again.

That's not all. I think he might be having an
affair. It's only a cyber-affair so far, but I
am sure something is going on between them.

Her name is Carol. She's in Ireland. She works for an ancestry Web site. That's all I know about her, but he seems to be Skyping and e-mailing her constantly. I don't know what to do about that either. How to stop it happening. How to fix our marriage.

Her sudden tears took her by surprise. She had to blink them away before she could keep typing.

I can't stop thinking about how good it used to be with him, what we used to have. I'm not imagining it. It was special between us. He was my best friend. Now, he and I scarcely say good morning anymore. We don't spend any time with each other, even though we are in the same house. When the children are away, we can be the only two people for literally hundreds of kilometers, yet it feels like we've got nothing left to say to each other. And I miss him so much, but I don't know how to make things better.

It feels so selfish to say this, but to make matters worse, his elderly aunt Celia is coming to stay, for a whole month at Christmastime. I feel sick at the thought. Not just that we'll have someone staying with us for so long, but that it's her. I've tried, I really have, but she doesn't like me. She never has.

The truth is, I don't like her either. If I was asked to sum her up I'd say this. She's an insufferable snob and an interfering old bat. I'm sorry to be so harsh but it's true. I've never met anyone with so much to say, and all of it critical. She stayed with us for a fortnight earlier this year, around the time of her eightieth birthday. I hosted a lunch for her, inviting some of our neighbors to join us, but she found fault with every part of that visit too, from the food I served to the cake I baked to the fact that the weather was so hot, as though that was somehow my fault too. Her husband (Nick's father's brother) died two years ago—henpecked to death, Joan joked one night. (It was actually lung cancer, he was a very heavy smoker.) He asked Nick to please take care of Celia after he was gone and Nick was always so loyal to his uncle, and so fond of him too, he's done his best to keep his promise. Celia's due here in a week, coming up from Adelaide on the bus. There are flights into the Hawker airstrip, and I know Nick offered to pay (even though she is comfortably off and could afford it herself) but she hates flying. She hates lots of things: spending her money, music, vegetarians, politicians. My cooking. My housekeeping. My marriage to Nick. My children. Me. I keep imagining the person who has to sit beside her on the four-hour bus trip. She'll fit in a lot of complaining in that time. Celia could suck the joy out of Christmas, to borrow a phrase from my own dear late mother. I just hope she won't suck the joy out of our Christmas this year.

It now took Angela longer to find the right words.

Which brings this letter to me.

I think something is wrong with me. Something serious. Not just with my marriage, with my children, with these headaches I keep having. It feels deeper than that. Not just physical. I feel so out of place these days. Overwhelmed. Not myself anymore. I seem to be yearning for something all the time. For everything to be different. To be a different person in some way. To go back and start again, somehow make things better, make the right choices.

Draw up a list, Joan advised me recently when I was trying to explain how I felt. Put what you really want down in black and white and see what is actually achievable. A wish list, she called it. I'll try it here now.

1. I wish Nick would start talking to me again, properly, like he used to. I wish he would tell me that I am imagining things, that he

isn't having an affair, that he does still want to be married to me. That he still loves me. I wish I could turn back time to when we had a good marriage, a beautiful marriage. Because we did. We really did. And I am so sad and so scared that he doesn't want to be with me anymore.

2. I wish the children were all happy and healthy and independent (Ig aside, I'm happy for him to stay at home for a few more years). I wish I could feel I'd done the best job possible raising them. I always expected that when I got to my age, when I'd been married for this long and had grown children (half-grown in Ig's case), I would have everything sorted; I would be calm and wise and content. Instead, I feel like I have nothing under control, that I haven't been a proper mother let alone a proper wife, that everything going wrong with my family is somehow all my fault.

3. I wish I had ignored my mother-in-law's advice. I wish I'd insisted that Nick involve me more in the business side of the station. I couldn't have stopped the drought or the drop in wool prices, but perhaps if I'd insisted he talk to me about it, we would have come up with a different solution than this mining lease. I don't even know how much debt we're in—Nick won't ever tell

me—but surely it can't have been so bad that we couldn't have worked through it together?

4. I wish I was more artistic. I wish I could create a piece of pottery, even one piece, that I could be really proud of. It's taken me by surprise, how much it matters to me. I only took that pottery course in Port Augusta to fill in the gaps between my station stay guests. I was feeling so lonely out here, with Nick so distant, Ig at school and the girls living their own lives. But I loved it from the very first lesson. It felt so good to work with the clay, to learn how to make practical things like vases, and be encouraged to try small sculptures too. And it felt like a sign, an omen of some sort, when I heard that the college was selling off their old kiln for next to nothing and I was able to set up my own tiny studio here on the station. I've spent hours out there since. I've made dozens of pieces, taking my inspiration from the landscape and wildlife around me. I'm still a bit shy about them. (The first few looked more like collapsed cakes than pieces of art.) But I took my teacher's advice (Aim high, he said) and contacted some ceramic galleries in Adelaide about possible representation. I haven't heard back from any of them yet. I wish I would.

5. Most of all, right now, this minute, I wish
   my headaches would go away. Actually, not
   just my headaches. Sometimes I wish everything and everyone would go away. Just for
   a little while. Not permanently. Please
   don't misunderstand me. I love my husband.
   My children. My life here on the station,
   here in Australia. I really do. But I just think
   if I could press a pause button for a while,
   have some time to myself, a little peace, a
   lot of quiet, time to reflect, I would be
   a much better mother, a much better wife, a
   much better person. I think I just urgently
   need a little bit of time off from worrying
   about everything, from being me, all day,
   every day, months and years on end. Is that
   too much to ask? Is that selfish of me?

She paused. But not for long.

Have any of you seen that film *Sliding Doors*?
Where the woman lives two parallel lives, all
hinging on her missing her train or not? Ever
since things have become so bad between Nick
and me, I've turned into that woman. I can't
stop thinking about how my life might have
been. If somewhere along the line, I took a
wrong turn, that I should have taken a different
path. I keep wondering what might have happened
if I hadn't been working in that bar in Sydney

that night, more than thirty years ago. Would everything be better now, for everyone?

Because if I hadn't been in that pub that night, I wouldn't be on Errigal now, would I? I wouldn't have met and married Nick. I wouldn't have my four children. I wouldn't be living here on an outback sheep station. I feel so guilty even thinking it, but I can't stop asking myself the question, "what if?" I would have done as I'd planned, stayed in Australia for another month, then gone back home. Back to my childhood sweetheart, Will. We were lovers, proper boyfriend and girlfriend, for more than two years, from when I was nineteen until he decided he needed to travel, explore the world and the world's architecture, before he settled into college. I decided to go backpacking too. But we had an unspoken understanding. When he came back, and when I came back from my own travels, we would meet and we would see how we felt about each other.

I can't stop thinking about that lately. I might have gone home to London after my few months in Australia, met Will again, decided I loved him and married him. And then what?

I can tell you. I've pictured it all. I'd have supported Will as he studied to become an architect. I'd have pursued my own love of art, really been serious about my own creativity. We'd have had one child. Just the one. A daughter called Lexie. A lovely, bright, stable child. A sweet-natured, polite child. We'd have stayed in London, in the house in Islington that Will inherited from his parents. We'd have saved all our money for full-scale renovations. Will would have done all the plans, of course, and turned it into a special family house. We'd even have had a big rambling garden, in the center of London, with an oak tree. An oak tree with a special tree house in it, designed especially by Will for Lexie.

We'd have been so happy. Will would have become a sought-after, award-winning architect. Lexie would have excelled in school and at university, and gone on to set up her own community theater group, outside of London. In Bristol, perhaps. I'd have become an artist of some kind, quietly successful, my work in constant demand.

Angela came to a sudden halt.

Writing about her London fantasy life was one step too far. Because these thoughts were more than a harmless fantasy now. They'd become her lifeline. Over the past difficult year, as things had grown so tense between her and Nick, the refuge of this alternative fantasy life had kept her afloat.

It had been somewhere for her mind to dwell when anxiety threatened to overwhelm her. Somewhere restful to go. Soothing . . . Her own personal meditation.

She'd learned to switch over to it at a moment's notice. She wasn't really on an outback sheep station, trying to cope with all these worries about her husband and children, was she? Her real life was in London, where her real husband, Will the architect, was at home waiting for her, a glass of wine ready to be poured, perhaps even dinner cooking in the oven. No, even better—she and Will had a housekeeper! Of course they did. A housekeeper five days a week, because she and Will were so busy with their creative lives. But they cooked for themselves on weekends or, more often than not, dined out. They had plenty of money. And every three or four weekends their daughter, Lexie, would come home to visit, because even though she was in her late twenties and had an exciting, fulfilled life in Bristol, she loved nothing more than coming home as often as she could and spending time with her beloved parents—

"Ig, stop that! Get down from there!"

Lindy's voice snapped Angela out of her reverie. What was happening to her tonight? She'd never taken this long to write her Christmas letter. Or written as much.

She began to read it back. Not even halfway through, she stopped, shocked. She couldn't possibly send out even a word of this. Anyone who read it would think that she'd gone mad. That her children were unhinged. That she and Nick were on the verge of divorce. That everything she'd been writing about Gillespie family life for the past thirty-three years was a lie. And it wasn't, was it?

Was it?

Of course it wasn't. They were just a normal family going through some normal ups and downs, weren't they? Going through a tricky patch? Yes. All she had to do now was delete every word of this, this *rant*, and instead write one of her normal, cheery end-of-year letters. And then send it off, tonight, on December first, as always.

She was just about to press the delete key and start again when a scream filled the room.

"Mum! MUM! Quick! MUM!"

THREE

Angela was on her feet before she knew it.

"Mum! MUM! MUM! Quick!"

She ran as fast as she could, up the hall, into the kitchen.

Her first thought was that there'd been a murder. There was blood everywhere. In the middle of it, sitting on the floor, looking up at her, was Ig. It was his blood. Beside him stood Lindy. She was the one screaming. On the floor, in the blood, was something else. Could it be a finger? Part of a finger? It was a *finger.* The top of Ig's finger. She stared at it, at Ig, at Lindy. Ig blinked. He didn't speak but he blinked as he looked at her.

There was a buzzing in her head. The headache and something else. A voice telling her what to do. *Stay calm.*

Lindy was babbling. "He was standing up on the table.

With the carving knife. Cutting his hair. I told him not to, Mum. I told him. And he went to jump down, and he slipped and he landed right on the blade and Mum, look, oh God, look! It's *revolting.*" With that, Lindy vomited onto the floor.

"Nick!" Angela barely recognized her own voice, shouting.

He appeared at the door. "What's—" She saw him take it all in at a glance, heard him swear.

"Help me." She made her voice sound calm. It was an effort. "Get the car. Please. We need to get him to the hospital. Quickly."

Nick left immediately. Beside the door, Lindy retched again.

Angela ignored her, ignored the blood, the vomit. *Stay calm.* She fell onto her knees beside Ig, a tea towel in her hand. She took his bleeding hand in hers and firmly pressed the cloth against the wound. "It's okay, kiddo. Don't worry. Hold your arm up. Can you do that for me?"

He was still staring at her, white-faced. He didn't look at his hand. All he did was look at her and nod, then slowly raise his hand.

She spoke quickly, issuing directions to Lindy. "Get the first-aid kit, Lindy, as fast as you can. Pass me the sterile water. The bandages." *Stay calm.* "Good girl. Now, quick, ice from the fridge. Freezer bags. Kitchen towel."

Lindy did as she was told.

Angela got to work. She doused Ig's finger in the sterile water, trying to ignore the blood, the sight of the bone. *Stay calm. Stay calm.* She pressed a wad of cotton on the end, then wrapped a bandage tightly around his whole hand, putting as much pressure on his finger as possible, keeping his hand raised above his heart, trying to stop the blood flow. She picked up the piece of his finger from the bloody pool on the floor, wrapped it in a kitchen towel, put it into one of the freezer bags and then into another bag with the ice. She might have been watching herself from a distance. How did she know to do all of this? How had she known that she shouldn't put ice directly against the finger, for fear of frost damage? From a TV program? A long-ago first-aid class? No matter how, she did.

Lindy, sobbing, was watching from the other side of the kitchen. "Mum, will he be all right?"

"Of course he will," she said, too loudly, too brightly. "Won't you, Ig? Dad's just gone to get the car and then we'll take you into the hospital and everything will be fine, won't it?"

Ig nodded. Still no words, but a nod was something, wasn't it?

Nick appeared again, holding the car keys. "The car's outside. I'll drive."

"No!" It was Ig, talking at last. "I want Mum to drive. I want her to take me."

"Ig—," Nick said.

"I want Mum." Ig was crying now. More than crying. Wailing. The shock had passed; now he was frightened, and in pain. With Lindy crying too, the room was suddenly full of noise.

"I'll go," Angela said to Nick. "We could be there overnight, longer even. You stay here with Lindy. All the party gear is being delivered tomorrow. Someone needs to be here for that."

She couldn't believe she was thinking so clearly, remembering party deliveries at a time like this. She turned back to Ig, doing her best to soothe him, stroking his hair, his face, telling him over and again it was going to be all right, he was going to be fine. He was so pale. His blood was so red. There was so much of it. It would take at least forty minutes to get to the Hawker hospital. . . .

Stay calm.

"Keep your hand up high for me, Ig," she said over his cries, finding an even brighter voice from somewhere. "Pretend you're reaching up for something. That's it, good boy. Ready for a bit of a drive?"

He stood up, swaying slightly, wailing now that it hurt, it hurt, it hurt. More orders to Lindy. Painkillers, a glass of water, quickly. After he'd taken them, gulping them down, tears still coursing down his cheeks, Angela put her arm around him, steadying him, holding him tight against her. It was a warm night but he was now shivering. She issued more orders.

"Lindy, get a blanket please, quickly. Nick, can you call the hospital? Tell them we're on the way?"

Lindy managed to step past the pool of blood before she started to retch again. She put her hand to her mouth and ran out the door.

As Nick finished speaking on the phone, Lindy appeared again, blanket in hand. Angela took it, wrapped it around Ig.

They moved quickly then. Nick carried Ig out to the car, placed him on the passenger seat, fastened the seat belt around him, opening the window so Ig could lean his elbow on it, keeping his injured hand high in the air. It took Angela only seconds to put on her own seat belt, start the car, wind down the window.

"I'll call as soon as I can," she called to her husband and daughter.

Nick and Lindy watched as the car moved out of sight, away from the homestead, onto the long, straight dirt road.

Four hours later, alone in the kitchen, Nick hung up the phone after talking to Angela.

Ig was going to be fine. Everything was under control. The drive to Hawker had gone quickly, she'd told him. She and Ig had sung Christmas carols all the way, a good distraction. There'd been a group waiting for them at the hospital, alerted by Nick's call, including the doctor on duty, an intern from Adelaide doing her bush experience. According to Angela, the doctor had taken one look at Ig's blood-soaked bandage and the contents of the freezer bag, paled, and then immediately called for an ambulance to take Angela and Ig to the bigger hospital in Port Augusta, another hour away. Angela was calling from there now. Ig had already had emergency surgery to reattach his finger. There hadn't been serious blood loss, despite how it looked from the mess in the kitchen. He might lose some movement, but the doctors were optimistic. The ice, the pressure bandage, it had all helped. She'd just come from his room. He was sleeping peacefully. The only thing wrong was that in the hurry to get Ig to the hospital, she'd left her mobile phone behind. She'd use pay phones while she was in the hospital, and the UHF radio in the car once they were on their way home.

"And you? Are you okay?" Nick had asked.

"I'm fine." She'd sounded so calm. Almost too calm.

There was a long silence before she spoke again.

"I'd better go. I'll call again tomorrow as soon as I can."

It wasn't until he'd returned the phone to the cradle that he realized he hadn't asked her where she would be staying. In Ig's hospital ward? A nearby motel? He went to call her back, but stopped. She didn't have her mobile. If she was still in the ward, the nurses wouldn't appreciate a ringing phone this late at night.

"I'm fine," she'd said. But how could she be? He should have said more to her. Asked her a dozen more questions. *Are you sure you're okay? Do you want me to drive over to you? I can be there in a few hours. Lindy can look after the delivery tomorrow. You need me there. I need to be there with you.* But the moment had passed, as it always seemed to between them these days.

It was his fault; he knew that. There was so much he wanted to say to her, but he never seemed to have the words. Not just tonight. It had been that way for months now.

"Have you told Angela yet?" his doctor had asked during his last session. "She needs to know. You need to tell her."

"I don't want to worry her."

"She's your wife, Nick. She's probably already worried."

But how could he even begin to tell her? It was hard enough facing himself in the mirror each day, knowing how much he'd let her down, let his whole family down. He couldn't bear to see more disappointment in her eyes. He'd seen how shocked she was when he told her about the mining deal. He'd heard the worry in her voice. That night had confirmed it for him. It was better for her, for the kids too, if he kept the rest to himself. If he tried to keep himself busy with his family research. If he stayed out of their way. Her way, especially.

He went down the hall and checked on Lindy again. She was fast asleep. He'd sent her to her room, as if she were a child again, as soon as Angela and Ig had driven off. He'd assured her everything was going to be okay with Ig, that he was happy to do all the cleaning up. It had taken him more than an hour. There had been blood everywhere.

It was now nearly midnight. He should go to bed. But he knew he wouldn't sleep. He hadn't slept properly for months. He turned on the TV but there was nothing he wanted to watch. He checked the time, making the calculation. It was the middle of the day in Ireland. A good time to e-mail Carol. E-mailing Carol would take his mind off things. It always did.

As he walked into the office, the computer was displaying an Irish-themed screen saver, a photo of an historic castle. There was a large map of Ireland on the wall. The whole family shared the computer and the office, but these days he spent the most time in here.

He pressed a computer key. The castle disappeared and a document appeared on-screen. He frowned. Had he forgotten to save this earlier? Then he saw the border of Christmas trees and realized that Angela must have been in here doing her Christmas letter when Ig had had his accident. Nick was about to close it and save it in drafts for her when he saw the time. Four minutes to midnight, December first. The date she always sent her Christmas letter.

At last. Here was something positive he could do for Angela. He knew how much these letters meant to her, even if he had long ago stopped reading them. He had never really understood why she felt the need to share their family news with so many people. In the days when he had still read the letters, he'd often found it hard to recognize their lives in them.

Three minutes to midnight. He hoped their temperamental satellite Internet connection would hold steady. He opened her e-mail address book and saw a group titled "Christmas Letter Recipients." He wasn't surprised. He'd never known anyone as organized as Angela.

It didn't take him long to set up the e-mail and insert the names. After everything that had happened over the past year, even a small gesture for her like this one felt momentous. Important. He wouldn't tell her he'd done it, either. It would be a surprise when she and Ig came home again.

One minute to midnight. He knew Angela often called Ig in to the office to press the send button for her, getting him to call out, "Hello from the Gillespies!" as the e-mail went. He hoped it wouldn't matter if that tradition wasn't followed tonight.

Right on the stroke of midnight, he pressed send. As he leaned back in the chair, Angela's Christmas letter left their computer and flew out into the world.

FOUR

In New York, Genevieve Gillespie was having trouble juggling her phone, her handbag, her work bag and her raincoat as she negotiated her way through the crowds of dawdling tourists and brisk locals on the Greenwich Village street. One of her blue dreadlocks had fallen out of her topknot and was dangling in front of her eyes. The sooner she got rid of them, the better. In her ear, her twin sister thousands of kilometers away in Sydney was hard to hear but clearly upset.

"Victoria, I'm so sorry, but can you please hold that thought right there? Give me two seconds and I'll give you all the sympathy in the world, I promise."

She turned right into an alley, dropped her bags on the ground, moving them in close to avoid any opportunistic bag snatchers, then held the phone to her ear again. It was dirty here, but at least it was quiet.

"Sorry about that. Can you start again? And can you please speak very slowly? I've got the world's worst hangover."

"Again? You've definitely become an alcoholic."

"You're one to talk. Anyway, I'm not one yet. Two big nights in a month isn't exactly a life on the rocks, is it? Gin on the rocks, maybe. Vodka too, if my memory is correct. Which it isn't. Victoria, I met the most hilarious man last night. You should have—"

"Genevieve, can we please talk about me first and then talk about you?"

"Sorry. Of course. Definitely. But can you make it quick? I'm late for work already." As she spoke, the work cell phone in her pocket buzzed again. And again. She took it out— nine missed calls. "Holy hell. Victoria, seriously, I can't talk for long. Something must be going on at work. Everyone's looking for me."

"You and your glamorous two phones. Don't worry. I'll call you later for a proper supportive conversation. Can I just check what time you're flying into Sydney? Your text said six, but did you mean a.m. or p.m.? I'm trying to book our onward flights to Adelaide."

"P.m. 1800 hours. Mum will pick us up in Adelaide, won't she?"

"She'd better. I'm not sure I can handle four hours of Lindy's wailing. And apparently Dad is shackled to the computer these days and never leaves the station. Thanks. I'll book the flights today. Who was the man last night? Is he a possible?"

"No, gay as can be, but I'd marry him anyway. He was so much fun. You know those people who laugh so hard at your jokes that you want to be as funny as possible just to keep them going? He was like that. 'You are hysterical, Genevieve. Tell me another one, Genevieve.'"

"Was that supposed to be an American accent?"

"I'll have you know, people often think I am an American."

"An American who got lost in the Australian desert for twenty years, maybe."

Genevieve's phone buzzed again. "Another missed call. I better go."

"No, wait. What are you working on this week? I can't keep up with your show-biz life."

Genevieve named the TV series and the lead actress.

"Ooh, what's she like?" Victoria said.

Genevieve couldn't help herself. "You know I'm sworn to secrecy and can't divulge anything about my work." She waited a beat. "She's the most selfish, ill-mannered, foul-mouthed cow *ever.* She's also having affairs with the director *and* her costar, one of whom is male, one female. Both married. She constantly talks about them while I'm doing her hair. She also constantly and openly smokes dope, and the reason she looks *so* convincingly out of it on-screen is because she *is* out of it."

"I want your job. Here I am, in hiding, shamed, a pariah—"

"My poor darling. I'll teach you how to cut hair when I'm back home. We can go into business together. The Gillespie Gals: Hair today, none tomorrow. Better go. Farewell, Victoria."

"Farewell, Genevieve."

Genevieve hung up, glanced at her watch and grimaced. She wasn't just late; she was very late. Only by five minutes, but timekeeping was essential in her industry. It would never do if actors arrived in the trailer to have their hair done and found themselves waiting for the hairdresser or makeup artist. The other way round, sure. That was often the case. But this TV series was already overbudget, and the pressure was on, for cast and crew. The director had made that clear via his latest all-crew e-mail yesterday.

If only she hadn't had that final drink last night. She didn't just have a headache. She was nauseous too. But it had been such good fun, and such a treat to have someone listening so intently. Be so amused by her. He'd even given her his number. "Ring me anytime. You're fun."

She hailed a cab. Once she was in the seat, her bags in a jumble at her feet, she took out her work phone again. Ten missed calls. What was happening? She pressed the key to listen to her voice mail. All the callers were asking the same question. Had she seen the *New York Post* that morning? She brought up the online edition on her phone and scrolled down until she saw it for herself. The gossip page.

The photo byline leaped out at her first. It was the man she'd spent last night talking and laughing with. The fun gay guy who worked as a graphic designer at the *Post*, he'd told her. Who hadn't wanted to talk about himself. Unusual enough in this city. Perhaps he really was a graphic designer. But he was also the gossip columnist. The gossip columnist with either a perfect memory or a recording device that he took everywhere with him, including noisy nightclubs.

Word for word, everything she'd told him the previous

night was there. The inside story on the actress. The two affairs she was having. The drugs. The misbehavior. All the information supplied by what he called "an insider on the set."

Genevieve's stomach lurched. She called back one of the callers. Megan, her best friend on the set, the show's makeup artist. As she waited for an answer, she tried to stay calm. The columnist hadn't named her. No one she knew from the industry had been in the club last night. No one on the show would know it was her he was quoting, would they? Her call went to voice mail. Why wasn't Megan answering? Genevieve wanted to be sick, but she asked the driver to please hurry. She was only a few blocks away now.

Her phone rang. "Megan?"

"Genevieve? Where are you? You're missing all the fun."

"I've just heard about it. I'm a minute away. What's happened?"

"Someone is in deep, deep trouble. The set has sprung a leak. A waterfall. And our director isn't happy. Our producer isn't happy. And our star especially isn't happy. You'd better get here, but you won't have any work to do. She's just informed the boss man she's off the project."

"But she can't. She's contracted. We're nearly done."

"Apparently she can. She had a clause that if any negative publicity comes from the set, she can pull out. Why do you think we all had to sign that confidentiality clause?"

"But we always sign those things."

"This time they meant it. It's really serious. You should see everyone's faces. It's like a funeral around here. She'll only come back if there is a public beheading of the big-mouth, apparently."

"Do you mean they know who it is?"

"Not yet. The word is the columnist is shut tight as a vise. Said he never divulges his sources."

Genevieve started to breathe again. Until Megan continued.

"But then I heard that the studio will pull all their advertising if he doesn't say who told him."

The cab pulled up at the set. They'd taken over an entire street on the edge of Hell's Kitchen. Trailers, cables and technical equipment were crammed tightly on the sidewalks. Usually there would be movement and bustle by this time of the day. This morning, there were just huddles of people standing around, doing nothing.

All because of her.

"I'd better go," Megan said. "I'm spying on the director's trailer and his door's just opened."

"See you soon," Genevieve said. Her hands were now shaking. It wasn't just the effects of last night's alcohol. She was in trouble. Big, big trouble. She ducked in behind a lighting van and took out her phone again. The article was worse on repeated reading. She googled the actress's name. The article's contents were already all over the Web. The contents, her words, repeated as if they were the truth. They were the truth.

What could she do? Keep quiet? What would Victoria tell her to do? For a moment, she thought about calling her twin for advice, but this wasn't the time or the place. This was so serious there was every chance someone was now bugging their phones. It wasn't about the actress's career. No one cared about that. In fact, her notoriety worked in the show's favor—the more badly behaved she was, the more free publicity the show got. What mattered was money. Every hour the production was shut down cost the investors thousands of dollars. Which meant that her hour-long conversation with that charming, attentive man the night before, all those laughs they'd shared, those stories she'd told, had probably already cost tens of thousands of dollars in lost production.

She moved on, keeping her expression neutral by sheer will as she passed another huddle of technicians, an unused set of technical desks. *Stay calm*, she told herself. It might blow over.

She knew within a moment of stepping into the makeup and hair trailer that it wasn't going to blow over. Megan was up-to-date with all the news. She was sleeping with the assistant director and he was feeding the intelligence straight to her. She gave Genevieve the latest.

"They've got a language expert onto it now. The column had direct quotes so they're trying to see if there are any particular speech patterns that will give away who leaked it."

Genevieve felt what little color was left in her face drain away. She was the only Australian on the set. Yes, she spoke English. Yes, she'd been working in the US for more than two years and had picked up plenty of American slang, as well as a bit of an accent, but would it be enough to wipe out her native language patterns?

"What was it he or she said?" she asked, trying to sound relaxed.

Megan read the article aloud. Genevieve listened, even

though she already knew the words by heart. Perhaps she was safe. It wasn't as if she'd said the actress was a bloody drongo, a stupid sheila, or spoken in any recognizably Australian way. She was saved from having to comment by Megan's phone ringing. As her friend launched into a lengthy retelling of the morning's drama, Genevieve took the opportunity to set out her brushes, clips and sprays, pretending it was a normal morning.

Think, Genevieve. What could she do about this? What *should* she do?

Confess.

Where had that come from? The depths of her Catholic upbringing? It sounded like something her mother would say. Angela had always insisted on the truth at home. Throughout their school years—at the local school in Hawker and then their very Catholic boarding school in Adelaide—she and Victoria had often rolled their eyes about it, and challenged her too. Genevieve generally started it. "That's all very well, Mum, but if we do everything the Bible tells us to—"

"Always turn the other cheek and always think of others—," Victoria continued.

"And always stop to help every poor, unfortunate person we see on the side of the road—"

"We'll never get *anything* done," Victoria would finish.

"They're not rigid rules; they're guidelines," their mother would say.

Guidelines to a boring life, Genevieve and Victoria decided between themselves. So as teenagers, they'd come to the conclusion that what their parents didn't know wouldn't hurt them.

Megan was still talking to her friend, reading out the article again. Genevieve didn't want to hear it. She started rearranging her already arranged brushes, just for something to do.

Megan finally hung up. Her phone immediately buzzed again. "Sorry," she mouthed across to Genevieve. She wasn't sorry; Genevieve could see it. Megan loved being at the center of the day's top gossip story. As Megan launched into the tale yet again, Genevieve picked up her phone to call Victoria. Her number was ringing when the door of the trailer opened. It was Tim, the assistant director, Megan's current boyfriend. He knew something; Genevieve could tell from his expression. She hung up. Across the trailer, so did Megan.

"Well?" Megan said.

"We're about to be called together. In fifteen minutes' time, on set. They want a confession. If the person who blabbed doesn't tell all by eleven a.m. today, the whole unit shuts down. We get a surprise day off. Possibly a surprise week off. A couple of surprise months off, the way the industry is at the moment."

Megan's reaction was noisy enough to cover Genevieve's shocked silence. So she was now not just responsible for hundreds of thousands of dollars of lost investor money, but also the livelihoods of more than a hundred people? Her heart started beating faster.

"And if the person does confess?" Was that really her talking? That calm, quiet voice?

"They lose their job but we keep ours. The show goes on. One falls for the sake of many. That's what we're all about to hear. A no-brainer, really."

Genevieve thought of the bills on the table in her apartment. The credit card bill in particular. She thought of next month's rent, due in five days' time. She had already paid for her airfare to Australia. Could she cash it in, not go back? No, she was longing to see Victoria. And her parents. Lindy. Ig. Then she thought of Bill, the lighting guy. His wife had just had their first baby. She knew that Ron, in set construction, was trying to buy an apartment. The actress at the center of this would get another job, another role, another magazine cover. But the others?

Tim was right. It was a no-brainer.

"Coffee?" Again, she was surprised at how normal she sounded.

"You're a doll," Megan said. "Thanks."

"Back soon." Or possibly never again.

She went to the coffee van first. There was a line. With production stopped, everyone had time on their hands.

"Hi," she heard.

She turned. It was Coffee Guy, as she and Megan had dubbed him. A man in his mid-thirties, dark-haired, solidly built. Genevieve only ever met him here in the line. They had a running joke that they shared the same level of caffeine addiction. She wasn't sure what he did on set. A technician, she'd guessed, or maybe one of the security guys, since he wore the black waterproof jacket with the studio logo on the left pocket that they all sported. They never talked much— like today, the coffee makers always kept the line moving too quickly to allow in-depth conversations—but she always enjoyed their exchanges. He'd been to Australia once, he'd told her. He'd gone scuba diving on the Great Barrier Reef. She'd never even seen the Great Barrier Reef and she'd grown up in Australia, she said.

"Don't worry. I've never seen the Chrysler Building and I grew up in New York," he said.

"It's there—look." She pointed behind them.

He turned, raised his eyebrows. "So it is. Wow." He gave her a big smile. "Thanks."

"This is my tenth coffee today," he said to her now. "I may look peaceful on the outside but I'm like Niki Lauda on the inside. The race car driver? No? How about Nick Faldo? The golfer?"

She was too jittery to be able to joke back to him. She just smiled. His heart was racing? Hers felt like it was on warp speed. She collected her three coffees, smiled at him again as she walked past and then delivered the drinks back to Megan and Tim. They were still gossiping in the trailer. She couldn't join in. She couldn't even drink her coffee. Her pulse rate was at dangerous levels already. There was something she had to do. Right now.

"Back in a while," she said to Megan.

"More coffee? You won't be sleeping for weeks."

Genevieve had to ask for directions. She hardly knew what the director looked like, let alone where his trailer was. She'd had more dealings with the production manager, the person who decided on the look of the set, the backdrops, the actors. It had been going so well for her here in New York. She'd loved every minute of the past two years.

She'd worked on feature films, music videos, TV ads, one-off specials. She'd met film stars from her childhood, up-and-coming indie actors. Nice people, horrible people. She'd seen great actors with ordinary faces and poor actors with photogenic faces. She'd pinched herself every day to think that the career that had begun as an after-school job in outback South Australia had brought her here, to New York, to the set of an Emmy Award–winning TV series—

That she had brought to a halt.

Her final steps to the director's trailer felt like a prelude to an execution. Five people were standing in front of it. She knew just one of them, Laurence, the third assistant director. He was reading something on his phone that was making him frown. She waited, then took a breath and walked across to him.

"Laurence? Can I have a word? In private?"

"It's not a good time—"

"I know something about"—she made a vague gesture—"the situation."

"Sorry; who are you?"

Why would he know who she was? "Genevieve Gillespie. I'm the hairstylist."

"You know something about the article?"

She nodded.

"Stay there."

She'd thought she could tell him and he would then tell the director. But he'd gone up the stairs, spoken to someone and was now back in the doorway, beckoning her over. To talk to the director? The director who had won four Emmys and was rumored to be directing his first feature film for Harvey Weinstein as soon as this series wrapped?

He gestured again. *Hurry up*, it said.

She'd longed to meet the director. But not in circumstances like this.

She walked up the stairs. Laurence let her pass, then stepped outside. It was now just her, Genevieve Gillespie, hairstylist, age thirty-two, twin to Victoria, formerly of Errigal sheep station in outback Australia, standing in a small trailer in New York City, opposite one of the best-known TV directors in America.

She swallowed, so loudly they could both hear it. He stared at her, waiting. She started to talk. And talk. She told him everything, about the bar, the drinks, how she'd struck up a conversation with this man, how they'd laughed, how she couldn't seem to stop saying things to him, because he was laughing so much. The more the director stared at her, the more she told him. Until finally there was nothing to add. Nothing to do but stare at him staring at her.

She'd hoped for understanding. For a brief flare of anger followed by forgiveness, reassurance that this would all soon be forgotten, that she'd learn from it never to trust eager, listening ears in late-night bars, that this city thrived on gossip but gossip had a price.

She was wrong on all counts. Within seconds, a security guard was leading her back to the makeup trailer to collect her things. Her work phone was taken from her. Megan had the decency to give her a hug, to say, "I'll call you," even if she only whispered it in her ear. It was afterward she remembered Megan had her work phone number, and Genevieve no longer had her work phone.

She was brought back to the director's trailer. An assistant had appeared; a printer was whirring. With shaking hands, she was forced to sign a hastily typed-up affidavit that would be couriered across town to the actress's luxury hotel. It got worse. She was forced to film a confession, looking into the camera on the director's iPhone. They told her exactly what to say. "I, Genevieve Gillespie, was the source of the false and hurtful gossip that appeared in this morning's *New York Post*. I accept that it was wholly untrue and without foundation and I am deeply sorry for any hurt I have caused by my actions. I have handed in my resignation." It stuck in her throat, saying the words she knew were untrue, in front of the director she knew was having an affair with the actress. She also knew with sudden clarity that this confession, her stuttering apology, with her hungover eyes and hastily tied-back blue dreadlocks, would be leaked to Twitter, Perez Hilton, TMZ and every other gossip site in town, within minutes.

The door opened. Coffee Guy appeared. So she'd been right; he was a security guard. There was a quick exchange between him and the director. Genevieve heard just part of it. It was enough. "Get her off the set. Now."

Outside, people still stood in groups. She heard snatches as she made her walk of shame to the edge of the set. The usual early-morning tourists were lined up against the temporary cordon, waiting for a glimpse of a famous face. They gave her only a passing glance. They probably thought she was a trespasser being escorted off the set. They were right.

They reached the barrier.

She turned to him. "Are you going to throw me over it?"

He shook his head. "Unless you want me to?"

"No, thanks."

He moved it aside and then handed over her bag. Not her handbag, which she had with her, but her work bag, all her brushes, scissors, combs, the tools of her trade. She must have left it in the director's trailer.

"I thought you'd need it," he said.

"Thank you very much." His unexpected kindness almost made her cry. She hurriedly blinked away the tears. "I'm sorry to ask, but could you please do me another favor?"

"I'm not allowed to. Of course. What favor?"

"Megan, in makeup. She only has my work number. Can you please give her this?" She hastily scribbled her personal cell phone number on the back of a receipt.

He put it in his jacket pocket. "You did the right thing, by the way."

"What?"

"You saved everyone's jobs. Thanks."

She stared at him. "You're welcome." She had to say it. "I didn't mean to make all this happen. I'd had too many cocktails. I thought it was common knowledge. That it didn't matter."

"How long have you been here?"

"On this show? A few weeks."

"In New York?"

"Two years."

Behind them, a voice shouted, "Matt!"

He turned, gave a wave to say he'd be right there.

She'd taken two steps when she heard her name. She turned. He had his hand out. He wanted to shake hands with her? Then she realized.

"Your pass. Sorry."

She lifted it over her head and handed it to him. She'd loved that security pass. She'd loved what it meant. She was part of the American film and TV industry. Part of a closed world. Not anymore.

"Don't worry too much."

She made a sound, somewhere between a laugh and a sob. "Sure. Thanks."

"I mean it. It'll all blow over."

"But in the meantime, I'll never work in this town again?"

This time he gave her a proper grin. "Worse things could happen."

She stood and watched as he walked back onto the set. At least he'd been kind. Treated her with some dignity. The crowd near the barrier looked disappointed. Not only was she a nobody; she hadn't even been manhandled off the set. She stood for a moment longer. Beside her, two curious on-lookers were watching her. One of them came over.

"Did you get kicked off the set for doing something?"

She shook her head.

"So what were you doing in there? Do you work in TV?"

Not anymore, she thought. "I was delivering something."

"To that actress?" the woman's friend asked, excited now. "What?"

Oh, what the hell, Genevieve thought. "Drugs," she whispered.

As both women's eyes opened wide, she walked away.

Through a gap in the parked trailers, she saw signs of action, lights being moved, sets being shifted. The actress must have accepted her apology. The show was back on the road.

She had turned the corner when she heard a phone ringing. For a second, she was confused. They'd taken her phone, hadn't they? Then she realized it was her personal phone. She knew who it would be even as she scrabbled for it in the bottom of her bag. It wasn't something she and Victoria ever admitted to the twin-obsessed people they met, but this happened all the time, one of them phoning the other just when she was needed. As if they sensed something was wrong even as it was unfolding. Like right now.

Genevieve answered. "Victoria, you won't believe what's just happened."

"It's not Victoria. It's me. Lindy."

"Lindy?" Lindy never called her. She was always in too much debt to be able to make expensive phone calls. "What's happened? Is everyone all right?"

"No! You won't believe what happened to Ig! It was *disgusting*! Can you talk or have I called at a bad time?"

Genevieve was now unemployed. Untouchable in her industry. She dropped her bags and sat down on a nearby stoop. "Go for it, Lindy. I've got all the time in the world."

FIVE

It was a blue, cloudless day in Sydney. As Victoria had done every morning for a month, she pulled back the curtain and checked her front garden for photographers. It was ridiculous. The world was in economic recession, injustice was rampant around the globe, yet *she* had somehow made the news. *Her* picture had appeared on front pages. Entire columns had been devoted to *her.* And why?

Because she had been silly enough, trusting enough, stupid enough to believe a string of silky words from a man she knew was a coked-up, megalomaniacal, lying, egotistical married idiot.

Never again. She'd learned her lesson. She was the one paying for it, out of work, an untouchable in her industry. As for him—the whole incident had proved to be just one more rung on the ladder of success. If she chose to, she could turn on the radio beside her, tune it to a station she'd considered her competition, wait until after the nine a.m. news and there he'd be. His voice. His opinions. Mr. Radio himself, broadcasting all over Sydney, all over New South Wales.

While here she was, humiliated, hiding in her tiny rented flat. The scapegoat.

On the table beside her, the phone rang. She glanced at the caller ID. It was Lindy. It usually was at this time of day. Since Lindy had moved back home, she'd taken to phoning Victoria every morning, ostensibly to see how she was. It always turned into a Lindy Whine Fest instead. Victoria would call her back after breakfast.

It was Genevieve whom Victoria really wanted to talk to. They spoke every day, sometimes twice a day, even if there wasn't a drama in their lives. They weren't just twins. They were best friends. Unfortunately Genevieve had been distracted today. It didn't matter. They'd talk again later. Victoria knew what her twin would say too. She'd been saying it to her since it happened. "Yes, it was horrible, Victoria. Yes, it was unjust. But you have to get over it. And you will."

"But how could he do that to me?" she'd sobbed during one of their calls. She'd had too much wine that particular night and had become very maudlin.

"Because he's a cad, Victoria. And you've been lynched while he sails on to fight another microphone, if I'm not mixing my metaphors. It's the big bad media world, darling. It bit you. So you have to bite back or run whimpering into the bushes until your wound heals."

"Have you been drinking too?"

"Yes, but I'm still making great sense and being quite poetic too, if I may say so myself. Seriously, Victoria, you do need to get over it. Get over him."

"How can I? He's the one who came into work off his rocker, abused not just every advertiser, but every actor, sportsman—"

"Politician. Yes, I know. You may possibly have mentioned them before. And now he has landed a filthy new contract worth millions and you're hiding under the bed without a job."

"I'm not under the bed."

"Where are you?"

"On the bed."

"Under the covers?"

"That's not the point. It's all right for you, Miss Hair Queen. Miss Successful."

Genevieve laughed. "I love you in this mood. But you're right. It is all perfect for me. So why don't you come and stay with me for a while? You can't use work as an excuse now. Come back with me after Christmas. We can have New Year in New York together."

"I can't afford it. I haven't got any money left."

"Nor have I. I've spent all mine on my wild lifestyle. Let's borrow some from Dad, if Lindy's left any for us."

Victoria had thought about her sister's suggestion constantly since then. It was a great idea, she finally decided. She could get out of Sydney. Escape the media world. Leave behind all her friends who'd turned out to be her friends only when she produced Mr. Radio's show. She hadn't heard from any of them since the blowup.

She'd called Genevieve not only to confirm her flight time, but also to give her the big news: She'd go back to New York with her. Not just for a holiday, but to try for work. She couldn't wait to hear Genevieve's excitement. To start planning. She'd try her again soon. Once her usual morning routine was out of the way.

Step one, check the front garden. It seemed to be clear. There'd been no photographers for days, in fact. She'd sneak out, get her mail and be back inside lickety-split. Step two, something nice to eat. She'd already had a bowl of cereal when she first got up, but that was more to wake herself up. For fuel, rather than pleasure. What she was looking forward to now was a proper breakfast. A lovely fluffy omelet, she decided. With smoked salmon, cheese and chives. And buttered toast. And a pot of coffee. She had to take this crisis and turn it into an opportunity. It was time to spoil herself. She *had* been working too hard. She *had* been burning the candle at both ends.

She *had* been sleeping with Mr. Radio. She had nearly fallen in love with Mr. Radio. Yes, he was arrogant, egotistical, out of control at times. But he was also smart. He'd made her laugh. Told her she was a great producer. Given her other, sexier compliments when the two of them were alone . . .

But none of that changed her situation. She had clearly meant nothing to him. So she had to take Genevieve's advice and move on. And she would. Literally. To New York.

She was out to the mailbox and back within a minute. Three letters, and no photographer, thankfully. They'd probably gotten enough unflattering shots of her to fill their image files. She'd been shocked to see the photos. She knew she'd put on a bit of weight recently, and they were taken at a bad angle, and she was also in her pajamas, but still . . . Once she got to New York, she was seriously going to do something about it. Genevieve said she walked everywhere; that was how she kept her weight down. Victoria had laughed and said, "So it's got nothing to do with the coffee you live on? The fact you don't actually eat?"

She put the letters to one side for the moment, unable to get the image of that fluffy omelet out of her head. Yes, there were definite advantages to being publicly humiliated and losing her job. She now had time to enjoy cooking again.

The eggs were free-range. The omelet was soon a rich golden yellow at the bottom of the pan. The smoked salmon turned from orange to luscious pink as it cooked. She sprinkled on some grated cheese and some freshly cut chives, gently folded it over, waited a moment, then lifted it onto the warm plate just as the toast popped. Two generous spreads of butter, a hot cup of coffee. She took a bite. Heaven. Who cared about work? Who cared about humiliation? Nothing mattered when life still offered pleasures like this.

It wasn't until she'd eaten a third piece of toast that she opened her mail. Within seconds, she wished she hadn't.

Her landlord was putting up the rent. It was already expensive, but she'd justified it to herself. She had to pay high rents if she wanted to live close to the city and have a sliver of harbor view. Even if she'd still had a job, she would have been stretched to cover the new figure. She put the letter back in the envelope. Then she put her empty plate on top of the envelope.

The second letter was worse. Her lawyer was writing to tell her that she wasn't eligible for compensation from the radio station on account of her freelance status. He was also advising her that if she was to take the matter further, the station was within its rights to pursue her for compensation, on the grounds that she had "clearly been in error for allowing an intoxicated presenter to go on air." The presenter who had subsequently left the station and taken hundreds of thousands of advertising dollars with him. But what could she possibly have done to stop him? The bill for her legal fees was also enclosed. She gasped out loud when she saw the figure. It was more than she had expected to get in compensation. It was five times the amount she had in her bank account. She put that letter back in its envelope and put a different plate on top.

The last letter was from Ig. Postmarked Adelaide, sent more than a fortnight earlier. It had obviously taken the scenic route to her, due to the incomplete address. She'd received quite a few of these from him this year. The latest message was just five words. He'd cut the letters out of a newspaper.

GeT mE OuT of HeRE.

Victoria already knew his plea had been answered. She'd received an e-mail from her mother the previous week letting her and Genevieve know the latest about Ig's ongoing battle with boarding school. *On the principal's advice, we've decided to keep him home for another year and review the situation after that.*

Genevieve and Victoria had immediately forwarded it to each other.

He's run away a third time?? Victoria had e-mailed.

The Houdini of the South Australian school system strikes again! Genevieve had written back.

Dear little Ig, Victoria thought. Dear, mad little Ig. It would be so good to spend time with him over Christmas too. She clearly remembered the first time she'd seen him, in her mother's arms at the Port Augusta hospital. At twenty-two, she and Genevieve had been old enough to be having their own babies, not welcoming a little brother. Her mother—and her father—had looked shell-shocked that day, she recalled. Happy, yes, but definitely shocked. As Genevieve had said, too often and too loudly, that would teach them to still be having sex at their age.

She'd picked up her phone to try Genevieve once more when it rang. Their twin-ESP at work.

Victoria didn't waste time with a greeting. "Genevieve? I've decided. I'm coming back to New York with you after Christmas. But not just for a holiday. To live."

An unexpected voice replied, "It's not Genevieve. It's Lindy. And you can't do any of that."

"I can't? Why not?"

"Because I've just hung up from her. She's been sacked. She's coming home too. For good."

SIX

When Angela and Nick first married, he gave her a puppy as a combination wedding present and welcome-to-station-life present. It was a black-and-white collie with different-colored eyes, one blue, one brown. All day it followed her around. Every time she turned around it was there. At night it whimpered until she came to it. It whimpered during the day too if she didn't give it enough attention.

Having Lindy at home again was reminding Angela of that dog.

Especially at the moment, when it was Ig who needed her attention. Angela had been surprised at how quickly he was allowed home, only three days after the surgery, but the doctor was relaxed. "You'll be amazed how soon he'll spring back, thanks to you," he said. "The old finger-in-the-freezer-bag trick never fails." Ig would have to wear a finger splint and a sling for six weeks, have his dressings changed regularly and start physiotherapy down the track. It could all be done locally. For now, it was business as usual. She'd looked in on him just a few minutes before. He was in his room, working one-handed on a jigsaw. He'd glanced up, shaken his hair out of his eyes—she still hadn't gotten around to getting his hair cut—and smiled. "All okay, Ig?" she'd asked.

"No worries, Mum," he'd said.

As she'd walked away, she heard him talk out loud. Not to her. To Robbie. But that was a worry for another day.

Not for the first time, she was thankful she'd made the decision to host her station stay visitors only from March to November. There was enough going on without extra guests to look after. But she would still be getting inquiries via e-mail. She always made a point of replying to them all within a day or two. That hadn't been possible this week. She hadn't been near a computer since the night of Ig's accident, and hadn't had the opportunity since she'd come home either. When Nick wasn't on it, Lindy was. The one time it had been free, the satellite connection had been down. It was a regular occurrence up here, one she had long grown used to. The phone line often dropped out too. They weren't completely isolated, of course. All their vehicles were fitted with UHF radios, the main transmitter in the kitchen, but it was an open line, not one that Angela liked to use to conduct private business.

She'd get to her e-mails as soon as she could. For now, she was doing her best to keep up with Lindy's litany of woes. Had Lindy always been this needy? Angela had probably been too busy to notice. She knew she should make the time to sit Lindy down, have a heart-to-heart, give her the space and support she needed to feel comfortable and confident enough to share all her worries in one fell swoop. But there never seemed to be time. The day before, Angela had promised herself she'd give Lindy all the attention she needed once the party was over and the twins had left.

Except now the twins weren't going anywhere.

They'd delivered their bombshell news the previous evening. Nick had been away, checking fences halfway across the property with Johnny, their now only part-time stockman. One of the local Adnyamathanha people, he had worked with Nick for more than twenty years. Angela was in the kitchen when Genevieve called to say she and Victoria wanted her to Skype them. Ig set up the computer. The video part never worked, but she could clearly hear their voices. Ig told them about his damaged finger, describing the accident in gory detail, then went to his room. Lindy was in the living room working her way through a box set of DVDs. Watching TV and being upset seemed to be her main occupations at the moment.

Angela heard the twins' news alone. Genevieve had lost her job in spectacular fashion. She was very relaxed about it, or at least pretending to be very relaxed. "Google me, Mum. I'm an Internet sensation!" When Angela got over her shock enough to ask what it meant for Genevieve's working visa, she was blithely informed that Genevieve's visa had actually expired some weeks before. Now she was, in her words, a "social media dish of the day," and any chance of being sponsored by another film company was gone. She had no choice, she announced cheerily. She was coming home for good.

"It's like fate, isn't it, Victoria?" she said to her twin. "The universe telling us to spend more time together."

Victoria joined in. It was all brilliant news, in her opinion. As usual, the two of them talked as one, finishing each other's sentences. They were, of course, sorry to land all this on Angela on top of Ig's accident, and the big party, and Christmas, but they'd both made some life-changing decisions. They'd decided the time was right for them to come and live on the station again—

"Just for a while—"

"Until we work out our next step—"

"Until we save some money—"

"If that's okay with you, Mum?" Victoria asked.

"And if you or Dad don't mind loaning us some money," Genevieve added. "Quite a lot of money, actually. Just to cover our debts. We'll pay back every cent, though."

"We promise," Victoria said.

"Of course that's okay," Angela said. "Of course. I can't wait to see you."

And of course she meant it. They were her daughters. This was their home. But how much money? Would she and Nick have enough themselves to cover the twins' debts? And what did "just for a while" mean? A month? Six months? A year? And how could they save when they wouldn't be working? It wasn't like the old days, when they were little, when she and Nick could give the children odd jobs around the property in return for their pocket money. Sweeping out the shearing shed, tidying up the toolshed. There wasn't any of that work to be done these days, not now that the station didn't run any sheep, not even breeding stock.

Angela broke the news of Celia's extended visit to them.

"She's staying for a *month*?" Victoria said. "Mum, no! Quick, build a moat!"

"Don't be rude," Angela said automatically. "She's family. Your father's only aunt."

"Only by marriage," Genevieve said. "Does that even count?"

"Why don't her own kids ever have her for Christmas?" Victoria asked.

Genevieve answered, "Because they emigrated as soon as they found out she doesn't like flying."

Angela had a suspicion she was right. Celia's two sons had left Australia years earlier. One lived in France, the other in Singapore. They only rarely came home with their wives and children.

"Can't you tell her we need some family time?" Genevieve asked.

"We never get you to ourselves anymore," Victoria said.

"We haven't in years. Not since you had Lindy, let alone Ig—"

"*Please*, Mum. And will you please pick us up at the airport? Just you. Your long-lost daughters—"

"Your prodigal daughters—"

"Coming home at last. If anyone needs you, it's us."

Angela had been alternating between laughing and telling them off when the line disconnected. Minutes afterward, Nick had arrived home with Johnny, with the news that Johnny was staying for dinner and the night. The men went straight out onto the back veranda after they'd eaten. They were still out there talking when she went to bed. She still hadn't had a chance to tell Nick the twins' news. It was the pattern of their lives now. Ships that passed in the night and day.

She wished she could have called Joan to talk about all of this. But Joan and her husband had been away on a week-long cruise with their two daughters and their families. She wasn't due back home until later today.

Lindy, however, knew all about the twins. She'd known for days, it transpired, but Genevieve had sworn her to secrecy. All morning she'd been following Angela around, asking questions and expressing opinions.

"I think Genevieve sounded too cheery about losing her job. You don't suppose she's on drugs, do you? That makes you immune to real emotion, doesn't it? I talked to her for nearly an hour about it and she didn't sound upset at all."

"For an hour? Lindy, please don't make long overseas calls without asking. You know how expensive they are."

"I needed to talk to her about something else too. Something urgent." She paused. "About Christmas."

Lindy was lying. Whatever else she had phoned her sister about, it wasn't Christmas.

For the next hour, Lindy followed her mother back and forth from the laundry to the washing line, handing over pegs, still asking questions.

"So where will they sleep?"

"In their old rooms."

"But Genevieve's room is your ironing room."

"I guess it won't be anymore."

"But how can Victoria afford to take time off? I thought you said she wasn't getting a payout from the radio station."

"She isn't."

"Genevieve wouldn't have got one either, would she? Isn't it irresponsible of her to waste money on an international airfare? Shouldn't she cash that in and stay there and look for work?"

Oh, shush, Angela thought as they walked back to the line with another basket. You ran home the second you got into financial trouble, didn't you?

Lindy stopped. "Mum!"

"What?"

"Did you really mean that? About me running home?"

Angela blinked. She'd certainly thought it, yes, but had she said it out loud too? By the look on Lindy's face, yes, she had.

"I was joking," she said.

"It didn't sound like you were joking."

"I was. Pass me another peg, would you?"

They finally finished the washing. The clothesline that stretched from the side veranda right across to the boundary fence was now filled with sheets, pillowcases and tea towels. The wind was hot and gusty. Everything would be dry within an hour.

As they walked back inside the cool house, Lindy looked at her mother. "You've got very sharp-tongued lately, Mum, if you don't mind me saying. You're not pregnant again, are you?"

Angela gave a sudden, high-pitched laugh.

"That's why I rang Genevieve the other day, you know," Lindy said. "To talk about you."

In the kitchen, Angela filled the kettle, talking over her shoulder. "That must have been a dull conversation."

"I had to talk to someone, Mum. I hope you don't mind me saying this, but you really have been a bit, I don't know, different lately. Weird. Distracted. I've been worried about you."

"You didn't think you could just talk to me about it?"

"No. I thought you'd get cross. Like you are now."

"I'm not cross. So, which of my current symptoms did you and Genevieve discuss?"

Lindy counted them off on her fingers. "How you're preoccupied all the time. Talking to yourself a lot. How you and Dad are funny with each other. How you've got that sudden new hobby, the pottery, when you've never done anything like that before. You've been ringing Joan even more than usual too."

"And what did Genevieve say?"

"She just changed the subject back to her being sacked." Lindy sat down and sighed again. "Life's not fair, is it? Look at me. I'm nearly thirty years old. I don't have a career. I don't have a boyfriend. I know Genevieve and Victoria are in a mess now, but at least they've had a taste of success. I haven't even had that. I ruin everything I touch, don't I? No matter what I do, it never works out. All that cushion stuff outside, the money I owe Dad—"

Here we go again, Angela thought. Blah, blah, blah.

"Mum!"

She'd said that aloud too? "Lindy, of course you're not a failure. Everyone goes through ups and downs. As you said, look at the twins. Roosters one day, feather dusters the next."

"That's not very nice either."

"How about you go and check your Web site? Maybe

you've had an order this morning. Wouldn't that be great? You could get started on that."

"I can't. Dad's back on the computer again. Shall I tell him to give me a turn? Tell him you insisted?"

"Good idea. You do that."

Standing at the linen cupboard in the hallway, Angela heard Lindy ask to use the computer. Nick was midway through watching an online history documentary but she could have five minutes, he said. But she needed ten, Lindy said. Angela wanted to go in, turn off the computer and send them both to their rooms.

She closed her eyes instead and imagined herself far from here. It only ever took a moment.

She wasn't on a sheep station in South Australia, in the middle of a hot summer, listening to a family row. She was in London. In springtime. On a deck chair in her London garden with Will walking toward her, smiling, carrying a tray of iced tea.

"Here you are, darling," he said. "It's so good to see you taking a break. You've worked so hard lately."

She took the drink, had a sip and smiled gratefully at him. "That tastes wonderful. What's in it?"

"I couldn't possibly say. It's my secret recipe. But I may have accidentally added a touch of gin."

"Gin? At this time of day?"

There was a whisper beside her. "Mum?"

She kept her eyes shut. "Yes, Ig."

"Are you okay?"

"Yes, thanks, Ig."

"Have you started sleeping standing up? Like a horse?"

She'd just smiled and pulled Ig into a hug when Lindy came running out of the office.

"I've got an order! I've got an order!"

Fifteen minutes later, Lindy and Ig were on their way across the yard toward the stack of crates behind the woolshed. They'd come to an agreement. If he helped her dismantle the crates, she'd let him build a cubby house out of all the smaller cardboard boxes her cushion material was stored in.

Lindy's mood had changed completely. An actual order! This could be the start of her brand-new career! It was a simple order too, wishing someone well after an operation. The customer had requested specific colors (purple and green) and a brief message (*Get Well Soon!*).

Ig helped Lindy as she untied the tarpaulin covering the sixteen crates. It hadn't rained in weeks, but the covering helped keep the dust off. Everything on the station—the fences, the sheds, the homestead—was often covered in a fine layer of red dust this time of year.

Lindy checked through the order again. She'd need a blank cushion cover. Cushion filler. Purple and green thread for the cross-stitching of the letters and the decorative border. She'd ordered those colors, hadn't she? Yes. She'd ordered every available color. She untied the last of the tarpaulin ropes.

"Ready, Ig?"

"Ready."

They both tugged. The tarpaulin fell in a shimmer of plastic onto the dirt. The crates, each of them filled with cardboard boxes, reared above them like giant LEGO blocks. Lindy got a sick feeling in her stomach.

Ig leaped up onto the first crate, still nimble despite his arm being in a sling. Fifteen minutes later, they were surrounded by cardboard boxes and she had all the material she needed.

"All yours, Ig. Happy cubby making. I'll be on the veranda sewing if anyone's looking for me."

"They won't be. It's just you and me and Mum and Dad here. We all know where everybody is."

"It's just a saying, Ig. I'm going to work. I, Lindy Gillespie, am Going Back to Work."

Ig watched her go, talking to herself. What was it with girls and sisters and mothers? They seemed to do so much talking and crying about things. Even his dad was at it these days, talking to his new friend Carol in Ireland all the time.

That was the good thing about his friend Robbie. He only ever said what needed to be said.

"Okay, Robbie," Ig said to him now. "Cubby time. No, not heavy at all. It's just sewing stuff. I'll lift them one-handed. You can help me decide how to arrange them." He laughed. "Exactly. You're the brains. I'm the muscle."

SEVEN

The phone in the kitchen rang as Angela was on her way out to her pottery studio. At least, she called it her studio. Her family still called it the toolshed. She waited for one of the others to answer. The phone kept ringing. The answering machine wasn't working properly anymore; nor was the phone in the office, not since Ig had used them to try to record a rap song he'd written.

Angela came back inside and answered. "Gillespies. Hello."

"So, I head off on a cruise for just a week and look what you get up to."

"Joan?"

"Angela, you're my oldest friend. I thought I knew you, but what got into you? Were you drunk?"

Angela felt a sudden chill that had nothing to do with

the temperature. She reached across, shut the kitchen door and lowered her voice. "Welcome back. How was it? And what are you talking about?"

"Your latest 'Hello from the Gillespies.' Or, as you should have called it, your 'Bombshells from the Gillespies.'"

Angela frowned. What did Joan mean? She hadn't sent out her Christmas letter this year.

Joan was still talking. "I have to say, you shocked me and I'm not easily shocked. Did Nick mind you telling everyone about the mining lease? I'm not sure how Victoria will feel about your telling everyone your suspicions about her affair either. I'd quite like to have seen a photo of Genevieve with those blue dreadlocks, though. What did you say Ig called her? A feral Smurf?"

Angela felt an unsettling shimmer. "Joan, what are you talking about?"

"Your letter. I have it right here on the computer in front of me."

Joan started reading from it. Angela went hot, then cold, then hot again.

It was her letter. Her ranting letter. The one she had deleted just as Ig had his accident. She hadn't even thought about it again until two days later, as she sat beside Ig's hospital bed reading an old newspaper. The date had leaped out at her. December 1. The day she always sent her Christmas letter. A combination of exhaustion and worry about Ig had swept over her. She'd decided she wouldn't send a letter at all this year. See whether it mattered. Whether anyone even noticed . . .

So how had this happened? How on earth had Joan received it?

Joan was still reading aloud. Angela asked her to stop. Joan was her best friend. They'd shared secrets for years. Even so, the thought of her knowing all this—Angela's headache started up.

"Joan, I can't understand it."

"You want me to read more?"

"No, I can't understand how you got it. Yes, I wrote it, but I decided not to send it. I took your advice, wrote the truth for once. I even imagined you there beside me, urging me on—"

That was it! Joan had been on her mind as she wrote it. And in the fuss of Ig's accident, rather than deleting it, she'd somehow, accidentally, pressed send and e-mailed it to Joan. Relief flooded through her.

"It's okay," Angela said, smiling into the phone. "I think I've worked out what happened. Oh, thank God it was only you. Joan, please, can you delete it? Right now? Every word of it? Then forget you ever read it?"

"Of course." There was a pause. "But what about the others?"

"What others?"

"The other one hundred people on your mailing list."

"*What?*"

"Angela, it didn't just go to me. It looks like it went to everyone you know. All their names are right here on the e-mail." She began to read them. Angela recognized name after name. All their neighbors in the Flinders Ranges. Nick's relatives around Australia. Her old school friends and distant relatives in England. People in Port Augusta. Ig's school principal in Adelaide. Their local member of Parliament . . . Name after name after name.

Angela's hands were shaking. *Oh God, oh God.* How had this happened?

Her voice was just a whisper. "Joan, what can I do? Is there a way of sucking e-mails back to the original computer?"

"Like putting a vacuum cleaner on reverse? Oh, Ange, I'm sorry. No, I don't think so."

"I'm dead. Nick will kill me."

"Not only Nick. I suspect the twins will too. Lindy won't be happy either. Ig got off the lightest. He just sounds weird. The other three sound demented."

Angela knew Joan was trying to lighten the mood, but she wanted to cry. "What am I going to do?"

Joan's tone turned serious. "You definitely didn't mean to send it?"

"Of *course* not. I can't even remember doing it."

"No matter. It's done. So you have two choices. You can e-mail everyone again and say it was a mistake and could they please delete it. Instant backfire. Those who haven't read it will do so immediately. Or choice two, do nothing."

"Nothing?"

"Nothing. That would be my advice. Brazen it out. Do nothing. Say nothing. Hope it just sinks without a trace. Most people hate getting these Christmas letters and never read them anyway."

"You read it."

"You're my oldest friend. Usually I loathe them. They're nothing but smug lie recitals, in my experience. At least you told the truth this time. It is all the truth, I gather?"

"Yes, but—"

"Shush. Don't explain it to me either. Just say nothing."

Another awful thought struck Angela. "Joan, is Celia's name on the recipients' list?"

"Let me check."

A minute passed. Angela crossed her fingers.

"Yes," Joan said.

Angela's headache started to pulse faster. "Oh no. Of all the people—"

"Let me see what you said about her. Here it is. 'Insufferable snob. Interfering old bat.' Beautifully put. You summed her up perfectly. I've known her for years, remember. She's also got the hide of a rhino. This won't change a thing."

"But she's Nick's aunt. His only aunt."

"So let Nick deal with it. If he can take his mind off his family tree or his Irish girlfriend for long enough. Will they get married in Adelaide or Dublin, do you think? You Catholics are allowed to divorce now, aren't you?"

"You're not helping, Joan."

"Yes, I am. You can either laugh about it or kill yourself about it, and you're my best friend and I don't want you dead. So we're going to laugh about it and we'll get you through this together."

"I can't even go into hiding. Half the people on that mailing list are invited to the woolshed party. I'll have to cancel it. No one will want to come now anyway, will they?"

"Are you joking? They'll all come now. You'll be turning people away. And you can't cancel it. My freezer is full of cupcakes for that party. By the way, did Lindy get my cushion order?"

"That was you?"

"I used a friend's credit card. After reading your letter, I thought she needed all the help she could get."

"Is it for you? Are you sick?"

"God, no. I'm fit as a mallee bull. I just thought 'Get Well Soon' would be quicker for her to sew than 'Happy Birthday' or 'Happy Anniversary.' I'm getting her to send it to my cousin in Perth. She's a hypochondriac. It'll make a perfect Christmas present." There was the sound of another voice in the background. "Glenn's coming. I better go. I'll call you again as soon as I can. Don't worry. I mean it. We'll get you through this." With that, she was gone.

Angela stayed sitting at the kitchen table, the phone in her hand. She didn't want to put it back on the hook in case someone else who'd received her Christmas e-mail decided to call her. She was suddenly glad they had no mobile phone coverage out here. Glad they were so isolated.

She had a mental picture of their woolshed in ten days' time. All their neighbors, all those familiar faces, staring at her, knowing all of her secrets.

She couldn't bear it.

"Brazen it out," Joan had advised. "Do nothing. Say nothing."

How could she?

She had to do something. Most important, she needed to read the entire letter again, right now. Perhaps it wouldn't be as terrible as it had sounded. And of course Joan was right. It was just a letter. Words on a screen. Perhaps it wouldn't be necessary to say anything about it to Nick, to the girls, to Ig. It was Christmas, after all. People were so busy. And if anyone did happen to read it, perhaps they would think she was joking, that she'd joined some sort of creative writing class. . . .

As she moved down the hall closer to the office, she heard talking. Talking and laughing. Nick was in there, Skyping. Someone with an Irish accent. A female someone. Carol.

Angela couldn't stop herself. She stayed in the shadows and eavesdropped. He sounded like a different Nick. The old Nick. The one she hadn't seen or heard for months.

"Carol, that's great. You've made it all seem so real."

"It's not me; it's your family. I've just found their stories for you."

"But I'd never have found all of this detail without you. Those letters my great-grandfather—"

"Great-great-grandfather."

"The political letters he wrote to the newspaper, how did you even know these archives existed?"

"That's my job. That's why you pay me."

"You're worth your weight in gold."

"Why, thank you, kind sir." A musical laugh. "I've also found a new lead. It's still early days, but it looks like a journal belonging to one of your aunts could be in a small museum in Letterkenny, in Donegal. It's not online yet. The only way I'll be able to check for sure is if I go there, but that would add to your expenses, and so I needed to check first, before I—"

"Of course. Please, go as soon as you can. Do you need me to transfer some money in advance?"

"That would be helpful, if you don't mind. I've done a rough calculation, gas and accommodation expenses. I'll need to stay overnight, unfortunately. It's a five-hour drive from here. Such a shame you're so far away. You could come too."

"I've been thinking the same thing. That I should make a kind of reconnaissance visit to Ireland, to help me plan the reunion. I've already had a look at possible flights in late January or February, just for ten days or so. Carol, this is a lot to ask, on top of everything else, but would you—"

"Mum?" It was Ig, in the hall beside her.

She looked down and put her finger to her lips.

"What are you doing?" he whispered.

"I'm trying to hear what Dad is saying to the lady in Ireland," she whispered.

Ig listened for a moment too. "That's Carol. His girlfriend."

"His girlfriend?"

Ig nodded. "Lindy and I think he's in love with her."

From the office came another burst of laughter from Carol.

"No, of course I won't recommend a car hire company! I'll drive you around myself. I'd be honored. I'll need to charge you a daily rate or my boss will kill me, but it will be as low as possible, I promise. You're my number one client, after all."

Angela felt nauseous. Was Nick really talking about a spur-of-the-moment trip to Ireland? For ten days? On his own? Flying there on his own, at least. But meeting Carol once he got there. Traveling around with Carol . . .

Ig whispered again. "Mum, are you and Dad going to get divorced?"

"Of course not." She said it as firmly as she could at low volume.

"Mum?" It was Ig again, still in a whisper. "Can I please have some curtains?"

She was still trying to listen in. "Sorry, Ig. What?"

"Some curtains. For my cubby. Please."

As she heard more laughter from Carol, Angela was glad of the distraction. She steered Ig back down the hallway, trying to sound normal.

"Another cubby, Ig? How many is that this year?"

Ig counted under his breath. "Ten. But Robbie thinks this one will be the best."

She found some old curtains in the linen cupboard. He inspected them closely before nodding.

"So, how is Robbie these days?" Angela asked casually as he headed for the back door.

"Good, thanks."

"Is it nice to have him back again?"

"Yep."

"Great. Well, tell him I said hi."

"Tell him yourself."

"He's here now?"

Ig nodded, then stood, waiting.

Angela cleared her throat. "Hi, Robbie."

There was silence.

"He says hi to you too. Thanks, Mum. See you later."

Angela was on her way back to Nick in the office when Lindy rushed in from the veranda. She was holding the cushion cover. "Mum, look!"

"You've finished already?" Angela took it. There was one letter in the center of the cover. The *G* of Get Well Soon.

Lindy was beaming. "It looks brilliant, doesn't it!"

"It sure does," Angela said.

Nick appeared. "The reunion's on. I've decided to definitely go ahead with one."

"In Ireland?" Lindy said. "Cool! Are you still thinking October next year? Can we all come?"

Angela looked back and forth at them. "You know about the reunion too?" she asked Lindy.

"Sure," she said. "I've been working out on the veranda. I've overheard Dad and Carol talking about it. Or should I say flirting about it." She laughed. "Joking, Dad. That's great news. Well done. Sorry; you'll have to excuse me. I've got loads of work to do." Lindy slipped past them both, cushion in hand.

Angela tried to sound breezy. "Carol's helping you organize a reunion now? I thought she was just a genealogist."

"Carol seems to do everything. When she heard I'd already been in touch with Gillespies around the world, she even suggested where to hold the reunion. I was thinking of either Donegal or Mayo, where the two original Gillespie cousins came from. She had a better idea. Hold it in Cobh."

"Cove?"

"It's in County Cork. Pronounced 'Cove,' spelled 'C-O-B-H.' It's where most of the emigrants sailed from. Their final connection with Ireland. I've been researching it for the past few days. It's a beautiful port town. So much history there, even an emigration museum. The perfect place for a reunion."

Angela waited for him to mention his reconnaissance trip to Ireland. He didn't. She found a bright smile from somewhere. "That's great news."

Tell him about the letter, an inner voice said. *Now*. But she couldn't. Not until she'd reread it. This was her chance. "Would you mind if I used the computer for a minute?"

He hesitated. "That's fine. Of course. How long do you need?"

"Ten minutes. Less, probably."

"Fine. Sure. I need a break, in any case. Can I make you a coffee?"

"No, thanks. I'm fine."

They were talking to each other like work colleagues. Not husband and wife.

Ig's words flashed into her mind. "That's Carol. His girlfriend. Lindy and I think he's in love with her." They were wrong. Of course they were wrong. In any case, she had something more urgent than Carol to worry about now. More urgent than Carol, the party, the twins, Lindy, Ig and even Nick . . .

She was at the computer logging on to her e-mail account when Nick reappeared. He leaned across her, taking the mouse.

"Sorry; I meant to close that last e-mail. Carol's sent me through some new links." He pressed some keys and the e-mail disappeared. But not before Angela saw the final two lines.

```
                                    Love Carol
                                      xxxx
```

Her heart thumped. "Love and kisses from Carol? That's very informal of her, isn't it?"

"You know what they say about the Irish—charm to burn."

Her brakes were off now. "The kids call her your girl-friend."

"So I gathered from Lindy. I'd call it overactive imagi-nations."

"Should I be worried?" Her casual tone sounded so fake. "Are you about to head off to Ireland to meet your new lady friend?"

"Of course not. I'll be back in a few minutes. Take your time."

She watched him leave. Was this the moment she'd been waiting for? Was this her opportunity to go out to the kitchen, shut the door and say, "Nick, we have to talk"? About Ireland, about Carol, about their marriage? About her Christmas letter?

No. Not yet. She needed to reread it first. Remind herself just how bad it was before she tried to fix it. She opened her e-mail account and clicked straight to her Sent folder.

There it was. Her Christmas letter, right on top. *Hello from the Gillespies!* Sent on December first. She shut her eyes, feeling sick. She tried to recall that night, the shock and confusion of Ig's accident, imagining herself somehow, accidentally, pressing send, not delete. Right at midnight, according to this. She frowned. But she'd been in the hospital with Ig by then, nowhere near a computer. It only took her a moment to figure it out. The Internet connection must have dropped out just as she'd sent it. It happened often. Once it was back up again, the e-mail had transmitted. Right at midnight. Right on time.

Oh God, oh God, oh God.

She forced herself to read it. Phrase after phrase jumped

out at her. *Everything seems to have gone wrong for us. Fake TV world. Having an affair. Married radio announcer. A debt-ridden mess. A very weird little boy. Like a different man these days. Think he might be having an affair.*

It got worse.

I think something is wrong with me. I wouldn't have married Nick. I wouldn't have our children. I wouldn't be living here on an outback sheep station. Gone back home to my child-hood sweetheart Will. Married him. We'd have had one child. Just the one.

Her eyes filled with tears. What had she been thinking when she wrote this? It read as if she regretted them all, as if she wished away her entire life here in favor of a different life. As if she hated Australia and wished she were back liv-ing in London. And she didn't. Did she?

No. She loved them. She did. She and Nick had had a good marriage. A great marriage, until the past year or so. And that fantasy life of hers? It was just that, wasn't it? A kind of meditation for her. Respite. Everybody thought like that sometimes, didn't they? Looked back over their lives and wondered "what if"? Pictured how their lives might have been if they'd made different choices?

Of course they did. Of course.

She just needed to somehow explain all of this, to Nick, to her daughters, to Ig. And to the other one hundred people who had received this e-mail and were—

"Are you done?"

She jumped at the sound of Nick's voice. "Just need a few more minutes," she called back.

As she sat there, she noticed something else. Her in-box

was filling, e-mail after e-mail slowly coming in to her account. She had five new messages. Ten new messages. It stopped at thirty-seven new messages. All with the same subject line: *Re: Hello from the Gillespies!*

They were replies to her Christmas letter. She clicked on the first one. Read it. Clicked. Read. Clicked. Read. The e-mails were from all over Australia, across the world.

Thanks for the best letter ever! So glad we're not the only family having ups and downs!

Happy Christmas to you all too. (Please send these monthly if you're going to be this honest!)

Usually just toss these, glad something made me read it this time! Merry Christmas to you all too, if you get through it!

There were more specific responses:

OMG, Angela! Do you really think Victoria and that radio presenter were having an affair? I'm never listening to him again! That creep!! She should sell her story to the papers! Or I will if she won't. (Joking, Angela! I'll keep this between us, promise.)

Genevieve knows all the Hollywood gossip?? Can't wait to hear it at the party!!

Lindy's back home again? That's what I call a
boomerang kid!

There were comments about Ig too:

Don't worry about Ig, Angela. I work in a primary school and half the kids talk to themselves, it's just a stage.

If I lived out in the middle of nowhere like
you, I'd have a few imaginary friends too!!!
(No offense!!)

My second cousin had an imaginary friend until he was fourteen. He became a paranoid
schizophrenic. Not saying that will happen
to Ig too, but thought you should know, in
case you want to watch out for any other
symptoms.

There were reactions about the mining lease, from
people who hadn't heard the news until now:

Angela, are you serious??? Have you any idea
what a disaster that will be for all of us,
for the whole Flinders Ranges?

Angela, is this a joke? You and Nick have sold
out? I can't believe it.

Even as she was reading those, more came in. She clicked on them too.

```
Hope you don't mind, but have forwarded your
e-mail to friends and family. You make us seem
normal!!
```

```
Angela, very sorry to hear life is so tough at
the moment. Thinking of you. Call me if you
want to talk?
```

```
So I'm not the only one with a fantasy life!!
Thank God!! I'm married to Brad Pitt in mine
LOL!!!!!!
```

The final one was from the radio station manager in Port Pirie, where Victoria had first started working in radio ten years earlier. Angela had forgotten Keith was even on her mailing list.

```
Great read, Angela, thanks. Have been wonder-
ing how Victoria was getting on. Awful situ-
ation in Sydney, she's best out of it. Ask her
to give me a call if she's ever back in SA?
```

She jumped as Nick came in behind her, carrying a coffee. She hurriedly pressed a key. Instead of her e-mail closing down, a YouTube video started playing. One of Nick's. An online documentary about Irish emigration, a man on a waterfront talking into the camera, while sad music played in the background. She pressed some more keys. Finally, her e-mail closed down. This was how it must have happened on December first, she realized. Pressing something without thinking. Send instead of delete . . .

"We might need to think about getting another computer," Nick said. "It'll be like Grand Central Station in here once the twins are home, even temporarily."

He knew about Victoria's work situation, but Angela still hadn't told him Genevieve's news. Here was her chance. A moment to have a normal husband-wife conversation, be parents together . . .

She filled him in. She could see he was concerned.

"So they're both back for good?"

"For a while at least."

"That'll cause a stir around here."

Not as big a stir as her letter. She had to tell him about it. Tell all of them. It couldn't wait.

She cleared her throat. "I was thinking we should have a family meeting after dinner tonight. A proper catch-up. I could get the twins on Skype too. Just to talk over everything that's going on. We've a busy few weeks ahead of us, the party, Celia arriving—"

"I can't tonight, sorry. I've got a conference call with a few of the international Gillespie cousins, to talk about the reunion. It's been difficult to arrange, with all the different time zones."

"Of course. That's fine," Angela said. She'd tried. And failed. "We can leave it for now. Have the catch-up another night."

She stood up, went to the door and stopped. No, it wasn't fine. He had to know. Even if the others had to wait.

"Nick?"

He couldn't hear her. The YouTube video was playing too loudly. He was already back e-mailing Carol.

Angela left without speaking.

EIGHT

Twenty minutes later, Nick finished writing his e-mail to Carol and pressed send. There was no going back now. He'd just confirmed it. The reunion was going ahead.

It was hard to believe. Six months ago, he'd thought life held nothing for him. That it was all over. Every night, while Angela slept beside him, he'd lain awake for hours, trying to quell a rising panic, or lift himself out of the feeling of despair. Each day, his mind went over and over the same defeated thoughts. He was a failure.

It was all he could think about, yet he couldn't talk about it, to Angela, to his friends, to anyone. Until the sleeplessness got so bad, he went to his longtime doctor in Port Augusta to ask for sleeping tablets. Dr. Mitchell asked him why.

"Take your time," he said. "You're my last patient for the day."

That simple statement triggered something. Nick started talking. He told him everything. About the situation on the station. The money worries. The constant anxiety. The insomnia. The feeling of despair. The emptiness. What it was like to go from being constantly busy to having nothing to do.

Dr. Mitchell summed it up in one word. Depression.

"You're one of thousands, I'm sorry to say, Nick," he said. "You can't go through what you've all been through with the drought and not pay for it in some way. It can be as stressful having nothing to do as a lot to do. Humans need to be busy."

"How can I be busy?" he'd said.

Year after year, as the effects of the drought continued, the work that had consumed every hour of his life had decreased. His full-time stockmen had to be let go. There wasn't the work or the money to pay them. He'd also had to do what many neighboring pastoralists had been forced to do: gradually sell off his stock so he could pay even some of his bills.

He knew he'd let himself down. Let Angela down. The kids. Not just his own family. His ancestors. He'd always been conscious this was a fourth-generation property. It was on the homestead gatepost, under the Errigal nameplate, "Established 1887." It wasn't until he'd started on the family tree that he'd discovered they had been mispronouncing the station name. It was Erra-gull. Not Err-rye-gal. A mountain in Donegal, the home county of one of the original Gillespie cousins. A mountain he would soon see for himself.

All because of his doctor.

That afternoon Dr. Mitchell had discussed the treatments available for his depression. He also gave him some medication to get him sleeping again, to help calm his anxious mind. He stressed how important it was that Nick still get outside as often as he could, do some exercise every day. He also wanted him to think about talking to someone.

"A psychiatrist?" Nick said. "No, thanks."

"A psychologist," his doctor said. Not a local, but a good man from Adelaide who visited the area twice a month. Against all Nick's instincts, hating the idea of it, telling Angela he was in Port Augusta meeting his lawyers—more lies—he had already had three sessions. It was helping, even if sometimes there was more silence in the room than conversation. Jim, the psychologist, had echoed his doctor's advice. Stay active. Get outside. Eat properly. He'd suggested he find a new interest. Something to stop the despairing thoughts from taking over. "Think of your brain like a radio," Jim had said. "You've been stuck on a bad channel. A negative channel. You don't have to listen to it anymore. You can tune to different thoughts anytime you want to. Or need to. That's where a new interest will help. A hobby."

"Like what?" Nick had said. "Stamp collecting? We get three mail deliveries a week if we're lucky."

"You have a computer and the Internet out there, don't you?"

"Yes," Nick had said. It was an expensive satellite connection, but they did.

"Have you ever thought of tracing your ancestors? Irish, aren't you? Bet there's a few good stories."

The idea lodged in his mind. He'd thought about it over the next few days. He decided he wouldn't start on it until he heard back from the mining company. They'd done tests on four other properties in the area, he knew. All four shared the same rock formations, geological signs to what might lie below. Over the years, there'd been lots of speculation about what could be there—uranium, gold, copper, diamonds. He had actually prayed that they would find something of value on Errigal. Angela didn't know the extent of their financial problems. No one but he and his bank manager knew.

They owed nearly a million dollars.

He felt the sweat bead now, merely remembering what it had been like to hear that figure.

The crash in wool prices as well as the long drought had affected everyone in the entire state. But his neighbors had fared better. Not only because they were better graziers. It was luck as well. Their stations were on better land, with more water. Or they'd diversified. Or they had better management of feed, or stock levels. Better-quality wool, better profits. The variables were endless. The result was the same, though: When the rain did come, when wool prices started to rise again, his neighbors were ready. They'd scraped through. It was too late for him. He was in huge financial trouble.

He couldn't talk about it with Angela. It wasn't his way. He'd also made a decision from the very start not to burden her unnecessarily. It had been hard enough for her to settle in to a new way of life, a new country.

He knew there'd been a lot of gossip when he first brought Angela back to Errigal, so soon after meeting her in Sydney. He was considered one of the eligible men in the area. The only son and heir to a big property. Well educated, courtesy of an expensive all-boys boarding school in Adelaide from the age of ten to eighteen, and then a three-year university course in agriculture management. For four years he'd gone out with Diane, the oldest daughter of one of the neighboring station families, three properties away. He'd thought it was a casual arrangement between them, even though he knew their parents were keen. Celia had been even keener. She'd always been very conscious of the advantages of a good social and financial match. The pressure had been on for him to ask Diane to marry him.

Then he'd gone to Sydney for that rugby match, walked into a pub to get directions and met Angela. And that was that.

He knew all the reasons why it shouldn't have worked. She was six years younger than him. She was a Londoner, not an Australian country girl. She'd never even been on a sheep station. But she had looked at him—it felt so corny, but it was true—she'd looked at him with those incredible blue eyes and he'd fallen in love. He'd thought, This is the woman I'm going to marry.

People tried to talk him out of it, remind him of his responsibilities, not just to his family but to the station, to Errigal. His parents were about to retire, move into Port Augusta, and were relying on him to keep the station viable. He needed to choose his wife carefully, people told him. He was the sole heir, after all.

He shouldn't have been. He'd had an older brother, Anthony, who died when Nick was four years old. He'd drowned in one of the creeks, one winter's afternoon. Only eight years old. To his shame, Nick didn't even remember him. Sometimes, after his parents had retired off the station but were back visiting, he'd seen his dad looking at the photos of Anthony. He'd wondered what he was thinking. Would Anthony have been a better son? A better sheep farmer?

Yes. Anthony would have married a local woman. Anthony would have made the right stock decisions, negotiated his way through the wool crash, coped with the drought, diversified, prospered, been poised for recovery when the time came.

Most especially, Anthony wouldn't have gotten Errigal into this position, where the only option was to hand over half his land to the big enemy, one of the mining giants, who could afford to pay a fortune for it.

Nick remembered the day he'd gotten the news. They'd found something on Errigal land. He'd heard a lot of geological detail about drilling patterns, surveying techniques, surface indicators, volcanic basins, all in search of something called *diamondiferous kimberlites* or *kimberlite pipes*. In layman's terms, diamonds. The draft contract they'd given him had run to more than fifty pages. His lawyer had summarized it. They'd found enough evidence and enough micro-diamonds during their exploration to warrant further, more extensive testing and drilling. They wanted a five-year exploration lease on 65,000 acres of Errigal. Nearly half of the property. In return, they were offering him a lump sum. Crazy money. Enough to pay off his main debt. Not only that. They were offering him a paid position as caretaker on their share of the property. It had nothing to do with sheep. They had no intention of running it as a going concern. They wanted him to do fencing work, windmill and floodgate maintenance, firefighting. Work he had done all his life. Work he could do without thinking.

It was like winning the lottery. Or was it more like a pact with the devil? The mining company mightn't touch the land for years. There might not be as much wealth in the land as they hoped. It was speculation on their part. For days he'd wrestled with the decision. What was the alternative? Saddling all four of his children with a huge debt for the rest of their lives? What kind of a father would do that? What kind of inheritance would that be? Day after day, night after night, he'd tried to think of another way out. He could think of nothing else, but he couldn't talk about it with anyone. Especially Angela. He felt too guilty, too ashamed, too helpless, too hopeless. This was his fault. His problem, not hers. She was busy enough taking care of her tourists, running her own business. Her successful business.

The night he'd told Angela about the deal had been one of the worst of his life. The shock in her eyes, the disappointment, the disbelief. He had registered it all. He had expected it. He had felt that way about it himself. She'd asked question after question. He couldn't answer them. He still didn't tell her the size of the debt. He'd been worried that if he started talking, he wouldn't be able to stop. Every worry, every doubt he had would come pouring out. So that night, and since, he'd said as little as possible. Hidden his own doubts from her. It was the only way to get through it.

As a family, they'd kept the news to themselves for as long as possible. It was Angela who had convinced him he needed to tell their closest neighbors. If it was up to him, he'd have said nothing to anyone. She was more linked in socially in the area. She heard more than he did about what people thought of mining deals. Jealousy from some. Anger from others. No one wanted what the mines would bring, the noise, the trucks. No one believed the mining companies when they said there would be minimal damage to the environment. They'd be ripping up rocks and earth that hadn't been touched in hundreds of thousands of years. Tearing down three-hundred-year-old trees. Spoiling the land for everyone.

He knew that. But he could see no other way out.

As news of the sale spread, he stayed put on the station. Angela was in town more often, either in Hawker or in Port Augusta or Port Pirie. She was the one who bore the brunt of it. She hid a lot of the comments from him; he knew that. But she didn't need to say anything for him to guess how she felt about it, and about him. Disappointed. Ashamed. He could see it in her eyes.

It hadn't always been like this between them. He'd thought they had a good marriage. Better than good. A great marriage. He wasn't a big talker. That wasn't his way. But they'd had plenty to say to each other. They'd laughed a lot too. She was great fun. A hard worker. A wonderful mother. His sounding board. His best friend.

But all of that had now changed. Because of him.

He knew she'd already had enough to concern her this year. Victoria. Genevieve. Lindy. And Ig, all his problems at

boarding school, the running away. One more worry, on top
of all the others.

Nick had hated his own first years at boarding school.
He'd gone there at the age of ten too. Even now he could remember the lonely nights in the dormitory. All the jostling
for position, the wrestling, physically and emotionally. Maybe
it had been good for him in the end. Got him out of his shell.
And he'd liked that his father and grandfather had gone to
the same school, that their names appeared in roll books and
on honor walls and trophies. It helped that he was good at
sports, that his name started appearing on a few of those trophies. He'd also secretly liked the idea of his only son following in his footsteps, a new generation of Gillespies.

Except Ig hated it even more than Nick had. Hated it so
much he kept running away. It caused more tension between
him and Angela. She'd already thought Ig was too young to
leave home. She understood it had been the Gillespie family
tradition, that all the Gillespie males went to boarding
school from a young age, but traditions could be changed,
couldn't they? she'd argued. They'd gone back and forth
about it, without any resolution.

In the end, it hadn't mattered anyway. After Ig ran away
a third time, the principal made the decision for them. When
the new school year began in February, Ig would be back at
the small school in Hawker.

It was Angela who'd dealt with all of that, while he had
what felt like endless meetings with the mining company, his
lawyers, his accountants. He knew she'd assumed the meetings were about restocking the station, getting the property
up and running again. When he and Angela did talk, meeting

in the kitchen at breakfast time, or briefly in the evenings before he locked himself away with the accounts and the stock sheets, he could see only blame and hurt in her eyes.

Around then, she'd started taking pottery classes in Port Pirie. She'd not only signed up for a three-month course; she'd put in a successful bid for the school's old wheel and kiln. He still didn't quite understand why. She'd never shown an interest in anything like that before. He hadn't said it to her, but he also wasn't sure what she was making. He'd expected cups and mugs and vases. Instead, she seemed to be producing shapes of some kind. She'd shown them to him in the early days, but he hadn't known what to say. He'd just tried for the best and said they looked great. He'd seen even more disappointment in her eyes. Later, he'd heard her describe them to Joan as sculptures, artwork based on the birdlife she saw around her in the Flinders Ranges. "Good for you, love," Joan had said. "I wouldn't have a clue about art."

It was while Angela was at her pottery class one day that he first took his psychologist's advice. Tried to distract himself from the despairing thoughts. He'd started with a Web site simply called "How to Trace Your Family Tree." He sat down with the documents that had been in the house for years. His own father hadn't been interested. His grandfather had wanted to talk about his ancestors, but back then Nick had had other things to do. As he started to delve deeper into the family history, he wished he had made time.

These weren't dry, dusty tales. They were adventure stories. These were his ancestors living their lives on this same land, in this same house, trying to get to grips with all that he had spent the past decades coming to grips with. Weather battles. Stock problems. Life in this wild part of the world. He kept thinking about those two Gillespie cousins. What had gone through their heads when they found themselves in Australia, swapping gray Irish clouds for the huge blue sky, exchanging damp, minuscule fields for massive open paddocks? Were they homesick? What had they left behind? What had their farms in Ireland been like? Their families?

Question led to question. It became a treasure hunt. He never knew what he would find next on the Internet. He'd always thought he would have to go to Ireland to learn anything more about his ancestors, but it was extraordinary how much he'd been able to unearth from his desk, in their office, on the old, shared computer.

He joined chat rooms, all of them frequented by amateur researchers like himself, everyone expressing frustration at the unpredictability of Irish record keeping. He got in touch with Gillespies all over the world. They started talking about a reunion in Ireland. He offered to coordinate it. Following others' suggestions, he posted his e-mail address, with a general call for information about two cousins with the surname of Gillespie who'd emigrated to South Australia in the 1880s. Three days later, he had a reply.

Dear Mr. Gillespie.

We were very interested to see your recent post regarding your Gillespie ancestors in Ireland and believe we can help you. For a monthly fee,

```
you receive expert, on-the-ground support from
an appointed genealogist, who will answer your
questions and help you find all the photographs,
records and stories of your family for your
personalized family history.
```

He was impressed with the letter. He checked out the company's equally impressive Web site. He read the testimonials. There were dozens, all glowing. It did make sense to have someone in Ireland doing the hard graft, visiting the archives, phoning the parochial houses, everything that was too difficult and time-consuming for him to do. It was expensive, though. Not just the monthly fee—he was also expected to cover any traveling and accommodation expenses incurred during the research.

But perhaps, just perhaps, his grandparents and his father would approve. They might even forgive him for what he had done to their property.

He filled out the online form. He set up the bank transfers. Two days later, Carol came into his life. Even thinking about her now made him feel better.

Better. Not guilty. Despite what the kids thought, what Angela had asked him, he had nothing to feel guilty about. It wasn't an affair. Carol was simply a voice on Skype, on e-mail. A scholar, an historian, a trained genealogist. In the past few months, she'd found so much information for him. His great-great-uncle had been a political activist. A great-great-grandmother was a poet. Carol had sent him pages of records, old family photographs. When he'd mentioned the idea of staging a reunion, she had immediately offered to help.

They'd negotiated an increased monthly rate. Money was still tight. The lump sum from the mining company had paid off the debt, but his wage as a caretaker still had to cover a lot of other costs. After long deliberation, he'd decided it was worth it. He hoped his ancestors would approve. He was in charge of bringing together Gillespies from all over the world, after all. He wanted to do it properly. He couldn't just rent out a room in an Irish pub and stick up a photocopy of a ship's log on the wall. Carol had already suggested many good ideas, of tours they could take, ancestral places they could visit.

It was now more than a hobby for Nick. More than a way to fill long, empty hours. He'd discovered a love of history. The research had given him purpose again. A sense of adventure. It seemed incredible that he was even making plans to visit Ireland. To travel overseas for the first time in his life. Not just for the reunion, but on a reconnaissance trip before that. And not on his own.

With Angela.

He'd been planning it for weeks. He hoped she would say yes. He'd decided the best time to ask her was after the twins had arrived home for Christmas. After he'd had the chance to ask Victoria in person whether she would stay on and look after Ig, and keep an eye on Angela's station stay Web site, manage any bookings and answer any queries.

Of all his kids, Victoria would be the best choice. She shared his love, and Angela's love, for the land around here. In the days before things went bad, he'd often thought she would be the one to take over from him. There'd even been casual conversations between him and Kevin Lawson, joking about Fred and Victoria getting married one day and combining Errigal and the Lawson property into one mighty one. Until Fred and Victoria had broken up so suddenly and her career had gone in a different direction. Nick had long ago ruled Genevieve out as his successor. She'd made it clear from early on that she wasn't sticking around. It would never suit Lindy either. She'd lose interest too quickly, start something but never finish it. And Ig? Despite being the only son and traditional heir, Ig's interest clearly wasn't on the land. Computers, yes. Station life, no.

In the meantime, Nick knew he could trust Victoria to take care of things while he and Angela went traveling. They could afford to go for three weeks, he'd decided. Ireland for ten days, and then on to London, her home city. And then to somewhere else in Europe, wherever she wanted to go. Just the two of them.

The trip couldn't come soon enough. He missed her. He missed what their marriage had been like. He hoped that going away together might help bring them back together. Help her to forgive him for the mess he'd made of the station.

As he turned to look at the map of Ireland on the wall, his e-mail pinged. It was Carol, working all hours as usual. She'd already researched a list of Gillespie places he and Angela could visit.

He was smiling as he wrote his reply.

NINE

Angela was in her pottery studio. She'd been there for the past hour, ever since she'd reread her letter. She wasn't working. She was hiding.

On her way out there, Ig had called her over to admire his latest cubby. It was very impressive, she told him honestly. He'd arranged all of Lindy's cardboard boxes, still filled with thread and stuffing, into an elaborate structure. After he'd pointed out all the features, she told him she was just going to do some work on her new sculptures.

"Do you need a spider check first?" he asked.

She'd been too distracted to even think about spiders. Thank God he'd remembered. She nodded. In her three decades living out here, she'd grown accustomed to snakes, to kangaroos, to lizards, locusts, mice and rats. But never to the spiders.

Especially not the huge, hand-sized spiders that seemed to lie in wait in dark corners just for her. Nick had rescued her from them for years. So had the girls, who had grown up fearless. Lately, it had become Ig's job. He wasn't keen on snakes, she knew, but he was very relaxed about spiders.

He opened the blue-painted door of the studio for her, tugging at it three times before it opened. The hinges needed oiling. The climbing red rosebush that grew around it, the one Nick had planted for her on their first wedding anniversary, needed pruning too, she noticed. One more item for her to-do list. She waited in the doorway as Ig fetched the flashlight she kept inside for just this purpose. He started to shine it around the shed, which had just enough room for her compact kiln, the pottery wheel, two tall racks of shelves and an old wooden bench. All perfect spider hiding places.

"You'd better look away," Ig said from inside. "It's pretty big. A huntsman, I think."

She shuddered. A huntsman. Huge, hairy. Not poisonous, but still . . . She moved several meters back, resisting a temptation to go even farther. She shut her eyes too, but was still able to picture what she knew Ig was doing in there. Picking up—actually picking up, in his bare hands— a spider. Another shudder. She heard his footsteps, knew he was taking the spider down to the other shed. He could have killed it, but as he'd told her solemnly once, it wasn't the spider's fault she didn't like it.

She opened her eyes as he returned, wiping his hands on his shorts.

"All clear," he said. "You can go in now."

"What would I do without you, Ig?" she'd said.

He'd given her his shy, sweet smile, then headed back to his cubby, talking to Robbie as he went.

Since then, she had been sitting here, on the bench, rolling the same ball of clay round and round in her hands. She hadn't even made a start on shaping it into any discernible form. All she'd been doing was fighting an urge to run away. To get into the car and drive as fast as she could away from this mess she had created.

Reason took over. She couldn't run away. There was too much to do. Party food to make and freeze. The woolshed to decorate. All the party gear had been delivered, the chairs and the trestle tables. She could start unpacking those. Or perhaps she could drive over to Joan's, get some face-to-face advice. An hour's journey across dirt roads. No. She had to try something else.

She took five breaths in, five breaths out. Again.

She let her mind drift. She used all the tricks she'd learned over the past months.

Slowly, surely, it began to work.

She wasn't on a sheep station in outback South Australia on a hot, dusty December day. She hadn't somehow sent out her innermost secrets to one hundred people around the world. She didn't have four children in various states of disarray, or a husband who had lost interest in her. She wasn't about to host two hundred people in a dusty woolshed, all of whom probably hated her and her family. She wasn't sitting in a small stone shed full of pottery equipment she didn't know how to use properly, beside shelves of half-finished sculptures that looked like they belonged in a kindergarten. No, that wasn't her and this wasn't her life.

She was Angela Richardson. It was midmorning in London. She'd been up since seven a.m. It was a cold and frosty December day, but her little studio at the end of the garden was warm. Her husband, Will, had turned on the heater before he left for an early breakfast meeting. Not only that, he'd made a thermos of coffee for her and left it on the shelf beside her kiln. Not just the coffee, but a note too. *Have a great day. I love you, Will xx.* Had there ever been a husband as thoughtful as Will? As loving? As demonstrative?

On her way to the studio, she'd picked up the pile of mail from the mat. One bill that they would have no problem paying, because they had plenty of money. More than they knew what to do with. An invitation from a gallery asking—actually, almost begging—her to consider them for her next ceramics exhibition. And a card from her daughter, Lexie. Lexie often put little notes in the post, postcards, photographs of objects or shapes that she thought her mother might find inspirational. Today's card was no exception. It was a card with a drawing of a robin on the cover, a gloriously bright red, plump little bird, with a gleam in its black eye, standing jauntily on its matching black legs. Inside Lexie had written just one line:

To add to your collection! Love you, Lexie xxx

Could Lexie get any sweeter? Angela doubted it. She had told Lexie two months ago that she was thinking about using robins, her favorite birds, as the theme for her next collection. She'd loved them since she was a child. Their curiosity. Their territorial natures. The way she needed only to step outside and pull up a single weed and one would appear, as if to keep an eye on her as much as on a lookout for a worm. She especially loved robins in December and January, when the garden was so bleak. Sometimes it would make her feel sad to look out from her studio and see the flower beds dormant, the old oak tree bare, the roses that were so glorious in the summer now just branches in the gray light. But then, in the corner of her vision, a flash of movement, a splash of color. A robin! She'd watch it for as long as it was there, loving the darting, bobbing movements, the little pecks at the food she had left on the bird table for it, and most of all, loving the life and color it brought into the garden.

At that moment, Angela's mobile rang. It was Suzy, the manager of the gift shop in Islington's Camden Passage, just three streets away.

"Angela, how are you? Look, darling, this is beyond cheeky of me, but I'm ringing to ask, do you have anything up your sleeve gift-wise this year? I was expecting a delivery of clay angels, lovely little things, but they're stuck in transit in Antwerp of all places. Won't get here until mid-January. Fat lot of good they'll be to me then. But I thought, angel, Angela, maybe you've had a burst of inspiration and have exactly what I need? You remember those bells you made a few years ago? The little ones? You don't have any of those left, do you? Or anything Christmassy at all? My loyal and rich customers will be arriving any day now, arms outstretched, credit cards ready, and I can't bear to think they might leave empty-handed and me empty-tilled."

"Yes, I do," Angela said, confidently, clearly. "But not bells."

"No? What?"

"Robins," she said. "I'm making robins this year. A simple

design. Clay base color, with a burst of red glaze on the chest. I can have a sample to you tomorrow." She hadn't even made one yet, but she already knew it would be a success.

"I love robins! Everyone loves robins! You're a genius! I don't even need to see them. I'll order as many as you can make."

Angela started work as soon as she hung up. It was as if her fingers already knew what they were doing. She molded the little round body, the delicate head. She used wire for the spindly legs. She had plenty of that in the garden shed. The clay was light; the whole object would be light too, perfect to hang on a tree or to rest on a windowsill. . . .

By seven p.m. she had a dozen made. She was around at Suzy's early the next morning. Suzy *loved* them. They were *divine*, she said. They had such *personality*. Such *charm*. How quickly could she make more?

"Angela Richardson, you are incredible," Will said that night, raising a glass over the set table, the rich, spicy smell of the beef casserole he'd cooked filling their warm kitchen. "May I propose a toast to you and your robins?"

"To robins," Angela said, laughing, clinking her glass against his.

"Who's Robyn?"

Angela opened her eyes. Lindy stood in the doorway, holding her cushion cover.

"I thought Ig was bad enough, talking to Robbie all the time. Now you're at it. Who's Robyn? Robbie's sister?"

"Not Robyn. Robin. As in the bird."

"You were talking to a bird? It's worse than I thought." She held out the cover. "Look, Mum, two words down, one to go."

"Beautiful, Lindy. Well done."

"You hardly looked at it. Does it matter that the 'W' is a bit wobbly?"

"Of course not. We don't have robins in Australia, Lindy; did you know that?"

"What?"

"There aren't any robins in Australia. The early settlers tried to introduce them, and then scientists more recently, but it's never worked. The climate's wrong for them. The robins that people call robins here aren't actually real robins. They're from a different bird family altogether."

"Really? That's amazing." Ig appeared beside her. Lindy gave him a look, raising her eyebrows. "Mum's talking about birds, Ig. You like birds, don't you? I'll leave you both to it." She left.

Ig came in and sat on the bench beside her. "What birds, Mum?"

"Robins, Ig. They were my favorite birds when I was growing up in England. Do you know the ones I mean? The little ones with the bright red breast?"

He thought about that for a moment. "I think I've seen them in films."

"I used to really love them. When I was a little kid, like you. We always had them in our garden."

"Do you still miss them?"

She nodded. "I thought I didn't but I really do."

"Do you want me to go and get some paper and draw you one? You'd have to tell me what to draw but I could try."

She didn't know who was more shocked, herself or Ig, when her eyes suddenly filled with tears.

"I'd love that, Ig. Thank you."

TEN

In New York, Genevieve had almost finished packing. Not that it had taken long. In her time here, she'd lived in what she would have termed *dog kennels* back in Australia. Tiny apartments in the East Village. They'd all been up several flights of stairs, with small windows looking down into either similar apartments or brick walls and fire escapes. Nothing like the vast rooms she'd seen on *Friends*. She'd learned to keep her wardrobe small. She'd bought some artwork, but again, small paintings only, knowing one day they'd have to be shipped home. Her expired visa had been a ticking time bomb. Even if she had still been legal, competition in the industry was rife. She already knew from Megan that her job had been snapped up within two hours of her being escorted off the set.

Megan had called her the night of her sacking. Coffee Guy, the kind security guard, had obviously kept his word and passed on Genevieve's personal phone number.

"Girlfriend!" Megan had shouted. "It was you all along! We have to meet!"

They'd met the next night, in a bar they knew film folk didn't go to. Megan's idea. At least she was honest. "You're radioactive, darling; sorry. If I'm seen with you, I might get sacked too."

The set had been in an uproar after her revelations, Megan told her in technicolor detail. Work on the surface, of course, but gossip at every opportunity.

"The director's brother, Coffee Guy, said—"

"His *brother*? I thought he was just the security guard."

"He's a man of many talents, I discovered. He was also asking lots of questions about you today. His name is Matt, by the way. I told him he should ring and ask you himself if he was that concerned. I said he'd better be quick, before you disappear into the outback. I still can't picture it. You and your dreadlocks back there. Won't you scare the kangaroos?"

"They're not easily scared." Genevieve tried to imagine walking down the streets of Hawker looking like she did. Perhaps if she were just home on holiday she could brazen it out. But skulking back, with her tail between her legs . . . "Megan, would you come back to my place and do me a favor?"

"And fix up that blue rats' nest of yours? I thought you'd never ask."

Back at the apartment, Genevieve's phone rang as Megan was midway through her new hairstyle. They'd opened a bottle of wine. Everything that had previously seemed worrying seemed hilarious now. Genevieve was giggling as she answered.

"You sound okay," a man's voice said. "I'm glad."

"Pardon me?"

"It's Matt. Matt from the film set."

"Well, hello, Matt from the film set," she said.

Megan gave her a thumbs-up.

"Yes, I'm great, thanks. It was the best thing that could have happened to me. I'll get to spend more time with my family now. Isn't that what politicians say when they've been publicly humiliated?"

Megan was waving at her, mouthing at her to clam up, slow down.

Genevieve took her advice. "I'm sorry, Matt. Please excuse that little rush of bitterness. I'm fine. Really. Thanks."

"Megan tells me you're going back to Australia?"

"On Tuesday, yes."

He'd been so kind. She'd really enjoyed talking to him on the set. He was also great-looking.

They talked over each other.

"Would you like to meet for a drink before I go?" she said.

"Can I buy you a farewell-to–New York drink?" he said.

More thumbs-up from Megan.

"Tomorrow?" Genevieve said. "At nine. Great. Yes, I know that bar. Thanks, Matt. That's great."

Megan whooped as she hung up. "A date! That calls for dancing. Come on, let's go out again."

As they left, Genevieve caught sight of herself in the

hallway mirror. Her hair was half-finished, blue dreadlocks on one side, an emerging pixie cut on the other.

"Could you finish this first, do you think?" she said.

The following night, she was regretting not just the last glass of wine with Megan, not just the haircut, but also accepting the date. She'd woken up that morning with another hangover, in a pit of dread. This date with Matt was probably a setup, to find out what else she knew about the director. The more she thought about it, the more sense it made. Why else would he get in touch with her?

She called Megan, using the code name they'd decided on. "It's me. Ophelia." She talked quickly, comparing hangovers and then airing her theory.

"I think you're wrong," Megan said. "I talked to him again today. He's a really nice guy. I've also asked around. Everyone had only good things to say about him. Smart, funny, decent. Much nicer than his brother. Chill, Ophelia. Enjoy."

She called Victoria, of course. He sounded gorgeous, Victoria agreed. Kind too. That was always important. She gave her blessing as well. She also asked for a full report, via phone call or e-mail, as soon as possible after their date.

It took Genevieve only five minutes to fix her new-look hair. She'd given herself a fright when she looked in the mirror first thing, expecting to see the blue dreadlocks and instead being greeted by this dark brown pixie cut. It felt like years since she'd seen her natural hair color. She liked it. She liked the style too. She quickly applied more eye makeup than usual. Lipstick. Sparkling earrings. She had a big collection of costume jewelry, including some pretty hairpins. They'd been lost in her blue hair. They looked great with this new short look, if she did say so herself.

She was at the bar five minutes before nine. She found a table at two minutes to nine. She was taking a sip of a glass of red wine at nine o'clock, steadying her nerves and quelling her hangover. At ten minutes past nine she realized she had been stood up. She'd been toying with her phone, pretending to text while waiting for word from Matt, but there'd been nothing. Was she angry? Maybe. More disappointed. He'd seemed nicer than that. Decent. She'd picked up her glass to swallow the rest of the wine and then go home when she heard her name.

"Genevieve?"

She spun around with the wineglass in her hand. So quickly that her drink flew out of the glass. Not onto her. Onto Matt. Matt and his white shirt.

An hour later, she sent that wine a big thanks. If she hadn't spilled it, his shirt wouldn't have been covered in a large red stain. There wouldn't have been three minutes of flustered conversation as he apologized for seeming to be late. (He'd been in the bar since before nine, looking out for a woman with blue dreadlocks. It was only on his fifth circuit around that he noticed her on her own in a corner and recognized her.) She wouldn't have laughed and apologized for not warning him about the haircut, and for spilling the wine. He wouldn't have asked whether she minded being with someone who looked like he'd just been shot. She wouldn't have suggested he come to her apartment to rinse out the stain.

If they hadn't been in her apartment, perhaps they wouldn't have begun talking so easily, laughing so readily. About work. About her family. His family. Australia. America.

Films they liked. Books they liked. Music they liked. If they hadn't gotten talking, and laughing, they wouldn't have started kissing. And normally she didn't have sex on the first date and this wasn't even a date, it was just a drink, but he was there in her living room which doubled as her bedroom, courtesy of the fold-down bed, and he was so lovely, and she was leaving and she suddenly wanted a final New York adventure, something great and romantic and fun and carefree.

She kissed him first. Or did he kiss her first? Whoever started it, it set off a wave of lust and urgency that seemed to surprise them both. Was this what all those casual, friendly chats in front of the coffee van had been leading to? If she had known he knew how to do this with his lips and his fingers and his body, she would have locked him in the trailer with her long ago.

After the second time, she lay her head back on the pillow and said the first word that came to mind.

"Wow."

"Wow yourself," he said, with the smile that she'd already fallen a little bit in love with.

"Would you like a drink?" she asked. "A cigarette?"

"Do you have to move to get either of those things?"

"No, I have a butler. He'll be here any minute with it all on a silver tray."

"Can he bring me a smoking jacket too?"

"Of course. And a footstool?"

"Marvelous."

They were both attempting and failing to speak in very

upper-class English accents. She turned her head so she was looking directly into his eyes. His lovely eyes, now that she was close enough to see them. Dark brown but with golden flecks in them. About to make a joke, her usual approach at intimate moments like this, she had the sudden urge to tell him the truth.

"That was great, Matt. So great. Thank you very much."

"That was really great, Genevieve. You're very welcome." He gave her another one of those beautiful smiles.

She wanted to keep telling the truth. "I wish I hadn't waited until I'd shot myself and my career in the foot and spread scurrilous gossip about your brother and his unorthodox private life before I asked you out for a drink."

He tensed slightly. She felt it. "I'm sorry, Matt. I won't mention your brother again."

"It's fine. And I asked you out for a drink first, remember. And I'm sorry you lost your job."

She moved closer. He put his arm around her, and started to slowly stroke her skin, from her shoulder down, his fingers featherlight and so, so sexy.

"That really does feel good," she said, feeling her eyelids grow heavy, desire starting to build again. "In fact, everything you do feels good. Even though normally I wouldn't do anything as brazen as this on a first date, of course."

"This isn't a first date. We're work colleagues. We've known each other for months."

"Weeks," she said.

He shrugged. She liked the look of the muscles on his shoulder as he did that. She reached up and kissed him. He kissed her back. She moved until she was lying on top of him, skin on skin. He felt very good indeed. Another kiss, a long, searching kiss, accompanied by his hands stroking her back, slowly, gently, moving lower, holding her tight against him. There was no more talking for a while.

"You're some kind of superman," she said, after the third time.

"I am? Damn. I always wanted to be the Incredible Hulk."

They lay head beside head on the one pillow. She felt wonderful, she realized. Every cell in her body had enjoyed every moment of every one of those three orgasms. She felt sensual, sexy, reckless. She was leaving in three days. There was no time for games, playing coy or waiting for him to make the next move. She told him the truth again, but this time masking it in a joke, borrowing a line from a film she'd grown up watching.

"Looks like I picked the wrong week to go back to Australia."

His lip twitched. "Surely you can't be serious."

She grinned. "You know *Flying High!*?"

"Of course. Except we call it *Airplane!* over here."

"My sister and I can quote that entire film to each other."

"I can quote that entire film and the sequel."

"Really?"

"Is that a shock? Because I seem so serious. So auteur?"

"Exactly. So intellectual."

"You want intellectual? I know lots of intellectual film quotes too."

"Me too. You say one and I'll guess the film," she said.

"And if you get it right?"

"You get to do what you've just done to me again. And then we go out for another drink. My treat."

"Right," he said. "I've got one. Sure you're ready? It's very obscure."

She nodded.

He paused. "'You're a wizard, Harry.'"

She bit her lip. "Gosh. That is difficult. I hope I don't embarrass myself with the wrong answer." She reached up and whispered it in his ear.

"Well done!" he said. "Right the first time. You really do know your cinema. So, then, a deal is a deal." He shifted position, lying facing her. He kissed her lips. Then her neck.

"When do you fly out?" he murmured, as he kissed her shoulder.

"Tuesday," she said, trying to concentrate.

"I'd take you to the airport—"

"You don't have to."

"I would, but I can't. I'm sorry. I'm flying to Costa Rica tomorrow. Location scouting."

"You do that as well? For your brother?"

He kissed her other shoulder. "Not this time. A friend from film school. He and I are going into production to-gether. A dystopian comedy drama." His lips went lower.

It was now getting extremely hard to concentrate. "Really? Vampires? Werewolves?"

"Rabbits."

"Rabbits?"

"Zombie rabbits. It's the new horror genre."

She closed her eyes in pleasure. "Sounds scary."

"It will be. Wait until you see the action figures."

She was now kissing him too. In between kisses, they were still trying to talk.

"If you're ever in outback Australia doing any location scouting, do drop in, won't you?"

"Sure. Do I need an address or do I just stand in the middle of nowhere and shout your name?"

"That's one way. Or you could always try my phone number."

"Thank you. I like the new haircut, by the way. Did I tell you that yet? I liked the blue hair too, but this is even better."

"Why, thank you. I like your hair too. And your body." She showed him just how much.

Their visit to a bar was delayed for another hour.

ELEVEN

In Sydney, Victoria was cursing herself. Stupid, stupid, stupid Victoria. Why had she said yes? Why had Mr. Radio only to send her a text for her to leap up like some overeager dog, keen to do his bidding? She was so stupid. She should ring him right now, this minute, tell him to forget it, she didn't ever want to see him again.

But she did.

It was foolish and she knew there was no future and she knew he would never leave his wife and kids. But he was just so fantastic in bed, so unexpectedly brilliant and inventive and gentle and sensual, and he made her feel so good and sexy that she couldn't stop herself. He was why she had put on weight. He was why she had turned to food. Not out of unhappiness. Because one day he had said there was nothing he loved more than a shapely woman. And the first time they had gotten drunk and ended up in bed together, he had made it clear that he meant every word of it. He talked about how much he loved the curve of her waist, the heaviness of her breasts, the plumpness of her thighs. Her body image changed in that instant. She had felt womanly, Rubenesque. Even now, knowing he was just fifteen minutes away, she could feel the desire start to build inside her. She was already wearing the black lingerie he had bought her, under a silk robe that tied with ribbons, because she knew how much he loved to untie them.

Out of nowhere, she had a memory of another man. Her first boyfriend. Fred Lawson. The oldest son of their nearest neighbors. Sex had been wonderful with him too. They'd been each other's first lovers, enjoying a heady combination of shyness and eagerness, which had soon turned into passion. She'd known him all her life, watched him grow from being a stocky, blond-haired boy into a stocky, blond-haired man.

At the age of nineteen, she had fallen hard for him. It took him a little longer, but four months after they'd started dating, he'd told her he was in love with her too. For three years, they'd been inseparable. They'd started talking about what they might do when they finished their degrees. He was studying agricultural marketing and economics; she was doing an arts degree, but already thinking about continuing her studies, looking at environmental science, something that would be helpful on the land. It was an unspoken understanding between them—they were still young, after all—but she could already picture them married, living on the Lawson station, having children while young, like her own mother. And perhaps one day, if all her dreams came true, taking Errigal over from her father.

But her dreams hadn't come true. Four years to the day after they had first gotten together, Fred had arrived at her share house in Adelaide unexpectedly. She'd known even before he started talking that it was bad news. It was worse than she'd expected. He'd been offered a scholarship to go to Canada. He wanted to take it. On his own. "I love you, Victoria. I've loved being with you. But I'm sorry—I'm not ready to settle down yet."

A month after that, he was gone. Six weeks later, the same week Victoria needed to put in her application for the environmental science course, Genevieve had sent her the ad for the rural reporter job at the radio station in Port Pirie. She'd applied. She'd gotten it. And so her media career had begun. She'd risen through the ranks, gained experience, all of it leading her day by day toward this job in Sydney, this situation in Sydney. This mess in Sydney.

Along the way, she'd learned to be tougher, though. She'd had to. Even if some days at the radio station all she'd wanted to do was run home to Errigal, to give up what sometimes felt like nonsense work, producing hours of babble that served no real purpose. Even if some days she still thought about that course she'd never taken, that she might have ended up working on Errigal. That if she had been there, with or without Fred by her side, she might have been able to help her father.

Of all of the family, she had been the most shocked at the news about the mining lease. On her last visit home, for a weekend in October, she'd tried to talk to her father about it. They'd gone out for a long walk across the property to-gether, the way they always did whenever she was home. It was her way of grounding herself, of reconnecting to Erri-gal, shaking off her city life even for a few days. As they'd walked, she'd tried to find out more about the deal, about why he had accepted it. "It's complicated" was as much as he would say. In subsequent phone calls home, she'd tried to ask him again. He'd cut the conversation short each time, just as she'd been about to ask, putting her on to her mother. She loved her dad. Trusted him. She knew he loved the land as much as she did, that he felt as strongly about preserving the landscape as she did. But for him to accept a deal like this? He must have had no choice. She still wished it hadn't been the case. That somehow, one day, her childhood dream of running Errigal herself could have come true.

She had to stop thinking like that. Stop worrying about what might have been. What was Genevieve's mantra? Or mantras? *Seize the day. You only live once. No regrets.* All her life, Victoria had tried to be more like her twin, fearless and brave, taking risks, not caring what people thought. It was one of the reasons she had applied for work in Sydney, even when the thought of it terrified her. One of the reasons—a secret reason, but part of it—that she had begun her affair with Mr. Radio. It had made her feel all those things she thought she should be—bold and reckless.

Thinking of him now concentrated her attention. She checked her appearance in the mirror again. She looked just the way he loved her to look. Voluptuous. Sexy.

By the time the doorbell rang, she was pacing the floor.

She didn't let him speak. He opened the door, stepped inside. She was kissing him before he'd even put down the bottle of wine.

An hour later, she was sated. On an intellectual level, she hated him again. But her body didn't. Her body felt full, exhausted, wonderful. It already wanted more.

They finally spoke. "I'm sorry all this happened," he said.

He didn't care a bit—she knew that—but at least he was pretending to. "Thanks."

"Once the fuss dies down, maybe you can come and work with me again."

"I don't think that would be a good idea, would it?"

"No, probably not. What are you going to do?"

"I'm going home."

"Back to Woop Woop?" He'd always thought his nickname for any place in country Australia was funny. She'd never laughed with him. She didn't laugh now. She just nodded.

He sat up, reached for his clothes, began to dress. She didn't say anything. She just lay and watched him.

He didn't take long to get ready. He never did. "It's been fun, Vic."

She'd always hated him calling her Vic too. But that didn't matter now either. "It sure has."

"Take care."

"You too."

"I'll let myself out."

"Thanks."

"Enjoy the wine."

"I will."

That was it. She lay there, the tousled sheets around her, scraps of lace on the floor beside her, her body white and plump in the lamplight.

She wasn't going to cry. She wasn't. But she suddenly wished she were home. With her mum and her dad. With Genevieve. Lindy. Ig. With nothing outside but space and trees and rocks and creeks all around, that huge and beautiful sky above.

Yes, she wanted to go home right now.

On the veranda of the homestead, Lindy decided she felt quite like Jane Austen. Admittedly, she was in Australia in the twenty-first century, wearing jeans and listening to the radio, but those facts aside, she was feeling very old-fashioned and ladylike. So busy in simple, gentle pursuits. She pulled at the last stitch and held the cushion cover out so she could admire it properly. All three words were done now. With practice, she hoped to get faster, but there was no denying her needlework was very delicate, very suited to well-brought-up young ladies.

Yes, this was all very Jane Austen–ish and English-ish. If she could just ignore the fact the magpies were making a racket outside the old toolshed, that she'd just seen a kangaroo hop by the fence, that it sounded like her dad was in the office Skyping his Irish girlfriend again, and especially if she could ignore the fact her little brother was a hundred meters away playing in a giant cubby made out of dozens of cardboard boxes, while simultaneously talking to an imaginary friend. Jane Austen never had to worry about those kinds of distractions, did she?

She put down the cushion cover. "Mum? Mum?" She waited. "Mum?"

After a while, as always, came the reply. "Yes, Lindy?"

"Are you making tea?"

"No, Lindy."

"Oh, Mum, please."

"Yes, Lindy."

Good old Mum. Even with that huge party to organize, and with Celia on the way, and Genevieve and Victoria dropping their bombshells, she'd stayed perfectly calm. Her mum was like one of those swans, Lindy decided. Always so serene on top, gliding along, getting everything done, while underneath she must surely be paddling like mad. If it were her, Lindy, she'd be running for the hills in a panic. She had every intention of giving her mother a hand, of course, but thank God she wasn't in charge of anything.

Her mother came out onto the veranda with a cup of tea and a plate of biscuits.

"Thanks, Mum. Look, I'm getting there." She held it up. "I just need to do the border now. I'm going to do a row of purple cross-stitch first, then another row of green inside it. What do you think?"

"Lovely. I'll leave you to it."

Her mother was back inside before Lindy had a chance to stop her. Drat. She'd wanted a longer chat. It still felt like such luxury to have her mother all to herself like this, Ig and her dad aside. Herself away from the twins, she meant. Lindy loved her big sisters; of course she did. But they did take over the family when they were around.

For the hundredth time, Lindy wished she had a twin. Or

even an extra non-twin sister who was her special friend and ally. Because it was hard not to feel left out sometimes around Victoria and Genevieve. They were like a mini-family within the larger family. They had so many in-jokes. That way of calling each other by their full names all the time, for example, which was also very Jane Austen–ish, now Lindy thought about it. But mainly it was their sense of a united front, the two of them against the world, even when they were on opposite sides of the world. That was something Lindy would like. Someone who was always on her side.

Yes, the more she thought about it, the more she realized she was the outsider in this family. The loner. Her mum and dad had each other. The world's most perfect marriage, it sometimes seemed. Friends of hers with divorced parents said they had grown up hearing arguments all the time, the house full of tension. It had never been like that with her parents. She'd grown up hearing them talking and laughing with each other. She'd always loved lying in bed and hearing them sitting up in the kitchen, their voices filtering down the hall. It was what she wanted when she got married, she'd decided. Someone who looked at her the way her dad looked at her mum. As if he couldn't believe his luck. Not that he ever went on about it. Her dad was definitely one of those strong, silent types, but it was obvious he really loved their mum. And the way they had met, that chance meeting in Sydney, their whirlwind courtship, it was all so romantic too.

So they had each other. Victoria and Genevieve had each other. Ig had his own special friend, even if Robbie was invisible. And imaginary. She was the only one on her own. It was no wonder she had to find solace and companionship in her own creativity like this. Perhaps that was going to be her lot in life. Never to be lucky in love, but instead to give pleasure to many through her artistic pursuits. Yes, she quite liked the sound of that.

Lindy sewed in silence for the next while. The border would take only a day or two, she hoped. If she kept at it full-time. She edged her chair around to avoid the view of the boxes of cushion material behind the woolshed, not to mention the sight of Ig standing hands on hips, chatting to nonexistent Robbie about where best to hang the curtain or bedsheet or whatever that green thing was he was dragging around. In just over a week, the woolshed would be filled with people for the party. The thought of that was making her feel a bit sick too. Not about all the guests. Just one.

She could still recall the horror she'd felt when she saw the name on the RSVP list two weeks earlier.

"Mum, no! You've invited Horrible Jane Lawson to the party?"

"Of course. I've invited all our neighbors and all their kids. Why? Didn't you want me to?"

Lindy didn't mind if Mr. and Mrs. and the other Lawsons came. Or even Fred Lawson, though he'd broken Victoria's heart all those years ago. Or she'd broken his. One or the other. It was Horrible Jane, Fred's younger sister, whom Lindy never wanted to see again in her life.

Genevieve had given Jane the nickname many years before, when Jane first started bullying Lindy at primary school in Hawker. The nickname made Jane easier to handle, in a funny way. It also gave Lindy a dart of happiness to hear every member of her family casually refer to Jane as Horrible Jane. Unfortunately, it had no psychic effect on Jane herself. She'd gone on to be even more horrible when she and Lindy found themselves at the same boarding school in Adelaide.

It had been five years of hell. Subtle insults. Vicious remarks wrapped up in a teasing tone. Casual ostracism. Dig after dig about Lindy's looks, her figure, her family, her school grades, her lack of boyfriends. Relentless, but played under the radar so Lindy never felt able to go to her teachers about it. After her sisters graduated, she had three years at the school on her own. She had no choice but to retreat into herself, away from Jane's malice and influence. She spent lunchtimes in the library. Stayed in her room rather than sit in the common room where Jane held court. The only positive was the amount of studying she'd gotten done. She'd been worried she wouldn't pass her final exams. She did surprisingly well, enough to get easily into college in Adelaide to study for an arts degree. As soon as she'd graduated, she'd headed across to Melbourne to look for work with some of her college friends. Adelaide was too small for her, she decided. There was surely a wider range of interesting jobs in Melbourne too. Also, she'd heard a rumor that Horrible Jane was planning on staying in Adelaide once she'd finished her dental studies. Lindy wanted to put as much distance between them as possible.

In the years since then, she'd never googled Horrible Jane or looked her up on Facebook. She'd followed Genevieve's advice: "Wipe her out of your life. You never have to see her again." Her sister had been right, for years. Until

Horrible Jane had come crashing back into her life in Melbourne, three months ago.

Lindy still hated thinking about it. The evening had started so well, a night out with her two flatmates at a band venue in Prahran. She'd dressed up for once, pulling her long hair out of the two bunches and into a sleek ponytail, borrowing her flatmates' clothes, urged on by both of them. They'd known she needed cheering up after her latest bout of unemployment. They'd been listening to her moaning for weeks, after all. As they walked into the bar, she had felt pretty, confident, as if she were in costume. The night sped by. By ten p.m., they were on their fourth cocktail each. She'd gone up to the bar for their fifth one, feeling even prettier, even more confident, ready for anything. She'd started talking to the man standing beside her. She introduced herself by her full name, Rosalind. He told her his name was Richard.

"And what do you do?" he asked.

She couldn't tell him the truth, that she was currently between jobs. She often was between jobs. "I'm a lawyer," she said. She named a well-known Melbourne firm.

"Snap!" he said. "I'm a final-year law student. I'm looking for work experience. Do you think they'd have me?"

"If they wouldn't, I would," she said, thrilled with her own cheekiness.

Over her shoulder she saw her friends grinning and giving her thumbs-ups.

Twenty minutes later, she and Richard were still talking. Forty minutes later, they were in a dark corner of the bar, kissing. He was there with his flatmates too, he told her. They were in the next room, listening to the band.

He was very cute, she realized. Tallish. Sturdy. She liked his hipster T-shirt, with its picture of Big Bird from *Sesame Street*. In the haze of five cocktails, she suddenly decided she had met the man of her dreams. After a five-year boyfriend drought, here he was at last! It was fate that they'd stood next to each other at the bar! And all right, he was pretty drunk, but so was she.

They were still kissing, very passionately by this stage, his hand on the bare skin under her top, right there in the bar, when the lights flickered on, signaling closing time. They blinked at each other in the sudden bright light. Then he smiled. A sweet, shy smile. Or maybe just a drunken smile, but it was still sweet and shy. "Can I please have your number, Rosalind? I have to go now, but I'd really like to see you again."

She was just about to key it into his phone when she heard a familiar voice.

"Oh, my God! Lindy Gillespie! It is you, isn't it?" It was Horrible Jane. She didn't look happy, either. She frowned as she seemed to notice how close Lindy and Richard were sitting to each other. "Do you two know each other?"

"We've just met," Lindy said. "Tonight."

It was as if Jane hadn't heard her. "Richard, let me introduce you. This is my neighbor and old school pal from South Australia, Lindy Gillespie. Lindy, this is Richard, my—"

Lindy waited, expecting the worst. My fiancé. Richard was Horrible Jane's fiancé.

"—flatmate," Jane finished.

Lindy glanced at Richard. He was smiling at her. "It's lovely to meet you, Lindy. Or should I keep calling you Rosalind?"

"Rosalind?" Jane said. "No one calls her that."

"I like it," Richard said. "Rosalind's a great name. Not only that, she said she might be able to get me some work experience at her law firm."

Jane laughed. It wasn't a nice laugh. "Law firm? Lindy, a lawyer? Well, I suppose it's the one career Lindy hasn't tried, if my memory serves me right." She turned to Richard. "Lindy's mother sends out the most detailed Christmas letter every year. You should see it. My family absolutely loves it. We act it out; it's become a family tradition for us. It's so bad it's hysterical. So I can tell you for a fact that since we both left school, Lindy has worked as a nurse, a nanny, a waitress, um, a barmaid. . . . What have I missed, Lindy?"

Lindy was struck dumb. She could only stare at Jane.

"Ah, I remember now," Jane said, laughing. "You worked in a petting zoo for a while, didn't you? Until you got bitten by a galah—or was it a parrot? In front of that kindergarten group? That one made me laugh till I cried. I can't wait for this year's letter from your mum. She does know about your law career, doesn't she?"

Lindy had gone beyond embarrassment. It was one thing to realize Horrible Jane now lived in Melbourne, another thing to be outed as a lying nonlawyer. But to have all her career failures reeled off like that? To hear she was a laughingstock among Jane's family? Not just her, but her whole family the brunt of the Lawson family's jokes? It was awful. Awful.

She stood up, mumbling something about having to find her friends. She left the bar with them minutes later, without talking to Richard again, without giving him her number. If he was a friend of Horrible Jane's, then she wanted nothing to do with him. The next morning, she called her mother and begged her not to do the Christmas letter this year.

"But I always do it," her mother said calmly. "I've done it for thirty-two years."

"Then can you please take the Lawsons off the mailing list?"

"But I always send it to them," she said just as calmly. "Why, Lindy?"

She couldn't tell her.

That incident had led to the cushions Web site. Humiliated, Lindy had stayed home for the next two weeks, spending too much time browsing craft Web sites, filling her shopping bag with items she couldn't afford and wouldn't take to the online checkout. Why didn't she try this craft business herself? she thought one night. She was creative, wasn't she? And best of all, she wouldn't have to actually deal with any customers face-to-face. There was no chance of public humiliation.

One of her flatmates worked in IT. Lindy had some IT experience herself. Between the two of them, they set up a Web site. It was so simple. That same night, over a bottle or possibly even two of wine, they downloaded photos of pretty cushions and wrote an almost-true biography, making Lindy sound so creative, approachable, friendly. All she had to do now was wait for the orders to pour in. Oh, and buy some cushion material. After her flatmates went to bed, she stayed up, googling suppliers. The Chinese companies were definitely the cheapest. After five glasses of wine it had seemed like such a good idea to buy in bulk too. And put it all on her credit card.

Now here she was. Back home, humiliated, broke and just meters away from the fruits of her mistake. Dozens upon dozens of boxes of cushion material. Wait until Horrible Jane saw them on the night of the woolshed party. Because she would see them. She was the nosiest person in Australia. She'd see them and she'd find out what was in them and why they were there. Lindy didn't think she could bear more mockery from Horrible Jane, or any of the other Lawsons.

Lindy suddenly put down her needle, recalling the night of Ig's accident. The date of Ig's accident. She ran inside, still holding the cushion. "Mum? *Mum?*"

"In here, Lindy." *Here* was the old governess's quarters, the guestroom off the veranda that her mum used only for her overseas visitors or when Celia came to visit. She had just finished making up the bed.

Lindy was breathless. "Have you sent out your Christmas e-mail this year? Can I read it?"

Angela looked at her. There was a long pause. "No."

"No, you haven't sent it, or no, I can't read it?"

"No, you can't read it."

"Why not?"

Another pause. "It's too boring."

"Boring? How can it be boring? It's about us, isn't it?"

"Not this year. I did a quick one this year. Mostly about the weather. All about the weather."

"Can I read it anyway?"

"You never usually want to read it. Why this year?"

"Just because."

"Lindy, 'just because' didn't work when you were six and it doesn't work now."

Lindy spoke in a rush. "I need to see what you said about me. So I can prepare myself for what Horrible Jane Lawson will say to me at the party. I ran into her in Melbourne. She told me that her family acts out your Christmas letter every year and makes fun of us. Of me, especially." It was an edited version, but it was the truth. "Please, Mum, can I see this year's letter? Just to prepare myself?"

Another hesitation. "Your father's on the computer."

"He won't mind me interrupting him. This is important."

"He might be in the middle of something important himself. Did you hear the reunion's going ahead? In a place called Cobh. It's where all the Irish emigrants sailed from, apparently, where—"

"Mum, are you all right?"

"Yes. Why?"

"You seem a bit agitated."

"I'm fine. I'll get the letter for you later, I promise."

Nick passed by the doorway. "Computer's free if anyone wants it."

"Mum does—don't you, Mum?" Lindy said. She held up the cushion. "Look, Dad, I've nearly finished the first one. I'll be able to start paying you back soon. Here, take a look."

Angela took her chance. "Back in a minute," she said.

She practically ran down the hall and into the office, where she shut and locked the door, then logged on to her e-mail. Another twenty replies had come in, all with the same subject heading. *Re: Hello from the Gillespies!* She clicked on the first one.

```
Best Christmas letter ever, thanks! Talk about
letting it all hang out!!
```

She didn't need to reread it to remember what she'd said about Lindy. Phrases leaped into her mind. *Debt-ridden mess. Floods of tears. Was she always so needy? Such a drama queen?* She couldn't possibly show it to Lindy. But she had to show her something. Buy herself some thinking time.

It was wrong but she did it. She had no choice. She clicked on her template letter with its cheery border of Christmas trees. She typed as quickly as she could. It took only a few minutes. She pressed print. Deleted the file. Double-checked she'd deleted it, and double-checked she'd closed down her e-mail account too. Only then did she go back to the guest quarters and hand Lindy the piece of paper.

"There you go. Short and sharp this year. Nothing for you or Horrible Jane to worry about at all."

Before Lindy had a chance to read it in front of her, Angela went out to her pottery studio to hide again.

TWELVE

The day before Celia was due to arrive, Angela woke up at dawn. She knew what she had to do today. Tell Nick about the letter. Then tell the children. It was now urgent. She needed to deal with the fallout while it was just them, without Celia's presence or interference.

It was Murphy's Law that now that she'd decided to tell Nick, he wasn't there. She was alone in the bed. He and Johnny had camped out overnight on the far side of the station, chopping trees or was it fixing fencing? She'd been too distracted to take it in when he told her.

In the past twenty-four hours, she'd received forty new e-mails about her Christmas letter. They varied between concern or amazement about the mining lease to sympathy and amusement about her other troubles. Joan said she'd been getting lots of calls too, from people in the area wondering whether Angela was all right. They hadn't dared to phone the Gillespies themselves. There had also been a flurry of new RSVPs to the party. Joan had been right about that too. From worrying whether anyone would come, Angela now wondered whether they'd have enough room or food for everyone.

The day passed slowly. Nick finally arrived home at four p.m. She had a pot of tea ready for him after he'd showered and changed out of his work clothes. Sandwiches. Cakes. He looked surprised but drank and ate everything she'd prepared. He was always ravenous when he returned from an overnighter. She asked the questions she'd asked so many times over the years, feeling like she was playing the part of the dutiful station wife. Was that what she'd been doing all those years? Playing a part? No. She had always loved hearing all the news of station life. Theirs had been a good marriage. A great marriage. There hadn't always been this tension between them.

A tension that was about to grow worse.

She waited until he'd taken a last sip of tea.

"Nick, I need to tell you something. Something serious."

"Is it about the kids? Ig?"

"No. They're all fine." She hesitated. "It's about me."

He waited. She began to talk, then stopped. They had the kitchen to themselves, but she knew that wouldn't last. At the back of the homestead there was a wooden bench that caught the last of the sunshine in winter and was shaded in summer. It had a perfect view of the rosebush Nick had planted for her. It was one of their talking spots. She asked him to come there with her.

She waited until they were sitting down, trying to delay the moment for as long as possible. She turned and gazed at him, at that tanned, lean face, the dark hair only touched with gray. His face was so familiar to her. So handsome to her. Again, she felt that longing for him. The feeling of homesickness.

"It's about something I've done. Something that happened the night of Ig's accident." She paused. "I was writing my Christmas letter, and I was having trouble with it. So I started a kind of stream-of-consciousness letter instead. I poured out everything that was on my mind. I wasn't going to send it, but then Ig had his accident, and I still don't know how it happened—"

"I do."

"What?"

"I know what happened. I've been waiting for you to notice."

Why was he smiling? "Notice what?"

"That it was sent out. To everyone. Right on your deadline, midnight, December the first."

"But, Nick, that's just it. I don't remember sending it. I'd never have sent—"

"You didn't send it. I did."

"You what?"

"I sent it out for you. After you'd left with Ig, after I cleaned up, I saw your letter on the computer. I knew how much it meant to you to send it to everyone on December first, so I sent it out."

She stared at him.

"I was going to give you until the weekend to realize and then tell you." He was still smiling.

"Oh, *no*. Oh, Nick. Have you got any idea what you've done?"

His smile disappeared. "I thought you'd be pleased."

She stood up, walked away, came back, trying to take this in. Another thought struck her. "Did you read it before you sent it?"

He looked uncomfortable. "Sorry, no. There wasn't time."

She knew it wasn't because he hadn't had time. "I wish you had."

"Why? It was just your usual letter, wasn't it? Here's what we all did this year?"

"Not exactly. Nick, you need to read it. It wasn't meant for anyone's eyes but lots of eyes have seen it. Everyone on my mailing list. And more, I think. People keep forwarding it on."

She'd printed it out that morning. She gave the copy to him. Her hands were shaking.

As he took it, they heard a voice.

"Mum?"

It was Lindy, calling from the side veranda. "Mum?"

"Go," Nick said. "I'll read it while you're gone."

She shook her head. She needed to be here, trying to guess how he was feeling as he read it.

"*Mum?* Where are you?"

"Go, Angela," Nick repeated.

It felt wrong to leave him, but Lindy was coming closer. Angela met her halfway.

"What's Dad reading?" Lindy asked.

"Just some business letters."

"From the mining people?" At Angela's nod, Lindy lowered her voice. "It's still hard to believe, isn't it? Do you think anyone will turn up to our party now? Everyone hates us, don't they?"

"Of course not," Angela lied. "What's wrong? Do you need some help?"

"How much cushion stuffing do you think I should use? So it's flat or plump? I didn't ask in my order form and I can't get any answer when I ring the customer's number. Can you help me decide?"

"Of course," Angela said.

It took longer than expected. More than fifteen minutes had passed by the time she returned. Nick was still sitting on the bench. He was holding her letter.

He looked up at her. She was shocked at his expression. He wasn't angry. He looked desolate.

"It's that bad?" he said. "You hate your life here that much? You wish you'd never met me?"

"Nick, it's not true, none of it—"

"I read every word, Angela. Three times. I recognized everything you said about Ig. About Genevieve. About Lindy. Victoria too, even if I didn't know she and that bastard were having an affair. If everything about them is true, then what you say about me has to be true too. About how you feel about me."

"No, Nick."

"It's all there. Everything you think. That I've made a big mistake leasing the station. That I'm having an affair—"

"No—"

"Who is Will?"

"I knew him before I met you. I told you about him, when we first met. He was my first boyfriend. Years and years ago."

"Are you in touch with him now?"

She shook her head.

"You're not? So what's this about your house together, your life with him, your daughter. In all this detail?"

"I haven't seen him since I first left England. I promise. I made it all up."

He picked up the letter. He started to read out a section about her fantasy life with Will, Lexie—

She couldn't listen. It was too personal, too humiliating. She had to stop him. "What about you and Carol, Nick? I've heard you talking to her every day. Laughing with her. All the plans you're making together, under the cover of a family reunion, family research. You're going to Ireland to meet up with her, aren't you? Early next year. She's organizing your itinerary. I overheard you talking about it with her. Were you ever going to tell me about that?"

"Yes, I was. The same day I was going to ask you if you'd come with me. Once I'd had the chance to ask Victoria if she'd look after Ig and your Web site while you and I were away."

Angela went still.

"You really thought that I'd make my first overseas trip without you? I've been planning it for weeks. I'd worked it all out. I thought we'd start with a week in Ireland; then you and I would go on to London. Maybe Italy or France after that. Wherever you wanted to go."

"But I thought you and Carol—"

"That we were what? Going to run away together?"

"I've heard you talking to her. Her flirting with you."

"It's just her way." He picked up the letter again. "Who else has read this?"

"Joan. Everyone on the mailing list." She wanted to say, "Because of you. Because you sent it out." She couldn't. She didn't.

"How many people?"

"One hundred. At least."

He looked down at the pages again. She knew what he was seeing. That she thought he was a failure. An adulterer. That she didn't want to be married to him.

It felt impossible to even begin to explain. All she could do was apologize. "I'm so sorry, Nick."

"So am I," he said.

He stood up. For one moment, one hopeful moment, she thought he was going to come close, take her in his arms. Perhaps even smile at her. Say, "It's a mess, but we'll sort it out together. Don't worry." Instead, he walked away; not toward her, not into the house, but away, across the house yard.

"Nick—"

He didn't answer and he didn't look back.

By nine o'clock that night, he still hadn't returned. Ig and Lindy both asked where he was. She said he was out working on the station somewhere. He wasn't working. He was walking; she knew that. It was what he always did when he needed to think. Walked for miles under that big sky.

The three of them were in the living room watching

TV when they finally heard him come in. He stopped at the doorway. "Angela?"

She turned, trying to read his expression. His face was in shadow.

"Would you come over to the chapel with me?"

His quiet request nearly broke her heart.

"Ooh," Lindy said. "A romantic walk under the stars. Dad, you smoothie."

Neither of them answered her.

As they crossed the paddock they didn't speak. They reached the chapel and took a seat on the one remaining pew. They were both silent at first. Out of sight, a windmill turned, its iron sails clinking rhythmically. In the darkness, Nick's voice was low, quiet. Sad.

"Why, Angela? Why didn't you say any of this to my face?"

"We never seem to talk anymore. About anything."

He turned and looked at her. "Is it that bad being married to me?"

"No."

"I always thought you'd leave me. Did you know that? That you'd decide you hated it here and would go back to England. When you first came, and it was so hard and you were so lonely, I used to pray, and I don't even know if I believe in God, but I would come here and pray that you wouldn't find it too hard. And then when we found out you were having twins, I thought it was a sign, a double sign, that you would stay. And then Lindy too. And then Ig. I almost thought there was something mystical at work. Because whatever problems you and I might ever have had, I always thought you loved the kids."

"I do love the kids."

"I thought you loved me too."

"I do love you." But did he love her anymore? *Ask him*, a voice in her mind said. She couldn't find the words.

"Do you want to leave now?" he said. "Leave us all? Go back to London? Is that what this is about?"

His question shocked her. Did she? She must have thought about it, to have been able to write that letter. But no. She didn't want to leave. Her mentions of London had been just one more detail of her fanciful thoughts about Will and Lexie. It all seemed shameful now. She couldn't bear to see him so hurt, so serious beside her. She shook her head.

There was a long silence. He broke it again.

"Have you ever been happy here?"

"Of course, Nick. Of course."

"But not for a long time. And not now. I annoy you. I disappoint you. Not just me; the kids too. You want a break from us—is that it?"

"It's not that. I just need a break from myself. I'm sick of myself. Sick and tired of everything about myself."

"So I gathered from your letter. As everybody who got it now knows as well."

Her hackles suddenly rose. "We're both to blame for the letter. You were trying to help me, I know, sending it out, but—"

"I'm not talking about how the letter got out. I'm talking about our family. Our marriage. What everyone now knows about us. It went to all our neighbors? Everyone coming to the party?"

She nodded. "We can cancel it."

"We can't cancel it," he said.

"So do you want to leave me?" she said.

"What?" he said.

"Do you want a separation?"

"We've got more to worry about than that at the moment. This party—how many are coming?"

She told him about the increase in numbers in the past few days. "Ghouls, Joan called them."

"Joan knows about all of this?"

She nodded.

"Do the kids know?"

"Not yet. They don't read my letters. And I don't think they've heard about it from anyone else."

"Has Celia read it?"

"She's on the mailing list. I don't know if she's read it yet."

"We say nothing to any of them for now. Only if someone asks do we mention it. Otherwise, we ignore it."

It felt like he wasn't asking her, but telling her. Something bridled inside.

"Please don't talk to me like that. You're the one who sent it out."

"You're the one who wrote it."

They sounded like children.

He continued. "We have to at least appear united, in front of the kids and at the party. And while Celia's here."

"And after that?"

"After that, we'll talk about it again."

He stood up, waiting for her.

She needed time on her own. Time to think.

"I'll follow you in," she said.

Again, she saw that expression in his eyes. Not anger. It was hurt.

Twenty minutes passed before she stood up too, and started walking back across the empty paddocks toward the light of the homestead.

She finished the dishes. She swept and washed the kitchen floor. She cleaned the bathroom. When it was all done, she joined the children in the lounge room, as if it were a normal night together. She knew he was in the office. As they finished watching their TV program, she heard his steps in the hall. She didn't turn off the TV until both Lindy and Ig had gone to bed, until the house was quiet.

For once, he was the one asleep by the time she came to bed.

THIRTEEN

It was two days later. Angela was on her way to Adelaide to collect Genevieve and Victoria from the airport.

It was the quietest few hours she'd had in months. In the first half of her four-hour journey, she'd passed less than a dozen cars, one semitrailer and an elderly couple towing a caravan. She'd waved and all of them—all strangers—had waved back. The country salute. She remembered noticing it for the first time while driving with Nick along this road three decades ago. She'd thought he knew everyone.

Celia had arrived the previous day. Nick had collected her from the bus in Hawker. She had been all charm and girlish giggles with him, all icy politeness with Angela. She was as perfectly groomed as always, her petite frame in an elegant, well-tailored dress. As Angela carried in her bag, helped her settle into the guestroom, she waited for a sign that Celia had read her Christmas e-mail. There had been nothing, until she heard Lindy ask her about the bus journey. "It was fine, thank you," Celia had said. "Especially because there was no one sitting beside me." It had to be a reference to the e-mail. But Celia had said nothing directly to Angela, nor Angela to her.

She wondered whether Celia had noticed the tension between her and Nick. How could anyone not notice it? They had barely spoken since their conversation at the chapel. Polite exchanges in the kitchen, no conversation at all in the bedroom. She wouldn't have thought it possible to be so physically close to someone, yet so far apart.

"Give him time," Joan had advised. Angela was talking to Joan as often as she could, as difficult as it was when the only phone was in the kitchen. She'd told her some of what had happened with Nick. Not all of it. Some of it hurt too much to share. Some of it was still sinking in.

"I was going to ask you if you'd come with me."

A trip with Nick was something she had wanted for years, the two of them traveling overseas together. Both times she had been back to the UK, for her parents' funerals, she'd gone on her own. He had offered to come with her, tried to insist, but she'd known it made the most sense to go on her own. Nick needed to be home, looking after the children, the stock, the station. She'd first made the long journey home to London after her father died suddenly. The twins had been seven, Lindy four. She'd spent three weeks with her mother in her old family house in Forest Hill, trying and failing to convince her to come to Australia to live.

Her mother had all her friends in London, she'd said. She was happy here. It was too hot in Australia for her. The second trip three years after that had been even sadder. Her mother had died in the nursing home. A quick and painless death, the matron assured her. Angela had hoped it was true. She'd sat in the small chapel, with only the staff around her, wishing that she had a big family to share this with. She'd called Nick that night and wept. "I'm an orphan now, aren't I?"

"You've got us. We're here waiting for you. We can't wait for you to come home."

When she'd landed at Adelaide airport, Nick and the three girls had been there. She'd never felt anything like the hugs the four of them gave her. The drive home in her jet-lagged state felt like a dream. Nick holding her hand with his left hand as he steered with his right. The three girls in the back, singing the songs they always sang on long trips, "Kookaburra Sits in the Old Gum Tree," and "Ten Green Bottles," over and over again. Nick had been right. She had all of them.

She arrived at Adelaide airport now to discover the twins' flight from Sydney was delayed by forty minutes. She wandered through the airport, past the shops and cafés. She saw a bank of public computers. One was free. She was logged on within a minute. Another twenty-two e-mails.

I hope you don't mind but I forwarded it on to some friends. Yours was EXACTLY what these Christmas letters should be like!

Great read, thank you!! Can you send these
monthly?? Happy Christmas to all the Gillespies.

There was another one from Keith, the station manager
at the Port Pirie radio station:

Angela, just a follow-up—there might be something here at the station for Victoria sooner
than I expected. Can you ask her to call me?

One from their neighbors to the east, the Ryans, a
family of seven:

If Genevieve is back, don't suppose she'd like
to drop over for an at home hairdressing session?? We won't be able to pay Hollywood
prices but we can pay her in eggs???

As she was about to log off, she saw an e-mail with a
different subject line. *Re: Inquiry re sculptures.* It was from an
art gallery. A big gallery in Adelaide. Six weeks earlier,
she'd sent them four photos of her most successful clay
sculptures. Her only successful clay sculptures. Her heart
began to beat faster.

Dear Mrs. Gillespie
I have always made it my policy not to mince
my words and give unfair hope to artists if I

genuinely felt their talents were best served elsewhere. I therefore write this to you in the spirit of artistic honesty and personal integrity. You say in your e-mail that you have been working in the medium of clay for some time now. Your sculptures appear amateurish and ill-thought-out. This may sound harsh, but believe me, a critic of any show I might be foolish enough to stage with your work would be harsher. You mention you plan to send your portfolio to other galleries too. My advice is not to bother. I have personally fostered the careers of some of the country's most successful ceramic artists and I know what I am talking about. I say this in the best possible spirit. Please stop.

Yours,
James Billington

She deleted it. She didn't need to keep it. She already knew that what he said was the truth.

Back on Errigal, Lindy, Ig and Celia were in the office, Celia in the chair in front of the computer. Before their mother left, she had asked Lindy and Ig to be nice to Celia. They were trying.

"No, I'm sorry," Celia said to Lindy. "I still don't understand. Can you explain again?"

Lindy tried not to sigh. "So, I set this cushion Web site up. People find it, read about all the things I can do and then order a cushion from me. They pay in advance. I make the cushion and then send it to them. Simple."

"And this is how you make your living?"

"Not yet, no. But that's the plan."

"How many cushions have you made?"

"I'm doing the finishing touches to the first one."

"Still," Ig said.

"And your profit margin will be?" Celia asked.

"Five dollars."

"So your annual wage so far is five dollars?"

"That's it so far, yes."

"I see. And what if you get so much work you can't fulfill the orders?"

"I don't think there's much chance of that."

"That's a very defeatist attitude."

"It's a realistic attitude. If I didn't have a semitrailer's worth of material out there, I'd forget the whole thing. But I owe it to Dad and Mum to somehow sell it, pay them back."

"Well, that's all very interesting. Thank you, Rosalind."

"Aunt Celia?"

"Yes, Ignatius?"

"Would you like to see my cubby now?"

"Thank you, yes, I would."

Lindy waited until they'd left before she pressed refresh. It didn't make any difference. She still hadn't had any new orders.

Outside, Ig was conducting his tour with the solemnity of a museum guide. He'd thought of a few ways to be nice to Celia. This cubby house tour, for a start. He'd ask Celia to play Scrabble later on too.

"This corner is the living room," he said, gesturing to it with his good arm. He still had the sling on the other one. He'd gotten used to being one-armed. He quite liked it actually. Robbie had started wearing a sling too. They both removed them now and again, though. When there was no one around to tell them off. "And that corner is the bedroom."

"And will you sleep out here one night?" Celia asked.

Ig nodded. "Especially when Genevieve and Victoria are home. They can be very noisy."

He stood back beside Celia. Yes, he was happy with his cubby house now. He'd made many of them over the years, out of sheets and chairs, old tents, and corrugated iron. He'd even had one in the broken-down station truck once, until a snake slithered up through the disused engine and gave him a fright. He hated snakes as much as his mum hated spiders. But none of those cubbies had compared to this one.

"Have you given it a name yet?" Celia asked.

He shrugged. "It's just my cubby."

"It's not just a cubby, Ignatius. It's like a castle. So you should give it a noble name."

He shot her a suspicious look. She wasn't usually this nice.

"The Gillespie Fortress?" he suggested.

"Very good. You'll need a flag too. To fly over the castle, to warn off would-be invaders."

"Can you help me and Robbie make it?"

"Robbie? You still believe in that nonsense about an imaginary friend?"

He went still. "It's not nonsense."

"Ignatius, it is. Robbie isn't real. You need to make real

friends, with real boys. You're too old for all this business and it isn't healthy. I'm sure your parents agree with me. Now, come on, come inside and I'll show you how to make the flag."

"No, thank you," Ig said.

"What do you mean, 'No, thank you'?"

"It won't have a flag. It doesn't need one."

"But it would look much better with a flag."

"No, thank you," he said again.

"Very well. Suit yourself."

He waited until she was back inside and out of earshot before he spoke.

"You're right, Robbie. That's exactly what she is."

Angela was waiting at the gate as her daughters' plane taxied in. A crowd formed just before the passengers began to appear.

She saw Genevieve and Victoria immediately, and was taken aback by the rush of love she felt. They hadn't seen her yet. They were too busy talking to each other. Genevieve had to be jet-lagged after her long international flight, but she looked radiant. The blue dreadlocks were gone, replaced by a chic pixie cut, her dark hair glossy. She was so tall, willowy, dressed all in black. Beside her, yes, Victoria was slightly overweight, but she looked so pretty too, glowing, with her blond curls and rosy cheeks. Why had Angela worried about the pair of them coming home again? They were her girls. Her two beautiful girls who had just noticed her too.

She was nearly pushed over by the force of their hugs, one on either side. Squashed in the middle, she could see other passengers watching, smiling. She hugged one, then the other, the feeling so familiar, wanting to gather them both up in one big hug. It had never been possible, even when they were babies. They'd squirmed too much. They still had that same energy, the urge to keep busy, to talk, to laugh. They were moving now, dragging their hand luggage, pulling her along with them down to the baggage hall, talking nonstop, about the flight, how they couldn't wait to get home to Errigal again, was she embarrassed by them, two of them coming home to lick their wounds, two unemployed, publicly humiliated thirty-two-year-olds; it was a scandal, wasn't it?

They scarcely drew breath. As always, one started sentences; the other finished them. They switched back and forth between calling her *Mum, Mama, Mother, Angela.* They'd always had dozens of names for her.

At the car, they stowed their luggage, then clambered into the backseat. Victoria had been home several times recently, but this was Genevieve's first visit since she'd left for America. She'd always been too busy to come, even for a brief holiday. "It's been more than two years. Can you believe it?" Genevieve was saying to Victoria.

"You should have spread scurrilous gossip and got sacked months ago if you missed your homeland so much," Victoria said to her.

"You should have slept with your boss and—" Genevieve stopped abruptly. "You should have let your maniac radio host off the leash months ago and come home more often yourself."

Angela pretended she hadn't noticed the slip.

They were soon on the highway. The familiar towns

passed by. There was no letup in their chatter. She'd thought they might doze, that Genevieve might succumb to jet lag in the dark comfort of the car. If anything, she was the more talkative. She told story after story from the film and TV world. "All brakes are off now," she said. "I've already been sacked. What can they do? Kill me?" She made them both laugh with tales of affairs, of stars misbehaving, director antics, all the gossip she'd collected over the past two years. She talked about life in New York, told a story Angela hadn't heard before about the first week she was there, when she and her flatmate had met a friendly, charming guy at a gig, who invited them up for a drink in the rooftop bar, pouring them what he called his "special cocktail for special ladies." Beside her, Victoria was laughing. She obviously knew this tale already.

"Genevieve, stop. Don't tell Mum this story. She won't even let us go to the Hawker pub on our own if she hears this."

Genevieve continued. "He'd spiked our drinks, Mum! Imagine! If there hadn't been two of us, helping each other to get out of there and get home, he might have kidnapped us and cut us into tiny pieces."

Angela was shocked. How could she sound so relaxed about it? Had she gone to the police?

"Of course I did. You know how law-abiding I am." More laughter.

The American accent Angela had heard during their phone and Skype conversations was already disappearing. Genevieve sounded like she'd been in Sydney, not New York, for the past two years, apart from the occasional use of *y'all* picked up from a Texan friend. It was clear Victoria was already teasing that out of her.

They passed through the final small towns, Jamestown, Orroroo, Carrieton, Cradock, Hawker, then turned off the main highway onto their dirt road. There was now just open space. The girls quieted down, still talking but in softer voices. Fifteen minutes from home, as Angela drove around the familiar bends, over familiar creek crossings, they came to life again.

"Quick, fill us in on everyone," they said to her. "Dad. Celia, Lindy. Ig. All the headlines."

Angela gave brief details. They asked about the latest reaction to the news of the mining lease. About the guest list for the party. About Joan.

Everyone was standing in front of the house as the car pulled in. The twins leaped out and ran over for hugs. Even Celia got one. Angela stood back, watching, smiling. Her whole family, together again. Her big girls back home, safe and sound after all their adventures.

She didn't allow herself to dwell on the fact that during the entire four-hour journey, they hadn't asked her one question about herself.

FOURTEEN

The party was now only four days away. The twins had been back for five days. The entire house was in chaos. Joan had practically moved in, coming each morning before nine and staying until late, supervising the cooking. A tall, strong woman, with gray hair kept short for practical reasons, she'd arrived each day dressed in work clothes, an old shirt of her husband's, patched trousers of her own. She'd stepped out of her car with her apron already tied on.

There had been a very happy reunion between her and Genevieve on her first morning.

"You look wonderful, Joan," Genevieve said, hugging her close. "Even if you have been cutting your own hair again. And don't tell me you haven't. I'm a professional; I know these things."

"What was I supposed to do? You were gone for more than two years. I'd have been like Rapunzel if I waited for you to come home again."

"I'm back now. As soon as your poor hair grows enough for me to cut it, call me."

"Oh, I'm too boring after all your film stars and actors," Joan said, smiling. She'd always loved Genevieve's cheekiness. "You look like a film star yourself with that haircut. As skinny as one too. Though I was dying to see the blue dreadlocks."

"You know about the dreadlocks? I only had them for a month. You are a diligent godmother."

Angela shot her a glance. Joan had only read about the dreadlocks in her Christmas letter.

Joan didn't miss a beat. "I had you under surveillance the whole time you were away; didn't you know that? A young innocent like you, in a big city like New York. I've been worried sick."

"I wondered who those men in the trench coats following me were. I thought they were just my usual lovelorn stalkers."

As soon as Genevieve had left the room, Joan and Angela had a whispered conversation. Joan thought it was a big mistake that Angela still hadn't told the girls and Ig about the letter. Angela promised she'd tell them before the party. She just had to choose the right time. Joan didn't think delaying it was a good idea, but she'd agreed to keep quiet in the meantime.

"I'm starting to wish I'd hired caterers," Angela said now, looking up from the oven, where she'd just placed another fifty sausage rolls to bake.

Joan was rolling pastry. "Of course you couldn't hire caterers. People are already gossiping about you Gillespies swimming in money now. Money and diamonds. You'd better serve badly cooked food and cheap wine at this party or you'll be in even more trouble."

"In trouble? With who? The neighbors?" Genevieve asked, wandering in. All four children were doing a lot of wandering through the kitchen, picking up just-cooked sausage rolls on the way past. "Mum, do people hate us because of that mining lease?"

"I don't know. I haven't been in town much recently." Angela had deliberately stayed away, traveling in only for Ig's checkups at the hospital, coming home straight afterward.

"So will there be strapping young miners strolling the land soon, a smorgasbord of possible husbands for Victoria, Lindy and me? Now that we don't have any strapping young shearers or stockmen to ogle?"

"Don't hold your breath," Joan said.

"Joan, please. We have to get husbands somehow. Unless you want us to live here for the rest of our days, Mum?"

"Join an online agency, would you?" Angela said. "As quick as you can."

Genevieve laughed, stole a sausage roll and left the room.

"Has there been much talk about us lately?" Angela asked Joan once they were alone.

"Of course. Between your letter and the news of that lease, you're topic number one around here. Everything from people wondering how much you've been paid, to how Nick pulled it off. Jealousy from some. Admiration from others. Lots of unspoken fear about what it means for the future. It's not every day there's the possibility of a diamond mine appearing in our backyards, Ange. People have to react to it."

"What do you think?"

"What I thought when you first asked me that question three months ago. Do you think Nick had any choice?"

"I don't know. He still won't talk about it. About anything." She crossed the room and shut the door, in case any of the children were listening. "It was bad enough between us before he heard about the letter. It's even worse now."

"You just need to stay patient, Ange. Let him come to terms with it all in his own time, in his own way. It was always a trait of the Gillespie males to keep their troubles to themselves. His father was the same. And his grandfather, apparently."

"I thought we were different, though. He always took care of the financial side of the station, but we used to talk about everything else. Not anymore. I can't stop going over and over everything that's happened over the past few years, wondering what I could have done differently, how I could have helped him to fix it—"

"Ange, you can't change the past. None of us can. All any of us have is the future. So we just have to get on with it. Make the best of things. Onward and upward, and all that."

As she reached for a new packet of pastry, Angela wished it were that simple.

"I'm bored," Genevieve announced, flopping onto the well-worn sofa in the living room.

"Only boring people get bored," Lindy said, not looking up from her sewing. She was redoing the cross-stitch border on the Get Well Soon cushion. She hadn't been happy with her first attempt. If she didn't get it in the mail to Perth the next day, she'd miss the customer's operation. As it was, she was going to have to pay for premium shipping. Her profit was now down to two dollars for a week's work.

"Are you daring to call me boring?" Genevieve said.

"I didn't make up that saying. It's one from school."

"And school is where it should stay." Genevieve sighed. "It's not just boring. It feels weird here too, don't you think? No sheep, no stockmen. It's like some postapocalyptic film setting. The only sheep station in the world without any sheep."

"They didn't all just disappear overnight, Genevieve. If you'd bothered to come home anytime in the past two years, you wouldn't be so shocked now."

Genevieve shifted position again, ignoring the dig and swinging her long legs onto the other arm of the chair. "It's hard to believe, isn't it? All these years and we had no idea there were diamonds lurking in the ground beneath us. I wish they'd hurry up and find them. I was hoping to have a sparkling necklace to wear at the party."

Lindy rolled her eyes. "God, Genevieve. Didn't you pay any attention when Dad told us? He's signed an exploration lease, not a mining lease. They're pretty sure the diamonds are there, but they could be hundreds of kilometers down. It could be years before they start digging, and even then it might not be worthwhile financially to try to bring them to the surface."

"Thank you, Lindy, for that potted history of the mining process. Next time, can you get a blackboard and do me some diagrams? Forget diamonds; let's talk cushions. Have you had any more orders yet?"

"I don't know. Once Dad's off the computer I'll check."

"Am I imagining it or is Dad addicted to that computer?" Genevieve said.

"To that computer, his history books, the family tree—"

"And to Carol," Ig said, from his spot on the floor. "He's in love with Carol."

"I know, Ig. You keep telling me about this great love affair. You're very relaxed for a child who's about to go through his parents' divorce. As if Mum and Dad will ever split up. I've never known a couple so in love. It's sickening. Scarring too. How can I ever measure up to their example? No wonder I'm still single. And me, such a catch."

"Didn't you meet anyone in New York?" Lindy asked.

"Of course I did. Thousands of men. Battalions. I was like catnip to the eligible young blades of New York. I turned them all down. You know how choosy I am." She turned back to her brother. "Enough about me for a few minutes. Where's Celia, Ig?"

"Having a lie-down," Ig said.

"Thank you. That's everyone accounted for. Ig, can I time how long it takes for you to go and get my phone? It's by my bed."

"I'm ten. That doesn't work anymore."

"I'll let you climb the ladder to do the decorations in the woolshed later."

"Promise?"

"Promise. Ig, please, get my phone. I'm too jet-lagged."

"You've been home for days."

"It was a very long flight. So who wants to hear some more about my exciting life in America?"

"I'll get your phone," Ig said, leaving the room.

Victoria came in. "Finished. What do you think?" She moved her head from side to side, showing off her newly plucked eyebrows.

"Perfect arch, perfect brow," Genevieve said. "Lovely."

"I can't find it," Ig called from Genevieve's bedroom.

"Try under the bed, Ig," Genevieve called back. "Victoria, why are you doing your eyebrows when you're going there to talk about a radio job?"

"You're about to do my hair too. Because I need this job. Because I'm trying to look as impressive as my CV sounds."

"I still can't believe it," Lindy said. "You get sacked and before you even get home someone approaches you about a job. It's not fair."

"You've got a job," Genevieve said. "One in a personalized sweatshop, but it's still a job."

"Knowing my luck, the person who is having this operation will die on the operating table and never get to see his or her cushion."

"That's the spirit, Lindy. I hope you're sewing all those positive vibes into the cushion."

Ig returned, holding Genevieve's phone.

"At last," she said, taking it. "Thank you, small and loyal servant."

Ig flopped onto the floor and turned on the TV.

"No volume, Ig."

"How can I hear?"

"Read their lips. You manage to hear Robbie all right, don't you?"

He muttered but he turned down the volume.

Genevieve held up her phone and groaned. "Still no

signal. How did I ever live out here in the back of beyond? It's primitive, isn't it? Thank God for the computer and satellite technology or we'd be completely cut off from the outside world."

"You could always get in the car and go to Hawker," Lindy said. "You can get a signal there."

"It's too hot. I'm too jet-lagged. I'll just read all my old messages instead." She scrolled through them, while Lindy kept sewing and Victoria put on her makeup using the big mirror over the fireplace. Ig picked up the remote and slowly increased the volume.

"I saw that, Ig," Genevieve said without looking up. "Down, boy, down. Lindy, did you hear the Ryans want me to do a bulk haircutting session on their station? All seven of them."

"You've got work too? That's really not fair."

"You should have gotten a degree in something useful, not just arts, if you wanted to be like us."

"I've done lots of jobs since I left college."

"You certainly have."

"Don't tease me. It was bad enough from Horrible Jane." Genevieve looked up then. "You've seen Horrible Jane lately? Oh, no. Is she back home?"

"Not yet, but she will be. She's coming to the party."

"No way! Who invited her?"

"Mum. She invited all the Lawsons. They're coming too. I saw their RSVPs."

"All of them?" Genevieve said. "Even Fred?"

"I don't know about Fred. He's still in Canada, isn't he?" Victoria didn't say anything.

"Forget about the rest of them for now," Genevieve said,

shooting her twin a glance. "Where did you see Horrible Jane, Lindy?"

"In Melbourne. It was hideous. Ig, I'm telling a story but you're not allowed to tell Mum. She'll only get cross with me. You can listen but then you have to forget it, okay?"

"I won't even listen," he said. He put his hands over his ears. Over one ear, at least.

Lindy told Victoria and Genevieve about meeting Richard in the bar. Kissing Richard. At first, they teased her. As she told them about Horrible Jane and the Lawsons mocking their mother's Christmas letters, they became serious.

"How *dare* they?" Genevieve said. "That's it. I'm putting thumbtacks on their road so they get flat tires and miss the party."

"Is Mum still sending those letters out?" Victoria said. "I haven't read one in years."

"She's still at it," Lindy said. "At least this year's was so boring the Lawsons won't be able to laugh at us. It basically said, 'Happy Christmas, everyone. Isn't it hot?' and that was it."

"You actually read it this year?"

"Only after she showed me a printout. I don't even know if she e-mails it to me anymore."

"I still get them, but I never read them. If you want to tell lies about how perfect your family is, what's wrong with Facebook?" Genevieve scrolled through her phone. "Hold on—this year's might still be in my Trash folder. Yep, here it is."

"Can I stop not listening now?" Ig asked.

"Sure, Ig," Victoria said. "Genevieve, which lipstick should I wear? Pink or this red one?"

Genevieve was looking at her phone and frowning. "Lindy, did you say Mum's Christmas letter was short? And boring?"

"Really short, really boring, thank God."

"Then what's this?"

"What's what?"

"This e-mail I got from her on December first. Her 'Hello from the Gillespies!' one. Ig, turn the TV off, would you?"

"Turn it off yourself. Stop bossing me around."

"Please, Ig. You can have some of the alcoholic punch at the party if you do."

"I'm ten years old."

"The nonalcoholic punch. Ig, come on—turn it off, get up and shut the door, then come back, sit down and pay attention. This is serious."

He got up, shut the door, returned to his spot and flopped down on the floor again.

"Victoria, you too. Wear the red lipstick. But listen to this first."

Genevieve started to read. "'Hello. It's Angela back again. Can you believe a year has passed since I last wrote to you all? I hope you've all had a great twelve months and are now looking forward to special family Christmas celebrations together. It's been a terrible year for the Gillespies. Everything seems to have gone wrong for us.'" She stopped there and looked up.

"That's not the letter she showed me," Lindy said.

"Keep reading," Victoria said.

"Keep reading," Ig said.

Genevieve kept reading.

FIFTEEN

It came without warning. From the kitchen Angela had heard the voices of her children in the living room, registering them on her mother radar. She'd heard some laughter, talking, and then Genevieve's voice for a long time. If she had known what Genevieve was reading aloud, she would have put down the sausage rolls and run out the kitchen door, gotten into the car and driven down the highway. She would have done anything to avoid what she was now facing.

Her four children, her four furious children, standing across the table from her and Joan, shouting at her. At least, her three daughters were shouting at her. Ig was trying to take Genevieve's phone. "Let me see what she wrote about me again. Genevieve, let me see it."

"Mum, what were you *thinking*?" Genevieve said.

Victoria was in tears. "That was all *my* private business, Mum. How can I face the station manager this afternoon?"

"So I'm a drama queen, am I?" Lindy said. "I can't *believe* you think that. I'm emotional, not dramatic."

"Genevieve, please," Ig said, jumping up as his sister held her phone aloft. "Give it to me!"

"Ig, no. You already heard what she said about you. You're a weirdo but at least she still loves you. She seems to think her three daughters are just basket cases."

"Oh, for God's sake, calm down, all of you, would you?" It was Joan speaking.

"Easy for you to say, Joan," Genevieve said. "Your mother hasn't just broadcast your family secrets to dozens of people around the world."

"One hundred," Joan said.

"What?"

"It went to one hundred people. I counted the names when I received mine."

"You got it too?"

"Of course. I've got your mother's Christmas letter every year since the first one. I've read it every year too. Unlike all of you."

"Have they been like this every year? Mum? Have they?" Angela found her voice. "No, this was kind of a one-off."

"Has Dad seen it?" Victoria asked. "Has he read what you said about him?"

Joan and Angela exchanged glances.

"Yes, he has," Angela said.

"And he's still living in the same house as you?" Genevieve said.

Lindy started crying. "Wait until Horrible Jane and her family see this. They already laughed at these letters. They'll be in hysterics now."

"So what?" Victoria said. "You care too much what everyone thinks. You'll never please everyone; you'll just keep tying yourself in knots and what's the point of that?"

"Says you! Look what Mum told everyone about you, having that affair."

"So it's true, then?" Joan said.

"No!" Victoria said. "Well, actually, yes. Ig, go outside."

"No," Ig said.

"But isn't he married?" Lindy said. "With kids and everything?"

"*He's* married with kids. I'm not. I didn't do anything wrong. Don't take the moral high ground with me, Lindy. At least I didn't come running home dragging a huge debt behind me."

"Actually, you did," Genevieve said. "So did I. That's why we're here, remember."

"Well, we can't stay here now, can we?" Victoria said. "After being publicly humiliated like this."

"By our own *mother*," Lindy added.

"Sit down, everyone. Please." It was Joan again. "It's good to have this out in the open, if you ask me. Your mother was going to tell you today, in any case."

"I was?" Angela said. "Yes, I was."

"A lot of people who will be at the party received it, so she thought you may as well be prepared."

"Forget the party. We have to cancel it," Genevieve said.

"We can't," Angela said. "It's too late."

"Mum, come on! How can we stand there smiling and pretending we're a normal happy family when every single person knows what a mess we all are?"

"It was an accident, I promise. I never meant to send it."

"And on the bright side, she has had some very nice replies," Joan said. "From all sorts of people. Even your old boss, Victoria."

"Keith got the letter too? That's why he wants to see me. Oh *no*."

"What's that saying? Every cloud has a silver lining?" Joan said. "That's why the Ryans want you to cut their hair too, Genevieve."

"That's it. I can't go there now."

"Of course you can," Joan said. "Everyone around here got it, anyway. And those that didn't have probably had it forwarded to them by now."

Ig had slipped away, unseen. He came in again now with a handful of paper. "Here's some printouts if anyone wants to read it again."

"Ig!" Angela said. "Where did you get those?"

"Off your e-mail. I know your password."

Angela suddenly sat down, holding her head.

"Mum, are you all right?" Victoria said.

"Of *course* she's not!" Lindy said. "I've kept trying to tell you both. She's losing her mind."

"Lindy!" Joan stepped in again.

"Look what she's just done to us, Joan! I can't go to the party. I'm never leaving this house again." She ran out of the room in tears.

"Oh, stop being such a drama queen, Lindy," Genevieve

called after her. "Hold on. If Mum was right about Lindy—"
She grabbed a printout from Ig, ignoring his squawk of protest.

Sitting next to Angela at the table, Joan gave her friend's hand a quick squeeze.

Genevieve read a few sentences under her breath. "Actually, I sound quite cool. Shallow, but cool. Thanks, Mum. And your dream has come true too. I'm home for good. It's like you cast a spell on me."

"It's not funny, Genevieve," Victoria said.

"Yes, it is. And you sound very sweet in your section, Victoria, if you ask me." She read on, then frowned, looking up. "Mum, has Celia read this?"

"I think so."

"And she still came? She's still here?"

Angela nodded.

Victoria was now reading it over her twin's shoulder. "'An insufferable snob and an interfering old bat.' Mum, what were you thinking? Were you trying to scare Celia off?"

"It didn't work, did it?" It was Celia speaking.

They all turned around. She was standing in the doorway.

"Am I imagining it," she said, "or do I smell something burning?"

Thirty minutes later, Angela and Joan were standing in front of the house. Joan was leaving, but had promised to return later that day.

"Can you please hurry back?" Angela said. "I need you here."

"No, you don't. You know what to do. Don't explain too

much. Don't apologize. You can't change it, so now you just have to deal with it. And it could have been worse."

"It could have? How?"

Joan smiled. "You could have said something mean about me."

SIXTEEN

It was after three by the time Joan returned. The kitchen was empty. She called out a hello. There was no answer. She went into the living room. Empty. She eventually found Genevieve in the dining room, wrapping plastic cutlery in paper napkins.

"Thank God someone's alive," Joan said. "I was starting to think you'd all run away or killed each other."

"It might happen yet," Genevieve said. "This is either the calm before the storm, or the calm after the storm. Victoria's gone to meet her radio station man, very upset. Lindy's sewing, very upset. Ig's sulking somewhere because he had to dismantle his cubby to help Lindy find more thread. Celia's either reading in her room or secretly sipping sherry in her room."

"And your parents?"

"Dad's gone off in the 4WD, presumably also upset. Mum's out in her studio, either hiding or making more of those sculptures, which, between you and me, don't look like anything I can recognize. Fun, aren't we? Hello from the Gillespies, indeed."

Joan took a seat and started wrapping cutlery too. "Genevieve, I'm worried about your mother."

"Join the club. Seriously, Joan, what got into her, writing all that stuff? You know her better than anyone. What was she thinking?"

"It really was an accident. She wrote it, but she never meant to send it. Then in all the fuss with Ig's finger, your father accidentally—"

"I know *how* it happened; it's *what* she wrote that's the worry. I read it again after you left. As I said, I got off lightly. But all that stuff about her and Dad? It was so personal. What happened to them while I was away? I thought they had a good marriage."

"Marriages go through stages. All couples have their ups and downs—"

"Joan, it's me. Your goddaughter. Don't give me a saccharine answer. This is more than ups and downs. Mum made it sound like they haven't spoken to each other in months. What do you think is going on? Who's this Will? Has Mum been having her own little cyber-affair?"

"I don't know. She's never mentioned him to me."

"Is he even real? Does she actually know someone in London called that?"

"I've no idea. We've been busy with the other parts of her letter. We haven't gotten to Will yet."

Genevieve put down the cutlery. "Right. Let's find out now. Come with me."

Joan followed her down the hall to the office. Genevieve took a seat at the computer and called up a search engine. "So, let's begin."

"Genevieve, I don't think—"

"Joan, come on. You're worried about her; I'm worried about her. We need to arm ourselves with information. What do we know about him so far?"

"Just what was in her letter," Joan said. "His name's Will. He's an architect in London."

Genevieve typed. Pages of entries appeared within seconds. "Too many, too vague. We'll need to narrow it down. Where exactly did Mum grow up? I know it was London, but do you remember the suburb or the street name or anything? Actually, what am I doing?" She spun around in the chair. "Forget Google. I'll get Ig to hack into her e-mails and we can see for ourselves if she and this Will are in contact." She was about to call for Ig when Joan stopped her.

"That's going too far."

"Don't worry. I'll pay Ig for his time. She's out in the studio if you want to keep her distracted while I do it. Because you know I will, don't you? Even if you tell me not to?"

"You're incorrigible."

Genevieve grinned. "I know. And I've gotten worse since I was away."

In her studio, Angela wasn't working with clay or firing any of her sculptures. She was just sitting on the old bench.

Joan came in and sat beside her. "Well done. The worst is over."

"It's not over. It's just started."

"No, you're dealing with the fallout, but the main explosion is over."

"Nick still won't talk to me. Victoria is furious. Ig is hurt. Lindy's being Lindy and—"

"Genevieve's having the time of her life. I think she was worried things might be a bit dull for her back here. You've certainly changed that."

Angela managed a smile.

"I think you should know she's in there googling that Will you wrote about. She's also about to bribe Ig to hack into your e-mail account."

"She won't find anything. Not on my e-mail anyway."

"But he is a real person?"

Angela nodded. "He was my first proper boyfriend. I was going out with him before I came to Australia, before I met Nick."

"And lately you started wondering what would have happened if you hadn't met Nick? If you'd stayed with Will?"

Angela nodded.

"There's nothing wrong with wondering 'what if,' Ange."

"You're telling me you have a fantasy life too?"

"Not quite as elaborate as yours, no. But what woman hasn't sometimes wished she was someone else? Or wondered how her life could have been different, if she'd made other choices?"

"Nick doesn't agree. He thinks it means I never wanted

to stay with him. That I never loved him, or the kids or—"
She stopped there, her voice faltering.

Joan patted her hand. "Give him time."

"He's not just furious, Joan. He's so hurt."

"Understandable, I suppose."

"We were on shaky ground before the letter. Even when
it was only the two of us, when Ig was at school and the
girls away. He's changed, Joan. It's like he's put up a barrier
between us. As if he's run out of things to say to me."

"How long have you been together now? Thirty-plus
years? It's a long time."

"So is that it for us, then? It's over? What about you and
Glenn? You've been married even longer. Did this happen
to you?"

"Oh, Ange, every marriage is different," Joan said.
"We've settled into what I'd call easy companionship. I'd do
anything for him; I know he'd do anything for me. We still
have the kids and the grandkids to talk about. What more
can I expect? Heated arguments about French philosophy
or world politics as we relax in the parlor after our gourmet
dinner each night?"

Angela smiled, picturing taciturn, gruff Glenn engaged
in a parlor discussion.

Joan continued. "I said it to Genevieve and I'll say it to
you too. Long marriages go through stages. All couples
have their ups and downs. It's just your turn to have a stage."

"I hope you're right," Angela said. She rubbed the back
of her head, closing her eyes.

Joan gave her a concerned look. "Are you still getting
those headaches?"

Angela nodded. "I'll go to the doctor again after Christmas. He said he'd send me to the specialist in Adelaide if I was still getting them."

"You can't wait until after Christmas."

"There isn't time before then. The party. The house full of kids. Celia. All this with the letter—"

Joan stood up. "We're making time. If ever you needed to be in good health, it's now."

"I can't. I've got cooking to do. Two hundred people coming in a few days' time."

"Too bad. We're going to the doctor in Port Augusta. You and me. Now."

"Joan, I can't. The sausage rolls—"

"Angela? Pardon my language; I'm about to say a sentence I may never say again in my life."

Angela waited.

"Fuck the sausage rolls."

Angela sat in the car while Joan went inside. She told Genevieve that she and Angela were going to Port Augusta, deliberately making it sound as though it were a shopping trip for the party. Genevieve was busy googling. She didn't look up. "Have fun. Try to get more info about this mysterious Will out of her, can you? There seems to be about two hundred thousand architects in the UK with the first name of William. Ig couldn't hack into her e-mail either. She's changed her password. Try to get that out of her as well, could you?"

Nearly two hundred kilometers away, Victoria was in the radio station in Port Pirie. She had started as a cadet there ten years earlier, after doing a three-year journalism degree in Adelaide. She'd done her first radio bulletins, reading from newspaper clippings as well as wire services. She'd produced her first segment, researched one-off specials. Then she'd moved back to Adelaide and worked as a producer on statewide programs there before taking the big step and moving to Sydney. Where it had gone so well before it had all gone spectacularly, publicly wrong.

At least her old boss, Keith, didn't beat around the bush. "That was one hell of a letter your mother sent out. You didn't mind?"

"She only did it so you'd hire me again," Victoria said lightly. At least he'd raised the subject right away. "And look, it worked. Here I am."

"So you are. And what's that saying? It's better to be talked about than not talked about? Sorry I can't make your party, by the way. It's my youngest's fourth birthday that day. Okay, to business. So you're back. For how long?"

"I don't know yet."

"I'll give you a six-month contract now if I know you'll stay here for it. But if you're going to head off as soon as you get a job offer in Adelaide or interstate, forget it. I want you to make a documentary series, family life on the land, told through different generations. Good interviews, good editing, good time slot. But if you start it, I want you to see it through to the end."

"That sounds brilliant, Keith. Thank you. But do I have to decide now? Right now?"

"Yep."

She tried to ignore a mental image of Genevieve standing in front of her shaking her head and shouting, "No, don't do it! Six months? We'll go mad out here!"

She blinked. Genevieve disappeared.

"I'll take it," she said.

There was a brief discussion about her salary and conditions. Keith made it clear it would be her project, and she could do it her way. She couldn't believe it. She wouldn't be hostage to anyone else's rampant ego or out-of-control drink and drug problems. Keith was so straightforward. He always had been. Thank God any kind of affair with him was out of the question too. He was happily married, with a few kids now, she'd heard. She'd learned her lesson with married men. He was still good-looking, though, in a lanky way. Once upon a time, she'd had a bit of a crush on him, in fact. Twelve years older than her, her first proper boss, he'd even initiated a kiss one drunken Christmas party, the first year she started working here. She'd known it was nothing serious, though. A year later, she heard that he was engaged. She'd even gone to their wedding. What was her name? Jenny? Jilly? She glanced at the desk. Yes, there was a photo of three very cute-looking children.

"So, how's Judy? And the kids?" she asked, when their business discussions came to an end.

"Julie's great, thanks. We split up, though, unfortunately. She's living in Quorn now. With her new husband."

"Keith, I'm sorry. And your kids?"

"They're with her. Her and him. I have them every second weekend. That's one good thing. If she was going to have an affair, at least she chose someone who lived within an hour's drive."

"I'm really sorry."

"Me too." He stood up then. The meeting was over. "Okay. Go and see Bert in operations for your equipment. And see you back here next week with your first interviews. We'll edit the first segment together. After that you're on your own."

She'd forgotten he could be like this, relaxed one second, abrupt the next.

She stood up too. "Great. Thanks. See you then."

She was at the door when he said her name.

"Sorry, a journalistic lapse on my part. I didn't ask you to verify your own story."

"My story?"

"In your mother's letter."

As she felt the blush rise, she cursed her pale coloring. About to come back with a flip answer, she decided to tell the truth. "She was right. I was having an affair with him. And he was out of his mind on drink and drugs that morning, but I got the blame. Mum was right about something else too. I'm not cut out for the Sydney media. I was completely out of my depth."

"You were also hung out to dry, from what I heard. He got the big new job and you got—"

"An unexpected holiday." She was trying to make light of it again.

"And are you still having an affair with him? If you don't mind me asking."

"No, I'm not. If you don't mind me not giving you any more detail."

"Good." He stood up abruptly. She'd forgotten how tall he was, well over six foot. "He's an idiot. You're too good for him."

"You know him?"

"I've known him for years. We started out together in Newcastle, twenty-five years ago. I didn't like him then either."

"Oh. Right. Well, thanks."

"Anytime. Sorry I was too late with my fatherly advice." He smiled then. A good, genuine smile. "Well, not fatherly. You have a father. My friendly advice."

"Next time I'm about to do something really stupid, I'll check with you first."

"You do that. Welcome back, Victoria. It's good to see you again."

"It's good to be back," she said.

As she left his office, she had to fight an urge to click her heels, do a little skip. Her life wasn't a complete disaster after all. She had a job, even if it was only a contract one. She was back home again. Not just back on beautiful Errigal, not just back with her family, but with Genevieve too. And all right, her mother had temporarily taken leave of her senses and shared all their family secrets, but maybe it wasn't the end of the world. Maybe a bit more honesty wouldn't do any harm. And yes, her father had leased out half the station, but they still owned half of it, didn't they? And at least it was diamonds they were searching for, not uranium or coal. And perhaps it might not even turn out to be a viable mine. Maybe in five years' time the lease would lapse and all of Errigal would be theirs again. Life suddenly felt more positive. All because she had a job. A fresh start. Even before she'd left the building, she'd taken out her phone to call Genevieve with the good news.

Ninety kilometers away, Joan and Angela were at the medical center in Port Augusta. Yes, it was urgent, Joan told the receptionist. Extremely urgent.

Thirty minutes later, they were sitting opposite Angela's

GP, Dr. Lewis. Joan had known him since he was a boy. She had not only insisted on accompanying Angela into the consultation; she also filled him in on Angela's headaches.

"Enjoying having an official spokeswoman, Angela?" Dr. Lewis said.

"If it wasn't for me, she wouldn't be here," Joan said. "And you should be thanking me for bringing you an unexpected extra customer. Not that you need any more money. It's scandalous how much you charge."

"Thank you, Joan," Dr. Lewis said. "But we do prefer to call them 'patients' rather than 'customers.'"

"Go on, then. I've done my job. Now you do yours."

His examination was brisk. He rechecked the scans he'd taken previously. After a brief discussion with Angela about her headaches, he picked up the phone and called an Adelaide number.

"Right, then," he said, putting down the phone several minutes later. "You have your specialist appointment. Not for three weeks, unfortunately. First week of January, the day he reopens after the Christmas break."

"Isn't it more urgent than that?" Joan asked before Angela could. "What if it's a brain tumor?"

"I don't think it is. The scans were clear four months ago, as I told Angela then. I still think the headaches are being caused by something else. It could be muscular. Or it could be stress. But you need reassurance as well as a second opinion at this stage, Angela, and the specialist will give you both."

"It's not just the headaches, though," Joan said. "Tell him, Ange."

Angela had no choice now. "I'm having other symptoms,"

she said. "The kids say I keep talking to myself. Saying odd things. Speaking my thoughts aloud. And I've done a few other things out of character lately, like—"

"Your Christmas letter?" the doctor asked.

"You know about that?"

He gave a quick smile. "I'm on your mailing list too. Don't worry. I'll make a note of those symptoms," he said, writing on the pad in front of him. "Again, all of those could be due to stress. You're not long out of menopause either. Hormonal changes can have a big effect on mood swings. The specialist will look at all the possibilities."

"And I'll drive you to Adelaide, Ange," Joan said. "I'm due a trip down there."

Angela remembered her journey to collect the twins. The peace, the quiet. The thinking time. "I'll be fine, Joan. Thanks anyway. I might even stay overnight."

"A four-hour trip on your own? Doctor, should she do that?"

"You haven't had any blackouts, Angela?"

She shook her head. "Just the headaches. I'll pull over if the pain gets too bad."

"Make sure you do."

He saw them to the door, touching Angela's shoulder as he said good-bye. "Don't worry. We'll sort this out. In the meantime, see you at the party."

In Port Pirie, Victoria was now in the supermarket. After talking to Genevieve, she'd decided to take the opportunity to do some grocery shopping. Living in Sydney, she'd gotten used to being able to nip round the corner to her local deli to get fresh bread, fresh fruit. The freezers on Errigal were always fully stocked, party or no party, but the family relied on frozen fruit and vegetables, frozen bread. If it was urgent, they could drive into the general store at Hawker, but even so, there were fruit and vegetable deliveries there only a couple of times a week. She filled four bags now with apples, oranges, strawberries, bananas, even some mangoes. And croissants, crusty rolls, baguettes. There was a surprisingly good cheese section too. She chose some lovely, runny Camembert and a creamy Tasmanian blue cheese. She also bought a selection of biscuits, sweet and savory. And a freshly baked apple pie. Ig would love that, she knew. So would she. She had every intention of going on a diet soon, of getting fit again, walking on the property for an hour every morning before the sun got too hot. But she was only just home. It had been a stressful few months. There was plenty of time for that yet.

She'd just packed the groceries in the trunk of the car and was walking around to the driver's side when she heard her name being called. She stopped. She hadn't heard that voice in ten years. It had taken her nearly that long to forget it. To force herself to forget it.

She heard it again. She turned around. She hadn't imagined it.

It was Fred Lawson.

Walking toward her. Smiling.

SEVENTEEN

It was the morning of the party. The entire family was gathered in the kitchen, sitting around the big wooden table. Not just the Gillespies. Joan was there too. This meeting had been her idea.

Over the past few days, while setting up chairs and tables, putting out glasses, organizing the bar, she'd become everyone's confidante. She'd heard everyone's worries about the party. Everyone but Nick's, and she'd tried to guess how he might be feeling. She'd decided it was time to bring their concerns out into the open.

She stood up and waited until she had everyone's attention. "Now, then, all of you. I've got something to say. I've known you four kids since you were babies. I've known you since you were a kid, Nick. And I've known you for thirty-three years,

Angela. So I think I have some right to speak up now. You all have a decision to make about this party tonight. It's happening, even though I know some of you wish it wasn't. It's a big deal. You've been waiting years for your turn to host it. What you have to decide now is how you're all going to behave at it."

"Who cares how I behave? I don't even want to be there," Lindy said, looking like she might be about to cry.

"Yes, Lindy, I've gathered that," Joan said. "But you *will* be there. Because it's a big party in *your* woolshed and all your neighbors will be coming."

"Unless they decide at the last minute to boycott it," Genevieve said under her breath.

"I heard that, Genevieve. No one's boycotting it. I did a ring around last night. Everyone's coming. But ever since you all read Angela's letter, you've been carrying on as if you're about to host a mass execution. I think it's time to stop being victims. Seize the day. Don't fear being talked about behind your backs. Step out in front of their backs."

"Does that even make sense?" Victoria said.

"Don't interrupt, Victoria," Joan said. "Yes, most of your guests will have read the letter. Those that haven't will want to read the letter. What they'll be expecting is a family in disarray. I say, don't give anyone that pleasure. Stand united, side by side. Face your battles."

"What have you been watching?" Genevieve asked. *"Game of Thrones?"*

"Yes, as a matter of fact. But I've also had an idea. Once everyone arrives tonight, I think each of you should stand up and make a short speech. Mention the letter. Make a joke out of it. Trust me, you'll not only stop the gossips in their tracks; you'll present a united front. Lindy, stop sniffling. If you get a sample cushion finished in time, you can even hold it up as an example of your fine needlework."

Lindy stopped sniffling.

Joan continued. "Seriously, all of you, what's the alternative? A party canceled at late notice? Impossible. Going ahead with it, frozen smiles all night, conversations stopping each time you come within earshot? Horrible. At least your mother told the truth in that letter. How often does that happen these days? I say, stand up, be proud, get the gossip out of the way and then give your neighbors a party they'll never forget."

They'd expected two hundred people. By seven thirty, it was closer to three hundred. Half the sausage rolls were already eaten. A third of the sandwiches were gone. It looked like locusts had visited the salad bar.

Standing in the doorway of the woolshed, Angela knew that Joan had been right. There was a definite air of anticipation and mischief among the party guests. Everyone was obviously expecting to see the Gillespies ignoring one another, or having an all-in fight.

At the family meeting, they'd eventually agreed with Joan's suggestion to make speeches. Lindy had been the most reluctant, but she'd finally agreed too. They'd do it at eight p.m., they decided, after everyone had had their first couple of drinks.

It was now five minutes to eight. Angela stood apart from the crowd and looked around. The mood was festive. There was a loud buzz of conversation. The music they'd chosen—Frank Sinatra and Ella Fitzgerald for now, Motown for later—added a cheery layer of sound. There had been nice comments about the food. No mention of the mining lease, not to their faces yet, at least. All things considered, so far so good. Her headache was back, but it was a dull ache rather than a shouting roar.

"I think you should do it now," Joan said, coming up beside her. "Nip the gossip in the bud."

Angela caught Genevieve's eye and nodded. Victoria and Lindy came over too.

Ig appeared beside Angela. "Ready when you are."

"Oh, Ig, you don't have to make a speech," she said.

"But you said I was weird."

"In an affectionate way."

"I'd still like to say something."

"Let him, Angela," Joan said. "One in, all in."

Angela led the way to the front of the woolshed, where they'd arranged a dozen pallets into a small stage. The others came up beside her as she switched on the rented microphone. It squealed, getting everyone's attention. She looked around. Her hands were shaking but she managed to keep her voice steady. At the edge of the stage, Joan gave her an encouraging smile.

"Welcome, everyone, and thanks for coming tonight," Angela said. "We've been to so many of your parties over the years, it's great to be the hosts again." She paused. "Some of you here may have received my Christmas letter. Thank you for your replies. That's definitely the last time I take truth serum." There was a ripple of laughter. "It's already a few weeks out-of-date, though, so we thought this was the perfect opportunity to give you all an update. So, firstly to Genevieve."

Genevieve stepped forward, taking the microphone. "Thanks, Mum, and hi, everyone. It's great to be home. You'll be as glad as Mum is, I'm sure, to hear that I left my fake American accent back in New York, as well as my dreadlocks. I've always been a good and obedient daughter, so just as Mum hoped, I've finished working in the film and TV world in America and come home for a while. Less said about that, the better, but what it means is I'm back here, scissors at the ready, have car will travel, so please do get in touch if any of you fancy a new do. That's all from me. Thanks. Here's Victoria."

Victoria stepped forward, not as confidently as her twin. "I'd like to add my thanks to Mum for updating you all about my time in Sydney. I'd also like to take this opportunity to let you know I'm doing some freelance radio work here, a documentary series about station life. So if anyone has any family stories they'd like to share, please get in touch with me. And yes, everything Mum said was true, and no, I'll be making no further comment, on the grounds that it might incriminate me and cause the publication of even more unflattering photos of me in my pajamas." There was laughter. Victoria gave an awkward curtsy, then stepped back.

"A curtsy?" Genevieve whispered. "What do you think this is, *The Sound of Music*?"

"Be quiet, or I'll tell them you slept with the director's brother."

Lindy was next. She stepped forward, a cushion tucked under her arm. She stared straight ahead, to a spot just beneath the woolshed roof. "I'm very happy to be home and I'd also like to thank Mum for being so honest with you all about my new venture. I'm happy to say my cushion business is now up and running. I've had a one hundred percent increase in orders this week. From none to one." There was laughter again. "But if anyone here would like to order a cushion as a handmade and unique family keepsake, please visit my Web site, type the code 'Woolshed Party' and you'll get a ten percent discount. Thanks. Have a great night."

As she moved back, she passed the microphone to Ig. Angela's heart turned over at the sight of him, the solemn face, that dark red hair. It was still too long. He'd refused to let Genevieve cut it.

He shook the hair out of his eyes and then spoke in a clear voice. "Hi, everyone. I just wanted to say to the other kids here tonight that Robbie and I will be outside in the cubby after this, if any of you want to come and play with us."

It was Angela's turn again. "Thanks again to you all for coming. Eat, drink and be merry, and have a great night, I hope."

She was taken by surprise when Nick appeared beside her, hand outstretched. He didn't say anything. She gave him the microphone.

He stood tall, straight-backed. Angela's heart turned over again.

"Welcome, everyone. My turn. I had a starring role in that famous Christmas letter of Angela's, so it would be wrong of me not to talk now too. First of all, I'm not having an affair with an Irish woman. Or any other woman. As for the rest of it, many of you already know I've leased half of Errigal to a mining company. I had no choice. But it was my fault, not Angela's, not my kids. So if any of you are angry, be angry at me, not them. It was my decision. My bad management to blame."

"It was the drought's fault, not yours," a man near the front called up.

"I should have handled it better," Nick said.

"Mate, there but for the grace of God and the rest of it," another man called out.

Nick shook his head. "I need you all to know I didn't make the decision lightly. I know what a mining lease means. I know how worried you all are about the impact. I grew up here. I've spent my whole life here. I love this land as much as any of you do. I know its history, my own history here, four generations of Gillespies. But I——" He stopped. After a few seconds, he spoke again. "I had no choice. I'm sorry."

"If I thought I had diamonds in my land, I'd have done the same," someone called.

"You weren't the only one in trouble, Nick," another added.

He stopped talking. He just stood there, looking out at his neighbors.

"Oh God, I think he's going to cry," Genevieve whispered to Victoria.

He didn't cry. But his voice faltered as he thanked everyone again for coming.

The room filled with applause. Victoria put the music back on. Ella Fitzgerald's voice soared into the shed. Conversation surged again.

Angela whispered to her friend, "Thanks, Joan."

"Anytime, Ange."

Off to the side of the stage a short while later, Genevieve and Victoria were talking.

"Is he here yet?" Genevieve asked.

Victoria shook her head. "Maybe he's decided not to come."

"I can't see any of the Lawsons, though. Maybe they're just running late. I still can't believe you waited until now to tell me he was back. That you've talked to him. You're supposed to tell me everything."

"I didn't think you'd approve."

"Of course I don't approve. I'd have punched him on the nose if I saw him. He broke your heart, Victoria, remember?"

"It was a long time ago. And he didn't mean to break it. He did explain. I just never told you everything he said."

"You seem to have become very sympathetic about him all of a sudden."

"Genevieve, don't be mad. We spoke for about half an hour; we had a coffee—"

"So what did he say? Is he back for good? Has he got a Canadian wife? Canadian children?"

"I don't know. I didn't get to ask him. He wanted to talk about me. He'd read Mum's letter. He wanted to know if I was all right. He was worried about me."

"He should have worried about you ten years ago."

"Genevieve, please. He needed to leave. I think I always knew that. He's not evil. He's not."

"How did he look? How old is he now, thirty-two, thirty-three? Has he gone to seed, grown bald from all that striding over the prairies? Fat from all that maple syrup? Those big steaks?"

Victoria started to laugh. "He's been working in farm economics over there, not striding the prairies. I don't even know if they have prairies in Canada. And he looked just like he used to look."

"Which was how? I've done my best to block any memory of him."

"Truthfully?" Victoria asked.

"Truthfully," Genevieve said.

"He looked gorgeous."

Horrible Jane and the rest of the Lawsons arrived at eight forty-five p.m. Lindy had been keeping an eye out for them all night. She was secretly glad they'd missed the speeches. She watched them all come in now, making quite an entrance. They'd always been a good-looking family, tall, blond, all four children—the three boys and Jane—in their twenties and early thirties, all successful. Lindy counted them coming in behind their parents, one, two, three, four. The fourth one was Fred. Wow, Lindy thought. So he was back from Canada. She wondered whether Victoria knew. About to go and find her, she watched as one more person came in with them. It wasn't an extra Lawson kid. It was Richard from Melbourne. Jane's flatmate.

Lindy raced over to the bar where Genevieve was telling Hollywood tales. "Oh, yes, everyone knows she's gay. It's an open secret, but the sad homophobic truth is she wouldn't get those romantic comedy roles if people knew it. The marriage is all for show."

Lindy pulled her aside. "I thought you vowed not to gossip anymore."

"I'm not gossiping. I'm telling the truth. What's wrong? You look like you're about to explode."

"I am. Horrible Jane is here. So is Fred Lawson. You'd better warn Victoria. And that's not all. Richard is here too. Richard from Melbourne. My Richard. Help me. Please."

"Of course. Step one, stay calm. Step two, stay here. And breathe. Victoria!"

Across the crowded, noisy room, Victoria looked up. It always amazed Lindy to see her sisters in twin-action. They were like dogs who could hear whistles at a pitch beyond the human ear.

Victoria came over. Genevieve filled her in. Over by the door, Horrible Jane seemed to sense the three Gillespie sisters looking across at her. She made a beeline for them, Richard in her wake. Her brothers and parents had already disappeared into the crowd.

Lindy felt a pinch from Genevieve, or maybe it was Victoria. "Shoulders back," one of them whispered.

"Hi, Lindy!" Jane said. "Great to see you again so soon!"

"Hello, Jane," Lindy said, her tone like an undertaker's. "Hello again, Richard."

"Hello, Jane! Hello, Richard!" On either side of her, Genevieve and Victoria spoke in unison. Lindy felt another pinch. She straightened her shoulders.

Jane turned her attention to the twins. "Well, you two, welcome back! You've both had an action-packed year, I hear."

Genevieve smiled. "Is that 'I hear' as in you read it in Mum's Christmas e-mail? Hilarious, wasn't it? One of her best yet. We've had so much fun reading it to each other and acting it out, haven't we, Victoria and Lindy? But then, we do that with Mum's letters every year. The old-fashioned entertainments are the best, don't you think, Victoria?"

"Undoubtedly, Genevieve." Victoria smiled. "So, Jane, you're home for Christmas? And you've brought a friend, I see."

"He's my flatmate. He's a Christmas orphan. His parents are overseas, so I invited him here."

"Lovely," Genevieve said. "Just your flatmate? Not your boyfriend?"

Jane's eyes narrowed. "What's it to you?"

"You might know this already from my mother's letter, but I'm a terrible gossip," Genevieve said. "I also like to make sure I have my facts right before I start spreading stories about people."

"He's my flatmate." Jane's tone was chilly now.

"Thank you for the clarification," Genevieve said cheerily.

Jane turned away from her. "So, Lindy, how are the cushions going?"

Victoria answered for her. "Flying through the roof! Mum's e-mail really did the trick. That's what I call a successful viral campaign."

With perfect timing, they were interrupted by a family friend from Hawker. "Love the sound of those cushions, Lindy. Can you do one that says 'Happy Birthday to Me'? It'll make my husband feel guilty every time he looks at it."

"You bet. I'll call you on Monday," Lindy said.

"So, you're back home for a while too, Victoria," Jane said. "Sydney got to be too much?"

"That's right—you missed our speeches earlier, didn't you? Yes, I'm doing freelance work for the radio station in Port Pirie. A series on well-known families in the area, those who have made their mark, added to the community in some way, or whose families have a long history in the area."

There was a pause. Jane was waiting for her family to be asked. Victoria didn't ask.

Lindy couldn't bear the tension. She turned to Richard. "Are you staying long?"

"For a couple of weeks, until early January. I—"

Jane took over. "He's coming camping with us over New Year's. His first camping trip. He's such a city boy; aren't you, Richard?" She looked directly at Victoria. "Fred's back from Canada too. We're a full house at the moment."

"Fred's back?" Genevieve said, sounding surprised. "What wonderful news! For a holiday or for good?"

"For good," Jane said.

"And with a Canadian wife and a troop of Canadian children?" Genevieve asked.

"No," Jane said. "He's single."

"Imagine that!" Genevieve said. "Someone as handsome as Fred, single. You're a font of knowledge, Jane; thanks so much." She gave a big, fake smile and then spoke to her sisters. "Mum's giving us all death glares. We're supposed to be handing out sausage rolls. I hope you didn't miss out on food as well as the speeches, Jane. Richard? Help yourselves, won't you?"

Victoria grasped her younger sister's elbow. "Lindy, coming?"

Lindy turned back to Jane and Richard. "See you later."

Jane just nodded.

"I hope so," Richard said.

"'I hope so,'" Genevieve echoed once they were out of earshot. "Ooh, Lindy, I think he likes you."

Lindy ignored that. She let her shoulders fall. "Thanks, both of you."

"Anytime," they said in unison.

EIGHTEEN

Outside the woolshed, Ig was showing a group of the younger kids around the cubby. One of them wanted to dismantle it and start again. He was pulling at one of the boxes. Ig stopped him.

"My cubby, my rules," Ig said.

At the end of the tour—it didn't take long—they sat on the ground in a huddle.

"Is this where you and that imaginary friend play?" one kid asked.

"Here. Everywhere," Ig said.

"How do you get an imaginary friend?" another asked.

"You just decide to have one."

"So we could get one too?"

"Of course."

"When? Now?"

"If you want."

"What's yours called?"

"Robbie."

"I'm going to call mine Spiky."

"That's your cat's name," one of the other kids said.

"It can have the same name as a cat, Ig, can't it?"

"It's better if it doesn't. Otherwise they get confused when you call their names."

"Oh. Right."

They fell silent as they tried to come up with suitable names for their new imaginary friends.

Nick was at the bar with three neighbors. He hadn't seen a lot of them recently. He said it was because he'd been so busy researching his family tree. They nodded. They'd read Angela's Christmas letter too. In the days when Nick was working full-time on the station, once a week he'd go into Hawker for a few beers at the pub, a chance to talk about life and work, family and sports. He hadn't been there in months. He hadn't had much to say lately. No good news, anyway. He'd also heard too many stories over the years of men around here drowning their sorrows in the bad times, being too damaged to work again when the good times returned. He'd made the decision several months earlier to stop drinking. He'd had only Coke so far tonight.

He thought of the latest session he'd had with Jim, his psychologist. His doctor had been right. Their talks were helping. Jim looked like a farmer, sturdy, a bit younger than him. Like someone he'd see at the Hawker races. It made opening up easier. He'd been half expecting someone who resembled a professor, an intellectual, someone who would look down on him. Instead, Jim had been very down-to-earth.

He'd asked Nick questions. Listened. He'd talked more about Nick learning to take charge of his thoughts. About the importance of staying fit, keeping up the walking, any exercise at all. About staying careful around alcohol.

Nick had talked about the trip to Ireland. How he'd considered canceling it when he'd read Angela's letter. How he'd thought it over, realized how much money he'd spent on the research already, paying Carol to set up his itinerary, how it would all go to waste. More waste. He'd cut the trip short instead. He would go only to Ireland, not to London, Italy or France. There'd been no more discussion with Angela about her coming with him.

Jim had asked about Angela too. About their marriage. That had been harder to talk about. Nick had tried, but then the words had stopped coming. "We'll take it one step at a time," Jim had said. They'd made another appointment, for after Christmas. On the way out, Nick had felt something he hadn't felt for a long time. A faint stirring of hope.

"Beer, Nick?"

It was another of his neighbors. One he hadn't seen in months.

"I'm all right, thanks, mate," he said, holding up his glass of Coke. "Let me get you one."

Celia was in a corner of the shed, sitting in a row of chairs with three women of her age. A disco of sorts was planned for the younger ones later, but for now, the music was still quite low.

All their talk was of Angela's Christmas letter.

"I think you're taking it very well," one of the women said. "I'd be livid."

Celia remembered this woman being livid most of her life. "If you can't have a sense of humor, where would you be?"

"But Angela called you an interfering old bat. How can you even stay in her house?"

"It was that or be home alone for Christmas. What choice did I have?"

The woman went quiet.

Lindy was at the bar when she felt him beside her. Richard.

"Great shed. Great party," he said.

He smiled at her and she suddenly wanted to tell him everything.

"I'm sorry if we seemed strange before. Genevieve and Victoria were just protecting me from Horrible Jane."

"Horrible Jane?"

"It's what we call her. We always have, ever since she started bullying me at school."

"So she hasn't changed much over the years, then?"

Lindy blinked. "You're talking about your girlfriend like that?"

"She's my flatmate, not my girlfriend. And she's a great flatmate, actually. A bit bossy at times, but she lives with three guys. Without her, the house would be chaos."

"You're sure she's not your girlfriend?"

"Let me just think about that. Yes, I'm sure."

"She must want you to be her boyfriend or she wouldn't have invited you home."

"She felt sorry for me."

Lindy scoffed at that. "She just wanted to arrive here with a handsome man so everyone would think you're her boyfriend."

"You think I'm handsome?"

"I think you're very handsome," she said mournfully. She shouldn't have had that last drink. Gin always made her gloomy.

"I wish you'd given me your phone number that night," he said.

"Why?"

"So I could have rung you."

"Oh," she said, blushing.

"Would you give it to me again now, instead? Maybe I could ring you when we get back from the camping trip. Come and visit you here before I go back to Melbourne."

Lindy could see Horrible Jane making her way across to them. She would have said yes anyway. But knowing Jane was watching made her put on an even brighter smile. And possibly also made her speak that little bit louder as she gave him her number.

"I'd love you to come and visit, Richard. Anytime you like."

"You okay?" Joan asked Angela.

"Fine. I think. How can that be?"

"Maybe you're drunk?"

"I haven't had a drop yet."

"Have you and Nick talked much tonight?"

Angela shook her head. She massaged her temple.

"Is your head hurting again?"

"No," she lied.

Joan gave her a skeptical look. "You take a break. Have a glass of wine. I'll go and get some more sausage rolls."

Angela took her advice. She went across to the bar and poured herself a glass. She was alone for only a moment. People started coming up to her to talk about her letter. Not just to say they'd read it, but to share their own stories. She heard about one neighbor's difficult husband. "You should be glad Nick doesn't talk to you. My husband never shuts up." She heard about another neighbor's difficult children. "At least yours went away before they came back. Mine have just never left." Another neighbor had strong opinions about family reunions. "The devil's invention. Who wants to be stuck in a room with a hundred people who look just like you, only worse?" Another knew someone who had run off with someone they'd met on Facebook. "Or was it on Twitter? Can you even meet someone on Twitter?"

"And Nick's actually going to Ireland?" one asked. "On his own? You don't mind?"

Another neighbor joined in. "I heard him talking about it too. He called it a reconnaissance trip. In late February, is it?"

So he was still going. He hadn't told her yet. "It's a great idea, I think," she said brightly. "Someone needs to make sure the hotel doesn't have holes in the roof before two hundred demanding Gillespies arrive for their reunion."

"He's holding it in Cork, isn't he? My great-great-uncle was from Cork. Or was it Carlow? It's a fascinating story, actually. He came out to Australia in 1840, after he and his—"

Angela took her chance. "Can you excuse me? I just need to heat up some more sausage rolls."

On her way out to the kitchen, Angela looked around for the twins, hoping one of them could give her a hand. She spotted Genevieve in a far corner, a crowd around her, hanging on her every word. Angela could only imagine what Hollywood gossip she was sharing. It took her longer to spot Victoria. She eventually saw her at the edge of the woolshed. She was sitting down on one of the long benches, deep in conversation with someone. Not just in conversation, but smiling and laughing. It was a man. A blond-haired man. A familiar man.

Angela stopped and stared. Could it be? She recognized him just as she saw Victoria throw her head back and laugh, as if she was the happiest person in the room.

It was Fred Lawson.

Angela hadn't seen him in years. It had to be ten years, at least, since he'd up and left, leaving Victoria in tears. Angela had been surprised when they broke up. She'd always thought Fred and Victoria had something solid.

She walked over to them. Fred stood up, smiling. He's changed, Angela thought immediately. Not in height or build. He was still as stocky, still a little shorter than average. Still with the same blond hair, round face. But he seemed more sure of himself. More quietly confident.

"It's really good to see you, Mrs. Gillespie," he said. "Thanks for the great party."

"It's lovely to see you again too, Fred. Welcome home. How was Canada?"

"Awesome." He smiled. "That was a deliberate Canadian accent, by the way. It was awesome, though. But it was time to come home again."

"And what's next? Will you be staying around here?"

Before he had a chance to answer, they were interrupted.

"Fred Lawson, as I live and breathe. Who let you back into the country?"

It was Joan. He gave her a hug.

"Look at you, all grown-up," Joan said, beaming at him. "I thought we'd never see you again. So, have you brought a Canadian wife home with you? Left a dozen brokenhearted Canadian women behind?"

Beside him, it was clear Victoria was waiting for his answer too.

"Of course not," Fred said. "They never had eyes for me. Not with all those strapping Canadian mounties around the place."

"Glad to hear it," Joan said. She turned to Angela. "I need you. We have to thaw out our emergency food supplies. It's as if these people haven't eaten in weeks."

Angela smiled at Fred again. "Great to see you, Fred. Come and visit anytime."

"Thanks, Mrs. Gillespie."

As they walked away, Joan whispered under her breath, "Talk about two blushing lovebirds. Are they back on, do you think? Already?"

Angela looked behind her. Fred and Victoria were in

deep conversation again. "It's beginning to look like that," she said.

Nick was heading to the bar to check on the beer supplies when he heard his name. He turned. It was his neighbor Kevin Lawson. Nick hadn't seen him in weeks. Maybe even months. He'd never counted Kevin as one of his close friends. The problems with Jane and Lindy, then Fred and Victoria, hadn't helped. No matter what, though, they'd stayed good neighbors. If Kevin ever needed Nick's help, he gave it. It worked both ways. That was how it was out here. You helped one another, be it with the stock, during the floods, the fire season, the good times and the bad. That was how it had been, at least. Over the past year or more, Nick hadn't shared his worries with anyone, let alone his neighbors.

"Great party," Kevin said. "Hell of a turnout."

Nick nodded.

"Been a rough year for you too, mate. Hear I missed your speech earlier."

"You didn't miss much," Nick said.

"One of the blokes said you reckoned you'd had no choice. That you had to accept the mining offer."

Nick waited. Here it was, what he'd been expecting all night. The anger. The lecture.

Kevin Lawson surprised him. "Wish you'd talked to me first."

"About what?"

"An idea I've had. Got a few minutes now?"

Nick nodded.

The party was still going strong at midnight. If they'd had close neighbors, they would have complained. As it was, their neighbors were at the party. The family's speeches and Nick's almost-tears had become the night's big talking points. The women approved. It was good to see a man showing his emotion, several said.

Angela knew that people had been watching her and Nick all evening. There'd been nothing to see. They hadn't exchanged a word. It had nothing to do with the letter or the tension in their marriage. They'd both simply been too busy, keeping the food coming, the drinks flowing, the music playing, their guests happy.

Angela knew that people had been watching her and Celia all evening too. The speeches at the start of the night had definitely helped defuse the situation, by making her letter out to be some kind of joke, but afterward Angela had realized none of the family had mentioned Celia. She'd decided it was probably for the best. Why draw any more attention to what she'd said about Celia in her letter? Angela had avoided talking to her so far tonight. Not just tonight either. In the days since Celia had arrived on Errigal, through accident or design, she and Angela hadn't been alone together. It was time they did speak to each other. Hopefully there was enough conversation and music that no one would overhear if Celia decided to attack her. Which she had every right to do, Angela conceded.

"Can I get you anything, Celia?" she said, sitting down beside her. There was almost always an empty chair beside Celia. People didn't tend to sit next to her for long.

"No, thank you, Angela."

"Are you tired?"

"Not yet." They sat in silence for a moment, watching the people on the dance floor.

Celia spoke. "You're not the first person to call me an interfering old bat. Though, in fact, I think she called me an interfering old bitch."

Angela wasn't sure whether she'd misheard. "I'm sorry?"

"My daughter-in-law. Peter's wife. The French woman."

Angela kept her mouth shut.

"Cat got your tongue?" Celia said.

The old-fashioned phrase almost made Angela smile. But she stayed quiet. Maybe this was the key to getting on with Celia. Stay mute. In the glow of the party, the evening almost over, the worst shock about her letter gone, Angela could feel a stirring of sympathy for the older woman. She was about to apologize for what she'd written when Celia turned to her.

"You should think yourself lucky you have a husband like Nick. You don't appreciate him. Oh yes, my henpecked husband was probably glad to get away from me, as Joan so kindly said and you so kindly wrote to one and all in your letter. But not as happy as I was to see him go. He was never a good husband. Too weak. Lazy. I ran the business; he didn't. I'm the reason it was a big success."

Angela still said nothing. She had heard a lot over the years about the success of Celia and her husband's spare parts company.

Celia kept talking. "That's what sticks in my throat with you. Nick has always been the kindest, most considerate person, ever since he was a boy. And now, when he most needs your support, what do you do? Embarrass him with that letter of yours. You should be ashamed of yourself. It was a sad day for this family when he walked into that Sydney pub and met you. If he'd married a local girl, a girl who had farming in her blood, he wouldn't be in this position."

Angela found her voice. "I'm responsible for the drought? How is that, Celia?"

"It wasn't just the drought. Every farmer needs his wife to support him, through bad times and good. You've always been distracted by selfish pursuits, like those tourists you have to stay, or that pottery carry-on. He needed good, sensible children to follow in his footsteps. No chance of that with yours. Your daughters are running wild. As for what you've done to Ignatius—"

"What have I done to Ig?"

"Indulged him. Turned him into a pet. That child needs to toughen up, stop all that daydreaming, not to mention that nonsense about that imaginary friend. He's what we would have called a 'mummy's boy' in the olden days. And don't think I don't know where he got the idea to run away from boarding school. I'm sure it was you."

"I had nothing to do with it. He's ten years old, Celia. Too young to be away from home. Not just away from me."

Celia made a dismissive sound. "Me, me, me. There you are. If anyone should be feeling guilty about the mess your family is in, it should be you, not Nick."

Angela stood up. People nearby were watching; she could sense it. She put on the brightest smile she could. Then she walked away as quickly as she could. Before she gave in to temptation and called Celia an interfering old bat to her face.

By two a.m. there were still a few dozen people left in the woolshed. Ig was in bed. So was Lindy. Victoria and Genevieve were sitting outside on the log by the fire, under the stars, talking. Fred Lawson was with them, sitting close to Victoria.

Nick was nowhere to be seen. Angela asked Joan, who was starting to stack the chairs. She thought she'd seen him head toward the house.

Angela guessed where he would be before she found him. The light from the office spilled into the hallway. She heard their voices. Nick's first and then Carol's.

"That all sounds good," Nick said. "I fly direct into Dublin. We can go straight across to Mayo and Donegal from there."

"Perfect. I'll pick you up at the airport in the rental car. And I'm sorry again to have to ask about that increase in the daily rate. My boss insisted."

"Don't worry. Your service is worth twice that."

"I've almost finished the itinerary. We'll spend the first few days visiting the different Gillespie home places so you can take all the photos you need; then I've booked us into the hotel in Cork I think would be great for the reunion, right on the waterfront in Cobh. I stayed there last weekend to try out the facilities. I'm sorry; I had to add that to your bill as well."

"No worries. Of course I should pay for that. And then we—"

Angela was tempted to leave without saying anything. But then she felt a sudden dart of anger. Give him time, Joan had urged. She'd been trying to. But what had he been doing with his time? Not thinking about her, she now realized. He'd been too busy planning his trip to Ireland. His solo trip.

Angela interrupted. "Nick?"

He turned and looked at her.

"Shall I say good night to our guests from you, or are you coming back?" she asked.

"Can you say good night from me?"

She was walking away when she heard it. Carol's voice. "Who was that?"

"Just my wife," Nick said.

Just my wife.

The phrase was still in her head three hours later as she tried to get to sleep.

NINETEEN

It was four days before Christmas, day five of a forecast two-week heat wave. The temperature hadn't dropped below 95 degrees in the daytime, 77 degrees at night and had topped 108 degrees for three days running.

The homestead was built to be cool, with foot-thick stone walls and a deep veranda providing shade and insulation in normal weather conditions. These weren't normal weather conditions. There were fans in every room, going all day long. An air conditioner in the living room. Throughout the heat wave, all six Gillespies and Celia had done little but lie prone in various parts of the house, napping, reading and complaining.

Angela was first up. It wasn't six o'clock yet. In the kitchen, she made a cup of tea and a start on her final

Christmas shopping list. Their freezer was huge and already filled with food, but none of it was Christmassy. She couldn't put off the trip to Port Augusta any longer. She imagined wheeling her cart up and down the aisles of the supermarket, bumping into other harried mothers with their own long lists, all of them shopping for winter-style food while the sun beat down outside and the last thing any of them felt like doing was cooking.

She put her pen down, rested her head in her hands and shut her eyes tight.

She wasn't in the kitchen of the homestead, in the middle of one of South Australia's hottest summers on record, trying to make a shopping list that was threatening to run to more than three pages.

She was in London.

Christmas in London was always special. She, Will and Lexie loved celebrating it. Like all families, they had their own traditions. They kept it simple, but elegant. It had already snowed in London this December, a soft white coating on all the trees outside. They'd started lighting the fire in the front room first thing in the morning rather than just at nighttime. The real fir tree in the corner of the room sent out a glorious foresty scent. Lexie had decorated it, coming home from Bristol especially early. Their decorations were kept in the attic, carefully packed away each year by Angela, unwrapped by Lexie. Will and Angela watched her from the sofa, glasses of sherry in hand. They only ever drank sherry at Christmastime. It amused them both. As she unpacked the big box, Lexie exclaimed over each decoration. "Oh, remember this one! We bought it in Spain when we went hiking together, didn't we? Look at this little clay angel; isn't she gorgeous! Was this the first one you ever made, Mum?"

The house was filled with Christmas cards. More than a dozen arrived every day from their many friends around the world. The mantelpiece above the fire was decorated with a row of candles, which sent a soft light out into the room. This year, the mantelpiece held something else too: a selection of Angela's little ceramic robins. She'd kept her favorites of the three hundred she'd produced for Suzy. They were the most popular items she'd ever made for the shop. Suzy could have sold each of them four times over, apparently.

The birds on the mantelpiece weren't the only new tradition this Christmas. She, Will and Lexie were doing something else for the first time—going out for Christmas lunch. Will had had another successful year, but it had been tiring too, finding and keeping his many new clients so happy. Angela was exhausted from her sudden end-of-year workload. Happy but exhausted. Lexie was full of energy, as usual, and always up for a new experience. It was just one of the many joyous things about her. She'd leaped at the idea. "Why not? No washing up either!"

They had booked into Claridge's. Not just for Christmas lunch but for three nights in a luxurious two-bedroom suite. A proper, festive mini-break in their own city. All the luxury, none of the hassle of traveling too far. "We all deserve it," Will said.

"Mum?"

Angela opened her eyes. It took her a moment to bring herself back to the kitchen, to Errigal, to South Australia.

"Are you okay?" It was Genevieve, in her pajamas.

"I'm fine. I just couldn't sleep."

"No? It sounded like you were sleep-talking, then. Something about Claridge's and Christmas." Genevieve grinned. "Ah, I get it. You were away in your fantasy life in London, weren't you? With Dreamy Will, the man without a surname because you won't tell us who he was. And your perfect daughter—what's her name? Flossie? Trixie?"

"Genevieve, I'm so sorry. You should never have read that. I should never have—"

"Mum, come on, don't apologize! If I could choose between noisy old us in outback Australia and a rich architect and perfect though boring-sounding swot of a daughter in London, I'd do it too." Genevieve took a seat beside her mother. "Did I hear that right about Claridge's? Is that where you used to go for Christmas when you were a kid?"

"I've never set foot inside Claridge's," Angela said. "I was just thinking about our Christmas. All I still have to do—"

"And you thought, what a nightmare. I wish I could hand it all over to the chefs at Claridge's and never see a shopping cart or a sink full of dishes again. Admit it, Mum. You can tell me."

Angela smiled. "You're right. I wish I never had to see a shopping cart or a sink full of dishes again."

"Shazam. Your wish has come true. Leave it to me. To me and that adorable twin of mine. You did the party. We'll do Christmas. It's only fair."

"Genevieve, you can't. You've just got home—"

"So what? Even more reason to do it."

Could Angela actually feel her headache starting to lift, even slightly? "Do you mean it?"

"I mean it. And to prove what a special child I am, I'm now going to make you another cup of tea. With my own bare, hair-dye-stained hands."

Several minutes later, they were sitting outside on the veranda, cups of tea in hand. The birdlife was just getting into full song, the squawks of the galahs tempered by the trilling of the blue wrens.

"Did you miss this?" Angela said.

"Not for a minute," Genevieve said. "I've always preferred the sound of burglar alarms and ambulances." She smiled and then turned so she was facing her mother. "Mum, are you okay?"

"I'm fine," Angela said. "Just those headaches, but I'm getting them looked at in January. I'm sure it's nothing serious."

"I'm not just talking about your health. Are you okay? You and Dad? Because I'm worried about you."

"You are? Why?"

"I can't help noticing that the two of you don't talk to each other anymore. That Dad stays up as late as possible in the office each night and you go to bed as early as possible. That he seems distracted. That you seem sad. I can go on, if you like. How you didn't talk to each other at the party either. Compared to the last woolshed party when the two of you danced all night, and we were embarrassed to see our parents carrying on like that. I could also mention your letter, all you said in that, about—"

"Please don't, Genevieve." Angela hesitated. "I appreciate your concern; really, I do. And I'm sorry you had to read all of that as well. I know we did our best at the party to make a joke about it, but if I could do anything not to have written it, not to have so many people read it—"

"But it was all true?"

Angela didn't reply.

"Mum, I know it's none of my business, and Joan's already told me that all couples go through ups and downs, but is there anything we can do to help? I know it's been tough financially and I'm sorry we've all landed back on top of you as well, and we'll try to get work as soon as we can, I promise, but if we can do anything, will you please just ask?"

"Thanks, darling."

"And you and Dad will be okay, won't you? Joan's right? It is just a rough patch?"

Angela started to speak, then stopped. She was trying hard not to cry. She reached over, took her daughter's hand and squeezed it, hoping to sound relaxed. "Of course. We're fine, I promise. Really."

Genevieve smiled. "Good answer. I'll let you off the hook about Dad for now. And in the meantime, you leave Christmas to me. Me and my loyal army."

"She was definitely lying."

It was two hours later. Genevieve and Victoria were in the woolshed. They were packing up the last of the party glasses to return to the rental company in Port Augusta. They were also having a private discussion about their parents.

"They're not fine," Genevieve said. "And I'm not imagining it, Victoria. You've seen it too, all that tension, the silences. You read her letter too."

"I'm still trying to forget that letter. But there are two sides to every story, remember. It's been a rough year on the station. A rough few years. Dad won't talk about it with me, but it had to have been a terrible decision to sell off the last of his stock and accept the mining lease. No wonder he's been distracted. And then to have their problems aired publicly. He's so private, he must have hated that. No wonder they're tense with each other."

"Are you taking sides?"

"Of course not. But it's their business, not ours, Genevieve. We have to give them the time and space to work it out themselves."

"What time and space? We're all back here, filling every available space and we're running out of time. Dad's about to head off to Ireland. I think we need to get them fixed up before he goes or we might never see him again."

"Now you're getting carried away. It's a research trip."

"You're just not as worldly or suspicious as I am. I definitely think we should do something before he leaves. Try to remind them both of how good things used to be between them. You know what they used to be like, how close they were, how we used to tease them about it. They talked all the time, for starters. Laughed a lot together. And you know how he looked at her, as if she was the most beautiful woman he'd ever seen. And the way they'd hold hands when we were all watching TV, and they thought none of us were looking."

"Until you'd pretend to vomit about it?"

"I was a teenager; it was embarrassing. But not just that. What about all those little traditions they have, not just the annual photo they take, but the thing they do with the birthday card? And the way they go over to the chapel together for those private talks? And Dad's so proud of her with the station stay business—I know it. He told me. But maybe he didn't tell her. Maybe he should have. Maybe if we could somehow remind them of all the good times, that would help."

"I think you've been working in TV for too long. What are you suggesting? We go through the photo albums, put together a flashback montage of the highlights of their marriage? With a soundtrack of weepy music? We were kids for most of it, or away at boarding school. We'd have to make up half the stories."

"No, we wouldn't." Genevieve was now smiling. "We have the perfect source, right here."

"Who? Joan, you mean?"

"Better than Joan. Have you forgotten something, my dear Victoria? The little matter of more than thirty letters in a file in the office?"

"Mum's Christmas letters?"

"Exactly. I knew they'd be good for something one day."

"What were you thinking? Getting them all bound into a book? Have we got time?"

"No, I've had an even better idea, thanks to Horrible Jane. If the Lawsons can do it, then why can't we?"

"Act them all out? Thirty-three years' worth? That would take days."

"I don't mean acting out every word. And we might skip this year's letter, don't you think? I thought we could read through them and pick out the mentions of Mum and Dad.

Some edited highlights of their lives together. Ig and Lindy can help too. We could turn it into a kind of a play, stage it as our Boxing Day entertainment."

Victoria was laughing. "You're mad. With costumes and everything?"

Genevieve grinned. "Why not? I'll do hair and makeup. You can be in charge of the musical soundtrack. If a trip down memory lane staged by their four beloved children doesn't get the two of them smooching again, I don't know what will."

"Have we got time?"

"We'll make time. What else have we got to do out here? Hunt kangaroos?"

"What are you two laughing about?" It was Lindy, at the woolshed door. "I could hear you from the veranda. We need to get going. I've just seen the shopping list. It's going to take us *hours*."

Genevieve put her finger to her mouth. "Hush, dear Rosalind. We're hatching top-secret plans."

"You are? About what? Getting Victoria and Fred Lawson back together?"

Victoria went red.

Genevieve didn't miss a beat. "No, that's New Year's secret plan. This is our Christmas plan. Code name: Save Mum and Dad's Marriage."

Lindy's eyes widened. "Really? What are you going to do?"

"Go and get Ig and we'll tell you all about it."

TWENTY

They discussed it all the way to Port Augusta and back. Once they were home again, the Christmas shopping done, they got to work. Genevieve appointed herself stage director. Victoria was in charge of music and voice-overs. They'd realized there was no chance of anyone having time to learn lines. They decided on a different approach. Ig would play the part of Nick. Lindy would play the part of Angela. Victoria would read their lines from the side, out of sight, while Genevieve managed the music and props and costumes.

Ig was put in charge of smuggling his mother's letters out of the office. He did it with ease, bringing them over to their meeting place in the woolshed. As they began to read them, their reactions ranged from embarrassment to amazement to hilarity. They read about Angela's earliest days on the station, the first years of her marriage. There were many descriptions of Nick, how hard he worked, what a great husband he was. His "manly manliness," as Genevieve dubbed it, after reading for the tenth time about how fit he was, how strong, how kind, how handsome. "We should send these letters straight off to Mills and Boon," she said after reading a particularly effusive description of Nick helping to fight fires on a neighbor's property. "'Nick Gillespie, the He-Man of the Outback.'"

They divided up the letters among them, taking turns reading bits aloud. At first, they were more interested in hearing about themselves. They found the descriptions of their own arrivals, the twins, then Lindy, then, out of the blue, all those years later, Ig. He got Genevieve to read that section aloud twice, smiling to himself as Angela described what a wonderful surprise he was, what a beautiful baby he had been, how Nick had nearly cried when he first saw his newborn son. They heard stories about their school days, tales of station life, about all of them helping out with the sheep mustering, going out with Nick to check the water in the bores, the dams, the windmills. Helping out in the woolshed at shearing time. Days out at the Hawker races. There were stories of their family holidays, usually by the seaside in Adelaide. Funny things each of them had said over the years. Detailed reviews of the concerts the three girls had often staged for their parents during school holidays.

Finally Genevieve announced they had to start skipping their own bits, and concentrate on any mentions of their parents. They soon had an abundance of material. When Nick wasn't being manly, he was being romantic, it seemed. They read about the rosebush he'd planted for Angela on their first anniversary. How he brought her a cup of tea in bed every morning.

They also read about the origins of Nick and Angela's birthday card tradition, now in its thirty-third year. In the first year they were married, Nick asked Angela what she wanted for her birthday. She said she already had everything. Nick said she must want something. She joked that all she really needed was five dollars to buy herself some sweets. (*Except they call them lollies over here!* she'd written.) Then, on the morning of her birthday, he presented her with exactly that—a card addressed to *My darling Angela,* with a five-dollar bill inside. *For some sweets for my sweetheart,* he'd added. Four months later, a week before his birthday, she asked him what he wanted. He told her that he already had everything he wanted. So on the morning of his birthday, she gave him the same card back, with the same five-dollar bill inside, simply crossing out her name and writing his, *My darling Nick.* Year after year, they did the same thing. Growing up, the three girls had always loved the presentation of it, taking turns to hand-deliver the now-yellowing envelope to their mother or father, laughing as each of them pretended to be surprised and touched. "It's just what I wanted, Nick! Thank you!" Angela would say. "You're so thoughtful, Angela," Nick would say, kissing her as the children shrieked in pretend embarrassment. The card looked so old-fashioned now, the inside crowded with all the crossed-out names. The five-dollar bill was out of date too, in the long-discontinued design. Did they still keep it up? Genevieve wondered. She hadn't been home for either of her parents' birthdays in years.

By the time they'd finished reading through the letters, they had more than enough material. Now all they had to do was start rehearsals.

Later that same day, keeping to another tradition, they decorated the Errigal Christmas tree. Not their inside plastic tree. That had been up and decorated for days. The gum tree in front of the homestead. Ig was chief decorator, even with his arm in the sling. He spent three hours clambering one-handed up and down the ladder, hanging the lights and decorations on the branches he could reach. It unfortunately meant only the lower third of the tree was decorated, but they all agreed it looked beautiful.

Usually it was Ig's job as the youngest to turn on the lights too. To everyone's surprise, he asked Celia to do it this year.

"You're the oldest," he said solemnly. "And I've got plenty more years ahead of me."

They all couldn't help but notice she went pink-cheeked.

"Thank you very much, Ignatius," she said, the slightest tremor in her voice. "I'd be honored."

That night, Angela remembered she'd promised to e-mail Joan some recipes for leftover turkey. She had deliberately stayed away from the computer. She'd read enough e-mails about her Christmas letter and she'd have been hard-pressed to get any time on the computer in any case. Nick was spending hours on it, closely followed by Lindy, then the others.

Even Celia had asked to use it, something about wanting to send e-mails to set up her next book club meeting.

Nick was out on the far side of the property, checking the solar pumps. He'd taken Ig with him. Ig had never been interested in the sheep, but he did like the technical equipment. The three girls and Celia were in the living room watching a program of Christmas carols. She took the opportunity.

In a moment she found the recipes online and e-mailed them to Joan. She decided to print out copies for herself. It looked like the kids had gone overboard with their Christmas food shopping. They'd be eating variations of turkey for days ahead. It was as she was picking up the pages from the printer that she saw it.

Her Christmas letter, tucked under a pile of Nick's papers.

It was the copy she had given him just over a fortnight ago. It was creased, as if it had been read, folded and reread many times. There was also writing on it. Nick's writing. Beside the section about her fantasy life. About Will.

Her heart started to beat faster. They were notes about architects in London. Different ones with the name of William, with question marks beside them, some of them crossed out.

He had been trying to track down Will. Why?

She knew the answer. Because his wife of thirty-three years had announced in the most public, humiliating way that she daydreamed about being married to another man. What husband wouldn't want to know about that other man?

She shut the door. She didn't know how long she'd have the office to herself.

She didn't google Will. She didn't want to know about his life. She never had wanted to know. Her fantasy life with him had been nothing more than a distraction, a refuge. The last thing she wanted to do was confuse it with real facts. Instead, she looked up the Internet search history. She already knew from Joan that Genevieve had been in here googling Will, the day they heard about the letter. But that had been two weeks ago.

The findings came up. Over the past week, someone had spent what looked like hours trying to find details about an architect in London called Will.

Not someone. Nick.

She knew then why he couldn't talk to her. Not because she'd written about the mining lease, or their family. It was what she'd written about her fantasy life. It must have hurt him so badly. As if she really had had an affair.

She heard the 4WD pull into the yard, heard two doors slam. She pressed the keys swiftly, clearing the history, shutting down the computer, leaving the office as quickly as she could. She was in the lounge room with the others by the time Nick and Ig came in.

She watched as he stood beside Ig, his hand ruffling his son's hair. He smiled at a cheeky comment from Genevieve, answered a question from Victoria, even took a look at Lindy's latest cushion. He'd always been a good father. A great father.

She was the only one he couldn't talk to anymore. And who could blame him?

She excused herself and walked outside, across the paddocks, over to the chapel, with only the moonlight to show her the way. She sat there, crying, until she had no tears left.

TWENTY-ONE

Christmas Day dawned hot and bright. By nine a.m. it was already eighty-six degrees. The Gillespies followed their usual tradition, going into Hawker for Mass, then straight back home afterward to open their presents on the front veranda. It was always one of the coolest spots in the homestead.

As a family, they'd long kept a limit on how much they spent on their presents. This year, in light of Ig's being only ten, and all three sisters on financially shaky ground, the budget had been set to a record low. A maximum of five dollars each. Even so, they all declared they were genuinely delighted with their gifts. They ranged from cans of baked beans (Ig's presents to all three of his sisters), vouchers for cushions (Lindy to each member of her family), bags of mixed lollies (Victoria to everyone) and vouchers for haircuts (Genevieve to everyone). Celia gave them books. Secondhand ones. As she always had done.

Their parents had been declared exempt from the limit. They gave Ig computer games, books, some new clothes. Genevieve kept a close eye on her parents as they exchanged their presents. A shirt, a book and some aftershave from her mother to her father. A silk scarf, a book and some perfume from their father to their mother. Nothing new there. That was what they'd always given each other for Christmas. But their thank-yous were as polite as if they were strangers.

After the present giving, the four children took over the kitchen. They'd spent hours there during the previous few days. When they weren't in the kitchen, they'd been in the woolshed. Helping Ig to build an indoor cubby out of the sun, they'd told their parents. Rehearsing their secret Boxing Day performance was the real reason.

Christmas lunch was a big success. They served a choice of prawn cocktail or Parma ham and melon for starters. Roast turkey and all the trimmings for the main course. Plum pudding and fruit salad for dessert, with a cheese plate for after. Victoria had taken charge of that part of the menu, serving a perfectly ripe Brie, a tangy cheddar and her favorite, the creamy Tasmanian blue cheese, all served with chilled grapes, quince paste and crisp biscuits. Dieting was definitely more of a New Year thing, she'd decided. They ate outside, judging it was still cooler on the veranda than in the dining room. After lunch they all dozed. That night, they played board games. Even Nick and Celia joined in.

"We've almost been like a normal family today, haven't we?" Genevieve said.

It was even hotter on Boxing Day. Nearly eighty-six degrees by eight a.m. After an early, already sweaty meeting, they changed the plans for their performance. They'd do it before lunch instead of in the heat of the afternoon.

By quarter to eleven, everything was ready. A stage of sorts was set up on the front veranda, the same pallets they'd used at the woolshed party. The stereo speakers were out of sight, Victoria's music soundtrack cued and ready. Genevieve had her costumes and hairstyling equipment arranged on a table, also out of sight. Ig started to complain of stomach pains, but Genevieve reassured him it was just stage fright.

"Once you're up under that spotlight, you'll forget all about them," she said.

Lindy was sent inside to fetch her parents and Celia. She led them out onto the veranda like a theater usher, pointing to the three chairs lined up in front of the small stage, all of it reminiscent of their childhood concerts. Just as they were about to start, Celia called Lindy over. She was looking quite pale, even in the heat.

"Would you please get me a glass of water? I'm feeling a bit clammy."

"Could I have one too?" her mother asked.

"Me too, please," their father said.

The performance was delayed while Lindy got the drinks. Meanwhile, it was getting hotter. Everyone was now wearing a sheen of sweat. Ig, dressed in his Nick costume, had gone even paler than Celia. The sooner they finished and got inside into the cool again, the better, Genevieve decided as she quickly helped Lindy to climb into her Angela costume—one of their mother's old dresses, and a matted black wig they'd found in the dress-up box in the cellar. It was actually part of a long-gone witch's costume, but they hoped their mother wouldn't mind.

Genevieve nodded to Victoria, who was also looking quite clammy now. She seemed to be holding her stomach. Genevieve was starting to feel the beginnings of cramps herself. She'd never realized stage fright was so contagious.

At Genevieve's nod, Victoria projected her voice. "Welcome, one and all, to this year's Gillespie Players performance, 'A Trip Down Memory Lane.' Subtitle, 'A Long and Glorious Marriage.' The time, thirty-four years ago. The place, a pub in Sydney."

Genevieve gave Lindy the thumbs-up. Lindy stepped onto the stage. The borrowed dress was too tight on her. Her black wig was already slipping sideways. She was holding a glass in one hand, a tea towel in the other. They'd decided they'd do their own lines for this first part of it, before Victoria took over the narration.

"Hi, everyone," Lindy said, in her attempt at a London accent. "My name's Angela Richardson. I'm from London. I sure love it in this beautiful country of yours." She sounded more Texan than English.

Genevieve peeked out. Her mother looked like she was either trying not to smile, or trying not to be sick. She'd gone a funny color. Beside her, Celia wasn't even smiling. She seemed to be doing a lot of swallowing. At least her father was watching, even if he was bathed in sweat too.

Genevieve nodded at Ig, who stepped out from behind the veranda pillar onto the stage. He was dressed in a pair of his own dark jeans, but wearing one of Nick's white shirts, the sleeves rolled up over his elbows the way Nick always wore them. The shirt was many sizes too big. On his head he was wearing one of Nick's old station hats, an Akubra, also far too big. His face was barely visible underneath. Genevieve hissed at him. He pushed it up, walked over and stood beside Lindy and gave her what could only be described as a leering smile.

"Hi, sugar," he said. "What beautiful eyes you have."

Angela gave a snort.

Genevieve frowned. Sugar? Ig hadn't said that in rehearsal. "Introduce yourself," she hissed.

"My name's Nick Gillespie," Ig said, in a strange growling voice. "Give us a beer, love."

There was another snort from Angela. Even Nick was grinning. Celia, however, wasn't. She didn't seem to be finding it funny at all. She seemed to be clutching her stomach as much as Ig had been. And Victoria now was. As if in sympathy, Genevieve's stomach gave a sudden cramp.

Ig and Lindy continued with their lines. They'd all grown up hearing how their parents had met.

"I'm lost, love," Ig growled. "Can you help me?"

"Sure. I can draw you a map," Lindy said, her accent now more Irish than English.

"That'd be beaut," Ig said, still in the strangely deep voice. "Did I tell you how beautiful your eyes are?"

Genevieve looked out at their audience again, expecting to see her parents laughing. Perhaps even staring affectionately at each other. Instead, they just looked sweaty and uncomfortable. Celia appeared to be in real pain. As Genevieve watched, she stood up, swaying slightly.

"Can you all please excuse me for a moment?" She walked quickly into the house.

Seconds later, Angela stood up too. "Sorry," she said. "Could you please wait for me?"

Celia didn't come back. Angela came back briefly, just as Nick left. When he returned, Angela left again. They all kept apologizing. Genevieve felt another cramp in her stomach. She looked over at Victoria. She looked terrible. So did Lindy. She'd taken off the black wig and was bathed in sweat.

"Is it just me," Lindy said, "or do you feel as if you—"

She didn't get a chance to finish. Beside her, Ig threw off the hat, ran to the edge of the veranda and was violently sick. Two minutes later, on the other side of the veranda, so was Lindy. Victoria made it as far as the sink in the laundry. They could hear her retching.

The performance was abandoned. There was no one left to perform it or watch it. They were all too busy taking turns in the bathrooms.

Two hours later, during a brief respite from her own violent cramps, Angela worked out what had happened. Food poisoning. The prawns were most likely to blame. Genevieve had talked her through their shopping trip to Port Augusta. It seemed that she had bought the prawns first and left them in the trunk of the car while they did the rest of the shopping, while it was one hundred degrees. The prawns went back into the fridge when they got home, but it was too late. The rot had literally started. The prawns were so smothered in Marie Rose sauce they hadn't noticed any difference in the taste.

They were all sick for the next two days. Any plans to go for post-Christmas walks, drives, even camping overnight, were canceled. The heat wave continued. There were daily fire risk warnings, reports of blazes in the nearby Flinders Ranges National Park for three days running.

By the morning of the third day, the Gillespies were all finally recovering, able to eat small bits of toast. Celia, however, seemed just as bad, if not worse. She was still unable to keep anything down. She was only able to take sips of water. She seemed to be sleeping all the time.

Now over the worst of her own cramps, Angela called the hospital for advice. Within an hour she was driving Celia into Hawker. She was back four hours later, on her own. Celia had been admitted. She was severely dehydrated, the doctor had said. He agreed it sounded like the prawns were to blame. Most likely a bug called *Vibrio parahaemolyticus*, he said. Bad enough for healthy people like the Gillespies, but dangerous in elderly people, children, pregnant women. Ig was recovering quickly, Angela had been glad to tell him. But she'd been right to bring Celia in.

When Angela got back to Errigal, she reported that Celia had already started to look brighter. She was in a ward with two other women, both of whom she knew from her years of visiting the area. She'd be there for at least three days, the doctor thought. Possibly longer, depending on how she responded.

Angela didn't say she thought Celia seemed happier in the hospital than she had been with them. She also didn't say that she felt the same way.

Two nights before New Year's Eve, the weather finally broke in one wild storm. The signs were there from early morning, the sky an ominous deep red. Huge billowing clouds came into view throughout the day, increasing in depth and size, shifting shades from gray to black. Even after all these years Angela still marveled at the buildup to an outback storm. Nick checked the generator. During the last big storm, the whole town of Hawker had lost power for nearly twenty-four hours.

Celia was back home again. One or two of the Gillespies had been into Hawker to visit her every day. Angela had brought her home again that afternoon. Celia was still frail, but there was no mistaking her much-improved mood. She'd clearly loved all the attention in the hospital.

They gathered on the front veranda to watch the storm hit. It was a spectacular show, a huge sky of black clouds split by sheets of lightning, the air echoing with the thunder, and then the rain. A great onslaught of water. Ig ran out into it, as he always did during storms, leaping and jumping, holding his face up to the sky. He was drenched in seconds. The girls joined him, standing out in the downpour, their arms outstretched.

They all welcomed the end of the heat wave. Ig played outside in his cubby for hours. The three girls started another TV box-set marathon. Celia seemed content to stay in her room and be brought her meals on a tray, occasionally joining the family to watch a little television. Nick had taken up residence in the office again. When he wasn't there, he was over at the Lawsons'. He'd been asked to lend a hand with some stock work. For several days running, he was gone before dawn.

In the meantime, Angela did what she'd always done when everyone was home. She cooked, cleaned, did the washing, swept the veranda, did more cooking and more cleaning. Not for the first time, she realized it took less work to look after her visitors than it did her own family. Her station stay visitors were much more appreciative too, willing to lend a hand as needed. No matter how independent Genevieve, Victoria and Lindy had been, or not, off the station, they turned back into teenagers once they were home. Helping when they thought of it, cooking the occasional meal, but otherwise content to let Angela take care of them.

Not that Joan had been sympathetic when Angela brought it up during one of their phone calls. "Why would they do anything when you do everything for them? You've dug your own grave. Stop cooking and cleaning for a few days and see if that spurs them into action."

"I wouldn't last a day," Angela said. "I couldn't bear the mess."

Joan had laughed. "Then you've only got yourself to blame."

No one mentioned restaging the concert. The moment had passed.

TWENTY-TWO

The morning of New Year's Eve, Genevieve, Victoria and Lindy set their alarms for six a.m. to watch the sun rise on the last day of the year. If their parents had their traditions, this was their own.

They left the house wearing their pajamas, sneakers on their feet, following the dusty path from the homestead gate. It was a fifteen-minute walk. They were quiet until they reached their destination, a hill that looked out over the entire Errigal property and beyond, from the jagged lines of the Chace Range across to the distinctive curves of Wilpena Pound.

They'd first made this journey the year the twins turned seven, when Lindy was four. Angela and Nick had woken them just as the sun was rising. All five of them headed out across the yard, in pajamas and assorted footwear. "But where are we going?" Genevieve had kept asking. "It's a secret," Angela told her. It was too long a walk across bumpy ground for them to be blindfolded, but Nick kept telling them not to look. As they walked hand in hand across the stony soil, they'd felt the ground rising under their feet.

"Okay, girls," Nick said when they stopped climbing. "Look up now."

"Surprise!" he and Angela chorused as the girls opened their eyes.

Before them stood a set of three swings built especially by Nick. The bars were painted a bright red. The three wooden seats were in their favorite colors: blue for Genevieve, green for Victoria, yellow for Lindy. Nick had even painted their names on the seats. They rushed to try them out, calling to their parents to give them a push, squealing as they swung higher and higher.

Back then, the swings were the main attraction. As the girls grew older, it was the view that became special. If friends came to stay, the visit always included a dawn walk in pajamas and sneakers to what they all now called Swing Hill. Angela had even brought some of their station stay visitors here over the years. It was the perfect place for spectacular photographs.

Genevieve, Victoria and Lindy took their seats now, in their assigned swings. It was a tighter squeeze than when they were children, but they were still able to fit—just, in Victoria's case.

"It's magnificent out here, isn't it?" Lindy said, starting to swing slowly back and forth.

"Sure is," Genevieve said, still half-asleep.

"Beautiful," Victoria said.

"We took it for granted when we were young, didn't we?" Lindy said. "All this space, this wildness. It makes me wish I could fly or run, run as fast as a gazelle. Or write an amazing song or paint an incredible picture, create something out of myself. It's so inspiring."

"At least it will be until all the mining trucks arrive," Genevieve said.

"But they won't be digging on this part of the property, will they?" Lindy said.

"They've leased this half of the station, Lindy. If they find what they're looking for right here, they're not going to say, "Oh, what a shame, millions of dollars of diamonds are just waiting for us, but we can't dig them up. That's where the swings are.""

"They won't find anything out here," Lindy said. "I just know it."

"Because you've got supernatural powers of mineral detection?"

"It's just a feeling I have. I'm trying to learn to trust my feelings. Also, this half is where the Aboriginal paintings are. They'll never be allowed to dig near them, no matter what they find."

Genevieve raised an eyebrow. "Such innocence. How refreshing."

Lindy kept swinging. "You have to stay positive, Genevieve. That's my New Year's resolution. To stay focused and turn optimistic thoughts into a positive future. I've already got a good feeling about next year. My cushions have taken off better than I could have hoped."

"How many new orders now?" Victoria asked as she swung past Lindy.

"Four, all from the party. And I'm sure I'll get even more soon, once word of mouth starts."

"Well done," Genevieve said. "One box of cushion stuffing used, only five hundred to go."

Victoria shot her twin a stern glance. "Any word from Richard, Lindy?"

"Not yet, but he's still away camping with the Lawsons."

"Lucky old Richard," Genevieve said.

"Any word from Fred, Victoria?" Lindy asked.

"Very funny," Victoria said.

"I'm just teasing you. I know he's camping too. He's gotten really handsome, hasn't he? It would be so romantic if you did get back together, wouldn't it? Do you think you will? I mean, not that I'd like to be related to Horrible Jane any more now than I would have ten years ago, but Fred's always been different from the other Lawsons, hasn't he? Nicer. And she wouldn't be my sister-in-law anyway, would she? Would it just be that Fred was my brother-in-law?"

Behind Lindy's back, Genevieve rolled her eyes at Victoria.

Victoria ignored her. "We've only talked to each other twice, Lindy. But if I do decide to marry him, I promise you'll be the first to know."

"I bet I won't be. I bet you'll tell Genevieve before you tell me."

They swung in silence for a minute, competing with each other for height in an unspoken contest. The sky around them began to change color as the sun rose higher.

The dark blue began to lighten, a band of red around the horizon started to disappear.

Lindy was the first to stop. "I'd better go back. I told Mum I'd cook breakfast for everyone today." She dragged her sneakers on the ground to slow the swinging, sending up clouds of dust. "It's great having you both back, by the way. I was worried it might be tricky, all of us home again at the same time, but it's working out so well, isn't it?"

"It sure is," Genevieve said, coughing at the dust. "It's brilliant to be back."

"Don't talk about me while I'm gone, will you?" Lindy said.

"Of course not," they said in unison.

They waited until she was out of earshot.

"I was lying then," Genevieve said. "I hate being back."

"Genevieve! You don't, do you? I love being back. Being back with you, especially."

"I'm not talking about that. I'd live in hell with you if I had to. What I hate is having nothing to do. At least you've got a job, some contact with the outside world. You're not marooned out here like me, in the middle of nowhere, with no prospects, parents with a marriage in crisis, tension so thick you could cut it with a knife—if your little brother hadn't fallen onto the knife already."

"Can't you try to look at it as a holiday? Lindy's right. It is beautiful out here. Look at the view. The colors of the rocks. The huge sky. The clear light. Mum's tourists pay a fortune for this. We get it for free."

"It makes me feel sick."

"Genevieve! How can you say that? I love it out here. If

Mum hadn't already started up her own station stay business, I'd have been tempted to try it myself. Wouldn't that
be a brilliant job? Taking people out on walks and drives,
answering all their questions, camping miles from anyone
or anywhere—"

Genevieve gave a mock shudder. "Maybe I've been away
too long or maybe I've seen too many of those apocalyptic
films. All this space makes me think a murdering lunatic is
going to drive up any minute and stab us to death."

"Thanks. I'll really sleep well tonight."

"I mean it. At least in New York if someone tried to attack me, I could scream and a thousand people would be in
earshot. Here it's like being in outer space."

"That's what people love about being here," Victoria
said. "The isolation, the wildness—"

"Sure, when it's temporary, when they have real homes
with real people around them to go home to afterward. If
they're not trapped here like we are."

"Do you want to move away already?"

"I can't afford to. And I don't want to leave you all yet.
I'm just bored; that's my problem. I need something interesting to occupy my long, lonely days."

"Apart from sniping at all of us and doing your best to
undermine Lindy's confidence?"

"I don't have to undermine Lindy. She manages it perfectly well on her own."

Victoria laughed. "Give her a break. Stop being mean."

"Mean is my default position. I was born mean. Don't
you remember? I pushed you out of the way so I could be
born first."

"I let you. I had better manners."

They swung in silence for a few more minutes.

"So, then, what about you and Fred Lawson?"

"What is it with all of you and me and Fred Lawson?"

"You're hiding something, aren't you?"

"I thought you'd stopped doing that ESP stuff on me."

Genevieve just waited.

"He gave me a letter. The night of the party."

"He *what*? And you didn't tell me?"

"I needed to think about it."

"No, you didn't. You needed to tell me about it. Immediately. What did he say?"

Victoria stopped swinging, then reached into her pajama pocket and took out an envelope.

"You carry it with you? Even in your pajamas?"

"You think I'd leave anything like this lying around? With Ig and Lindy in the house?"

"You sure you want me to read this?"

Victoria nodded.

Genevieve brought her swing to a standstill. She read the letter twice. When she looked up, her eyes were glittering.

"Oh, my God," she said.

"Yes," Victoria said.

"Did he tell you any of this ten years ago?"

"Not like that. I knew he needed to get away from his family for a while. He'd talked a lot about how domineering his father could be. About how his life had been mapped out for him."

Genevieve read aloud.

Going to Canada ten years ago was the best decision I could ever have made. I felt like myself there, Victoria. Not one of the Lawsons, the oldest Lawson, Kevin Lawson's son. I was able to make mistakes. Do stupid things. Do good things. On my own two feet. But ten years ago I also made the worst decision of my life. I should have asked you to come with me. I should have begged you to come with me. I should have asked you to marry me, and maybe we could have started a life over there together. But back then I didn't think that was fair. I knew how much you loved Errigal, that you wanted to take over from your father if it worked out that way. I didn't want you to have to choose between your family and me.

I was ready to come back. It was the right time. Not everyone around here knows this, but Dad's got big plans for the future. Expansion. Diversification. He wants me to be involved. I've got lots of ideas I want to try, and Dad is backing me. But I can't stop thinking about something else I wanted but didn't have the courage to ask for ten years ago. And I'm too scared to ask you this face-to-face in case you say no. I loved being with you for those four years, Victoria. As soon as I saw you in Port Pirie, I realized nothing had changed. I know you don't know what your plans are yet, and I know we need to get to know each other again, and I wouldn't even expect any kind of answer from you for weeks or months or even years, if that's how much time you needed. But maybe you'd think about it at least.

I haven't even told you what the question is, have I? I feel like a teenager asking this, but I can't think of another way to put it. Can we start seeing each other? Go on dates? Have dinner? Get to know each other again? And this time I promise I won't suddenly up and go. This time I'll be staying around. And I hope that's what you'll want to do too.

With love,
Fred

Genevieve folded it gently and handed it back to Victoria. "I think I want to cry."

"I did."

"What are you going to do?"

"I don't know. I need to take it slowly."

"But why? It's a declaration of love, Victoria. It's almost a proposal. And you loved him, didn't you? You were heartbroken when he left. You never heard from him again."

"Because I told him not to contact me."

"What? Why are you only telling me all of this now?"

"It was a big deal for me back then, Genevieve. I needed to be sure I was doing what I wanted, not what you thought was best for me."

"But I always want what's best for you."

"I know that. But sometimes we want different things."

"Did he try to stay in touch with you?"

Victoria nodded. "He e-mailed. I didn't read them. I just deleted them. I eventually wrote to him to say he'd already made his decision by leaving. That he couldn't have it both ways. That we had to move on."

"But what if you were wrong? What if after a year of him being away, you staying in contact, you'd decided to go and join him?"

"But I didn't, did I? I'd gotten the job in the radio station by then. I'd started my own new life."

"But you loved him. I used to be so jealous of the two of you. You were so solid. So well matched. I was more shocked than you were when you broke up. Why are you having to think about this? Okay, you're both ten years older, but you're still the same people, aren't you? Can't you pick up where you left off?"

"We're not the same people. We've both been through a lot in the last ten years. And I also thought I was in love with Mr. Radio, Genevieve. And look what a mess that was. I'm still working through that. Yes, I know I loved Fred. I don't think I ever stopped loving him. But I can't just forget ten years, or go back to where we were. I need to think about it."

"Are you going to make him wait ten years for your answer? Punish him?"

"I'd never do that. He's punished himself enough as it is. He's changed since he went away. In good ways. I could see it immediately. He's grown up."

"I thought so too. I wanted to hate him when I saw him at the party, but I couldn't. I always really liked him. I like him even more now."

"You do? Really?"

"Really. You have my approval. Now or in ten years. Whenever you want it."

"Thanks, Genevieve. And please don't tell anyone else about the letter. About Fred."

"You really have to ask me that?"

They swung in silence for a few minutes more.

It was Genevieve who stopped first, dragging her heels on the ground, sending up another cloud of dust. "We better go back. If Lindy really is making breakfast, I don't want to miss out."

They started walking down the hill and across the paddocks to the homestead.

"I have had a small idea about some work," Genevieve said, as they picked their way through the scrubby salt bushes to the path. "It might get me into trouble but I figure I'm in trouble already. You know that gossip I passed on about the actress, the stuff that got me sacked?"

"I remember something about it, yes."

"Do you know how many hits that piece got on the Internet? Two million. For a sliver of news about an actress. I'm sitting on a gold mine. I think I should start a gossip Web site. I heard so many stories that would make your hair curl if it wasn't already curly. It suits you like that, by the way. Don't start straightening it again, will you?"

"Did you really just combine a hint of salacious gossip with unwanted hair advice?"

"That's an even better idea. I'll combine the two, play to my strengths. Isn't that the thing to do in times of crisis?"

"I thought your response to times of crisis was to get drunk and sleep with a security guard."

"He wasn't a security guard. He was the director's brother and also a location scout."

"You still haven't heard from him?"

"No."

"Are you okay about that?"

"The truth? No, I'm not. I liked him, Victoria. Really liked him. And I hoped I'd hear from him. Not only hoped. I really thought I would."

"Maybe he's been trying your mobile. He wouldn't know there's no signal out here, remember."

"But there is one in Hawker. I've driven in a few times to see if there have been any messages from him. Nothing. Sad, aren't I?"

"I'm really sorry."

"So am I. That's why I need a project. Even if I have to make up half the gossip now that I'm stuck out here, a Web site would keep me out of trouble, wouldn't it?"

"Or get you into even more trouble."

Genevieve waited while Victoria opened one of the paddock gates. There were no sheep left to get out but they'd been trained since childhood never to leave a gate open behind them.

"No word from Mr. Radio? Or any of your Sydney media pals?" Genevieve asked as they walked on.

"Not a single one. Oh, I lie. I heard from one, asking if he could be the go-between if I sold my story to one of the women's magazines. He only wanted a thirty percent cut."

"Classy."

They were almost at the homestead now. In the big tree near the toolshed, a flock of galahs was squawking and fluttering. Victoria stopped as they reached the final gate.

"Genevieve, there's something else I need to tell you."

Genevieve waited. "That sounds serious. Not another old boyfriend declaring undying love?"

Victoria didn't smile. She shook her head. "You know how I told you about having sex with Mr. Radio one more time before I left Sydney?"

Genevieve nodded.

Victoria paused. "I'm overdue."

"I thought you were on the pill."

"I had been. I stopped when all that stuff happened at work. When I got sacked. I didn't think I'd need it anymore."

Genevieve blinked. "How overdue?"

"Six days."

"That's just stress; don't worry. Look what you've been through lately."

"Do you think?"

"Of course."

"You're right. Thanks."

They had just opened the gate when Genevieve spoke again.

"Victoria, you know how I talked about having sex with the security guard who was actually a location scout? In New York? About three weeks ago?"

Victoria looked at her twin.

Genevieve nodded.

"Seriously?" Victoria said.

"Seriously."

"But you always use condoms."

"We did the first three times. Just not the fourth time."

"Four times? In one night?"

Genevieve nodded.

"How overdue?"

"Five days."

"It's just the stress. The long flight. Jet lag. You couldn't be either."

"No. Of course not."

"We'll give it a couple more days, will we?" Victoria said. "Before we really start to worry?"

"Good idea. But then what? Ask Mum if she has any old pregnancy tests lying around?"

Neither of them laughed.

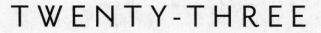

TWENTY-THREE

Angela was on her way out to the pottery studio. She hadn't been there since she'd read the e-mail from the gallery owner. She'd missed it. The peace. The cool, dark shed. The feel of the clay in her hands. She needed to get back to it, even if no one ever saw her finished work.

Inside the homestead, she knew that Nick was making his final plans for Ireland. They were still managing only the politest of exchanges. She could only follow Joan's advice. Give him time.

The kids were being especially noisy today. Lindy had heard from her friend Richard, who wanted to come and visit her. She was in a state. Victoria had taken over the kitchen phone, calling around to set up her radio interviews.

Genevieve was still trying to convince Ig he needed a haircut. She wasn't getting very far.

The old wooden door of the shed stuck as Angela tried to open it. It took three tugs. The blue paint had started to flake in the heat. Beside it, the rosebush was looking heat-exhausted. She filled a can with bore water and soaked it. Thirty-three years on, she couldn't let it die now. It didn't take much to draw parallels with her marriage.

Inside her studio, she hoped there hadn't been a visit from a new spider. She looked across at the shelves, crammed with her attempts at sculptures. None of them successful. She decided to forget about trying to make a piece of art for now. She'd make something practical instead. A cup, or a small vase. She cut some clay from the large block, took a seat at the wheel and set it spinning. The wet clay felt soft and soothing in her hands. She rolled it into a ball, inserted her thumbs, felt the shape of a cup begin to form, the surface smoothing, the layers getting thinner. Then she pressed too hard and it collapsed in on itself. She stopped the wheel from turning, picked up the clay and slowly, methodically, began to roll it back into a ball again.

As she went through the familiar movements, feeling the clay in her hands, the silence around her, the cool dim light, her mind began to drift. So quickly, so easily. With such relief.

She imagined herself in her garden studio in London, Radio 4 playing classical music, frost outside the window, the room snug and warm from the heat of the kiln, the shelves around her laden with the latest of her beautiful, sought-after ceramic birds. She imagined herself and Will going for a long walk beside the canal near their Islington house, getting inspiration from—

Out of the blue, her imaginary life disappeared. She stopped working the clay as she found herself recalling a real memory. An outing with Will that had actually happened when she was nineteen and he was twenty-one.

It was one of their first dates. They'd met in groups before that, going to the cinema together, or to bars to see bands or comedians. He'd always stood out, confident, knowledgeable. She had been thrilled when he singled her out one day. She'd thought he was more interested in another of the girls in their group. He'd come over and sat beside her, asked her questions about what she was studying, where she had grown up. She told him she came from Forest Hill, that she'd grown up across the road from the famous Horniman Museum, home to an eccentric natural history collection. It was her favorite place in London. He'd laughed at the name. People usually did. Then he told her he'd never heard of the place.

They met there the next day, just the two of them. She'd brought a picnic lunch. It was a beautiful spring day. He'd been impressed by the building, with its distinctive clock tower, sweeping stairs, the frieze on the front portico. The grounds were ablaze with flowers, the trees covered in fresh leaves after the long winter. The garden was busy with birds. She'd proudly shown Will around. He was always the one who seemed to have done so much and been everywhere. She felt like a tour guide as she led him inside to a big room containing dozens of glass cabinets, all filled with stuffed birds and animals, and over to the centerpiece of the museum, the famous stuffed walr—

"Mum?"

Angela blinked.

"Mum?"

"Sorry, Lindy. I was miles away."

"You're always miles away these days. Does this dress look all right?" It was a vintage-style blue cotton dress. "I'm trying to decide what to wear when Richard visits and I don't want to ask Genevieve or Victoria."

"You look lovely."

"Really?" Lindy beamed. "Thanks. But I can show you the other possibilities too, if you like."

"No need to," Angela said. "That one is perfect."

"I thought so too. What are you making?"

"Nothing, really."

"Yes, you are. I can see a sort of shape. What is it?"

Angela looked down. On the stationary pottery wheel was the beginning of a bird shape. She swiftly molded the clay back into a ball. "Just practicing a new technique," she said.

Lindy pulled up a stool beside the wheel. "Mum, can I please talk to you about Dad?"

"Lindy, I'd rather not—"

"Not about your fight with him. Genevieve and Victoria told me to leave you alone about that. I meant something else. How did you know Dad was the one when you met him?"

"Sorry?"

"When you met Dad that night in Sydney, how did you know he was the one for you?"

"The one for me?"

"You know, the man you were going to marry, the man who was going to father your children."

"I don't know."

"Mum, come on. You turned your whole life upside down for him, swapped countries, left friends and family behind to move to an outback station, and you don't know why?"

"Why are you asking?"

"I told you, Richard's coming to visit and I'm trying to work out how I feel about him. I've never felt like this with my other boyfriends. I feel all kind of, I don't know, nervous when I'm with him. Excited but kind of anxious too. And I can't work out if that's a good thing or a bad thing."

"Have you actually had a proper date with Richard yet?"

"Not exactly. I mean, we've talked, just the two of us. And we kissed. Once. It was so incredible, he—"

"Lindy, that's fine. You don't have to tell me everything."

"I just know I feel different with him than I've felt with any other guy I've gone out with. But how do I know for sure that it's love? That it's not just infatuation or lust?"

"Darling, I'm sorry. I don't know. It's different for every person."

"Mum, please, help me. You must have felt something amazing with Dad when you first met him. Because you got it right, didn't you? Whirlwind romance, married within a year, still together all these years later. You must have felt something that made you sure he was the one for you."

Angela bought herself some time. "Let me think about it. You could try asking your dad too."

"I did," Lindy said, with a sigh. "Just now, in the kitchen."

"And what did he say?"

"He told me to ask you."

TWENTY-FOUR

The morning of Angela's trip to Adelaide for her specialist's appointment, Joan called to wish her well. "You're sure you're happy to drive down on your own? I can be over to you in an hour if you need me."

"I'll be fine, I promise."

"No headaches today?"

"Not for two days. I'm starting to feel like a fraud."

"Ring and let me know how you get on. I'll be waiting to hear."

Ig carried Angela's overnight case to the car. He had been like a shadow all morning, checking she had everything. He and Genevieve had taken care of the hotel booking, doing it online, getting an excellent last-minute deal in a very nice city center hotel.

"You're a genius, Ig," Genevieve had said as he pressed print and handed her the booking confirmation. "Who taught you all this?"

"Robbie," he said.

In the kitchen, Genevieve adopted a serious expression as Angela ran through the details of her trip once more. "I think I've got it," she said. "You're leaving now, driving to Adelaide to see your specialist this afternoon. You're staying one night in a hotel, then coming back tomorrow, expected time of arrival five p.m."

"Or before. As soon as I can."

"And I'm in charge until then. How will I cope? Can you remind me, how do I switch on the lights? And that kettle thing, do I take it outside and wait for rain? Or do I use those silver things by the sink? What are they called, taps?"

"Very funny."

"Mum, just go, will you? Get in the car, drive away, see your specialist, then go out on the town tonight and dance the light fandango."

"Fandango?" Angela said.

"Fandango, fantastic, however you want." She hugged her. "Just go. Forget all about us."

Victoria was in her bedroom, practicing interview techniques. She came out and hugged Angela too. "You're sure you don't want one of us to come with you?"

"Thanks, but I'm sure," Angela said.

Lindy asked the same question. "I could be packed in a few minutes. Your hotel looks so nice. I'd love to stay there too. To help and support you, I mean. It's not just about the hotel."

"I'll be fine, Lindy, thanks," Angela said. "You stay here and do your sewing."

Lindy held up her latest cushion. Her second. "Look, I'm nearly done. Isn't it gorgeous? A perfect twentieth anniversary present."

Angela agreed. She decided this wasn't the time to tell her there were two *N*s in anniversary.

Soon after, Angela was ready to leave. She'd hoped Nick would come to find her. He knew her appointment was today. He'd been in the office all morning and the office window looked out onto the yard. He would have seen Ig carrying her luggage to the car. The guilt she'd been feeling about her letter was starting to twist into a different shape. The kids had managed to get over the letter, hadn't they? Even Celia had thawed a little over the past week or so, especially after all the attention she'd received thanks to her hospital stay. But Nick? There had been no change.

She kept her voice polite as she stood in the office doorway. "I'm off, Nick."

He turned around only slightly. "Safe trip."

"Thanks."

She was in the hall before he spoke again.

"Good luck at the doctor."

"Thanks," she said, without turning back.

That was it, she thought. After thirty-three years of marriage, that was the best they could do.

As Angela drove away, Ig ran beside the car as he loved to do, racing it, waving in at his mum as she waved back at him. He wasn't going to cry, even though he really wanted to. She was only going away for one night. She'd be back tomorrow. He wouldn't have time to miss her, she'd told him.

But he knew he would. He already had a kind of sick feeling in his stomach. He used to get it all the time at school in Adelaide too. Some of the boys there had teased him when the teacher asked once who was the person they most admired in the world. The others named sportsmen and pop stars. One named an astronaut. When it was his turn, he told the truth. His mum.

He stood at the homestead gate and waved until her car was out of sight, just a cloud of dust from the dirt road trailing in the air behind her. Genevieve joined him, tousling his hair. He half hated the way she did that, half liked it.

"She'll be back tomorrow, Iggy. Don't be too sad. Want to come and help me make chocolate biscuits?"

"Not yet. Soon," he said.

He stayed outside watching until even the cloud of dust from her car was gone.

In her bedroom, Victoria was doing some broadcast practice, recording her introduction for the third time. She hadn't done any presenting for more than two years, not since she'd moved into a producing role. It felt good to be back doing it again. Maybe Mr. Radio had actually done her a favor. Dropping her in that mess. Getting her sacked. Forcing her to run home, shamed, ashamed . . .

Pregnant?

No. She couldn't be pregnant by him. Of course not. It was just stress delaying her period. And it had to be the jet lag delaying Genevieve's. But perhaps it would be a good idea to get a pregnancy test the next time they were in Port Augusta. And perhaps they should go there soon.

She pressed the on switch of the microphone again. "Hello, I'm Victoria Gillespie. Welcome to Outback Lives, my new series on—"

"NO!" A cry from Lindy suddenly filled the room. "It CAN'T be wrong. It CAN'T!"

Victoria switched off the microphone and swore under her breath.

In the kitchen, Genevieve was trying to calm Lindy down. "I'm sorry, but it is. 'Anniversary' definitely has two 'N's. Didn't you check before you started?"

"I just sewed it exactly as they wrote it on their order form."

"Then they obviously can't spell either. So maybe they won't notice."

"Of course they'll notice. Or one of their kids will notice and I'll be a laughingstock again. I can't do *anything* right, can I? I'm a complete and utter failure!"

She snatched the cushion back from Genevieve and threw it onto the table. They both moved but not fast enough. They could only watch as the tin of cocoa powder spilled onto the white cushion.

Another wail filled the house. In her room, Victoria turned off the recorder again.

In the office, Nick shut the door to try to keep out the noise. He had no intention of going to see what was happening.

Once again, he cursed the fact they hadn't gotten around to getting the office phone fixed. If ever there was a time he needed to make a call out of earshot of his family, it was today.

A call to Angela.

He should have said more to her before she left. He shouldn't have let it go on like this between them. He might have made a bad job of keeping the station running, but he'd made a good job of staying angry with Angela. She hadn't even told him about the specialist's appointment until three days ago, when he'd found Genevieve and Ig in the office booking a hotel online for her. That was when it had hit him. He and Angela had become one of those couples who communicated only through their children.

The only option was to go out to the kitchen and use the landline phone, or call her on the UHF radio. But not with Genevieve and Lindy in there, making a racket about something. Or with Victoria, Ig and Celia all in listening range. He didn't want any of them overhearing him attempt to apologize to Angela.

Not just to apologize. To explain.

He'd read her Christmas letter again that morning. He'd read it so many times now he almost knew it by heart. He'd gone through every emotion—anger, hurt, embarrassment. Despair. He'd talked about it with his doctor. He'd talked about it with his psychologist.

It was Jim who had asked him the question. "Do you recognize yourself in what Angela was saying?"

Yes, he'd said. Eventually. In the past few days, he'd realized something else too.

278 | MONICA McINERNEY

Angela hadn't just written the truth about him. She had let him off lightly.

Because everything she'd written about him was the truth, he realized. He *had* shut himself away. He *had* stopped talking to her. He hadn't involved her in any of the decision making about the mining lease. His family research *had* become an obsession.

He recalled his speech at the party. Getting emotional like that, in front of all his neighbors. Once, he and Angela would have talked about it the next day. She would have made him feel better. Not this time. He'd been too ashamed to ask her about it. It had been easier to say nothing.

Easier.

Was that what had happened to him? He'd started taking the easy route, because it was just that, easier, safer? That was what the family research had become; he knew that. A safe hobby. At least when he was researching the past, there could be no nasty surprises, nothing that would actually affect him, hurt him. It was also helping him assuage his guilt. He might have had to lease out half the Gillespie land, but look how much he now knew about his Gillespie ancestors.

In the past week or so, he'd begun to look at that in a different way too. If he hadn't signed that contract with Carol's company, he might have stopped the research. Shelved his plans for the reunion. But he was committed now, not just to hosting a reunion with two hundred strangers, but to his first overseas trip in just a few weeks' time.

Without Angela.

His wife, his best friend, the woman who knew him better than anyone else in the world.

That was why her Christmas letter had hurt so much. He thought he had hidden his pain from her. The letter was proof he hadn't. She'd seen right through him. She'd seen him for what he had become. She was right. He wasn't the man she'd married.

Was it any wonder some old English boyfriend she hadn't mentioned in years had become her ideal, fantasy husband? Nick had been so angry about that at first. Not just angry. Hurt. Humiliated. Knowing their neighbors and friends had also read all about this guy Will. The successful architect: the soft, pen-pushing Londoner, who did all the cooking, who made her laugh, talked to her; who'd given her a life of luxury, of money, one perfect daughter, in a big city. There it was, Angela's ideal life laid out in her own words. All that she had really wanted. None of which Nick had been able to give her. Round and round his head the thoughts had gone. Angela didn't want to be married to him. She regretted meeting him. He hadn't been able to get past that.

Then he'd remembered something the psychologist had said to him. That just because Nick thought something didn't mean it was real. That for every negative feeling he had, there could be a stronger, positive one. It was a matter of choosing a thought that made him feel good about himself, not bad.

During his long walks on the station over the past weeks, he'd tried. Over Christmas, he'd tried. When the kids were acting out that concert, before they all fell sick, he'd tried. He'd heard afterward what their plan had been. To act out highlights from Angela's letters, everything she had written about the two of them over the years.

Four days after Christmas, alone in the office late one night, unable to sleep, he'd found the letters in the filing cabinet. He'd read them for himself. All of them. Yes, they mostly told the positive stories. And yes, sometimes Angela had used more flowery language or gone into more detail than he might have liked. That was one of the reasons he'd stopped reading them.

But Angela had also written about the tough times they'd had over the years. When his parents died. When Angela's parents died, and she had twice gone back home alone to London. About how their lives had started to change when the drought came. When the wool industry collapsed. What it had been like to wait for rain year after year, to have to start selling off the stock. She hadn't ignored any of the realities of their lives on Errigal. But she had always stayed positive. Every letter had remained upbeat. She'd always included the good things that were still happening, with their children, among their friends, in their community, with her station stay business.

With him.

In every letter, from the first one to the last, she had talked about him. Year after year, in letter after letter, he'd read, in her words, exactly what she thought of him. How much she loved him. How proud she was of him. How much she loved her life here on the station with him and their children. How much the two of them had gone through.

Together.

After he'd finished reading the letters, he'd gone outside and sat on the veranda, in the darkness. An hour had passed, maybe more. No wonder she had felt shut out. No wonder she had felt lonely. No wonder she had needed to take up pottery, invent a fantasy husband to keep her company. He had thought telling her nothing was the best way. The only way. That by keeping his troubles to himself, he was shielding her. He had been wrong. All he had done was cause her more pain.

He hadn't even had the decency to say good-bye to her properly this morning, before she drove off on a four-hour trip to find out once and for all whether she had a brain tumor. Enough, he decided. Enough silence between them. He needed to apologize to her. To explain. And, once more, to ask her whether she would come to Ireland, to London, to Europe with him.

He couldn't call her, but he could e-mail her. She only had an old-style mobile phone that didn't have the Internet, but there'd be a computer in her hotel. When she called later, he'd ask her to check her e-mails.

As he moved his chair closer to the desk, he realized something. This wouldn't just be the first time he'd e-mailed her. It would be the first time in thirty-three years that he'd written to her.

He stared at the blank screen for a long moment, and then he began.

TWENTY-FIVE

Angela was halfway to Adelaide. For the first hour, she'd been able to think of nothing but Nick. About that moment in the office. About what she should have said. Could have said. Wanted to say. Hadn't said. As every day passed, it was as if the gulf between them widened.

That morning, she'd tried to fix it. She'd woken early, Nick beside her, physically close. Once upon a time, she might have moved closer to Nick, put her arm around him, kissed him awake. Perhaps there might even have been more touching, caressing, leading to sleepy morning sex. But that was out of the question now. Their love life had been another casualty of the distance between them over the past months.

But was it out of the question? Perhaps it was exactly

what she should do. Sex had always helped them in the past, especially in the early years of their marriage, whenever they'd had rows. They'd always argued in different ways. She had a quicker temper than he did, was inclined to speak her mind, let it all out, whereas he moved more carefully through any minefield in their relationship, was easily hurt by careless words, inclined to fall into silence. Many times in their marriage it had been Angela who'd made the first move toward a reconciliation. It had bothered her at first. She'd always thought it should be a two-way street. She'd talked about it with Joan.

Joan had given her usual straight advice. "Marriage is a one-way street, love. Imagine you are two cars in a narrow alleyway, hood to hood. One can't move any farther without the other moving too. If neither of you move, you're both stuck there forever. But if one of you does move—and it doesn't matter which one does—voila, the road is cleared and you can get back to business. Just don't keep count of who said sorry first. Don't get into the habit of saying, 'But he never does this' or 'He never does that.' As long as one of you is making a move, that's all you need to get started."

It had been good advice. She'd decided to try it that morning in bed. She put her arm around his waist, inched closer against him. Again, the familiarity struck her. The feel of his skin. The shape of his body. The smell of him. The sound of his breathing. Even thirty-three years later, she still found him so attractive, tanned, lean and fit from all the outdoor work he'd done over the years. His hair was still dark, just graying on the temples. His face was lined now, but so was hers. Of course they could get through this.

Of course their marriage wasn't over. As she tightened her arm around him, he shifted in his sleep, a quick, sudden movement that felt like he was pushing her away.

She'd edged back immediately. Perhaps he was still deep in sleep. Perhaps he hadn't even registered she was touching him, his reaction just a reflex. But it had been enough to stop her. She'd gotten up, left the bedroom. When she saw him next, in the kitchen, the kids around, the noise level high; there had been no opportunity to even try to talk, let alone anything else.

She passed through all the familiar towns. The highway stretched out in front of her. Her car was an automatic. It almost drove itself. There was very little traffic. She had the air-conditioning on high. The sun was bright outside, shining in on her right arm, which was more tanned than her left from so many years driving in light as harsh and strong as this. In her early years in Australia, there'd been no talk of sun block or skin cancer. Everyone soaked up all the sunshine they could, especially the kids. She was paying for it now, with early wrinkles, older skin.

If she had gone back home and married Will, would she look different now too? Fewer wrinkles? More wrinkles? Gray hairs? Dyed hair? She'd certainly have been paler. Unless, of course, they had a home in Spain where they spent most summers, and quite a lot of time over the winter months too.

Her mind began to drift.

Yes, she and Will did have a holiday home in Spain. They had always loved to travel. They thought they'd satisfied their travel bug when they were young, when he went backpacking in search of architectural wonders and she came to Australia for a few months, traveling around, doing some bartending, but never any in Sydney, even though her friend in the hostel begged her to do her shift one night. Angela nearly said yes, but she'd been offered tickets to a comedy gig the same evening. She'd chosen the comedy. Her friend ended up losing her job in the pub. Angela always felt a bit guilty about that.

Recently, though, Angela and Will had begun to talk a lot more about traveling again, even farther afield this time. He was the one who suggested Australia.

"I'd love to go there again," she said. "But it's such a long flight. We'd want to stay a month at least. Six weeks, ideally. And you're so busy at work."

"I'm also the boss. And I could easily take that much time away, if it turned out I was doing some work while I was there."

She laughed. She should have guessed he was up to something.

Will explained that he'd been asked to work on a new ecotourism development. It was a company based in Italy, but with properties in Spain, Portugal and Croatia. Plenty of money behind them. Will had researched similar developments. The best of them just happened to be in Australia. Some in Queensland. Others in outback South Australia. "It would still be mostly a holiday, of course, but we could stay in a few of these eco-places as well."

"And then claim the entire trip as a business expense?"

"I hadn't thought of that," he said. "But you're right. I probably could."

He was teasing her, of course. Will was a very astute businessman.

There was nothing stopping them. Nothing except that Angela would miss Lexie so much. Once again, Will read her mind.

"I rang Lexie last night. She can't take a six-week holiday, but she can take a fortnight. She's going to come out and join us for the last two weeks. Wherever we decide to be, somewhere tropical or somewhere outback—she doesn't mind which."

They spent the rest of the evening in front of the computer, researching business-class airfares with stopovers in Hong Kong and making notes about their Australian itinerary. Will was right. The Australians were world leaders in the kind of ecotourism ventures his new client was planning. But there were also even more down-to-earth ways of seeing the real Australia.

"Look at these places," Angela said, clicking on a Web site for outback station stays. "You can stay in actual homesteads, with outback families. That would be something special, wouldn't it? Not just being in a luxurious eco-cabin, but living the real life."

"Sleeping in a bed that the youngest kid has just vacated? In a bedroom filled with sporting trophies? Seriously, Angela?"

"No, listen to this." She clicked on a station at random, situated in northern South Australia, near the Flinders Ranges National Park. She read aloud. "'You'll stay in the old governess's quarters attached to a hundred-year-old stone homestead, and be the personal guest of the station owners. Guided tours of the station, expert information on local Aboriginal history and culture, native Australian flora and fauna, overnight camping trips including dinner around a campfire, 4WD tours conducted by the wife of the station manager, a fourth-generation sheep farmer.' I've heard about these somewhere. Wouldn't that be fun! We could stay in a few of the eco-places as well, but why don't we have some time on a real station too?"

"Great idea," Will said. "You choose the station. I'll be happy to go wherever you want to."

Angela scanned the list. They all sounded great. But she kept being drawn back to the first one she'd looked at. The one called Errigal, with the one-hundred-year-old homest—

The blast of a semitrailer's horn made Angela leap. She swerved slightly before bringing her attention right back to the road. The truck driver had been signaling to a passing truckie, not her, but it brought her to her senses.

What on earth had she been thinking, bringing her fantasy life into her real life? The whole idea of her alternative life was to take her away from her real world, not imagine herself and Will sitting at the kitchen table on Errigal, being served dinner by—

By whom?

Because it wouldn't be her, would it? Because if she had gone back to London, married Will and had Lexie, she wouldn't have married Nick, gone to live on Errigal or had four children with him.

She'd imagined her alternative life, but she hadn't imagined Nick's. What would *his* life have been like if he hadn't walked into her pub that night? Who would he have ended up marrying? Diane, the woman he'd been going out with for a few years before he met her? How many children would he and Diane have had? Would they have lived happily ever after?

It was a sudden, unsettling thought.

For the rest of her journey, she concentrated on the road.

Once she reached Adelaide, it took her nearly an hour to find the specialist's rooms. The city's streets were laid out in an orderly way, grids and straight lines, but she didn't know it well. Her visits over the years had been confined to seeing the girls—and, briefly, Ig—at their boarding schools, and the occasional shopping trip.

She eventually found her way. The rooms were in a shady street on the edge of the central business district, a florist on one side, an upmarket café on the other. The reception area had a polished, designed look with expensive carpet, leather seating and original paintings on the wall. It smelled good too, of lemon or mandarin. The woman behind the desk was middle-aged, well-groomed, smiling. Angela gave her name.

"Welcome, Mrs. Gillespie. Dr. Liakos is unfortunately running a little behind schedule today. I hope you won't mind waiting."

That was fine, of course, she said. She declined tea or coffee, picked up a magazine and sat down. Four other people were waiting. Classical music played quietly. The receptionist was making calls, speaking in a low tone. If Angela didn't have the start of a headache, this would feel so relaxing, like a day in a beauty spa. Peace, music, magazines, a quietly spoken lady being so nice to her. Perhaps she should cancel the actual appointment and just sit here for the day instead.

The young woman across from her was called in first. What was wrong with her? Angela wondered. Two more people came in. The young woman left. Another woman was called. Angela felt her headache start to pulse. She now wasn't even looking at the magazine.

Finally her name was called.

She liked the specialist right away. Despite the waiting room full of people, he took his time with her, going through her GP's letter, looking at the scans again, examining her, asking her questions about the headaches, their severity and duration. When they'd started. What triggered them.

He was calm and reassuring. No, he told her, he didn't think there was a brain tumor. He was inclined to think the headaches were being caused by stress, or something amiss with her neck muscles or vertebrae. There could even be a connection with menopause. But for her sake as much as his, he wanted her to have more tests, another MRI, a different kind of scan. He would ask his receptionist to make the calls for her. It usually required several days' notice for a nonurgent case like hers—even that phrase was reassuring—but they hoped it would be possible for her to do them either later that afternoon or early the next morning, to save her having to make the long trip down again in the near future. He refused to talk about the what-ifs. "Let's get the facts and then go from there," he said.

Outside, his receptionist took over, confirming she

would be making calls on Angela's behalf to organize the new series of tests for her. She took down the phone number of Angela's hotel. "I've got your mobile number too. I'll try that first. We'll arrange your tests and get you on the road home before you know it."

In the car, Angela knew she should call home, let them know it had gone well, but she couldn't decide who to call. A year ago, it would have been Nick. Without question. But she was still hurt by his farewell that morning. She took the coward's way out and called Genevieve's mobile number instead. Even if her daughter wasn't in signal range, she could leave a message.

Genevieve answered after the third ring. "Mum! Your timing's perfect. I'm in Hawker shopping, with a signal for once. Civilization again! How did you go?"

"The specialist thinks it's nothing too serious, but he wants me to have some more tests. I might have to stay down two nights, not just one." Angela surprised herself with the sudden lie.

"Oh, Mum. Are you sure you don't want us there? Do you need me to book you into the hotel for another night?"

"No, thanks. I can manage it," she said. "What's been happening there?"

"Shall I tell you about Lindy's cushion tantrum? Ig's near accident with a rope ladder on his cubby? Victoria's sudden attack of work nerves? No, it can all wait till you get back. In fact, I might stay here in Hawker myself."

"And your dad?"

"He was still locked in the office when I left. He'd been in there since you left."

"I tried the house phone but it just rang out." The lies were coming too easily. "My battery's nearly run out too. Can you please fill him in for me when you get home?"

"Of course. Good luck with the tests. Book into the hotel for another night even if you don't need to. Enjoy the luxury. And steal all the soap, would you? Ig wants them for his cubby."

Her hotel was easy to find, near the Festival Centre, overlooking the river Torrens. It was more than twenty stories high. Inside, the lobby was airy, cool. The staff were immaculately dressed, all smiling. Once again, she heard the sound of soft classical music. And again, she had that feeling of peace. She asked about a second night even as she was checking in.

"Certainly, Mrs. Gillespie. Let me take a look." There was the click of beautifully manicured fingers.

The receptionist had such a friendly face. She was so calm and efficient. Angela felt an urge to talk to her. "This is my first night away from my husband and children in ten years."

"Ten years?" The young woman raised an eyebrow. "How many children do you have?"

"Four. Two sets of twins." She couldn't seem to stop lying now.

"*Two* sets! You definitely deserve some time off."

"It's my birthday next week too. A significant one. My husband thought I needed some spoiling. He's booked me theater tickets for tonight. I'm meeting an old school friend."

"Oh, how thoughtful."

"He is—very. He and I will have our own time away to-gether too, of course," she added. "This was just a special pre-birthday treat from him."

"I hope you enjoy every minute of it." Another rapid click of fingers and then a smile. "That's all fine, Mrs. Gillespie. I've booked you in for a second night at the same rate. Unfortunately I couldn't give you the same room, so I hope you don't mind that I've upgraded you to a suite for the two nights. At no extra cost."

Angela hadn't expected that. She had just been enjoying herself, making up a story. She reached for her purse. "Oh no, you don't have to do that. Let me pay the difference."

The receptionist smiled again. "It's my pleasure, Mrs. Gillespie. You don't need to pay anything extra." She lowered her voice. "I'm one of four too. I can't wait to tell my dad what your husband did. My mother's birthday's coming up too. Nothing beats a subtle hint!"

A young man in a uniform carried Angela's bag up in the elevator for her, even though she was capable of carrying it herself. He opened the door with a swipe of a keycard. She stifled a gasp as they stepped inside. The room was beau-tiful. Except it wasn't a room; it was a suite. As well as the bedroom, there was a separate living area with a sofa, two chairs and a desk. There were two enormous televisions, one in each room. The bedroom had the largest bed she'd ever seen, made up with what looked like the whitest, soft-est linen and six—*six*—pillows. There was an entire wall of windows looking out over the river and the Festival Centre, to Adelaide Oval and to parklands and suburbs beyond.

The porter showed her how to work the two large sets

of curtains, where the refrigerator was, the TV and DVD player, the CD sound system. He pointed out the menu for room service, for the spa downstairs. Then he was gone, before she'd even had time to wonder whether she should tip him. People always tipped porters in films, didn't they? It suddenly felt as though she were in a film. She was still standing in front of the huge windows, looking out at the view, when there was a knock at the door.

It was a different porter, holding a basket of fruit. "Welcome to the hotel, Mrs. Gillespie. We hope you enjoy your stay."

She tipped him, clumsily reaching for her purse, taking out the first bill she found. He seemed happy enough with the crumpled five-dollar bill.

She carried the basket across to the polished table. As well as ordinary fruit like an apple and a banana, there was also a mango, a passion fruit, a blood orange and an exotic fruit that she'd never seen before, a star-shaped light green one. She'd take that one home for Ig. She checked in the bathroom. Not even it was ordinary. There was a whole row of soaps, lotions and creams. Ig would love those for his cubby, for sure. Five-star toiletries in a cardboard cubby.

She reached for the phone and dialed reception. The young woman who'd checked her in answered.

"This is Angela Gillespie," she said. "I just wanted to say thank you again. It's all so beautiful."

"You're very welcome, Mrs. Gillespie. Have a great stay."

She had just hung up when her mobile phone rang. Who would it be this time? The porter offering to run her a bath?

It was the specialist's receptionist. "I'm so sorry, Mrs.

Gillespie. The soonest I can get you in for those tests is next week. It's good news in a way. Dr. Liakos is happy to wait as he doesn't feel it is urgent in your case. But it will mean you have to come back to Adelaide again."

"That's no problem at all. Of course I can come back."

"Thanks for being so understanding. I wanted to let you know as soon as I could, in case you decided to drive back home tonight."

"That's a great idea," Angela said. "I might do just that. Thanks very much again."

Angela called Genevieve's mobile again. Her daughter was just leaving Hawker, still in signal range. Angela waited until she had pulled over to the side of the road.

"I won't keep you, darling. This battery is still playing up. Just to let you know the specialist's receptionist called, and they've been able to fit me in for those tests. Yes, tomorrow and the next day. So I'll definitely book in for another night here. And maybe for a third night as well. No, of course you don't need to come down. I'll be fine. The specialist assured me they're all routine, not painful. They'll just take a long time. Can you let Dad know? Thanks very much."

She had one more call to make. Once again, the lies tripped off her tongue. Even to Joan, her oldest friend.

"Two days of tests?" Joan said. "Maybe three? Sounds like torture. Which ones are first?"

Angela floundered for a moment. "I can't remember. The list is in my bag."

"I hope it's not another of those MRI ones. You're not claustrophobic, are you? Apparently it's like being eaten by a snake. So, what's the hotel like?"

Angela could at least answer that truthfully. She told her about the upgrade, describing the view, the two rooms, the room service menu, the linen—

"That's enough," Joan said. "I'm turning green here. You're not having any tests, are you? You're just having a few sneaky days away in a swanky hotel, getting away from us all."

How had she guessed? Angela felt an urge to confess. Of everyone, Joan would understand. But it was too late. She could hear Joan talking to Glenn.

"I'd better go. His Lordship needs feeding. Good luck. Don't worry about the tests. You'll be fine. And enjoy the break from everyone. You deserve it."

Angela hung up, feeling better. Joan was right. She should enjoy this. Just stop worrying, take advantage of this beautiful hotel and step outside her own life even for a couple of days. She leaned down and took off her shoes. About to place them neatly side by side, she changed her mind, and threw one across one side of the room, the other in a different direction. They landed with satisfying thumps. She felt the carpet underfoot, the pile thick between her toes. There were only floorboards and rugs back at Errigal. It got too dusty for carpets. She stood in the center of the room. What should she do now? What could she do now?

Anything she wanted, she realized. Absolutely anything she wanted.

She could drink everything in the minibar. Order everything off the room service menu. Watch twenty-four hours of movies. She could go downstairs and have a massage, a facial, a swim. She could sit in the bar and drink cocktails.

She could go out for a walk, along the river path she could see from her high window. She could do anything she wanted and no one was going to interrupt her, ask anything of her, be angry with her, judge her or ignore her.

She needed to mark this moment in some way. It felt like she was in a film, so she decided to do something she'd only ever seen done in films. She ran barefoot across the room and threw herself onto the enormous bed, laughing out loud.

TWENTY-SIX

In the kitchen at Errigal, Nick had just hung up from Genevieve.

Celia walked in. "Was that Angela?"

"No, it was Genevieve." He filled her in on the news about Angela's tests.

"Two days of serious tests? Maybe three? On her own?"

"It's what she wanted."

"I'm not saying it wasn't." Celia gave a small laugh. "I did notice she couldn't get away from here fast enough this morning."

Nick didn't answer.

Celia was watching him carefully. "That's good that she's having the tests, at least. She'll get to the bottom of those headaches once and for all, hopefully."

Nick made a noncommittal noise.

"So, then," she said, in a bright voice, "tell me the latest about your reunion. Any more of those fascinating journals turned up in Ireland yet?"

Nick took a seat. "Are you being polite like the rest of my family or are you actually interested?"

"You are out of sorts today. I'm interested. Very interested. I've been a Gillespie for nearly longer than you, remember, even if it's only by marriage. Errigal's always felt like home to me. You know, your uncle did a bit of family research over the years himself. I could dig out his files for you, if you like. They're at home somewhere. I'd have brought them with me if I'd realized quite how, what's the word—"

"Obsessed?"

"Enthusiastic about it you are. There are folders full, in fact. I'll send them on to you when I'm home again. Before you go to Ireland." She glanced down the hallway. "There's something else I wanted to say to you while we're on our own. Nick, I can't help noticing there's a great deal of tension between you and Angela."

Nick stayed silent.

"No wonder, I suppose. That letter of hers was a terrible thing. All those things she said about you and me, not to mention her own children. If it doesn't turn out to be some kind of mental illness she has, the alternative is just as bad, really, isn't it?"

"The letter was my fault, Celia."

"I beg your pardon?"

"Angela was just letting off steam. She didn't mean to send it. I sent it."

"You did what?"

"I sent it out. By accident."

"Oh. Well. Be that as it may. She still wrote it, didn't she? And don't pretend you're not angry about it, Nick. Your loyalty is admirable, but I've known you since you were a little boy, remember. Angela is—"

He stood up. "My wife. And our marriage is our business, Celia. Excuse me. I need to send some e-mails."

The next day, Genevieve, Victoria and Lindy were gathered in Lindy's bedroom.

Lindy was doing her makeup. "How much should I put on? Or would it be better to look as if I haven't gone to any trouble at all, in case I scare him off?"

"It depends on his intentions," Genevieve said. "What did he say when he rang?"

"He said would it suit if he came over and visited today."

"And what did you say?"

"I said that would be great. Was that wrong, do you think? Too eager?"

There was a knock at the door.

"Come in, Ig," Genevieve called. "Perfect timing. We need a male opinion. Tell us, how does Lindy look?"

He inspected her. "You look really nice, Lindy. Your hair and makeup look great. If I was Richard, I'd think you were really pretty."

"Thank you, Ig!" Lindy said, beaming. "I'll be right back. I'm going to see if he's coming."

Ig waited until she was gone, then put out his hand to Genevieve. "Five bucks."

"No way. I said I'd give you four."

"I added the extra line about Richard myself. That was worth a dollar."

Victoria stared at her sister. "You bribed him to say that to Lindy?"

"You can bribe Ig to do anything. That's why he's fun to have around. Expensive but fun."

Twenty minutes later, they were all on the veranda waiting. Lindy was jumpy.

"Do I still look okay? Ig, do I? Please stay out of the way once he gets here, all of you. Or if you insist on hanging around at the start, just to be polite, can you please at least try to be nice?"

"We're always nice," Genevieve said.

"I am. You're not," Victoria said. "You can be really horrible."

"Stop it, please, both of you," Lindy said.

Another minute passed. There was still no sign of a car.

"What are you going to do with him?" Genevieve asked. "If he ever actually gets here."

"Oh, God, I don't know. Should I take him for a drive?"

"You could, but Mum's got the good car, remember. You could always take him in Dad's filthy old ute, I guess. If you don't mind getting mud all over that nice dress."

"I didn't think of that! Have I got time to change? What should I wear? Jeans? Shorts?"

"Too late. Here he comes."

They watched the dust cloud moving closer. It was one

of the advantages of living out here. There was little chance of anyone arriving unexpectedly.

Ig clambered up the ladder beside the water tank and started waving at the car.

"Ig, get down!" Lindy called. "Don't embarrass me."

"I'm not being embarrassing. I'm being friendly."

"You don't even know him."

"I do. I met him at the party. Anyway, I'm not waving to him."

"Who are you waving to?"

"Horrible Jane. She's in the car with him."

Two hours later, they were all out in front of the house again, this time waving good-bye.

It had been an excruciating afternoon. Jane had come bounding out of the driver's seat of the car, all false cheer. "I couldn't let Richard drive over on his own. He'd have got lost!" She started talking nonstop about her family's Christmas and New Year's camping trip.

As soon as she could, Lindy invited Genevieve into the kitchen under the pretext of getting drinks. She begged her not to go anywhere. "I can only handle Horrible Jane when you're around."

"But what about you and Richard? Your whirlwind romance? Your privacy?"

"Forget that. She's here as his bodyguard; can't you tell? It's a disaster."

An hour later, Genevieve conceded Lindy was right. Richard hadn't gotten a word in. Jane was still doing all the talking, about herself and how well she was doing in Melbourne.

Genevieve and Victoria tried to make it easier for Lindy, but Jane got to be too much for them as well. Victoria slipped away first, then Genevieve. Ig was long gone. As soon as she could, Lindy excused herself and went to find them.

"She's ruined everything," Lindy said. "It's over with Richard before it's even started."

"Not necessarily," Genevieve said. "You're doing really well. You're almost coming across as a normal person. And he wants to be here, I can tell. He's trying to talk to you."

"But she won't let him get a word in."

"Let me see what I can do," Genevieve said.

Back out on the veranda, Genevieve took a seat across from Richard and Jane. Jane was now talking about one of her brother's excellent cricket scores. Richard looked like he had heard about it before. Genevieve waited for Jane to take a breath and smoothly interrupted.

"So, Richard, how long are you staying up here?"

"Just a few more days," he said. "I leave on Saturday."

"We're leaving together," Jane said. "Work calls for some of us!"

"So soon? What a shame. Richard, you'll have to visit again before you go. Maybe we could all meet up for a drink in the Hawker pub tomorrow night? How about that, Jane?"

"Sorry, no can do," Jane said. "My cousins are coming down from Leigh Creek tomorrow, arriving about lunchtime, staying for a big family barbecue. It's my dad's birthday."

"How lovely," Genevieve said, smiling like a shark. "But Richard doesn't need to be there the whole day, does he?

Richard, how about we come and get you from Jane's place tomorrow morning? We can take you on a sightseeing tour ourselves, and drop you back to Jane's by late afternoon. So you can still meet all of her cousins, but have a brand-new outback experience with us too. There's an incredible view from Pugilist Hill—isn't there, Lindy? You go there a lot, don't you?"

"All the time," Lindy said, after a kick under the table from Victoria. "It's, um—"

"Breathtaking," Victoria said.

"Breathtaking," Lindy repeated.

"That sounds great," Richard said, slightly too quickly. "If you don't mind, Jane?"

"Of course Jane doesn't mind!" Genevieve said, ignoring Jane's stormy expression. "She knows all about country hospitality. And Richard will still get plenty of time with your family, Jane, promise. It's the perfect arrangement."

Genevieve played her final card as they were walking Jane and Richard out to their car. "Oh damn, I've just remembered Victoria and I promised to take Ig to Port Augusta tomorrow, didn't we, Ig? So you'll have to take Richard sightseeing on your own, Lindy. Is that okay? You don't mind, Richard, do you? It would be much more fun with all of us Gillespies, but Lindy's okay once you get used to her."

"I'm sure we'll be fine on our own," Richard said, smiling.

Jane said nothing. Her expression was enough.

"Well, that's wonderful," Genevieve said. "We're all organized. I love it when things fall into place spontaneously like that, Victoria, don't you?"

"I certainly do, Genevieve."

Richard leaned out of the passenger window as the car started to move. "See you tomorrow, Lindy."

"See you then, Richard!"

Lindy waited until the car was out of sight, then hugged them all enthusiastically, even kissing Ig. "Thank you! You were fantastic! If Richard and I get married, I want you all in the bridal party!"

After she'd gone inside, Ig wiped his cheek and turned to Genevieve.

"So is that true about Port Augusta?"

"It's a long drive, Ig. And it's so hot."

"I like driving. And the car has air-conditioning," Ig said.

"And we do actually need to go to a pharmacist, Genevieve," Victoria said pointedly. "Soon."

"Yes, you're right. We do," Genevieve said. "Okay, Ig, we're on."

"What about Celia?" Victoria asked. "Should we invite her?"

"Are you joking?" Genevieve said. "You didn't hear me say that, Ig, did you?"

"No," he said. "But can Robbie come?"

"Of course," Genevieve said, tousling his hair as they walked inside. "He can drive."

TWENTY-SEVEN

In her Adelaide hotel room at lunchtime the next day, Angela was still in bed. She'd had plans to go to a film, do some shopping, take a walk along the river, have lunch out. Instead, she hadn't left the room. She had slept in. Ordered room service breakfast. Slept some more. She had just eaten room service lunch too. She'd had only quick, polite exchanges with the two young porters who delivered her meals. The food was delicious. She'd left her tray out to be collected, as requested. Not even a dish to be washed.

She had watched two programs on the enormous TV. A chat show from America she had never seen before but found compelling. And a movie starring the actress who had demanded Genevieve's sacking. Angela had taken pleasure in switching that off as soon as she recognized her.

Around two, her mobile phone rang. She didn't answer it. Only when it stopped ringing did she check to see who it had been. Genevieve. She felt a flash of guilt, then remembered she was supposed to be having tests. Genevieve would assume that was where she was, not worry too much about the fact she hadn't answered. The missed call broke into her hotel room bubble, though. She thought about what lay ahead. The four-hour drive home tomorrow, back to the tension between her and Nick, Celia watching it all, sowing seeds of discord in her sly way. The fun but also the noise of the children. She thought of her Christmas letter too. It was still out there somewhere, possibly being forwarded on and on, like some virus that she'd unknowingly propagated. She'd stopped checking her e-mails in recent days, finding the replies too much to take. She wasn't going to check them here either. Why bring the outside world in?

But she did need to return a phone call.

Genevieve answered after three rings. "Mum, hi!"

"Where are you? Hawker again? It's a great signal."

"No, the big smoke this time. Port Augusta. We brought Ig here for the day because we are such kind big sisters. Lindy's at home hyperventilating. She's spending the afternoon with her dreamboat. Where are you? How are the tests going?"

"Great. Four down, four to go. But they can't do the rest until late tomorrow afternoon. So I do have to stay a third night."

"You're making this all up, aren't you? You actually haven't left the hotel room, have you?"

First Joan, now Genevieve. Were they mind readers? "I wish," she said vaguely. "Could you let your dad know?"

"Of course. And that makes great sense to stay another night. Enjoy yourself. Hang on, Ig's here. He wants to know, are you happy with the hotel or do you want us to find you a better one?"

"Tell him I love it. You chose the best one in town. I'd better go. Love to you all."

"Love to you too."

Her conscience niggled at her again after she hung up. How would she explain it when she had to come back again in a week to do the real tests? There was no point worrying about it now.

She jumped as her mobile phone rang again. It was Joan.

"So, how are you getting on? What were the tests like?"

"They were actually fine," she lied. "I'm just back in the hotel room now."

"Wish I'd insisted I come down with you. We could have been kicking up our heels in Adelaide together. So, what are you going to do tonight?"

"I might just order room service, I think. I can feel a bit of a headache again."

"I'm not surprised. Those tests have to be stressful. Why rush back? Why don't you spoil yourself and book in for another night? Let me treat you. You deserve it. You've had a big few weeks."

Angela was taken aback to find her eyes filling with tears. She wished she'd told Joan the truth from the start. She'd do it face-to-face, she decided. For now, she told Joan what she'd just told Genevieve.

Joan whistled. "Three full days of tests? They are being thorough. That's a good sign, I guess. But don't worry about those tonight. Forget about all of us too. Have some Angela time."

Angela took her at her word. She ordered room service dinner, at what felt like the luxuriously early time of six p.m. She even had a glass of wine. There were three films she'd have liked to see, but she didn't turn on the TV. Instead, she turned off the lights in her suite, opened the curtains wide and sat by the window.

The blue faded out of the sky. The sun slowly sank, sending up flashes of bright orange, red, even a dark pink. The buildings below changed from sun-kissed stone to darker purple shades. The lights along the river glowed, sending their reflections into the water. Beyond, she could see streetlights, houselights, moving car lights. People everywhere she looked, going home, heading to work, meeting friends, going for a drink, to see a film, eat dinner. All connected, so close to one another. Sometimes being in the city after all the space on Errigal was quite overwhelming. More lights came on. So many different colors—neon signs in bright colors, red lights from the backs of cars, the blinking orange lights of indicators.

The room was air-conditioned, but she could imagine the heat outside rising up. She'd seen the forecast earlier. Another heat wave was on the way: 110 degrees tomorrow, the high temperatures expected to last for a week.

She had a memory flash of her first summer on Errigal. They'd married in the autumn. It was six months before she discovered what a summer in the outback could be like. The ground that had been green turned brown. The sun beat down, day after day. She'd coped easily enough with the winter hardships—the frost, having to wait for pipes to thaw, cold rooms. She was used to that from her English background. In fact, the cold of the Australian winter had taken her by surprise. She'd written about it in one of her Christmas letters. *I thought the sun was supposed to shine all year round here in Australia. I've been had!* Nick had lit the open fires in their bedroom, the living room and the kitchen. The homestead was so big, but they stayed cozy in the main rooms. When summer did arrive, the thick walls and high ceilings came into their own.

It wasn't just the weather she'd grown accustomed to. In her early years on the station, she'd learned to drive not only the car, but also the 4WD, the tractor and the motorbike. She'd learned to operate the UHF radio in all the vehicles. She'd grown used to the kerosene fridge. She'd come to grips with the party telephone line they had had in the early days too, recognizing which series of rings was theirs, which rings to ignore. She'd learned to hang up if she picked up the phone and heard voices already on the line, hard as it was to fight the temptation to eavesdrop. She'd even learned how to use a gun, in case she ever needed to shoot a snake. She had another memory flash, of the day Nick had taught her.

"I'm not exactly Annie Oakley, am I?" she said at the end of that first lesson, looking at all the cans she'd managed to miss.

"Not yet," he'd said. "But you'll get there."

A week later, while he was out, she spent an afternoon practicing. She tried to remember his instructions. He'd told her to aim at the fence line, where the snakes were most often found. So she did, again and again.

"What happened to the fence?" he said as soon as he got home.

She stood beside him as he tried his best not to laugh. Their new corrugated iron fence now had hundreds of tiny pellet shots in it. It looked like a lace curtain.

"It looks quite pretty, don't you think?" she said. "Lets the light in now."

He'd just laughed, planting a kiss on her head.

Her memories were interrupted by a knock at the door. "Housekeeping," a voice called.

She opened the door, politely declined the offer of the turndown service but did take the chocolate. She moved back to the window, slowly eating the chocolate, looking out over the city, a blanket of lights beneath her. She was high up, on the twentieth floor, but she suddenly wished she were even higher, that she could open the window, feel the fresh air.

Another memory flash. This one from just before she and Nick were married. They had all been in Adelaide, Nick and his parents staying with Celia and her husband in their big house in North Adelaide, Angela and her parents, newly arrived from London, in a small, friendly hotel not far from there. There had been gatherings every night with Gillespie cousins, old school friends, many neighbors. A Gillespie wedding was a big deal, Angela had discovered.

Two nights before the big day, Nick had called her hotel room. She'd already been in bed. "See you downstairs in ten minutes," he said. He'd hung up before she had a chance to ask more.

She'd dressed again and gone downstairs, just as he

pulled up at the curb. "Where are we going?" she'd asked. "Wait and see," he'd said.

He'd driven her across the city center, through the suburbs, up into the foothills, then up even higher. Twenty minutes later, they were pulling into a car park high above the city. There were cars all around them, most with couples inside. Kissing couples. It was a lookout spot. The bright lights of the city formed a carpet of color below them, right out to the sea on the horizon. It was beautiful.

She felt like a teenager who'd sneaked out behind her parents' back, she told him.

"That was the idea," he said. "I feel like I haven't seen you for days. I missed you."

They kissed. A little more than kissed. She'd missed him so much too. It was wonderful having her parents there, exciting to be caught up in the wedding preparations, but she was longing for it to be just the two of them again. On their honeymoon first. They were going on a driving holiday, all the way along the coast to Sydney, taking their time, stopping when they felt like it. After that, it would be back to Errigal to start their new life together.

She told him how much she loved him. How happy she was to be marrying him.

"Not as happy as I am," he said.

He'd kissed her again. He'd promised that he would always love her, always look after her. No matter what.

At her hotel window, Angela had to blink away sudden tears. She must have cried more in the past weeks than she had in months. An urgent longing to talk to Nick took hold of her. She wanted to be close to him. To take him in her arms, kiss him, remind him of all they had been through together. Assure him that they could get through this too. Keep talking to him, keep telling him how much she loved him until she broke through that wall they had built between them.

She went as far as picking up the phone and starting to dial their number. But then she hung up. It was impossible to have a private conversation in their kitchen. She couldn't call him on his mobile either. But it suddenly seemed urgent to tell him how she felt. Tell him she still loved him.

She could e-mail him. Of course. She could go downstairs to the business center right now and write to him. And if he wasn't in the office tonight, he would read it in the morning.

She dressed hurriedly, pulling on her shoes, picking up her handbag. In the elevator on the way down, she realized something else. Even two days away from Errigal had helped her. She hadn't had a headache since the one in the specialist's waiting room. She hadn't had to once conjure up Will or Lexie.

Perhaps getting away from there would help Nick just as much. Even for a day or two.

As she stepped out into the foyer, she decided. She wasn't only going to tell him that she loved him, that she had never stopped loving him. She was going to ask him to drive down to Adelaide as soon as he could tomorrow. Even to leave tonight if he got her message in time. Drive down and join her here in this beautiful hotel. Just the two of them. For one night. Two nights. More, if necessary. For however long it took for them to start talking to each other again. The way they used to.

The business center was closed. Angela went over to the receptionist. The woman was very apologetic, but they were doing maintenance work on the computers. There'd been a network crash. But they would be up and running again in an hour, if Angela didn't mind waiting. If it was urgent, if she just needed to check her e-mails, she was of course welcome to use the reception computer.

Angela didn't think she could write the e-mail to Nick with someone standing beside her waiting. She'd liked the idea of sitting on her own in the business center, taking her time, carefully choosing her words. Thank you but no, she said. She'd come back in an hour instead.

She took a seat in the foyer, trying to decide what to do next. Go back up to her room? Go for a walk? Then she saw a sign by the elevator. "Garage Downstairs." Her car was there. She hadn't been outside the hotel in nearly two days. She knew exactly where she wanted to go.

She asked the concierge for directions. Just a half-hour drive, he assured her, marking the way on a map. A beautiful view. Well worth the journey.

"Have you ever been up there?" he asked.

"Not for years," she said.

"Nothing like a trip down memory lane, then," he said.

"Exactly," she answered.

She was smiling as she waited for the elevator to take her down to the garage.

TWENTY-EIGHT

On a stretch of highway outside Port Augusta, Genevieve, Victoria and Ig were sitting in their car with half-eaten fries and hamburger wrappers on the seats beside them. They were parked outside a McDonald's. Genevieve and Ig were in the front, Victoria in the back. She hadn't been happy about it all day.

"I'm the adult; Ig, you're the kid," she'd said as they set off that morning. "Kids sit in the back."

"No, it's my special day out. Robbie and I want to sit in the front."

"But there's more room for you and Robbie in the back."

"We've got all the room we need in the front."

She'd had to give up when he buckled himself in, locked the door and pulled faces at her through the window.

"Can I please have a sundae?" he asked.

"Can you actually physically fit any more junk food into your body?" Genevieve asked.

"I've only had a bit."

"KFC for brunch, McDonald's for afternoon tea. And now you want a sugar hit as well."

"I never get this stuff. It's a treat. You said you'd spoil me today."

"I said I'd spoil you, not stuff you to the gills with dangerous additives."

"So can I have a sundae? I'll get you both one as well."

In the backseat, Victoria groaned.

"No, thanks," Genevieve said. "I can't move as it is. All right, Ig. But you have to go in and get it. I'm not your slave."

"Cool," he said. He took the money from her and was out of the car in seconds.

Victoria was rummaging in Genevieve's handbag. She took out a paper bag and looked inside at the contents. "Do you suppose we should use these pregnancy tests now?"

"In the McDonald's toilet? Lovely idea."

"It could still be stress, couldn't it? Or jet lag in your case? Even this many days late?"

"I hope so," Genevieve said.

"I really hope so," Victoria said.

A few minutes later, Ig returned. He was carrying three sundaes in a cardboard tray.

"That was nice of you to buy all of those with my money, Ig," Genevieve said. "But I told you I couldn't eat another thing. Nor could Victoria."

"I thought you were joking. Sorry. I'll have to eat them all myself." He started on the first one.

One hundred kilometers away, on the road between the Pugilist Hill lookout and the Gillespies' homestead, Richard was watching while Lindy changed the tire at the front of the ute.

"I'm very embarrassed," he said.

"Why?" she said, looking up.

"I'm the man. I should be doing that."

"But you don't know how to change a tire. I do."

"I'm embarrassed I don't know how to change a tire."

Lindy shrugged. "You probably know how to do stuff I don't know how to do."

"What else do you know how to do?"

"Kill a snake. Shoot a gun. Muster sheep. Just ordinary stuff like that."

"Can you really do all those things?"

"I grew up out here, Richard. We didn't just sit around praying for rain."

"No, I guess not."

They were silent for a moment as Lindy took off the flat tire and moved the spare into place.

"That was a great trip today," he said. "Thanks again. It's incredible out here."

"Jane will kill me for bringing you back late."

"We won't be that late. And she knows why. It's not as if we deliberately got a flat tire."

Lindy had used the UHF radio in the car to contact the Lawsons. She hadn't spoken to Jane but to her brother Fred, who'd been very warm and friendly. He'd also asked after

Victoria. She was brilliant, Lindy had said, laying it on thick.

As she started to tighten the last bolt, she heard a noise from the radio.

"Lindy? Are you there?"

"Richard, can you get that? Just pick up the handset and press that button."

He sat in the front seat and fumbled for the handset, dropping it and disconnecting the call. "I'm really failing on the macho front, aren't I? Can't change a tire. Can't use a walkie-talkie."

"It's a UHF radio, not a walkie-talkie," Lindy said, wiping her hands on an old piece of cloth. She leaned past him and picked up the handset again. "Jane?"

"Lindy? Where are you?"

"On the side of the road with Richard. About ten kilometers from our house."

"He's supposed to be back here by now."

"I know. Sorry. We got a flat tire. Didn't Fred give you my message?"

"Yes, but how long does it take to change a tire?"

"As long as it takes. Why? What do you think I'm doing, Jane?"

"It's obvious. You're trying to keep Richard to yourself for as long as you can."

"Actually, you're right," Lindy said. "I am." She pressed the button and finished the connection. Then she turned to Richard and pulled a face. "She'll really kill me now."

"You can drop me off at the gate to their property and I'll run in."

"Their gate is about a kilometer from their house. You'll need to run fast."

"Has she always been jealous of you?"

"Jealous of me? Are you joking?"

"That's what it looks like. She goes to a lot of trouble to put you down. Why does she do that? Because she's threatened by you."

"You really think she's jealous of me?"

"Of your whole family, I reckon. She talks about you a lot. In fact, she hasn't shut up about the Gillespies since I got here. All of you and your mother's Christmas letter, especially."

Lindy shut her eyes. "Don't talk to me about that letter. I can't bear it."

"But it was a brilliant letter. The Lawsons had a whole file of your mother's letters. I read a few of them."

"How nice of Jane to show you."

"I enjoyed them, Lindy. Your family sounds like fun."

"Yes. So much fun. If you like asylums. I suppose they acted this year's letter out in front of you?" She could tell by his expression that they had. "It must have been hilarious."

"It was. But I was laughing at them, Lindy, not at your family."

"Sure."

"How can I fix this? I know—can I drive? Let me at least show you the tiniest element of masculinity."

"Do you know how to?"

"Please, Lindy, I'm trying to salvage some pride here."

"It's pretty hard on these roads. You have to go really slow, be careful passing other cars, watch out for stones—"

"Please."

She gave him the keys. He smiled at her and she felt a little thump in her chest.

"That last letter from your mum was pretty memorable," he said as they started moving again. "Maybe she'll start a trend. No one usually tells the truth in those letters, do they?"

"I don't know and I don't care. If she ever sends out another one, I'm divorcing myself from the family and never coming home for Christmas again. Slower, Richard. I know it feels like you're crawling but you have to take it really easy out here."

They drove on for five minutes. "See," he said, smiling over at her. "I do have some macho cells in my body."

"You're a very good driver. You're just going a bit fast again. And there's a car coming."

It was a tourist 4WD, also going too fast.

Lindy put her hand on the dashboard. "Richard, seriously. I know these roads. Can you slow down a bit; otherwise—"

The other car passed them. A stone flew up into the windshield. It shattered.

Richard slammed on the brakes. They skidded to a stop. He turned to her. "That happens?"

"That happens," Lindy said.

TWENTY-NINE

Angela was halfway to the lookout point. She wouldn't stay long, she decided. She was beginning to regret even deciding to come. She could have been back in her hotel room, enjoying the luxury and comfort while she waited for the computer. Not making this solo drive to what was probably still a late-night lovers' lookout. Some sight she'd be, there on her own as couples smooched all around her. She turned on the radio, a talk show filling the car with noise.

At least the concierge's directions were easy to follow. The roads were quiet through the suburbs. As she drove closer to the foothills, the houses grew farther apart. She drove around bend after bend, past road signs warning of corkscrew turns. She loved to drive but this wasn't easy, an unfamiliar road, at night.

Another sign appeared. One kilometer to go. More tight bends ahead.

She had slowed to the recommended forty kilometers when she saw it. An enormous huntsman spider on her windshield. Not outside the car, inside the car. Centimeters in front of her. The fat body, the long legs, as big as her hand. She screamed. She took her hands off the wheel for only a second. It was long enough. The car went out of control, veered to the left and slid off the bitumen.

The last thing she saw was a huge gum tree coming toward her.

The last thing she felt was a searing pain in her left side as her body was thrown against the steering wheel.

The last thing she heard was the car horn, blaring in response to her sudden weight against it.

The last thing she tasted was her own blood.

———

Angela's whole body felt so strange. So heavy. Her eyelids felt like they were glued shut. She couldn't seem to open them. Her left side hurt. A lot. Not just her left side. Her chest too. Her head. Her arms. Everything.

Had she just been in a car crash? She must have. That had to be why she was slumped against the steering wheel like this. But how had it happened? Had someone run into her? As she tried once again to open her eyes, she became aware of something.

Voices. Lots of voices from lots of people. Gathered around her car. All talking about her.

"Is she alive?"

"I think so. Look, she's breathing."

"I saw the whole thing! Her car just suddenly ran off the road and hit that tree. Is she okay?"

Yes, thank you, she wanted to tell them. But she couldn't seem to make a sound.

"What if the car explodes? Should we try to get her out?"

The car might explode? Oh yes, please, do get me out!

"No, don't move her. She might have spinal damage."

I don't think I have, she wanted to tell them. But my left side hurts. It really hurts.

"Should we risk it? I can smell gas."

"No, don't. Here comes the ambulance now. Let them do it."

She waited, listening for sirens. Nothing. All she could hear were the voices. But was *hear* the right word? No, she decided. It was more like she was "seeing" the words somehow, as though they were subtitles on a film, lines of words running across the inside of her eyelids. But how could that be?

Had she actually died in this accident? Was she having a peculiar out-of-body experience? Somehow drifting away from her physical self, looking down on the last moments of her life?

"Stand back, please. Everyone, stand back! Let the paramedics through."

She waited, wondering whether she would be able to feel them reaching for her. There was nothing.

Only more voices.

"That's it. Lift her out. Careful, now."

"Her pulse is low. It's gone. Stand back, everyone. Stand back. Defib!"

Pain, a rush of something, like sparks, fireworks behind her eyes, in her head, and a force of something. It felt like someone had shoved her, hard, in the chest. There was still that excruciating pain in her left side. She wished she could talk out loud, tell them about that pain, but she couldn't speak or open her eyes. There was just more of those voices, more talk of her pulse, her lack of pulse. They all sounded so serious. They were talking about the hospital. They were taking her to the hospital. She was in the back of the ambulance being taken to the hospital.

A short time later, or perhaps it was a long time later, there were more voices, more discussions.

"Can someone check for ID?"

"Here it is. I've got it."

Was she at the hospital now? It sounded as though the police were there too, as well as the paramedics. They'd found not only her driver's license but an In Case of Emergency card, listing all her personal details.

"Everything's here, names, numbers, addresses."

"If only everyone was that organized."

She couldn't remember filling out anything like that.

"Her name's Angela Gillespie. She's fifty-five years old."

Angela Gillespie? The Angela part was right, but that wasn't her surname. Her name was Angela Richardson. They must have found someone else's handbag. Someone who happened to have the same first name. She wanted to explain, but she still couldn't make a sound.

"Next of kin is her husband, Nick Gillespie. According to this, she's got four kids—three daughters and a son. She lives somewhere called Errigal via Hawker."

"Hawker? That's practically the outback, isn't it? Wonder what she was doing here in Adelaide."

Adelaide? The outback? A husband called Nick? Four kids? No, no. They had it all wrong. She was married to Will. He'd been her childhood sweetheart. She'd kept her own surname, Richardson. Will hadn't minded at all. He'd always wanted her to be independent. They had one daughter called Lexie. And what was this about Adelaide, the outback? She and Will and Lexie lived in London, not the outback. London, England. The other side of the world. There must have been a terrible mix-up. They were talking about another Angela. A different Angela. She tried once again to open her eyes, tried to speak. She couldn't.

Try the husband first.

Yes, please call my husband, she wanted to say, to shout somehow. Call Will. He'd sort all this out in an instant. He was probably already worrying where she was. Not that she could remember where she was going or where she'd been when she had the crash, but surely he'd be expecting her home by now.

She wished she could tell them that, tell them every-thing. But Will would get to the bottom of it all.

Beside her, one of the voices began to make a phone call. She had to strain to make out the words. It was as if the letters on her eyelids were growing smaller, fainter. As if she were moving away, drifting somewhere. Her left side was really hurting now. She felt like she was plummeting into velvety darkness. Not into sleep, but something deeper, heavier . . .

"Mr. Gillespie? Nick Gillespie? Is your wife Angela Gillespie, aged fifty-five? Does she drive a blue Holden Commodore? Mr. Gillespie, I'm sorry. I've got bad news. Your wife has been in a car accident. She's alive, but she's unconscious. . . . Yes, yes, I promise you, she's alive—"

Angela didn't hear the rest. She was already far, far away.

THIRTY

The landline rang ten times before Nick remembered he and Celia were the only ones in the house. The twins and Ig were in Port Augusta, due back soon. Lindy was dropping that friend of hers back at the Lawsons.

Celia was in the living room, with the TV turned up to full volume, watching a soap opera. "Phone's ringing, Nick," she said as he went past. "I thought there was no point getting it; it wouldn't be for me."

Five minutes later, he was back, ashen-faced.

She stared up at him. "What's wrong?"

"That was the police. It's Angela. She's had a car accident. She's in the hospital. It's serious."

"A car accident? Where?"

"In the Adelaide Hills."

"The Hills? What on earth was she doing there?"

"I don't know, Celia." He lowered his voice. "I'm sorry. I don't know. I need to get to Adelaide now, as soon as I can." He stopped. "I don't have a car. All the cars are gone. Angela in hers. Lindy's in my 4WD. Genevieve's got—Oh Jesus."

"Ring Joan."

"She's an hour away."

"Contact the girls. See how far away they are."

He took out his mobile phone and dialed. "No answer. No bloody answer."

"But you can't get a signal from here, can you? I meant their car radios."

"I'm not thinking straight." He went to the radio in the kitchen and tried Genevieve first. "Answer," he said under his breath. "Come on, answer."

Genevieve's voice filled the room. "Ten-four, Big Daddy, you're coming in loud and clear."

"Where are you? I need the car."

"Hello, Dad. We missed you too."

"Your mother's had a car crash. I have to get to Adelaide. Tonight. Now. It's serious."

"Oh, Dad. Oh, God. Is she all right?"

"She's in the hospital. They're operating. I don't know any more than that. I have to get there now."

"Oh, God. You don't have a car, do you? We're not far, Dad. Half an hour maybe. I'll be there as fast as I can."

"Hurry," he said.

Lindy and Richard were still on the side of the road, in the spot where the windshield had shattered. The other car had driven on, oblivious. Their intention had been to take out the broken windshield glass and keep driving—with Lindy at the wheel—but somewhere in the process, the idea of carefully picking out pieces of broken glass had been replaced with the idea of kissing. They had now been kissing for twenty minutes. Lindy couldn't believe how wonderful it felt. To be here, outside in the cool night air, pressed against the car, her arms around a man who had his arms around her. Any more of these deep, amazing kisses, and that blanket on the seat of her dad's 4WD would be on the ground beside them, and them on top of it. Richard's hands were already inside her shirt, on her skin. Her hands had long been on the bare skin of his back. She could hear small moans of pleasure. Her name, spoken again and again.

"Lindy, answer me. Lindy."

It was her father. Her father's voice coming out of the radio in the car.

"Can you ignore it?" Richard murmured.

"Sure," she said.

"Lindy, where the hell are you? Answer me."

She broke away, reluctantly. "Sorry. I'll be right back."

She picked up the handset. "Dad?"

"Get home now."

"But, Dad, I—"

"I need the 4WD. Your mother's had a car accident."

"What? Where?"

"In Adelaide. She's in the hospital. I need to get there and I haven't got a bloody car."

"Dad, the windshield, it's smashed."

"Fuck. Okay. Forget it, Lindy."

He hung up.

Richard had heard it all. "Lindy, what is—"

She got into the car and started the engine. "Get in," she said. "We have to go."

They'd gone only twenty meters when the radio crackled into life again.

Lindy snatched it up. "We're on our way. As fast as we can."

"About time, Lindy." It was Jane Lawson. "Is this some kind of joke? What now? Overheated engine? Another flat tire? My cousins are about to leave and—"

About to explain about her mother, her father, the windshield, Lindy lost patience. She said something she'd wanted to say to Jane Lawson for years, then replaced the handset.

"Wow," Richard said. "That told her."

Lindy just kept driving.

Genevieve saw the light ahead first. They'd turned off the main road and were now on the dirt road to Errigal, traveling at forty kilometers an hour, the fastest she dared to go. It wasn't a car or a truck coming toward them. "It's a motorbike," Ig said. Their father was coming along the road toward them on the station motorbike.

She pulled onto the side of the road. He did the same. He leaped off the bike, holding out his hand for the car keys. Genevieve handed them over.

"But we're coming with you, Dad," she said. "All of us."

He'd just started the car and was turning back toward

the main road when the radio crackled. It was Lindy. "Genevieve? It's me. Quick, answer."

"Does she know, Dad?"

Nick nodded.

Genevieve picked up the handset. "We're on our way, Lindy. You'll have to follow us."

"I can't. My windshield's gone. Wait for me, please. I can see your lights. I'm not far."

"Dad?" Genevieve put her hand on her father's arm. "Dad, please. She has to be with us too."

Nick took his foot off the pedal. They waited.

Lindy was parking behind them less than five minutes later. She ran across to the car, got into the back with Victoria and Ig. Then she got out again and ran back.

"Richard, sorry. Here are the keys. Just drive slowly. Keep going in that direction. Past our house for another forty minutes. The Lawsons is the only other station on this road. You'll be fine."

"But I don't know where I am."

"You'll find your way. Use the radio if you get lost."

"I don't know how to use it."

"You'll work it out. I'm sorry."

He stood watching as Lindy and her family drove away.

The car filled with voices as Lindy and Genevieve fired questions at their father. Ig started to cry. Victoria tried to soothe him. Nick eventually held up his hand to silence them.

"Stop it, everyone. Just stop it. Just shut up. Please," he snapped finally.

"Dad, please, tell us everything." It was Victoria, her voice quiet. "Now we're all here."

"The police rang. She had an accident. In the Adelaide Hills. She's been seriously hurt. They rushed her to the hospital. She's being operated on now."

"What do they mean by 'seriously hurt'?"

Nick glanced back at Ig. Victoria had both arms around him.

"He needs to know, Dad," Genevieve said. "We all do."

"She's had some kind of internal bleeding. It caused a sudden drop in her blood pressure." He hesitated. "The paramedics had to restart her heart."

Lindy gasped.

"Did she die?" Ig asked.

Victoria held him even tighter. "No, Ig. There were paramedics there. They kept her heart going."

"But if they hadn't been there—"

"They were there, Ig," Victoria said. "They got her to the hospital. She's in the hospital now. The very best place."

A mobile phone rang. They'd just come into signal range. Nick scrabbled inside his shirt pocket, took it out and gave it to Genevieve.

It was a nurse from the hospital with an update. Genevieve asked questions, listened for several minutes. She told the caller they were on the way, that they'd be there in less than four hours.

"Mum's still in the operating theater," she reported. "It's a ruptured spleen. That's what caused the bleeding and the lack of oxygen. They had to—"

"They had to what?" Nick said. "Genevieve, what?"

"Her heart stopped again. They had to use the defibrillator

on her in the hospital, in the operating theater. But she's alive. She's still alive."

In the backseat, Victoria held Ig tighter.

Lindy was crying. "Will she be all right? Dad?"

"Of course she will," he said. "Of course."

They prayed. All of them, for the rest of the journey. Prayers that they hadn't said in years, since school, since the days they used to go to Mass every Sunday. Hail Marys. Our Fathers. Over and over again, until they reached the outskirts of Adelaide. They made only one stop, for gas. Only Nick got out. In the light from the gas station, their faces took on a strange golden glow.

Ig spoke, his voice clear in the silence of the car. "Robbie says she'll be fine."

Lindy sobbed. "It's not the time for Robbie, Ig."

"He says she'll be fine!" He shouted the words.

Victoria held him tight again, stroking his hair, kissing his head. "It's okay, Ig. It's okay."

"He knows about this stuff," Ig said. He was crying again now too. "He told me to tell you."

"Tell him thanks, Ig," Genevieve said.

"He's here. Thank him yourself."

Their father was approaching. Genevieve exchanged a glance with Victoria, who nodded.

Genevieve turned right around in the seat and addressed a spot somewhere between Ig and Victoria. "Thanks, Robbie. We're really glad to hear that."

"Ready?" Nick said as he got back into the driver's seat.

"Ready," they said.

Thirty minutes later, Nick pulled up in front of the main hospital in the center of the city. All four doors of the car opened.

"Go, Dad," Genevieve said. "I'll find a garage. I'll find you all."

"I'll stay with you," Victoria said.

"No," Genevieve said. "Go now, please. One of us should be there if—"

"She's going to be all right." Victoria's tone was fierce.

"I know. Just go, Victoria. I'll be there as quick as I can."

Victoria turned and ran after her father, sister and little brother.

It took Genevieve twenty minutes to find a garage and then find her family. They were sitting in a small waiting room near the operating theaters. There were plenty of spare seats but they were in a huddle in the corner, sitting side by side. Her father was staring across the room. Lindy and Victoria were talking softly to each other. Ig was talking too. Smiling even. As Genevieve got closer, she realized he was talking to Robbie. About a TV program they both liked.

"What's happened?" Genevieve asked her father. "Is she—"

"They're still operating," Nick said.

Beside him, Ig laughed. "No, that's not the funny bit. The best bit is when the duck goes—"

Genevieve was shocked at her rush of temper. "Ig, no, not now. Tell Robbie to be quiet."

His expression turned mutinous. "No," he said.

"Then at least whisper to him, will you?" She turned

back to her father. "Have they told you anything else? How it's going? How long they'll be?"

Nick shook his head. "Nothing new."

Victoria reached up and took her twin's hand. "We just have to wait, Genevieve."

THIRTY-ONE

One hour went past. Two. Genevieve became the family's spokeswoman. After a third visit to the nurses' station, she had more news. Angela was out of the operating theater.

"She's in intensive care. They had to remove her spleen, but the operation went well."

Ig raised his hand as if he were in school. "I don't know what a spleen is."

Genevieve's expression softened. "It's here, Ig," she said, pointing to her left side. "I had to ask too. It cleans your blood. But you can live without it."

"So they think she'll be all right?" Lindy said. "That was all they had to do?"

"They think so, but they don't know. She hasn't regained consciousness yet."

Nick was quiet. Victoria touched his shoulder. He flinched.

"Dad, it'll be okay. She's come through the operation. She'll be okay. She will."

"It's my fault," he said. "I should have driven her down here. What kind of husband lets his wife be tested for a brain tumor on her own?"

"It's not your fault," Genevieve said. "It's no one's fault. She wanted to be on her own. And for whatever reason, she went for a drive tonight and had an accident. An *accident*. It's not your fault, Dad."

"But what was she doing up in the Hills?" Lindy said. "That's miles from the hotel, isn't it?"

"Maybe she just needed a distraction after all those tests," Genevieve said. "Maybe she wanted some fresh air. When she wakes up, she'll tell us everything. Lindy, can you ring Celia and update her? And you better contact Horrible Jane too, find out if your Richard got home safely, or if we need to call in a search party. I'll ring Joan."

Joan was shocked. "But why was she even up there? Should she have been driving after those tests? And is that it injury-wise? Do you want me to come down? What about Celia? Is she all right on her own?"

Genevieve didn't have any of the answers.

A nurse told them the doctor would be out to talk to them soon. While they waited, they ate and drank from the vending machines. Ig dozed, his head on Victoria's lap. Lindy kept talking about Richard. He'd made it to Jane's house two hours after she'd left him, a journey that usually took only forty minutes. She was interrupted by the arrival of a doctor, still in scrubs, and one of the nurses. The doctor invited them into a room down the hall.

As they followed them, Lindy became upset. "It's bad news, isn't it?"

"It's not, I promise," the doctor said, overhearing. "It's just more private in here." He waited until Genevieve had shut the door. He explained about the removal of the ruptured spleen. "She's come through the operation well. She's in stable condition."

"Were there any other injuries?" Genevieve asked.

"We're keeping a close eye on her, but her pulse is strong again. The bleeding has stopped. Once she regains consciousness we'll know more, but the tests so far are clear. The best thing you can all do for her now is go home and get some sleep."

"But we live four hours away," Lindy said.

It was Ig who suggested it. Aunt Celia's house was empty. It was only two suburbs away, in North Adelaide. Victoria made the call. It was well after midnight, but Celia was still awake. She called her neighbor, then called back. He'd be there waiting with the key. It was a five-bedroom house. Room for them all.

The nurse reassured them before they left. "You all need some sleep. We've got your number. You're ten minutes away if anything happens. But it won't. She's stable."

As they headed to the car, Genevieve hugged Ig. "That was a brain wave about Celia's house, Ig. Well done."

"Robbie thought of it, not me," he said.

Celia's neighbor was waiting outside the house. Ig had fallen asleep on the way. Nick carried him inside and put him to bed. Genevieve did all the talking, thanking the neighbor, filling him in on Angela's condition. He and his wife had already turned on the lights and air-conditioning, made up the beds. They'd also left a big plate of sandwiches in the kitchen. The Gillespies were touched by their kindness.

Soon afterward, Nick said good night and went to bed. Genevieve, Victoria and Lindy sat in the kitchen, eating the sandwiches, drinking tea, going over all that had happened, every detail the nurse and doctor had said. Lindy was checking her phone for messages.

She smiled. "There's one from Richard. 'Thinking of you. xx.' Two kisses. That's a good sign, isn't it? Two kisses? Should I write back now, or would it be better to wait for a while?"

"You are unbelievable," Genevieve said. "Don't let a little minor thing like your mother being in intensive care get in the way of a possible boyfriend, will you?"

"Genevieve—," Victoria said.

"No, Victoria, this needs to be said. Seriously, Lindy? 'Sorry about your accident, Mum, but look, some hipster boy sent me two text kisses—that's much more important.'"

Lindy stood up, eyes welling. "That's not fair! I'm as scared about her as you are, okay? I just had a nice thing happen to me today and it's helping me to think about him as well as Mum. But oh no, you have to ruin it like you try to ruin everything good that ever happens to me."

"That is complete garbage. You selfish, self-centered little—"

Victoria interrupted. "Genevieve, stop it. We're all tired. It's been a bad day."

Lindy snatched her phone. "I'm going to bed." At the

door, she paused, looking back at Victoria, not Genevieve. "Mum will be all right, won't she?"

"Of course she will."

Lindy looked at her other sister. "Sorry, Genevieve."

Genevieve rubbed her eyes. "It's okay, Lindy. I'm sorry too. Sleep well."

They waited until they heard her bedroom door close.

"Sorry," Victoria said. "I couldn't bear a fight. Not tonight."

"I'm sorry too. Thanks for stepping in."

"Mum could have died tonight, couldn't she?"

"She could have. But she didn't. Don't think that way."

They reached for each other's hands across the table.

"I don't even know what a spleen looks like," Victoria said.

"Then you won't miss hers, will you?"

They started to laugh. And then suddenly they were both crying.

Ig woke Genevieve just after dawn. She'd barely had any sleep.

"What is it, Ig? Are you okay?"

"Can I get in with you?"

"Sure." She moved over and he wriggled in next to her. He gave her a look. She moved again, making room for Robbie too.

They lay there holding hands until Victoria knocked softly on the door. She came in and sat on the bed. She had some news. Moments later, Lindy came in too, sleepy-eyed. Victoria had woken her as well. She'd knocked on their father's closed bedroom door but got no answer. She'd decided it was best to let him sleep. She'd called the hospital, right at seven a.m. Their mother's condition was still stable. She hadn't regained consciousness yet, but all her vital signs were fine. There was no need to hurry back in. Visiting hours were from ten a.m. They'd be welcome anytime from then on.

They tried to pretend things were normal, that it wasn't strange to be staying here in Celia's too-big, too-grand house while she was back in their homestead. They had showers and dressed in the same clothes. They had nothing else with them. Afterward, they sat around the kitchen table, eating breakfast, as if it were a normal day, a normal morning.

They heard the front door open. Nick walked in, fully dressed, carrying milk and a newspaper.

"Dad!" Lindy said. "We thought you were still in bed."

"I've been at the hospital. I couldn't sleep. I needed to be there with her."

The questions flew at him. How was she? Was she awake? Did she say anything?

She was still unconscious, he told them. There were drips and medical equipment around her, some bruising, but she still looked like herself.

"Can we see her too?" Genevieve asked.

"Later today, they said."

"But she's our mum," Ig said. "Why do we have to wait?"

"She's in a special ward, Ig," Nick said. "She has to be kept safe from any germs."

"I don't have any germs. I had a shower."

"Not those kinds of germs, Ig," Victoria said. "I know— what about you do some drawings for her? Some nice bright ones that she can put by her bed when she wakes up?"

"When will that be?"

They all looked to their father.

"They don't know. Sometime today, they hope."

"I'll draw her some robins," Ig said.

As he fetched pens and paper from Celia's office, the talk turned to practicalities. They needed clothes, groceries. They'd go to the hospital first, and then make further plans.

The eight a.m. news came on the radio. It was like a signal. Their phones started to ring. Word had spread quickly. Joan was first, calling Genevieve for an update. Celia called Nick. There was another message from Richard, on behalf of the Lawsons, saying Angela was in everyone's thoughts.

Genevieve followed her father as he went down the hall to Celia's study. As she watched, he started going through her filing cabinets. She was taken aback as he opened drawer after drawer.

"Should you be doing that?" she said. "Isn't that her private stuff?"

"She told me there's family tree info in here somewhere."

"What?" She felt the same rush of temper she'd felt the evening before with Lindy. "I don't believe this. Mum's lying in the hospital, she was nearly killed, and you're worrying about your family tree?"

He slammed a drawer shut. "Don't talk to me like that."

"Someone has to." She lowered her voice, speaking quickly, furiously. "You think none of us noticed what was going on with you two? That big freeze? We *all* read her Christmas letter, Dad. We all felt hurt. But we got over it. Can't you?"

"This isn't your business, Genevieve. This is between me and your mother."

"It *is* my business. When she wakes up again, Dad, the

minute she wakes up, if you don't sort it out with her and apologize, then I will—"

Lindy appeared at the door. "Has anyone got a phone charger?"

"In my bag," Genevieve snapped. "In the kitchen."

"I just asked, Genevieve. No need to—"

"Lindy, get out and shut the door, would you? Behind you."

Lindy shut it with a slam.

Genevieve turned to her father again. "I know what you're thinking. Who do I think I am, breezing back home again, saying all this stuff. I'm your eldest daughter—that's who. And I would have said something to you eventually, even if Mum hadn't had this accident. This only makes it more urgent. Something's wrong with her, Dad. It's not just the headaches. She's unhappy. Victoria and I noticed it as soon as we saw her at the airport. We think she's lonely. Depressed, even. It's all right for you; you've got a hobby, a new obsession, but what about her? What was she supposed to do day after day, night after night, while you were locked in the office, doing your research, flirting with your precious Carol—"

"That is enough. You've stepped over the line."

"No, I haven't. This is my family and it's my business."

The door opened. It was Lindy again.

Genevieve spun around. "For God's sake, Lindy, now what?"

Lindy held up a paper bag. "Why do you have two pregnancy tests in your handbag?"

THIRTY-TWO

It was nearly lunchtime. They were all back in the hospital. They had the waiting room to themselves. Nick was in one corner, reading through the family tree information he'd found at Celia's. Genevieve was in the other corner, reading a magazine. Ig was quiet, kneeling on the floor, using the seat of a chair as a desk for his drawing.

Lindy was whispering to Victoria. "I've already said sorry to her. What was I supposed to do, pretend I hadn't seen them? They were right at the top of her bag."

"You should have said nothing. Or at least said nothing in front of Dad."

"I didn't think. I was so shocked."

"Sure," Victoria whispered. "So much for the sisterhood."

"I didn't mean to get her into trouble," Lindy insisted.

"She didn't answer me when I asked her about them anyway. She just got even madder, said it was a silly joke and hasn't talked to me since, as if it was all my fault Dad saw them. And why did she have two, if it was just for a joke?"

"I've already told you why, and told Dad why. Because I dared her," Victoria said. "You know how we always dare each other to do embarrassing things."

"When you were fifteen, sure, not thirty-two."

"We're back home; we've regressed. Once and for all, Lindy, this is what happened. When we were in Port Augusta yesterday, I dared her to go into the pharmacist and buy either condoms or a pregnancy testing kit, whichever was the most embarrassing. She chose a pregnancy test. And she got two of them, just to show off. You know what she's like."

"Where was Ig when all of this was going on?"

"Stealing cars and buying drugs? I don't know—talking to Robbie, probably. What is this, an inquest?"

Lindy lowered her voice. "You're sure it's not because she thinks she's pregnant? Or that you are?"

"No, Lindy, I'm not pregnant and neither is Genevieve."

By one p.m. Ig was up to his twentieth drawing. He'd now done enough to cover a wall.

"That's probably plenty, Ig," Genevieve said.

"No, it's not."

"Ig, when they move Mum into the ward, she'll only have a little bit of wall space. She won't be able to display them all."

"She will."

"Ig, seriously."

He put down the pencil and stood up. "I want to see her."

"We all do, sweetheart. But we can't. Not just yet. Remember what the nurse said?"

"I want to see her now. I want to see Mum."

Nick looked up. So did Victoria and Lindy.

Genevieve moved to take Ig in her arms. He pushed her away. "I have to see her. Now."

"You can't, Ig," Nick said. "Not yet. They've asked us to wait until—"

Ig took off across the room and ran down the corridor toward intensive care.

By the time they reached him, two nurses had already caught him. He was crying and struggling. There was a hurried conference in the hallway as Lindy and Genevieve tried to calm him down.

"Ig, she's still unconscious," Genevieve said. "That means she—"

"I know what unconscious means, but she can still hear us, can't she? I just want to see her. I want to see my mum."

A different doctor appeared in front of them. He was young, sweet faced. "Hello, there. Ignatius, is it?"

"We call him Ig," Genevieve said.

"Ig, can you please calm down for me? And especially for your mum?"

Ig went still.

The doctor crouched down until he was at Ig's level. "Ig, I'm sorry you've had to wait. I know it's been hard and I know it feels unfair that she's just over there and you can't see her. You can all go in now. Usually we'd ask you to take turns, but you can go in together as long as you're as quiet as possible and don't stay long."

"Can I talk to her?" Ig asked.

"Of course you can. That's a great idea."

"Can I hold her hand?" Ig said.

The doctor nodded. "I'm sure she'd love that too."

It was Angela, but it wasn't her. She looked asleep, but more than that. There were more tubes than they'd expected, one in her nose, another going down into her throat. Her face seemed puffy. There were bruises on her hands. Nick stepped back, let the children go to her first. They stood close, staring down at her. Victoria reached for Genevieve's hand, and then for Lindy's too.

Ig was the first to touch her. He patted her hand, the tiniest of touches. "Wake up, Mum," Ig whispered. "We're here."

There was just the sound of the machines, the sight of her chest slowly rising and falling.

The girls followed Ig's lead, gently touching her hands, talking to her.

"Can I tuck her in?" Ig asked Nick. "The way she tucks me in?"

"Be careful," Nick said.

Ig gently pushed the covers in close on either side of Angela's body, as she always did with him. "There you are, now," he said. "Snug as a bug."

It was what she always said to him.

It wasn't until they were all back in the waiting room

twenty minutes later that Genevieve remembered. "Oh God. Mum's tests."

"Tests?" Victoria said. "They're just monitoring her for now, aren't they?"

"Not here. The tests she was supposed to have about her headaches. She had a third day of them today. We should have canceled them. Dad, what's the name of her specialist?"

He couldn't remember. None of them could.

Genevieve went out into the corridor and called Joan.

"His name's Dr. Liakos. You should go to her hotel room as well, get her things, check her out. You're sure you don't want me to come down, give you a hand? I can be there in four hours. Less, the way I drive."

"Not yet, Joan, thanks. We might soon, but we're okay for now."

"I'm ready whenever you need me."

Genevieve decided to go outside to make her calls. Ten minutes later, she was back on the phone to Joan again. "You're sure it was that specialist? After I finally convinced them I was her daughter and explained what had happened, they said they hadn't sent her to have any tests. That they couldn't fit her in anywhere until next week."

"It was definitely that one. She couldn't have had tests anywhere else? Organized them herself?"

"I asked the same question. Not without a referral."

"That's strange," Joan said.

"You said it," Genevieve agreed.

She decided to call the hotel next. She'd just dialed the number when she looked down the street. The hotel was in walking distance. It would be quicker to go there and explain in person. She could pack up her mother's belongings then too.

The hotel lobby was quiet. Genevieve introduced herself and explained why she was there. The young male receptionist was apologetic. "I'm very sorry. What a shock for you all. But I'm afraid I need to see your mother's ID before I can take you to her room. I'm sorry; it's company policy."

Angela's handbag was back at the hospital. One of the nurses had given it to them the night of the accident. Victoria had been looking after it since. Lindy and Ig were away buying sandwiches when Genevieve got back to the waiting room. Her father was still engrossed in the family tree notes. She didn't mention Angela's phantom tests to him yet.

Victoria came back to the hotel with her. The receptionist took a brief look at the ID. He apologized again.

Genevieve settled the bill. A young porter accompanied them to their mother's room. They were all quiet in the elevator on the way up. As he let them in, Genevieve felt her breath catch. Seeing her mother's handbag on the night of the accident had been bad. This was somehow worse.

There were signs of her everywhere. Her pajamas at the end of the bed. Her dressing gown draped across a chair. Her makeup and toiletries in the bathroom. Her book and glasses on the bedside table. There was just a small bag, an overnight case. It took them both only a few minutes to pack everything.

Neither Genevieve nor Victoria needed to say it out loud. It was as if she had died.

They held hands as they went down in the elevator again.

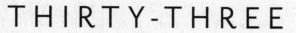

THIRTY-THREE

By the third day, Angela still hadn't woken up. The family was called together for another meeting. The doctors were concerned that she hadn't regained consciousness. They had called in a neurologist and wanted the family's permission to do more tests. The hospital's neuropsychologist, a woman called Ruth Morgan, would explain it to them all.

In her late thirties, with long curly hair, Ruth had a calm and gentle manner. "Your mother—your wife"—with a nod to Nick—"should have been awake and communicating with us by now. We're concerned the lack of oxygen caused by the sudden loss of blood after her spleen was ruptured may have caused some damage to her brain. She's not brain-dead; let me stress that. She's started breathing on her own. We've already done brain-stem tests, reflex tests.

They're all fine. But we've been reducing her levels of sedation for the past three days and she should have begun to regain consciousness by now."

Their questions came in a torrent. She answered each of them in turn. No, it didn't necessarily mean she had permanent brain damage. The fact she was starting to breathe independently was a good sign. But in cases like hers, where there had been a period of hypoxia, a lack of oxygen to the brain, there could be temporary issues relating to the frontal lobes, the hippocampus, the parts of the brain that affected the memory. That was why they wanted to do some more tests, including an MRI, to determine the extent of any effects.

"She might have amnesia, do you mean? But that's common enough, isn't it? People get over that, don't they?" Genevieve asked.

"We'll know more once we've done the tests," Ruth said.

Nick gave permission to do whatever needed to be done.

It was Victoria's idea that they have dinner in a nearby restaurant that night, rather than eat more vending machine food or try to cook in Celia's house. There was an Italian restaurant a block away, near Rundle Street. It was early. They glanced at the menu, ordering quickly.

"We have to stay hopeful," Lindy said. "Maybe the sedation just had a stronger effect on her than on other people. She'll wake up on her own soon and be perfectly fine."

"The tests Ruth mentioned are just routine, anyway, aren't they, Dad?" Victoria said. "They're not looking for anything really serious, are they?"

It was hard to make conversation. Their mobile phones

kept beeping. Word was still spreading about Angela's accident. Joan had obviously decided Genevieve was the spokeswoman and had given people her American cell phone number. She was getting text after text on that. She needed to get an Australian mobile phone, she realized. Such an ordinary, mundane thing to do while her mother was being tested for brain damage three streets away.

It was late-night shopping. She and Victoria decided to get her new phone now. They weren't hungry anyway. The phone was organized within fifteen minutes. On the way back to the restaurant, Victoria said what they were both thinking.

"What if she does have permanent brain damage?"

"We have to stay hopeful. What if she doesn't?"

"We have to prepare ourselves. She was clinically dead twice, Genevieve. No matter how quickly they got her heart started again, there had to have been some damage."

"Or maybe no damage at all."

"Then why won't she wake up?"

"She's catching up on all the sleep she missed out on when we were kids."

They stopped on the street before they got back to the restaurant.

"We need to do the pregnancy tests, don't we?" Victoria said.

Genevieve nodded. "But I can't face it at the moment."

"Neither can I."

"Can we wait until Mum wakes up? Do them then? A few days won't matter, will they?"

They agreed that they wouldn't.

For the next two days, all any of them could do was try to fill the time. Angela was transferred from ICU into the high-dependency unit. They moved between Celia's house and the hospital. Genevieve and Victoria went shopping for clothes and toiletries for everyone. They played games. Read magazines. Tried to read books, but returned to magazines, their concentration spans too jittery. Ig kept drawing. He now had more than sixty bird drawings ready for his mother. He also had the use of both hands again. It was Victoria who'd realized it was time the finger splint and sling came off. They were able to get him looked at in the same hospital their mother was in. Ig's finger was declared to be in good shape. It was welcome news in an otherwise worrying time.

They'd been told they'd have the test results the morning of the fifth day. The night before, Genevieve couldn't bear to sit around at Celia's watching TV any longer. She also needed to talk to her father, tell him about Angela's nonexistent tests. There hadn't been the opportunity yet.

"Dad, want to come for a walk with me?"

He looked up, wary.

"I won't fight with you. I promise."

They walked down the treelined street, the hiss of garden hoses the soundtrack to their steps. It had been another hot day. It was after eight p.m. and still in the seventies.

"Sorry about the other day, Dad. For shouting at you. And for what I said about you and Mum."

"It's okay."

"It's your business, not mine. Your marriage. And you're

right: I've been away. What right do I have to march on in and make judgments on your lives?"

"It's never stopped you before."

"No. I guess not." She hesitated. "Dad, there's something I need to tell you about Mum. Something a bit odd." She explained about the tests.

"Maybe she just wanted a break from us all for a few days," Nick said.

"Do you think so?" Genevieve said. "But what about where she was found? Up in the Hills? Why would she have gone up there?"

"I've been asking myself the same question," he said.

"And?"

Nick hesitated. That morning he had remembered something. A memory that belonged to him and Angela, not to the whole family. A memory of a trip to the Hills, a night or two before their wedding. Had Angela remembered that night too? Was that why she had gone up there?

"I don't know," he said. He wanted to keep that thought to himself for now.

Two hours later, Lindy was at Adelaide airport. Just after Genevieve and her father had gone out for a walk, she'd had a call from Richard. He and Jane were flying back to Melbourne that night. Mr. Lawson was driving them down. Was there any chance she could meet him there?

They met at the café nearest to their departure gate. The conversation was all about Angela initially. Lindy could tell Jane didn't like her being there at all.

"We're all thinking of your mum," Mr. Lawson said. He told her he'd also had their car windshield fixed. He'd even returned the car to Errigal. "Tell your dad to let me know if he needs anything done on the station."

Lindy thanked him. She knew her dad had already had lots of offers of help. That was one good thing about the station not running sheep anymore. There wasn't anything urgent to be done.

"Celia's doing okay up there on her own?" Mr. Lawson asked. "Want us to drop in to her at all?"

She was fine, Lindy told him. Joan was phoning her each day, and visiting every second day. Joan had even offered a bed at her house but Celia had insisted on staying at Errigal.

Jane and Richard's flight was called. Lindy cast a glance at Richard. They'd hardly said a word to each other. Jane and Mr. Lawson had done all the talking. It was minutes now before he boarded.

She surprised herself. "Richard, will you come with me to that souvenir shop over there? There's some great South Australian chocolate. You really shouldn't leave without any."

He sprang out of his seat. Lindy hoped Jane would stay where she was. To her surprise, she did.

"I'm really sorry about your mother," Richard said, as they walked to the shop.

"And I'm sorry for leaving you alone that night."

"I just kept wishing I hadn't seen *Wolf Creek*. Or any of the *Mad Max* films." He smiled at her. "Sorry. I promise I did find the beauty in all that open space. Especially once I was safely inside the Lawsons' house."

She bought him some chocolates, insisting they were a

farewell gift. Out of the corner of her eye, she could see Jane gathering her bags, sending glares in their direction.

"You were so great out there," Richard said. "Your tour guiding. Your driving. Your tire changing. Your kissing."

She felt a flame of color burn her cheeks. "You were pretty good too. Not the tire stuff. Or the driving. But the, you know—"

"Lindy, can we keep in touch?"

"Yes, please," she said. That sounded so lame. "But since Mum's accident—" She tried again. "I don't know what'll happen yet. If I'll be back in Melbourne anytime soon. We just don't know."

"Maybe I could come and visit one weekend. Once you know how things are with your mum."

"I'd like that. Really like that."

He moved to hug her. It went awkwardly. Their noses bumped. They skipped the hug. They kissed instead. They would have kept kissing if they hadn't suddenly felt someone else standing beside them. Jane.

"Come on, Richard, or we'll miss our flight."

Lindy stayed at the gate with Mr. Lawson, watching until they were both out of sight. It had been one of the worst weeks of her life. But in a funny way it had also turned into one of the best.

Back at Celia's, Genevieve and Victoria were in the living room. Victoria was watching TV. Genevieve was cursing at her father's old mobile phone as she tried to send some texts on his behalf.

"Which century did he buy this in? I'm starting to wish

he didn't have so many concerned friends. What did people do at times like this before mobile phones, anyway?"

"They didn't know as much, I guess. Or they waited to find out in other ways."

Genevieve swore again as she accidentally pressed delete instead of send and lost another message. "Forget it. There has to be a better way to do this. Could I just e-mail everyone? I'm quicker on e-mail. All I'd have to do is text them all first and get their e-mail addresses."

"We already have everyone's e-mail addresses. On Mum's letter."

"Dear, clever sister. You're right; we do." She reached into her bag and pulled out the printout she'd kept of Angela's Christmas letter. There were one hundred e-mail addresses on it, including those of all the friends who had been in touch over the past days.

She checked with her father first. He was reading Ig a story. Ig had become very clingy the past few days. They were all keeping a close eye on him. Nick thought the e-mail was a good idea. He was also happy to let Genevieve write the message.

Five minutes later, she and Victoria were in Celia's neat office, in front of her pristine computer. Genevieve opened up a new e-mail, and keyed in all the addresses as Victoria read them out.

"What do I put in the subject line?" she said, once the addresses were ready. "'About Mum'? 'The latest about Mum'? 'How Mum is'?"

"Do what Mum would do," Victoria said.

Genevieve started to type.

Hello from the Gillespies.

By now I think you've all heard the news that Mum was in a car accident five days ago. Thank you so much for your many texts and phone calls, they are helping us very much. She is in the best medical hands and we remain hopeful of a full recovery. We hope you'll understand if we keep in touch with you via e-mail rather than reply individually from now on. We also hope you'll keep her in your thoughts and prayers.

Thanks very much,
Nick, Genevieve, Victoria,
Lindy and Ig Gillespie

She was reading it back to Victoria when there was a voice at the door.

"What are you doing?" It was Ig, half-asleep, his dark red hair tousled, his pajama top buttoned wrong. He looked even younger than ten.

Genevieve explained. Ig came over and read it too.

"What about Robbie?" he said. "You left him off."

"Ig, people won't know who he is."

"Please," he said.

"Go on," Victoria mouthed. Genevieve added Robbie's name.

"Can I send it with you?" Ig said. "Mum always lets me help her."

"Of course you can," Genevieve said.

He came close, leaning up against her. She put her arm around him.

"Ready?" she said.

"Ready," he answered.

They pressed send together.

THIRTY-FOUR

They knew as soon as Ruth called them together at the hospital the next day that the news wasn't good. The MRI scan had showed up what she called "changes" on the brain. She did her best to keep the terms simple, but they were soon lost with the terminology: hypoxicischemic injury, white and gray matter junction, a diffusion weighted scan, a T2 scan showing the pattern of damage. Medial temporal lobes. Changes to the hippocampus caused by lack of oxygen to these areas.

"But what does it mean?" Genevieve asked. "That she definitely has some kind of brain damage?"

"It's still too early to say," Ruth answered. "We won't know what the effect is until she wakes up."

"Will she wake up soon?" Lindy asked.

"We expect her to, yes. The changes to her brain can

manifest in all sorts of ways. Her memory might be affected; there could be a period of confusion. Disorientation. We won't know for sure until she's conscious again. We just have to be—"

"Patient," Genevieve said.

Everyone was starting to hate that word.

They continued to take turns sitting by her bed, holding her hands, talking to her. There were three other women in the ward. They were conscious of crowding the limited space.

Ig stuck up his ten favorite bird drawings on the side of her locker. He'd cut out each bird, to fit more on, he said. It was like a little paper aviary: three robins, a magpie, a kookaburra and an emu. That would stop her feeling homesick, he said.

That night, Genevieve sent out another e-mail.

Hello from the Gillespies,

Mum is still unconscious and the doctors are continuing to run a series of tests. We are staying hopeful. Thank you for your messages; they mean a lot.

She signed all their names, as before. Robbie too.

Genevieve, Victoria and Lindy were in the waiting room the next day when they had a surprise visitor. Joan.

"I had to come. I felt useless up there, waiting for those daily e-mail reports. As if they would help me stop worrying. What's going on? What can I do?"

They spoke at once, explaining that Nick and Ig were in

by her bed now, that all they could do was wait, that it was a matter of her waking up.

"Nonsense. I'll go in and give her a good talking-to," Joan said. "She'll listen to me."

They let her go in on her own, watching from the doorway. Nick looked up, his exhausted expression changing to a smile. Ig threw himself into Joan's arms. Still holding him, Joan moved closer to Angela. She looked down at her for a long moment, and then gently touched her face.

It was too much for Genevieve. She turned away, back into the waiting room, her eyes filled with tears. Victoria followed her.

"She's not going to get better, is she? Joan touched her then, like she was—" Genevieve couldn't say the words. "Like she was dying."

Victoria pulled her into a hug. "Don't think like that. We have to stay positive. For Mum."

"I'm too scared. What if this is it? What if she never wakes up?"

"She will. We just have to be—"

"Don't say it. If I hear that word one more time, I will—"

A shout stopped her midsentence. It was Ig.

"She opened her eyes! She opened her eyes!"

By the time they reached the bed, Angela's eyes were shut again. But the others were adamant. She'd woken up and looked around for a few moments before closing her eyes again.

"I told you I should have gotten here earlier," Joan said. "She's just been waiting to hear my voice."

The nurse was now with her. They'd all been asked to

leave for the moment. In the waiting room, it was as if they'd been given a shot of adrenaline. Their quiet mood changed to chatter, even laughter. Their patience had been rewarded! This was the start of her recovery! She must have heard Joan, or maybe it was coincidence— "Of course it wasn't!" Joan said—but the days ahead suddenly didn't seem so bleak.

That night, Angela opened her eyes again. None of her family was there. But a young nurse was, checking her drip. Angela didn't just open her eyes. She spoke a few words.

Ruth filled them in the next morning. Genevieve had phoned at seven a.m. When they heard the news, they came in earlier than usual.

"The nurse said she sounded okay? She wasn't slurred or anything?" Genevieve asked.

"Not according to her notes, no. Angela was conscious for nearly a minute. She said a few words and then she closed her eyes again."

Yes, Ruth assured them, these were all very good signs. "I know you are sick of me saying this, but you just have to stay—"

"Patient!" Ig shouted. Genevieve shushed him.

"Actually, I was going to say positive," Ruth said, smiling.

At nine o'clock that night, Genevieve and Victoria were in the bathroom at Celia's house. They were whispering.

"She hasn't completely woken up," Genevieve said. "And we weren't there. Does that count?"

"We said we'd do the test when she woke up. And she's woken up twice. So we have to do it."

"I don't want to. I don't want to know."

"Nor do I."

There was a knock at the door. It was Lindy. "Are you two finished?"

"Not yet," Genevieve said. "Use the other bathroom."

"What are you doing in there?"

"Victoria's upset," Genevieve said.

"So am I. Can I come in too?"

They heard something else then. The front door opening. More voices. Their father's, then someone else's. A woman.

"Lindy? Who is it?"

Lindy went away but she didn't come back. They could hear her talking to the new arrival. It wasn't the right time to do the tests now. They needed to find out who the visitor was.

It was Celia.

She'd caught the bus from Hawker, after calling the Lawsons and asking Kevin to drive her into town. She'd taken a taxi from the Adelaide bus station to her house. She had all her suitcases with her. Nick came in from paying the taxi driver.

"Why didn't you at least ring from the bus station?" he said to her. "I would have collected you."

"You should have called me, Celia," Joan said. "I would have brought you down with me."

"I would have come with you, if you'd told me you were coming. Which you didn't," Celia said. "It just seemed silly to me, Nick, to be up there when you were all down here."

"But where will we all sleep now?" Ig said. "We've run out of bedrooms."

Celia looked too exhausted to make any arrangements. Joan took over. She put Victoria and Genevieve into one room and moved Lindy into a different bed, giving Celia her own room back. They were still one bed short. Joan checked herself into a nearby hotel. "I love you all, but I'm too old to live in a commune."

That night, Genevieve sent another update e-mail. It was the easiest one to write so far.

> Hello from the Gillespies.
>
> Mum woke up briefly today. Still hard days ahead but today has been a good day. Thanks again for all your messages and thoughts, please keep them coming.

Alone in the office, Genevieve was about to log out of her account when a new e-mail came in. It was from Megan, her makeup artist friend in New York. They hadn't been in touch since Genevieve had left. Their lives were so different now. A dose of NYC gossip was just what she needed, Genevieve thought.

Megan was full of chat. She'd finished on the TV show that caused the problems for Genevieve. She'd started work on a new film. She hated the hairdresser she was working with:

> Ham-fisted, bad-breathed. If I could fly you in, I would. Guess who's also on set??? Your Matt. Coffee Guy. I was super-surprised to see him. He was super-eager to see me. I haven't lost my touch, I thought to myself. Nope,

```
turns out he didn't care about me. All he
wanted to do was ask about you. Poor guy got
mugged on New Year's Eve in Costa Rica or some
such place. Somewhere exotic and dangerous
anyway. Hurt (broken ribs and black eye, was
in hospital for a week) robbed (completely—
phone, laptop, wallet). Hasn't been able to con-
tact you. So I hope you don't mind but I gave
him your e-mail address. Give him my love when
you hear from him. Tell him I'm much closer
than the wild west of Australia!
```

About to call out to Victoria, Genevieve heard the ping of another e-mail.

It was from Matt.

```
Hi Genevieve. I'm sorry for the long silence.
A combination of lost phone—actually, a robbed
phone—and no contact details for you. I goo-
gled Genevieve and Australia. Do you know how
many Genevieves there are in that country of
yours? A lot. So hopefully you get this and
hopefully you'll e-mail back. I'm in NYC again.
Wish you were too. Matt
```

Again about to call out to Victoria, she heard the sound of a phone ringing. Moments later, her father appeared at the door.

"Genevieve, get everyone. We have to go. That was the hospital. Angela's awake."

THIRTY-FIVE

Angela could hear something.

People's voices and the clattering of cups. As if she were in a café or a restaurant. But she was lying down. In a bed. She could feel a sheet under her hand. Was she in her bedroom? Who would be in her bedroom, clattering cups, talking? So many at once too. It wasn't Will. It wasn't Lexie either. These voices sounded different. They sounded . . . yes, Australian.

How very odd.

Still, there were so many Australians working in London these days. Maybe it was the radio coming from the kitchen, a sort of documentary. She tried to open her eyes again. It just felt too hard. It felt like they had been stuck somehow. She felt sore on her left side too. This really was all so strange. She tried calling out for her husband. He didn't answer but someone else did. Someone standing close to her.

"Angela? Can you hear me?"

She was no longer seeing the words on her eyelids. She could hear them loud and clear. Had she just heard someone say something about getting a nurse? Was she in hospital? Good heavens. It really did sound like that. She hadn't been in hospital since . . . since Lexie was born, surely? How long ago was that? Nearly thirty years? What on earth had happened to put her in hospital? She was supposed to be on holiday. In Australia. With Will and Lexie. Visiting eco-resorts. Staying on an outback station.

If only she could open her eyes and really work out where she was and what was going on. She had managed it earlier, hadn't she? Or had she? Was that hours ago? Or a few minutes ago? Time seemed to have gone so strange. She felt like she'd been asleep for days. Weeks. It had been quite nice, actually. Such a deep, deep sleep.

Her thoughts were all a bit jumbled, but she did seem to remember waking up now and then. Each time there seemed to be different people around her. She'd been having the oddest conversations with them too. One time it had been a young woman in a uniform. Another time, a pretty woman with long dark hair, who'd asked her all sorts of questions, as if she were interviewing her. Another time Angela was sure she'd seen a little boy standing there looking at her. And a tall, serious-faced man. A group of young women. All saying her name.

Who were these people? And where were Will and

Lexie? Perhaps they'd gotten caught up at work. They'd be joining her here soon. Yes, that was it. Will was so dedicated. So in demand. His architectural designs had won so many awards. Angela had been amazed when he said he'd be able to take six weeks off. As for Lexie ... Angela frowned as she tried to remember. That was right. Lexie was going to join them for only part of the trip anyway, wasn't she? She was so dedicated too. So enthusiastic about her work with the community theater group in Bristol. Angela was so proud of her.

She changed position in the bed. That was better. Yes, she was much more comfortable now. Come on, open your eyes again, she told herself. You can do it, Angela. On the count of three.

This time she managed it. There was a sudden rush of light. It hurt, but only for a second. She blinked, once, twice, and tried to focus. Above her, she could see fluorescent lights. A curtain rail of sorts. A curtain too. Yes, there was a curtain around her bed, but it was pulled back. She could see a drip stand, some tubes. She glanced down. The drip was attached to her. She looked around some more. She'd been right. She was definitely in a hospital bed, one with white sheets and a pale blue blanket. She shifted slightly and felt a quick dart of something, not quite pain, more a tightness of some sort. In her left side. She touched it. There seemed to be a bandage there. How odd. Why would she need a bandage?

She heard someone say her name. She looked around again. The people were back. The little boy. Or was it a little girl? Her or his hair was so long, it was hard to tell.

The tall, serious-faced man. The three young women. All looking at her, as if they were waiting for her to say something. She couldn't think of anything.

It was all getting a bit too confusing again. A bit too much. She'd just shut her eyes again for a while. Have another one of those lovely deep sleeps. Yes, that was what she'd do. Right now.

Hopefully it wouldn't be too long before Will arrived and sorted everything out.

THIRTY-SIX

It was the next day. The Gillespies once again gathered in the hospital meeting room. Ruth had asked them to join her there. Angela had woken again that morning, while Ruth was nearby. They'd had a conversation for nearly twenty minutes. Ruth wanted to tell them about it, but was finding it difficult to get a word in. They were all still talking about their experience with Angela the previous night.

"She didn't recognize us, did she?"

"She looked at me like she had no idea who I was! Has she forgotten us?"

"Why did she go back to sleep again? Is she in another coma?"

"Can we try to wake her again?"

Eventually, Ruth managed to quiet them down. "It's

still positive—I promise. She's woken up several times now. She is on her way back. When she woke this morning, I managed to have a long time with her awake and talking. That's what I need to speak to you about now."

"What did she say?"

"Did she ask about us?"

"Does she know what happened that night?"

"Why was she up in the Hills at all?"

Ruth glanced at Nick for assistance.

"Just wait and listen, all of you, please," Nick said.

They shut up.

Ruth spoke. "From what I can gather from our talk this morning, there does appear to be some memory loss. Some confusion. I asked her a series of questions. Standard ones. What's your name? Where do you live? What month is it? Who is the prime minister?"

"What did she say?"

"She said her name is Angela Richardson."

"That's nearly right," Nick said. "That was her surname before we got married."

"She also said her husband's name is Will, her daughter's name is Lexie and that she lives in London. That the prime minister is Margaret Thatcher and that her favorite newspaper is *The Guardian*."

There was an eruption of noise, questions and astonishment.

"She thinks she's in London?" Genevieve said, speaking over the others. "That it's the 1980s?"

"No, not consistently," Ruth said. "When I asked her about music, she mentioned a recent song. She was jumping from subject to subject, confused at times. But she was also lucid at times too."

"Should we go back in there now?" Victoria asked. "Stay beside her? Talk to her, tell her who we are, show her photos?"

"Not just yet. Please, let me explain. We talked before about amnesia. There are different forms. Some are caused by a blow to the head, a punch or a knock of some kind. That can create damage to either the left or the right lobe. That kind of amnesia can be more straightforward in some ways. What's happened to your mother is different. The loss of oxygen meant that both lobes have been affected. It's rare, but it does happen. And when it does, there can be some amnesia, but it's not just a matter of forgetting who she is, of there being a blank area in her brain. It can lead to other changes in memory and in behavior. To a state called confabulation."

"Which means what?" Genevieve said. "That she's forgotten us?"

"Not exactly. In Angela's case, when she regained consciousness, her brain couldn't readily tell her where she was or who she was. Our brains don't like it when there's nothing going on. We all need a personality, a story about ourselves. That's what our mind is made of, thousands and thousands of snapshots, memories, thoughts that tell us every second of our day who we are, what we are doing, what we want and need. In Angela's case, that knowledge, that memory of her real life, has been affected. So she is doing what we call confabulating.

"Her brain has created a new identity for her, a new story, made up of lots of different fragments of information that she's stored over the years. Anything to fill that blank

space. Underneath, the rest of her brain is working on re-
trieving her lost memories, putting the pieces of the puzzle
back together. What we expect will happen is that slowly,
gradually, her real story will emerge again, once her brain
has had time to adjust."

"But can't you give her something now, a tablet, some
kind of treatment?" Victoria asked.

"What if she never remembers us?" Lindy asked.

"We're her own kids and she looked at us like she had
never seen us before," Genevieve said.

Ruth's pager buzzed. She glanced down. "I'm sorry; I
need to see another patient. But please save your questions.
I'll do my best to answer them all."

They waited until she'd gone and then the room filled
with noise again. Joan called for silence. "Please, all of you, be
quiet. Not just for me, but for every patient in this building."

"We need to talk to Ruth again now," Genevieve said.
"Because this confiber—"

"Confabulation," Victoria said.

"Whatever it is, this new story she's creating, it's not
out of nowhere, is it? You heard what Ruth said. Mum talked
about a man called Will. A daughter. London." She reached
into her handbag and pulled out the creased printout of Angela's Christmas letter. "Listen to this: 'I'd have supported
Will as he studied to become an architect. We'd have had
one child. Just the one. A daughter called Lexie. We'd have
stayed in London.'" She stopped reading. "I think Ruth
needs to see this letter."

"No." It was Nick.

"Dad, this might be the key to what's going on with her."

"Too many people have seen that letter. It's done enough damage."

"I think it's important Ruth sees it," Genevieve insisted.

Victoria intervened. "Dad, maybe it will help. If that's part of who Mum thinks she is now, maybe it will make a difference to her treatment, if they know she had these thoughts—"

"Fantasies," Genevieve said.

"—before the accident. That they haven't come out of nowhere. It might be important."

"She's right, Nick," Joan said. "It could be important."

"Dad, please."

He looked at Genevieve for a long moment. "Go on, then. Give it to her."

Genevieve left the room, Victoria, Lindy and Ig close behind her.

In the silence that followed, Joan came across the room to Nick and sat beside him. His eyes were shut. She didn't say anything. She just touched his arm to let him know she was there.

There was another meeting with Ruth the next day. Angela had been conscious again during the night. Ruth had spent ninety minutes with her early that morning. She'd also read the Christmas letter Genevieve had left for her.

"Let me start with the good news," Ruth said. "Physically, she's doing well. Her reflexes are good, as is her eyesight, her hearing. She's off the drip now, eating and drinking normally."

Ruth shared details of her latest conversation with Angela. Again, there had been talk of London, different British politicians, place-names. Another mention of a husband called Will. A daughter called Lexie. She had also talked about Australia. A trip to Australia. A holiday on an outback sheep station. She had spoken about their sheep station, even named it. Errigal.

"So she's started to remember us? Remember where she lives? The old her is coming back?" Genevieve asked.

"Not yet. I'm sorry. It's not a matter of there being an Old Angela replaced by this New Angela. Both versions of her are still present. The best way to explain the idea of the amnesia and now this confabulation is to think of it as a protective shell her brain has put around itself. Her brain did receive some temporary damage, so while it's fixing itself up, it's operating on a different kind of system. Does that make sense?"

They looked blankly at her.

Ruth tried to explain some more. "Her brain is still her brain, her memories still her memories. But on the surface, there is this new story that she has invented, or at least her brain has invented. It will keep changing as she needs it to change, to help her to make sense of what is happening around her. In her case, she seems to be taking fragments from a preexisting fantasy life, the one you showed me in her letter. From what you've said, from what I read, it was very rich and detailed. The idea of a fantasy life, of retreating to your imagination to soothe or to calm, is perfectly normal. We all do it to some extent, especially when real life is a bit tough or times are hard. But we can usually differentiate between what is fantasy and what is fact. What's happening with Angela now is she's forgotten the factual part of her life, and believes parts of her fantasy life to be her reality."

"But can't you fix her?" Victoria said. "Hypnotize her or something? Tell her it's not real?"

"Should *we* tell her it's not real?" Genevieve said. "Tell her who we are, that we're her family? Isn't it only doing her damage if we go along with this whole other life of hers?"

"This is where you have to be patient. For the time being, she won't take in all that you say. It's a factor of this condition that the patient is able to easily discount anything that doesn't tally with their idea of reality. They simply ignore it. It will be the same if you point out any inconsistencies in her story. In the same way a child will ignore you if you tell them their teddy isn't alive. They'll appear to listen to you, but it's not sinking in. It's not what they are experiencing or what they know, so it simply doesn't register with them."

"So who does she think we are?" Genevieve asked. "How do we fit into this new life of hers?"

"Subconsciously, she's recognized you," Ruth said. "You're all familiar to her in some way. What I expect to happen is that she'll find a way to blend you into her confabulation. She might think of you as old friends. Talk to you as if she knows you. Or she might ask you to tell her all about yourselves. It will probably change from day to day."

"I still don't understand," Lindy said. "Can't we just tell her who we are?"

Ruth shook her head. "The fantasy life is what she believes at the moment. You could show her family photographs and she might not even recognize herself in them."

"So what happens next?" Genevieve asked. "Does she

stay in the hospital until she completely remembers us and can come home? Until she realizes there is no Will, there is no Lexie?"

"She doesn't need to stay in the hospital until she regains her memory. As I said, her vital signs are good. She's recovered well from her spleen operation. She's been told about that and she accepted it without any difficulty."

"Has she said anything about why she was in the Hills?" Joan asked.

"She said she was driving from the airport and got lost," Ruth said.

"She doesn't remember staying in a hotel for those nights?" Genevieve said.

"She was able to give me some details, but she thought it was an airport hotel in Hong Kong. I know you all hate the word, but it's a matter of being patient. She really is doing well after her operation. But she will still need hospital care for another week. She's a bit confused. Her attention and concentration will be poor. We'll need to assess and monitor how she copes with her self-care skills and daily living, but that can be done in a hospital closer to your home. So we're arranging for her to be transferred to the hospital in Port Augusta. For a week to begin with, and then depending on how she is physically, after she's been examined by a doctor there and also the occupational therapist, she should be able to go home with you."

"Go *home*?" Genevieve said.

"You *can't* let her out," Lindy said. "She's not herself."

"I want her to come home," Ig said.

As Ruth explained more, it was clear to them all that

she'd taken a personal interest in the case. She didn't see cases of confabulation very often, she told them. With their permission, she wanted to stay closely involved even after Angela went home. There would be a treatment plan put in place, devised by a team of people—doctors, nursing staff, psychologists, occupational therapists. There would be plenty of support available from her too, over the phone at any time. The safest place for Angela would be at home, with her family, she assured them. There was more chance of a speedy and complete recovery if she was in familiar surroundings, rather than in a hospital ward in Adelaide or Port Augusta.

What went unsaid was the other factor. They needed her hospital bed for other patients now.

"And you're still sure she will get better?" Genevieve asked.

"I can't tell you when, but I do believe she will. Whether she returns completely to her old self is difficult to say, but I'm hopeful. I can also assure you she's in good spirits. Happy, even. It's often a factor in confabulation. The patients can be quite jovial. It's not an unpleasant condition."

Ig put his hand up again. "Can I please go and talk to her?"

"Ig, she might not recognize you," Ruth said gently. "She will one day, but for now—"

"I don't care about that. I just want to talk to her now."

"Can I take him in?" Genevieve asked her father, and Ruth. "Even to say hello to her?"

Ruth nodded. After a moment, so did Nick.

"What do we call her?" she asked Ruth. "We can't call her Mum, can we? That won't make any sense to her."

"Just use her name," Ruth said. "All of you. Just call her Angela."

THIRTY-SEVEN

As they walked to the ward, Genevieve was clutching Ig's hand so tightly he yelped.

"Sorry," she whispered, loosening her grip.

Their mother was sitting up in the bed at the end of the ward, sipping a cup of tea. A newspaper lay on the covers beside her.

They stopped at the end of her bed. Angela showed no sign of recognizing them.

"Hello," Genevieve said.

"Hello," Ig echoed.

There was a long moment while they all just gazed at one another.

"Hello," Angela finally said, with a smile.

"I'm Genevieve. This is Ig."

"Hello, Genevieve. Hello, Ig."

"She sounds different," Ig whispered.

Genevieve thought so too. More English. She also seemed to be waiting for them to say something else.

"We're from Errigal. The outback sheep station," Genevieve said. She tried to think of a question. "Have you been in Australia long?"

"Just a few days. I had an accident."

She seemed very cheery about it, Genevieve thought. "And you're here for an outback holiday?"

Another big smile. "For six weeks. My husband and daughter will be coming soon too."

Ig spoke then. "What's her name?"

"I beg your pardon?"

"What's your daughter's name?"

"Her full name is Alexandra, but we've always called her Lexie."

"How old is she?"

"She's twenty-nine. She lives in Bristol."

Genevieve couldn't think of anything to say in response but Ig seemed unconcerned.

He leaned against the end of the bed. "I've got an imaginary friend."

"Have you? What's your friend's name?"

"Robbie."

"How long have you had him?"

"Ages."

"Lovely. It's been very nice to meet you." She put her cup on the bedside table. "Excuse me now."

She closed her eyes. They waited, but she seemed to have fallen asleep.

Back in the waiting room, the others were eager for a report.

"I can't even begin to explain," Genevieve said. "It's still her but it's not her."

"It's her," Ig said firmly.

"It's not, Ig. She didn't even know who we were."

"She was very nice."

Genevieve started to laugh. "She *was* very nice. Very English. Very polite. She'll do fine. We'll just have her as our mother instead."

"Can we?" Ig said. "Can she come home now she's awake again?"

"Not just yet," Genevieve said. "Dad, do you want to go next? When she wakes up again?"

He nodded.

"With me?" Lindy said.

"No, Lindy," Nick said. "I'm sorry. I need to see her on my own."

It was another hour before a nurse told them Angela was awake again. As Nick walked into the ward, his first thought was that Ig and Genevieve were right. She looked like Angela. She was sitting up in bed the same way Angela did, with two pillows behind her, one horizontal, one vertical. But as he watched from the doorway, hesitating, he saw her put two sugars in her tea. Angela didn't take sugar in her tea.

He stopped at the end of the bed. He forced himself to smile. She looked up and smiled at him.

"Hello," he said. "I'm Nick."

"Hello, Nick."

I'm your husband, he wanted to say. But he'd been warned against saying anything like that. Not to introduce the facts. Not yet. It would be too confusing for her.

"I'm from Errigal. The station in the Flinders Ranges. Where you'll be staying."

"I can't wait. I met your daughter and son! They're charming."

"Thanks," he said, fighting the urge to walk away, fighting a second urge to ask her to please stop this strangeness. It was her but not her. A different version of her. An unwell, confused version of her, from what the neurologist had said. Yet her eyes were bright, her smile wide. Nick had expected her to seem vague, disoriented. Instead, she looked happy. She was also very chatty.

"We looked at so many places to stay. I can't wait to go camping. My husband is an architect. This is a research trip. He's going to design a new resort in Portugal." She frowned. "I think it's Portugal. It might be Spain."

She seemed to be waiting for a response from him. "That's great," Nick said.

"Are you really in the outback? Lexie wants to see a kangaroo. I'm sorry about the fuss with the hospital. I should be better soon."

Nick felt he had no choice but to go along with all she was saying. "Yes, the doctors are pleased with your progress. How are you feeling? After the accident, I mean."

"I can't remember a thing about it." She laughed.

The sound of it hit him like a jolt. He had always loved her laugh. It felt like he hadn't heard it—or properly heard it—in months.

She was still talking. "So, is your station a long way away? It must get very hot there. Will is coming soon. Lexie's coming after that. Will is an architect. We live in London but we have always loved to travel. Lexie will join us soon. She's our daughter. She's twenty-nine." She smiled as she finished, gazing at him, as if waiting for him to answer.

Nick couldn't think of anything to say. All he was feeling was shock. Something more than shock. Something more like fear. This wasn't his Angela. This was a stranger.

He felt someone beside him. It was Ruth, with another doctor. "Sorry to interrupt. Nick, would you please excuse us?"

He was glad to leave. He couldn't pretend otherwise.

THIRTY-EIGHT

Over the next two days, they took turns spending short periods of time with her. She was bright, happy, talkative. She spoke to each of them as if they were from the host outback station. She still looked like the wife and the mother they knew. She almost sounded the same, just with more of an English accent. There had been an Old Angela. There was now this New Angela.

Each night, they spent several hours at Celia's computer. They googled and studied every similar case of confabulation they could find. In some, the person's memory had been altered for months. In others, only days or weeks. In one case, for years. Sometimes, the person's real memory had come back gradually. Sometimes, it had returned instantly, in one complete rush. By the end of their Internet sessions, they were as confused as they had been at the start.

Ruth advised them not to push any conversation with her. "Talk if she talks to you. Follow her lead."

Her main interests seemed to be reading and crossword puzzles and napping. She was doing a lot of napping.

"That's not a bad sign," Ruth told them. "The brain needs as much rest as the body. And she'll be unsettled the first few days in Port Augusta. It's good for her to get as much rest now as she can."

Genevieve was still the family spokesperson. "She's so amenable, though. She just goes along with whatever we're telling her is happening. We're strangers to her, yet she's happy to be told she'll be coming to live with us for six weeks or more. Is that a good sign or a bad sign?"

"It's part of the process. Somewhere in her brain, she's recognized you. That's why it's a good idea to bring her home as soon as possible. All sorts of things there might stimulate her memory. A familiar object, a smell, a piece of music, even a familiar taste. What's happening to her in real life now is close enough to what she's imagined for herself in her fantasy life, so this is all making perfect sense to her. She knows she had an accident, even though she can't remember it. But she's seen the bandages, knows about the operation; she's taking her medication—that all makes sense to her. She understands she needs to spend more time in the hospital too. She also believes she's in Australia on holiday, to spend time on an outback station. You are taking her to an outback station. So it's all happening as she expects it to."

388 | MONICA McINERNEY

———

Angela's transfer to Port Augusta went smoothly. She went by ambulance, with the Gillespies following in two cars, Nick's and Joan's. Her admittance was swift, the nursing staff friendly. The Gillespies were surprised by how relaxed they all seemed about Angela's memory issues.

"It's more common than you'd think," one nurse said to them. "We see it with Alzheimer's patients, dementia patients. We had a lovely lady here for two months who thought she was one of the Queen's ladies-in-waiting. She was frightfully grand." She said the last sentence in a very exaggerated British accent.

They booked into a motel near the hospital. They were less than two hours from Errigal now, but no one wanted to go home yet. Not without Angela. After dinner, using the motel computer, Genevieve composed another e-mail. It took her a long time to get the wording right.

Hello from the Gillespies.

Mum has now been moved to the hospital in Port Augusta. She's doing well physically, but she still has some memory issues as a result of the accident. We're glad to say her doctors think she will be able to come home soon. Her full recovery could take some weeks yet, though, and she'll need plenty of peace and quiet. So we hope you'll understand if she doesn't have any visitors or phone calls for the time being.

As the week in Port Augusta went by, they fell into a new routine. Each of them took turns spending time with Angela during the day. Over dinner, they shared their experiences. A pattern was emerging. Angela was friendly, but also reserved with them. She was happy to chat a little, but seemed to prefer to be left alone to read. She still slept a lot. She'd started to go for walks, just short ones on the hospital grounds. They'd all asked her whether she wanted company. Each time she'd declined the offer. She spoke about Will and Lexie as if she were in close contact with them, yet she hadn't asked to use a phone or a computer. Physically, she was in a good postoperative condition, the nurses told them. She took her medication regularly. Her appetite was also good. She was very appreciative of the food. "Anything's better than cooking," she often said. She was one of the easiest patients they'd ever had, the nurses said. So nice. So grateful. So peaceful.

Genevieve asked about the headaches. It had struck her after visiting Angela on the fifth afternoon in the Port Augusta hospital. Her mother didn't just look happy and content. She looked so well. Younger. Something was different. After some thought, she'd realized what it was. The tension had gone from her face. The frown she'd often had recently was nowhere to be seen. Had the headaches disappeared along with her memory?

She asked the nursing staff whether Angela had asked for any pain relief. Nothing for headaches, they confirmed. Could that have been the case? Genevieve asked Ruth next time she spoke to her on the phone. Could an accident wipe out an existing medical condition like Angela's long-suffered headaches?

It was certainly possible, Ruth told her. Especially as her recent tests had all been clear. There was no sign of a tumor or any other underlying cause of the headaches. They'd most likely been stress related. Now that Angela had nothing to worry about, and was living contentedly in this state of confabulation, the headaches were gone too.

Victoria had been out for a walk. For the fresh air. The thinking time. She also secretly hoped that the exercise might help her period to arrive. There was still no sign of it. For either of them. Everything had been so topsy-turvy with their sleeping, with their eating, it was still hard to tell if they had any other symptoms of pregnancy. It simply had to be stress delaying their periods, they'd decided. Stress on stress, their mother's accident on top of everything else. They couldn't both be pregnant. That would be impossible, surely.

As she came into the hospital foyer, she saw a familiar figure at the reception desk. Heard a familiar voice.

"I'd like to leave this here for the Gillespie family, please, if I—"

"Fred?"

He spun around. "Victoria?" He went red.

She knew she was blushing too. "What are you doing here?"

"I wanted to leave some things for you all. Not just from me, from Mum too." She could see a basket on the counter behind him. It was packed—cakes, books, even what looked like an iPad.

He followed her gaze. "It's my old one. I thought Ig

could use it. I loaded it up with games for him. I heard he's a computer wiz these days."

"Fred, I'm sorry. Your letter, I haven't—"

"I know, Victoria. You weren't even supposed to see me today. I was just going to drop these off. There's no pressure. No rush. Please, take all the time you like." He gave her a shy smile.

"I'm sorry, Fred. I haven't had time to think about it. With Mum, with—"

"Of course. I mean it, Victoria. There's no rush. How is your mum? We've been getting the e-mails—thanks for those—but if there is anything else we can do . . ."

She gave him a quick update, keeping the terms general, using the phrase *memory issues* as they had all decided to do.

"And how are you?" he asked. "It must be a very worrying time."

Seeing him standing there, so solid, so familiar, looking at her with such kindness, such concern . . . All the tension from the past few days, few weeks, few months, seemed to boil up inside her. As she burst into tears, he opened his arms wide. It felt like the most natural thing in the world to step into his embrace.

It wasn't until they were back in their hotel room later that night that Victoria had the chance to tell Genevieve the details of Fred's visit. Her sister already knew about the gift basket. They'd all seen it now. It had been so generous, so thoughtful, something in it for all of them to eat, read or be entertained by.

Victoria told her about her tears. The hug. How good it

had felt. How kind Fred had been. The conversation they'd had afterward. It was Victoria who had raised the subject of the letter. Not Fred. Yes, she would like to try going out with him again, she'd said.

She was regretting it now. "It was a mistake, wasn't it? I should have said I needed more time. I do need more time."

"But you don't, do you? It sounds to me like you should definitely have said yes."

She lowered her voice. "Genevieve, I might be pregnant. You might be pregnant."

"We're not. Of course we're not. We'll do the tests now. I've still got them in my bag."

Victoria shook her head. "I can't. Not here, not in a hotel room. With Mum in the hospital."

Genevieve felt the same way. They agreed they'd do it as soon as they were home again.

Six days after Angela arrived in Port Augusta, her discharge date was confirmed. She'd be going home the next day. It was nearly three weeks since the accident. Her treatment plan was discussed. There would be a support team available at all times, and visits to Errigal if needed, but it was up to time to do its work now. The Gillespies had met on several occasions with Angela's occupational therapist, who'd conducted a series of tests. She confirmed that Angela was what they called a "safe" patient. She wasn't at risk of harming herself or others. She was capable of washing herself, feeding herself, dressing herself. She was ready to go home.

The family had a video conference call via Skype with Ruth that night.

"Is it okay to admit I'm scared?" Lindy asked.

"Of course it's okay, but you don't need to be," Ruth said.

"But it's one thing visiting her in the hospital for an hour or so a day. How do we behave around her at home, every day?"

"You just have to be yourselves. All do exactly what you would normally do if you were living in the house together. Live your normal lives."

"But that's the problem. We didn't have normal lives before the accident happened. We definitely don't have them now."

"Perhaps you could fill me in on that. Ig, let's start with you. What's ahead for you?"

"It's still the school holidays for another week. After that, I'm going to school in Hawker again."

"That's quite a distance, is it? Who would normally drive you?"

"Mum," he said. "Angela," he corrected himself.

"Perhaps your dad or one of your sisters could do that now instead?"

They nodded.

"Are you happy with that, Ig?" Ruth asked.

Ig nodded.

"What about you, Lindy?"

"I'm back living at home again. I had a bit of a meltdown at the end of last year. In Melbourne. I'm now running an online cushions Web site."

"Can you continue to do that for the time being?"

"If I get any orders, sure. You don't need a cushion for a special occasion, do you?"

"I'll keep you in mind if I ever do," she said. "Victoria?"

"I had a bit of a meltdown at the end of last year too. In Sydney. I've now got a contract job with the radio station in Port Pirie. For six months."

"That's good news. Genevieve?"

"This will shock you. I had a bit of a meltdown last year too. So yes, I'll be sticking around as well."

"It's my plans that have to change," Nick said. "I was due to go to Ireland next month. A ten-day research trip to plan a family reunion. I'll cancel it as soon as I get home again."

"Why? You were only going to be away for ten days, did you say? You can still go."

"Leave my sick wife and—"

"Nick, she's not sick. It's important you all realize that. She's in a different mental state, yes, but she's not physically sick. Before this happened, did Angela know you were planning to go to Ireland on this trip?"

Nick nodded.

"Then my advice would be to go ahead with your Irish trip. It's only for ten days. She will still have plenty of support at home. Is she used to you being away? Before this happened?"

"Yes," Nick said. He explained he'd often been away on overnight trips, sometimes for longer if the work he needed to do was on the far side of their property, or on a neighbor's station.

"Then I don't see a problem with your trip going ahead. The closer you all stay to your normal routines, with all you'd planned to do, the better for Angela. Girls, I'm sorry about your various meltdowns, but it does mean you're all home and able to help out. To repeat that phrase again, she is in a safe state of mind, and being with her immediate family is the best place for her at the moment.

"I'd also advise you to let Angela settle in at home first before introducing any new people, apart from Joan. There might be some additional changes in behavior and it would be better to keep the group around her as small as possible to begin with. I'd also like you all to keep a note of anything you notice Angela doing that seems unusual, or remarkable in any way."

"She takes sugar in her tea now," Lindy said.

"That's a good example. A young man I worked with was a smoker before his accident. After he 'woke' again, he'd forgotten he was. He never smoked again."

"Won't she start to worry about her husband and daughter in London?" Victoria asked.

"She might. But patients with confabulation seem able to find reasons for anything inconsistent with their stories. If she does mention them, just reassure her. Tell her they are coming; they've just been delayed."

"But it won't just be what we say to her, will it?" Genevieve said. "There are photos of her all around the house. Won't that seem weird to her?"

"My advice would be to take them down before she gets home. In other cases, patients haven't recognized themselves or they've remarked on how similar they look to the person in the photos, in the way that we all have doppelgangers. But as you have the time to prepare, I'd advise you to keep any visual reminders like that to a minimum. We've learned that it's actually other stimuli that have a more profound effect on bringing memory back. Smells. Music. In the meantime, please stay optimistic. All of you. Take it day by day. I still believe she'll be fine again, in time. And I know you'll all be fine with her until then too."

There were no more questions after that.

THIRTY-NINE

Genevieve and Victoria drove back to Errigal together, in one of the station's 4WDs. Joan's husband had organized two of his stockmen to deliver it to them in Port Augusta.

The twins wanted to do a quick clean and, more important, to prepare their mother's new room. They were putting her in the old governess's quarters, where her overseas visitors always slept. It had a good view of the Chace Range, and French doors leading out onto the veranda. It was simply decorated, cream-painted walls, one wallpapered in a light floral pattern— chosen by Angela herself. There was a double bed, which they made up with crisp white sheets and a floral quilt, bought by Angela. On the bedside table, they placed a small glass vase holding two red roses from the bush near the pottery shed.

After her room was ready, they hurried through the

house, taking down any photos that Angela featured in. They gave the rest of the house a quick vacuum and dust.

They radioed their father, who was still thirty minutes away. They had the house to themselves for what would probably be the last time for weeks. This was their best chance.

They went into the bathroom. They did the tests, put them aside and waited the required time. On the count of three, they turned them over.

One was positive. The other wasn't.

The twins were in the kitchen drinking tea when the others arrived. As they all came in, it became clear that Ig had volunteered to show Angela around the homestead and the station buildings. Lindy kept saying that she wanted to help. Ig insisted it was his job.

Nick put down Angela's suitcase. The same one she'd had in the Adelaide hotel. "Let Ig, Lindy. He asked first."

"How nice to be fought over like this," Angela said, smiling. "It would be very nice if Ig showed me around today. And you can show me more tomorrow, Lindy."

Ig looked pleased with himself. Lindy relaxed. Genevieve stepped in. "Good thinking, Angela, thanks. But Victoria and I are showing you your room."

They all walked down the hall and out across the veranda to the guestroom. Angela looked around happily. It was beautiful, she told them. So elegant. What a wonderful view. The bed looked so comfortable. "And look, roses. What a nice touch," she said. She leaned down and breathed in the scent.

They all went still. Ruth had said her memory could be sparked by a smell. These were her roses. From the rosebush planted by Nick. The bush she had tended so carefully for years, even when water was scarce.

She straightened and smiled. "I do like roses. It must be hard to keep flowers growing out here. Is it?"

Genevieve was the first to answer. "It is, yes. Even harder to grow a lawn, as you'll see. Or not see."

Victoria continued the tour. "Here's your bathroom. Your wardrobe. If you need more coat hangers, just let us know."

They had filled the wardrobe with clothes from her own room. That had been Ruth's idea. "Don't make a fuss about them," she'd told them. "Just put them there."

Angela looked around again. "It's a lovely room. Thank you. Perfect. And where will Lexie sleep when she gets here?"

They hadn't thought of that. Victoria stepped in. "Lexie can sleep in here and you and Will will have the main room." She'd nearly said, "Your and Dad's room." "Our parents' room."

"Where is your mother?"

Ruth had told them to prepare for that question too.

"She's away," Victoria said.

"On holiday?" Angela asked.

"No. A sort of study trip."

Angela had lost interest. She was standing at the window exclaiming over the view. The view she had seen every day for the past thirty-three years.

"Do you ever get tired of this?" she said, turning around, her eyes wide. "Look at the colors! Do you mind if I step outside?"

She pulled at the nearest of the two French doors. The right door. There had long been a trick to opening these doors. She'd remembered it.

Outside on the veranda Genevieve and Victoria had placed a small table and a cane chair.

"You can have breakfast out here every morning if you like," Victoria said. "Our other guests often do."

"I might spend all day out here," Angela said.

Ig followed her. "Can I give you the proper tour now? This is just the house. The best stuff is outside."

"I'd love that, thank you," Angela said. "Remind me again, Ig—how old are you?"

"Ten."

"A great age. Can you ride a bike?"

"I can drive a car."

"Really? At ten? You do start early here."

He nodded. It was Angela who had taught him to drive.

"I'll take you for a drive later if you like," Ig said.

"I don't think so, Ig," Nick said.

"Ready, Angela?" Ig asked.

"Whenever you are," she answered.

Nick and the three girls watched as Ig led her across the yard and opened the gate. They couldn't hear what he was saying, but they could see him pointing out the different buildings, and across to the Chace Range. Beside him, Angela was nodding and listening.

"Is it just me, or is this the weirdest day of our entire lives?" Genevieve said.

"I think it's only the start," Victoria replied.

A short time later, Nick left the room to go to the office. He needed to catch up on some e-mails, he told them. Victoria,

Genevieve and Lindy stayed where they were, looking out the window, still watching Angela and Ig.

"What could they be talking about?" Genevieve asked. "They've been standing there chatting like that for ages now."

"They're probably talking about Robbie," Victoria said.

"Or to Robbie," Genevieve said.

Nick returned. "Is everything okay?"

"Fine," Genevieve said. "Still completely weird, but fine. Are you okay?"

He nodded.

"Dad, you have to say more than that," Genevieve said. "It's going to be strange at first. Ruth told us that. She also said we have to keep talking to each other about how we feel."

"I'm fine, Genevieve. That's what a nod means."

He left the room again.

"He's definitely not fine," Lindy said.

Back in the office, Nick shut the door.

He'd done his best to stay calm in Adelaide. In Port Augusta. For Ig's sake. For the girls' sake. They were watching him so closely, following his lead; he knew that. He couldn't let them see his true feelings.

He'd spent more time with Angela than all of them. Hours by her bed. This New Angela looked like his wife. Sounded like his wife. Smiled and laughed like his wife. But everything she said was tearing into him. She kept talking about this Will. About Lexie. London. Asking him the same questions about the station, the names of his children.

They're your children too, he'd wanted to say. It's your

home. I'm your husband. I am. Not this Will. He couldn't say any of it. He had to trust Ruth's advice, go along with it all.

If he could have done anything to turn back time, stop the accident from happening, he'd have done it. Was this memory damage of hers his fault too? If things had been better between them, if he had talked to her more, if he hadn't reacted the way he had to her letter, would her memories of their marriage, their lives together, have been stronger? Strong enough to cancel out this Will, this Lexie, her fantasy London life? He hadn't asked Ruth any of that. She already knew more than he would like anyone to know about his wife, his marriage, his family.

He felt the despair come over him again. Like fog, stealing in. No. He wouldn't let it. He closed his eyes. He tried to recall all the advice Jim, his psychologist, had given him. "Change the radio station. Don't listen to the bad thoughts."

It was harder than ever. Before Angela's accident, he'd been getting better at dealing with his negative thoughts about the station. About the mining lease. There had also been a new development to think about. The conversation he'd had with Kevin Lawson the night of the woolshed party. The offer Kevin had made. "No rush with your decision," Kevin had said. "We'd be talking next year at the earliest." Nick had said he would think about it. He was still thinking about it. But other things had priority now.

Not other things.

Angela.

The children were coping better than he was. Ig was

the most relaxed of all. The three girls were following Ruth's advice to the letter. He was the one at sea.

He stood up and turned to look at the wall of photos, as he often did when he was in here working. The photos of him and Angela over the years were gone. The wall was bare. He remembered then that Ruth had told Genevieve and Victoria to pack them all away. He was taken aback at the flash of sorrow he felt. His wife was no longer his wife. He no longer had any photos of her either. Tears came to his eyes. He roughly wiped them away.

While Angela had a nap, Genevieve phoned Joan and filled her in on how the homecoming had gone, how they were all following Ruth's advice, going along with whatever Angela said.

"And is that okay?" Joan asked. "Are you all coping?"

"Better than we expected. It's easier than we thought. She thinks everything is lovely. Wonderful. That we're the perfect hosts and all she has to do is be the guest. She hasn't done any of the things she'd normally do after being away: sweeping every floor, rummaging in the freezer, telling us to empty our suitcases, putting on a wash load. We gave her a tour, made her a cup of tea and then she said she was going to sit on the veranda and read. Making it very clear she didn't want any company at all. She wanted to know what time dinner was, and what it would be, and also managed to let us know very politely but firmly that she's also looking forward to a glass of wine, preferably on the veranda around six p.m."

"And what will you be having for dinner tonight?"

"That's why I'm ringing. You don't feel like coming over and giving me a few cooking lessons, do you? Now?"

Later, over dinner—a lasagna made from ingredients Joan had found in the freezer—they made polite conversation. It was nothing like their normal, noisy family dinners.

"Do you have children yourself, Joan?" Angela asked.

"Two grown-up kids. Neither of them wanted to stay on the station. One is in Queensland; the other is in Sydney. I've got five grandies."

"Grandies?"

"That's Australian slang for grandchildren. We shorten everything here. Footy. Barbie. It's like our national pastime."

"How interesting," Angela said politely. She continued to eat.

Joan seemed to be hitting the right note with her conversation, not batting an eyelid about Angela's odd questions or replies. Angela had been using the words *grandies*, *footy* and *barbie* herself for years.

"And what about you, Angela?" Joan asked. "You have just the one daughter?"

"That's right. Alexandra. We call her Lexie. She'll be here soon too."

"And whereabouts in London do you live?"

"Do you know London?"

"Only from films and TV shows. It always looks gray. Gray skies, gray buildings."

"It often is gray. But I love it. We live in Will's family home in Islington. His grandparents bought it before the war. His mother grew up there. She left it to Will."

"And you're from there too?"

"No, I'm from a much less grand area. Forest Hill, in south London. I grew up in a council house. My parents were in their forties when they had me. I was a surprise child." She gave a merry laugh. "What about you, Joan? Do you have children?"

They all stopped eating. "Yes, I do, Angela. Two grown children. And five grandchildren."

"How lovely," Angela said.

In her room soon after dinner, Angela finished getting ready for bed. She was very happy here. It all looked just like she'd expected an outback station to look. Her room was lovely. So peaceful. So quiet.

She opened the French doors and stepped out onto the veranda, to breathe in some of that fresh, clean air again. How beautiful it was. They seemed like such a nice family. She was very lucky.

She couldn't wait for Will and Lexie to meet them all.

Joan came over for dinner the next night too.

Genevieve had invited her to come every night if she wanted to. She'd also asked for her help in ways other than cooking. "I think you should get her talking as much as you can about her real life. See if that sparks any memories. It might be stronger coming from you than us."

Joan invited herself to join Angela for a pre-dinner glass of wine on the veranda. The sun was setting, the sky a vivid red, the air filled with birdsong. In the old days, she and Angela would have talked nonstop. Now Angela was content to sit quietly.

Joan began the conversation, talking about all the years she had come here to visit the Gillespies, what a great family they were. Not just Nick and the children. Their mother too.

"She's a lovely woman. Warm, friendly, talented. A dear friend of mine, actually."

"She's away at the moment?"

"That's right. A study trip." The children had coached Joan on that too. "I've known her since she first came here. She had the twins less than a year after their wedding. She was new to station life, on the other side of the world from her parents and friends. Not just a new city or country, either, but a new life in the middle of nowhere, really. Nick's a great husband and father, and he was a great pastoralist too. . . ."

Angela didn't react.

"But he was completely clueless when it came to looking after twins. I spent a lot of time here when they were small. After Lindy was born, just before the twins turned three, I practically moved in. I was here every day; sometimes I stayed overnight. Three little kids needed at least two pairs of hands, sometimes three."

Genevieve came out, carrying a bottle of wine. She refilled their glasses. Joan smiled at her.

"I was just about to tell Angela what a handful you were as a child, Genevieve. How hard it was for your mum to have three children under the age of three."

"She and Dad only had themselves to blame. No self-control. We were angels, Angela. Truly."

"Three devils, and this one was the worst," Joan said,

gesturing to her. "The ringleader from the start. Born first and bold as brass."

"Joan, you're not painting a very nice picture of me in front of our guest."

"Victoria was always so sweet. So was little Lindy. She wanted to be a twin so badly. She could never quite understand why she was always a bit smaller than the other two. And why they would always gang up against her."

"We didn't 'gang up.'"

"Yes, you did."

"Rarely."

"Often."

They glanced at Angela. She seemed to be listening.

"Do you remember those dolls of yours?" Joan asked. "And their names?"

"The ones you gave me for my fourth birthday?" Genevieve smiled. "I do, yes."

Joan explained to Angela that she had taken Genevieve out for a day trip once, to Port Augusta. They'd gone to the cinema and Joan had let Genevieve have a whole bag of popcorn to herself. Afterward, they'd visited all the shops, walking past the church on the way. Joan had pointed it out as Jesus's house. As an end-of-day treat, Joan had bought her an inexpensive pair of dolls. That night, Genevieve had announced the names she'd given them. Popcorn and Jesus.

"She was always losing them too. Especially when we were out and about in town or, even worse, in church together. You'd hear her shouting at top note, 'Where's Popcorn? Where's Jesus?'"

Joan and Genevieve both laughed. It was one of the Gillespies' favorite family stories. One of Angela's own favorites.

Now she just smiled politely.

Victoria called out from the kitchen. "Joan? What's the difference between sautéing and burning?"

"About thirty seconds. I'm on my way. Excuse me."

Genevieve and Angela stayed where they were.

"And what do you do for a living, Genevieve?" Angela asked.

Angela had asked her the same question four times now. Genevieve realized she could say anything. She could tell Angela she was a nuclear physicist. An Olympic hurdler.

"I'm a hairdresser," she said.

"A great job, I'm sure. There's always work for hairdressers. How did you get started in that?"

"In a local salon in Port Augusta. Then I moved to Adelaide, entered lots of competitions, and won a lot of them too. I met a famous stylist from Sydney at one of them, who told me to get in touch if I ever wanted to work in film and TV. So I did. For the past five years I've worked on film sets, in Australia, and then I tried my luck in New York for two years." It felt so odd to be saying all of this. It was Angela who had driven her to her first interview at the salon in Port Augusta. Who had encouraged her to enter those competitions. Who had convinced her father that it would be good for Genevieve to move to Sydney.

"That must have been exciting. Did you get to meet lots of famous actors?"

"I did, but I'm sworn to secrecy, of course. I can do your hair for you while you're here, if you like."

"That's very kind. I can't remember the last time I had a haircut." Angela frowned. "I actually can't. Do I need one?"

"You could do with a trim. I'll do it for you tomorrow if you like."

Angela smiled. "You really do offer all the services here—a warm welcome, beautiful views, lovely food and haircuts too. Thank you very much."

It hit Genevieve then. This wasn't just a joke. This wasn't a game of pretend. She was talking to her mother, but her mother had no idea who she was.

"You're very welcome," she said.

She excused herself and went inside before she started to cry.

The next day, Genevieve kept her word. She cut her mother's hair.

She set everything up in the kitchen, as she had done so many times over the years. Her scissors, her combs. The towel. The mirror. She'd done this so often, for every member of her family, ever since she was an apprentice. In recent years, she'd looked after film stars, models, actors, customers in Sydney, in New York. She'd taken all of them in her stride. She was good at her job and she knew it.

Today, her hands wouldn't stop shaking.

She had to excuse herself for a moment, go outside, take several deep breaths. When she returned to the kitchen, her mother was still sitting there quietly, the towel around her shoulders, gazing out the window at the view she had looked at for more than thirty years. Smiling as if she'd never seen it before.

"It's so beautiful here, isn't it? So peaceful."

"Yes, it is," Genevieve said.

One by one, the others came in and watched as Genevieve combed, snipped, combed, snipped, the sound of the scissors loud in the room. Genevieve had always loved that sound. It didn't take her long to finish the cut. She'd always known how to shape her mother's curls into the most flattering style.

She picked up the mirror and showed her.

"Lovely," Angela said. "Thank you so much. You really do have a gift, don't you?"

Genevieve tried to ignore the sudden lump in her throat. "Any other takers? Ig? Yours is almost getting long enough to plait these days. Come on, sit down. I'll be quick, I promise."

Ig was sitting up on the kitchen stool. He turned to Angela. "Do you think I should get it cut?"

Angela studied him for a long moment. "No," she said. "I think it looks great long."

Ig gave her one of his special smiles and stayed where he was.

FORTY

It was now four days since they'd returned home. Ig and Angela were out on a walk.

The previous night, after Ig and Angela had gone to bed, the rest of them had had a long discussion. As adults, they'd taken in most of what Ruth had explained to them about confabulation. They were worried Ig might not have. Victoria had volunteered to talk to him.

That morning, she had taken him aside. "Are you feeling okay about all of this, Ig?" she'd asked. "I know it seems a bit funny, but do you understand that Mum isn't quite Mum at the moment? That she thinks she's someone else?"

He'd nodded.

"And can you keep remembering to call her Angela, not Mum, so she doesn't get confused?"

"Yes," he'd said.

"And don't worry if she starts talking about London, or a different husband or daughter, will you? Or if she gives you any strange answers. She'll be all right again soon. Ruth promised. So don't be too worried, okay?"

"Okay," he'd agreed.

"Look," Ig said now, showing Angela a scar on his hand. "I cut my finger off."

"Did you? Ouch. When was that?"

"At the start of December. I was standing on the table with the carving knife. Then I fell off and I landed on the floor and the knife at the same time."

"Ouch again. What did you do then?"

"Mum was here and she took me to the hospital. She put my finger in a bag with some ice first. Look, they sewed it back on." He wriggled it for her.

"That's incredible. And it still works perfectly too. How did your mum know what to do?"

"She knows everything."

They walked on in silence for a few moments. There was a rustle in one of the bushes nearby, a fluttering sound and then the sudden quick call of a bird. A blue wren shot out in front of them, trilled again and then flew back into the bush.

"The birds are so different here," Angela said, smiling. "So colorful. The poor London birds seem very dull in comparison."

"My mum really likes birds too."

"Does she? I like them so much I even make them for a living. Little ceramic ones."

"Mum's got a pottery wheel here. And loads of clay. Do you want to see it?"

"I'd love to, Ig. Thank you."

———

In the kitchen, Genevieve and Victoria were looking out the window.

"He's taking her into the pottery shed."

"Is that a good idea?"

"I don't know what's good or bad anymore."

It took Ig three tugs to pull the blue wooden door open. He switched on the light and stood back as Angela looked around.

"This is nice. Much bigger than my studio in London."

"Do you like it better here?"

"I've just got here, Ig. And I'm on holiday. It's very different."

"But could you live here all the time if you had to?"

"I think I'd get a bit lonely without my husband or daughter."

"But they're coming soon, aren't they?"

"Yes, they are."

"Do you want to do any of your ceramic birds while you're here?"

"I don't know." Ig watched as she cut herself a piece of clay, held it in her hand, started to soften it. She rolled it one way, then the other. When she opened her hand again it still looked just like a ball of clay. She held it out to him. "Do you want to try making a bird for me?"

He shook his head. "But I can show you lots of real ones if you want. I know all their names."

"You'd take me bird-watching? Thank you. I'd like that."

"Want to take a picnic too?"

"That would be great."

"Wait here."

Genevieve and Victoria interrogated him as soon as he appeared in the kitchen.

"We were just talking," he said. "About clay and London and stuff. And now we're going bird-watching. I'm getting a picnic first."

"A picnic?"

"We might get hungry."

"You had breakfast about twenty minutes ago. So did Mum."

"We have to call her Angela, not Mum," Ig said.

They watched as he gathered a packet of biscuits, two bottles of juice and two apples. He put them into his school-bag, which he slung over his back.

Victoria reached up on top of the cupboard. "Want the binoculars too?"

He added them to his bag.

"Ig, are you sure you're okay?" Genevieve said. "You're not scared of her or anything?"

"Why would I be scared of her?"

"Because she's different at the moment. Mum, but not quite Mum."

Ig gave that some thought. "I'm not scared. I like this one too."

After dinner, Angela got up and yawned politely. "That was delicious. Thanks so much. Nearly as delicious as your picnic today, Ig. Excuse me; I might go to bed now and read."

They watched her leave. Lindy spoke first. "Mum never, ever did that, did she?"

"I bet she wanted to," Victoria said.

———

Once again, after getting ready for bed, Angela stepped out onto the veranda. It had become her routine, to sit out here on her own every night for a little while. She didn't turn on the light. She sat in the darkness that wasn't darkness. The stars were so bright out here. The moon so big. It sounded quiet at first, until you really listened and heard all sorts of sounds. Faint birdcalls. The scratching of animals. She'd even seen a kangaroo that morning, right at the homestead fence. Later in the afternoon, she'd spied an emu in the distance. Wait until Lexie saw them!

Yes, it had been another lovely day. It was so peaceful here. So relaxing. She loved spending time with that little boy too. He was such a quirky little fellow. Adorable. The girls were all so interesting too. Each so different. And their family friend, Joan, was so warm and friendly. Exactly the kind of neighbor anyone would want to have.

She thought about the man too. The children's father. Nick.

Over the past few days she had started to notice him more. Several times, she'd caught him looking at her. He seemed so sad about something. She wondered what it was.

"Have you noticed something about Angela and Dad?" Genevieve said later, once she and Victoria were alone in the kitchen, cleaning up. "She talks to us, but she's hardly exchanged a word with him."

"Have you put that in the book?" They'd done as Ruth suggested and started keeping a note of anything unusual that they noticed Angela saying and doing.

Genevieve nodded. "Of all of us, you'd think she'd remember him, wouldn't you? The man she's lived with for
thirty-three years? There'd be some physical memory of
him, wouldn't there?"

Nick came in. Genevieve wasn't sure whether he'd heard
or not.

"How are you doing, Dad?" she said. "Are you okay?"

"I'm fine," he said.

"I'm not," Victoria said. "It all feels so strange. She looks
just the same, but she's completely different. She's so relaxed. She reads; she naps; she goes for walks. Mum never
did those things."

"And she doesn't do any of the things Mum used to do,"
Genevieve said. "She hasn't swept the veranda once since
she got back. Or cleaned the bath. Done the dishes."

"That's because it's not her anymore," Nick said.

Genevieve heard a catch in his voice. "Dad? Are you
okay?"

Nick didn't answer. He had his back to them, reaching
up for a glass.

"There's beer in the fridge if you want one," Genevieve
said.

"No, thanks." He poured himself a glass of water, then
left the room. "Back soon," he said.

Fifteen minutes later, he was still outside. He'd planned to
walk over to the chapel, to sit quietly on his own. He hadn't
gotten that far. Halfway across the paddocks, he'd stopped.
The last time he'd been at the chapel was with Angela, the
day he'd read her Christmas letter. He didn't want to

remember that conversation. Instead, he went in the other direction and leaned on one of the empty sheep pen fences. It was a crisp, clear night, the stars bright, the moon huge. A night that promised hot weather the next day.

If he turned around, he would see the lights of the homestead, hear music, snatches of conversation, his children talking, getting ready for bed. He would go to bed soon too. To the bedroom that he and Angela had slept in for more than thirty years. To bed, alone. While she slept in the guestroom.

He kept trying to follow Ruth's advice. Act normal. Go along with what she says. He had talked to Angela less than half a dozen times since they'd brought her home from Port Augusta. About the weather, the scenery. He'd offered her a cup of tea on several occasions. She'd accepted it once and declined it twice, smiling at him each time in that odd, distracted way. As if they were strangers. As if they hadn't spent most of their lives together. As if she had no memory of him. No memory of their years as husband and wife.

"It's temporary," Ruth had told them. "It's her brain recalibrating. She'll come back to you again."

He hoped so. He hoped it was soon. Because it was breaking his heart to see her like this.

Back came the bad thoughts. The fog. He hadn't made a new appointment with his psychologist yet, but he needed help now.

In the homestead again, he went into the kitchen. It was empty for once. He took the opportunity, picking up the phone and dialing. He spoke briefly.

The answer was immediate. "Of course. Come now. I'll meet you halfway."

———

He left a brief note. He knew the kids wouldn't worry. They were used to him having to leave at all hours of the day or night. Station work, even caretaking work, was never nine to five.

He'd been driving for thirty minutes across the dirt road when he saw the headlights ahead.

They were almost exactly at the halfway point between their two stations. He parked and got out of his car. Soon after, the other car stopped. Joan got out and walked toward him.

It was easy to talk out here. They'd both turned their headlights off. The only light was coming from the stars and the moon. He had known Joan all his life. She was the closest person he had to a big sister. He had been so glad, so grateful when she had taken Angela under her wing all those years ago. He'd always trusted her. He trusted her again now. He needed her to tell him the truth. He got straight to the point.

"Did she want to leave me, Joan? Before this happened? Was she that unhappy?"

"Never. She loved you so much. Loves you so much. She's been worried sick about you."

"But her letter. Everything she said in it, about the man in London, about—"

"Forget about that bit for now. It's the other part you should read. The part about you. That's exactly how she felt, Nick. That you'd stopped talking to her. Closed yourself off from her. She couldn't understand why."

"I had to."

"Why?"

There was a long pause.

"Nick? What's wrong? What's been going on?"

He told her. Hesitantly, to begin with. Her silence encouraged him. He told her everything. About the debt. His depression. Why he'd accepted the offer from the mining company. He told her about the visits to his doctor. The psychologist. If she was shocked, the darkness hid her expression. When she spoke, her voice was as calm as ever.

"I wish you'd told Angela all of this. It would have helped you. It would have helped her."

"What do I do, Joan? I don't know how to handle this. How to be with her."

"Just be yourself, Nick."

"She doesn't know me anymore."

"Then let her get to know you again. That's who she fell in love with thirty-three years ago, remember. You haven't changed that much, apart from a few gray hairs. You're definitely as stubborn as ever."

He couldn't see her smile but he could hear it in her voice.

"Do you still love her?" Joan asked. "Do you still want to be married to her?"

"Of course I do."

"Good. Because I happen to know for a fact she feels the same way about you. You'll get through this. You heard what Ruth said. We have to stay hopeful, stay patient and let nature take its course. She'll come back to us. We just have to wait. And in the meantime, be nice to her. Really nice. Then go off to Ireland. And make sure you bring her back a really good souvenir."

"Thanks, Joan. For everything."

"Anytime, Nick."

They didn't hug. It wasn't their way. Nick waited until she had gotten back into her car. He waved good-bye, and stayed until her car had disappeared from sight. Only then did he head homeward himself.

Victoria and Genevieve talked through the night once again. During the day, someone always seemed to be within earshot. They needed to keep their news to themselves for now. The news they'd had for nearly a week.

Victoria was pregnant.

"*Might* be pregnant," Genevieve tried to reassure her again. "It might have been a faulty test."

"They're supposed to be fail-proof."

"There's always one that's broken, surely. Maybe you were just unlucky." She squeezed her hands. "We'll go to Port Pirie or Port Augusta tomorrow. Get another test."

"But what if that's positive too?" Victoria's eyes filled with tears. She asked the question she'd asked every night since she'd done the test. "Genevieve, what am I going to do?"

"Just wait. Wait and see. Wait until we know for sure."

The next morning at breakfast, Victoria and Genevieve casually announced they were going to drive across to Port Pirie after they'd dropped Ig at school. It was his first week back. They told their father they were going to buy groceries. He just nodded, distracted. He'd had a call from one of his neighbors that morning, asking whether he could lend a hand with some stock.

Lindy decided to stay on the station. She was trying to catch up on her cushion stitching. While they had all been in Adelaide and Port Augusta, she had received another three orders.

It was Genevieve's idea to ask Angela whether she'd like to join them. She'd like that very much, Angela said. She went to her room to get her bag.

Lindy looked alarmed. "Is that a good idea? Didn't Ruth say it's better to keep her here?"

"We won't let her out of our sight," Genevieve said. "We'll drive straight there, get some groceries and come straight back. She'll be fine."

They lost her within twenty minutes of arriving in Port Pirie.

"She was right here," Victoria said, standing in front of the supermarket. "Where did she go?"

"I don't know," Genevieve said, panicked. "And she hasn't got a phone. We can't even ring her."

"You go in that direction. I'll head this way."

Victoria ran down Ellen Street, past shops, pubs, a café, quickly looking inside each one. There was no sign of Angela. Then she saw the bookshop farther down the street. As a family, they'd called in there often over the years, chatting to the owners each time. Would the New Angela have felt drawn there as well?

Victoria was out of breath as she came into the store. Angela wasn't there. Had she just missed her? She sought out the dark-haired owner. Yes, she said, Angela had just been in. "I was serving another customer, so I gave her a wave and said I'd be with her soon. But she was gone before I could help her—sorry."

Victoria said thanks, excused herself and said good-bye. Outside again, she looked across the road at the old railway station. It was now a museum and tourist information point. Angela thought she was a tourist. Would she—

"Someone saw her head in there. Come on." It was Genevieve, panting beside her.

Their mother was inside, holding a large bundle of brochures.

She smiled at them. "Hello, girls."

"Is everything okay, Angela? Can we help at all?"

"No, thank you. I'm just getting some information for when Will and Lexie arrive."

Genevieve glanced at the brochures. They advertised the attractions of Wilpena Pound, the Angorichina gorges, the Yourambulla Caves, the Wilpena Panorama in Hawker—places Angela had been to many times with her overseas visitors.

"We thought we'd lost you," Victoria said, as they steered her back to the car. They passed a pharmacist, but decided without speaking that this wasn't the time.

Angela was unruffled. "Didn't I tell you where I was going? I can go for another walk now if you like, while you finish whatever you need to do."

"We're finished, thanks," Victoria said. "Let's go home."

"Already?" Angela said.

"Already," Genevieve said.

After Angela went to bed that night—again, straight after dinner—Genevieve called a family meeting and told them what had happened. Nick came the closest they'd seen to losing his temper since the night of the accident.

"Anything could have happened to her," he said. "What were you both thinking?"

"We're sorry, Dad," Genevieve said. "It won't happen again."

Victoria stepped in, changing the subject. "We need to talk about the cooking and the housework too. I think we need to get a bit organized about it." With Angela no longer in charge, it had all gotten very haphazard. The washing was piling up. No one had swept the veranda in days. As for the cooking—they had nearly emptied the freezer. If Joan hadn't kept dropping over quiches and casseroles, they'd have been eating toast for most meals.

Genevieve offered to draw up a roster. Yes, she assured Lindy, she would do her share too. She was a socialist, not a dictator.

Genevieve took out the notebook. "I'm due to ring Ruth on Friday. We need to tell her everything we've noticed. Ig?"

He shrugged. "I really like her."

"We know that. But have you noticed anything unusual about her behavior?"

"She says the same thing a lot," Ig said. "I've heard about her daughter's tree house about ten times."

Lindy had noticed she'd had breakfast twice one day that week. "I just thought she was hungry, but maybe she'd forgotten about the first one."

"Dad?" Genevieve asked. She was shocked by his expression. For a moment, he looked so desolate.

"Nothing more than you've all said. She and I haven't talked much yet."

Over the next two days, more items were added to the

notebook. One day Angela changed her outfit three times. Her T-shirt was on backward once. Another day she offered to make lunch for everyone. When it came time, there was no sign of her. They found her asleep in bed. Victoria made lunch instead.

On Friday, Genevieve waited until Angela was out with Ig on their daily after-school bird-watching walk before she called Ruth.

"How does she seem mood-wise?" Ruth asked. "Is she relaxed, happy? Not agitated at all?"

"She's fine. We're not. My heart is still racing after losing her in Port Pirie."

"It probably wasn't a good idea to take her to a new place so soon."

No, it wasn't, Genevieve agreed. She lowered her voice. "Ruth, is it odd that she's not talking much to Dad? You read her Christmas letter. They'd had a few issues lately. Would she remember that?"

"Subconsciously she might. But there's no anger, no fighting?"

"No. They mostly just ignore each other. Like they were doing before the accident."

"Again, all you can do is let that unfold in its own way too. Just be patient. Stay positive."

It was back to that again.

Victoria was away for several hours the next day. She told everyone she was visiting neighboring stations to do her interviews for the radio series.

That night, she and Genevieve waited until everyone

had gone to bed before they met in the bathroom. She hadn't just been doing her interviews. She'd also gone to Port Pirie to buy two more pregnancy tests. Genevieve didn't need to do one again. Her period had arrived that afternoon.

Victoria did both tests. Both were positive.

FORTY-ONE

"Are you okay, Victoria?" Lindy asked at breakfast the next day. "You look pale. So do you, Genevieve."

"We're getting a bit of a bug, maybe," Genevieve said.

"Does that happen between twins?" Angela asked them. "If one gets sick, the other one does too?"

"Don't start asking them for their twin coincidence stories," Lindy said. "You'll be here all day."

"I'd like to hear them," Angela said.

For the next hour they took turns telling her their childhood twin stories. The same ones she'd told many times over the years.

By the time Angela had been home a fortnight, they'd developed a routine. Genevieve or Victoria drove Ig to school in Hawker each day and collected him again in the afternoon. He liked being back at his old school, he'd told them. The three girls made sure one of them was always near Angela. They spoke to Ruth regularly. The occupational therapist from Port Augusta visited and observed Angela over several hours. She praised them all, reassuring them that everything was going as well as possible.

Joan visited every second day, delivering meals that she had either made herself or that neighbors had asked her to pass on to the Gillespies. She ate dinner with them and then spent an hour out on the veranda with Angela. Nick and the children left them alone, content to hear the murmur of conversation, occasional laughter. It seemed that New Angela got on with Joan just as well as Old Angela had.

"Is this getting to be too much for you?" Genevieve asked Joan as she walked her out to her car after one of the visits. The temperature was rising again—it was forecast to be more than eighty-five degrees for the next week—but for now, it was beautiful, the air warm, not hot, with a light breeze too.

"I'm enjoying it. That sounds strange, but I mean it. She's different but she's the same. I like her."

"What do you two talk about?"

"What we always talked about. Life. Our husbands. Our children."

"I guess she's got plenty to say about husbands, seeing as she has two."

Joan smiled. "Will sounds too good to be true, if you ask me. So does Lexie. I prefer you lot, faults and all."

"Does she ask about us much?"

"A little. But I talk about you even if she doesn't. As Ruth said, the memories are there somewhere. I figure it won't do any harm for her to hear all your family stories again."

"Which ones are you telling her?"

Joan counted them off on her fingers. "The one about you two and your pet lambs, Lambington and Lambert. The time Lindy drove off in the ute when she was only seven. I also told her about Ig running away from boarding school. She seemed interested in that one. In fact, the most interested I've seen her since she got back. She told me she couldn't understand how a parent could send such a little kid away."

"That's a good sign, isn't it? That's what she thinks? The real her?"

"Let's hope so," Joan said as she got into her car. "See you in two days."

Genevieve resumed her e-mail updates that night.

Hello from the Gillespies

Thanks as ever for all your e-mails and notes, they are all very appreciated. Mum/Angela is still doing well, and we and her doctor are all pleased with her progress. Unfortunately we do need to keep to the "no visitors beyond immediate family and her oldest friend, Joan" rule, but we're making sure she knows you are all asking about her. Thanks also for not telephoning. More soon and thanks again.

If Celia received and read the e-mail, she chose to ignore it. She continued to ring each day, insisting on full reports. She was also dropping hints to Nick about coming to stay while he was in Ireland in late February, apparently to help with the cooking and cleaning.

"No, Dad. She doesn't help. We wait on her hand and foot," Victoria said.

"She's eighty years old," Nick said. "Please show some respect."

"If she comes, I'm going, Dad," Genevieve said. "She only wants to be a vulture around Mum. Angela, I mean. And Angela's too vulnerable. I wouldn't trust Celia around her."

"Don't overreact, Genevieve," Nick said. "It might be good to have an extra person here while I'm away."

"Then let's ask Joan to stay."

"We'll talk about it later."

They all knew what that meant. Whether they liked it or not, Celia was coming.

Genevieve tried to keep her father talking. She was getting worried about him. They might have settled into a sort of routine with their mother, but he hadn't. There was still the strange tension between him and Angela. An awareness of each other, but a deliberate separation. He seemed different too. Quiet. Distracted. Sad. Genevieve asked him often how he was, but he only ever gave her brief answers.

"I really would be happy to drive you to the airport, you know," she said to him. "It doesn't seem right that you're catching the bus to Adelaide. Your first overseas trip. We should all be there at the airport to wave you off."

"The bus is fine."

"Are you nervous, Dad?" Lindy said. "I would be if I were you. My first overseas trip. Being personally responsible for planning a reunion for two hundred Gillespies."

"Thanks, Lindy."

"I bet it'll be great," Genevieve said. "It'll be good for you to get away from us too. Can you show me the itinerary again?"

"I haven't shown it to you at all, have I?"

"Then show me now. Dad, please, I'm interested. We all are, deep down. It's just the nonstop Irish folk music that's setting our teeth on edge."

"Lindy told me she liked it."

"Lindy is sucking up so you'll tell her to forget about the cushion money she owes you."

"I am not," Lindy said. "And I will pay Dad back."

"When? In 2045?"

"Thanks so much for your support and belief, Genevieve." Lindy stood up. "I'll have you know I got another order this week. Word of mouth is definitely spreading. No thanks to you. So if you'll excuse me, I have sewing to do."

Genevieve waited until she was gone before she spoke. "She still doesn't realize most of those orders are coming from Joan, does she?"

"Joan?" Nick said.

Genevieve nodded. "She said her kids will kill her if they find out she's spending their inheritance on a range of cushions. Mind you, the one Lindy's doing now is from me, Victoria and Ig. We clubbed together. It took us ages to come up with a message. 'Best of luck with your wisdom teeth extraction.' It worked, though. She's been sewing it for days now." Genevieve smiled at him. "Come on, Dad. Please show me the itinerary. I really do want to see it."

After a moment's hesitation, he agreed.

Half an hour later, she put the folder down. "You'll be exhausted by the end of this. You land in Dublin at dawn, head straight off to Mayo, Donegal, and then down to Cork. Carol will be exhausted too after driving you everywhere."

"Perhaps your mother was right. It's a ridiculous obsession."

"Dad, your research is a good thing. Really. One day we'll all be interested in Great-Uncle Seamus and Great-Great-Aunt Bridie. I promise. And Mum only said it was an obsession. She didn't say it was ridiculous." She walked over and shut the kitchen door. "Can we please talk about Mum? About you and Mum? I know this is harder on you than it is on any of us. And that you don't like talking about it. But we need to. I just wanted to say I'm here if you need me."

"Thanks, Genevieve."

"Would it help if we all went away for the day? If the two of you had some time on your own? Maybe that would help bring back some of her memories. You could even show her around the station. Take her for a drive. The way she does with her overseas visitors."

"I don't know if that's a good idea."

"What did you do when she first came here? When you first met her?"

"I took her on a tour. Lots of tours. She'd never been out in country like this before."

"Could you take her on one of those tours again?"

"She might not want to."

Genevieve looked at him. "Dad, are you shy of her?"

"Of course not."

"What about if I ask her for you?"

He agreed. Five minutes later, Genevieve was back, smiling.

"She said yes."

They left at dawn the next day. Genevieve had been right, Nick knew. He was feeling shy. Not only shy, but nervous too. About taking his wife of thirty-three years across a property they'd traveled together hundreds of times. He was nervous about being alone with her. What to say to her. How to be with her.

Genevieve came out, still half-asleep, as Angela was in her room getting her jacket.

"Have fun," she whispered, kissing her father on the cheek.

Angela appeared at the door, jacket in hand. "Ready when you are," she said, smiling.

She seemed to smile so much more these days, Nick thought. She was different in so many ways, her voice, her personality, but that smile was still the same.

She started asking questions even as they were walking across the yard to the 4WD. About his family, about his parents, about how long they had been on Errigal. Where the name had come from. He gave her a brief history of the Gillespie cousins.

He started up the 4WD and drove out through the gate,

feeling as nervous as he'd felt more than thirty years earlier, when he'd first taken her on a tour.

Her questions kept coming. She wanted to know why there weren't sheep anymore. She frowned when she heard about the mining lease. "Mining operations, out here? Won't it spoil things for everyone? I'm sorry; this is none of my business. It must have been a very hard decision to make."

"It was. But we had no choice." He would never dream of telling a complete stranger what the situation was. She wasn't a complete stranger. "We owed nearly a million dollars. I had no other way of paying it back. I couldn't do it to the kids, leave them with that debt."

"A million dollars." She looked genuinely shocked. "What went so wrong? What happened?"

"Me," he said. "The drought didn't help. Then the wool market collapsed. But I made bad decisions along the way." In a few minutes he'd told her everything they had been through together as a couple over the past years. The realization they were spending twice as much feeding the animals than they would ever make selling their wool, or the animals themselves. How he'd taken out loans. How he'd had no choice but to sell most of his stock, keeping just the minimum of breeding stock. Then more loans. By the time the drought broke and the wool market began to improve, it was too late. There had been two years when he'd felt like he was drowning, as he sold off the last of his stock. Then the mining company had approached him. He hadn't chased them. It had felt like a lifeline, a miracle, when they told him that there was something of value in his land.

She'd stopped asking questions. She was just sitting there quietly beside him, letting him talk. And talk. He hadn't talked about the past years in that much detail ever. Not even to her. When she had been his real Angela.

"And none of the children were interested in taking over? None of the girls? I know Ig is still so young, but even him, in the future?"

He shook his head. "I thought Victoria might have been, but then she went in a different direction with her career. It's not for the other two girls. Or Ig either. I've thought about that a lot. All the trouble my Gillespie ancestors went to, that long journey from Ireland, starting the station from scratch. And now it's all over."

"Is that why you're organizing your family reunion? To make up for it in some way?"

Old Angela had never asked him that. This Angela had gotten straight to it.

"Yes," he said. "That's exactly why."

He started up the car.

He drove her to all the special spots on the property. To the Aboriginal rock paintings, a small collection of ochre markings on a cluster of rocks thirty kilometers from the homestead. They had been cataloged by the museum in Adelaide, and all the Aboriginal stockmen he had worked with had been aware of them, but otherwise only the Gillespies knew their location. Angela spent a long time looking at the markings, asking him about the area's Aboriginal history as she did so. He answered everything he could. Yes, he had employed many Aboriginal stockmen over the years. Yes, there were serious problems of disadvantage in Australia.

Yes, he'd see whether any of his former stockmen were around when Will and Lexie visited. Yes, if this dry weather kept up, they could have a proper camping night, sleep under the stars.

It felt so strange to say it, but he followed the others' lead. "My wife, Angela, usually organizes all of this for our overseas visitors. They love it."

"I can see why. It's incredible out here," Angela said. "Your wife's name is Angela too?"

He went still. Had he made a mistake? Had none of them mentioned this before?

"It's such a common name, isn't it?" she said. "Is she from around here?"

"No," he said. He nearly said she was English too, but stopped himself.

"What's she like?" Angela asked.

Nick hesitated. "She's still in there," Ruth had said. "What you say to her will register in some way. Be stored in her memory."

"She's wonderful," he said. "Kind. Warm. Clever. A great mother. A beautiful wife."

"Wow," Angela said, smiling. "She sounds like some woman."

"She is," Nick said.

"I hope Will talks about me like that."

It was his turn to ask the questions, Nick decided. "What's he like?"

"He's an architect. In London."

He waited for more.

"He's—" She hesitated, frowning. "He's tall. As tall as

you. He's one of the kindest men I've ever met. We've been married a long time. We take a photo on the same day every year."

"You do?"

She nodded. "I love traditions like that. We have another one. On our birthday, Will and I always give each other the same card. The exact same one. All we do is cross each other's names out." She was laughing. "We give each other the same present too. A five-dollar bill. The same one every year."

Nick was choosing his words very carefully. "Where did you meet?"

"In a pub," Angela said. "A pub in Sydney. He walked in, he was lost, and I know this sounds like I am making it up, but I'm not. I took one look at him and I think I fell in love. We met for lunch the next day and that was that. We've been together ever since."

"You met Will in Sydney? In a pub in Sydney?"

"No. In London. Not Sydney." Another frown. "I don't think he's ever been to Sydney."

Nick didn't ask her any more questions.

It was past five by the time they returned home. As they drove into the Errigal yard, she gave him another one of those smiles. In the late-afternoon light, her eyes looked so blue. So beautiful.

"Thanks very much, Nick. I enjoyed every minute of that."

"So did I," he said.

"How did you go?" Genevieve wanted to know later that night, after Angela had gone to bed.

"I took her on the tour. She asked a thousand questions. I brought her home."

"Dad, come on."

"It went well."

"That's it? That's all you're going to tell me?"

"That's all," he said.

Angela still wasn't asleep. She was enjoying her usual bedtime routine, sitting out on the veranda, enjoying the peace, the clear air, the nighttime rustles and bird sounds.

She was also thinking about the day she'd had. They had seen so much. She had learned so much. Nick was so nice. No, *nice* was too soft a word for him. So good. Clever. Knowledgeable. Courteous. Kind. Definitely kind. She had felt so looked after today.

He was good-looking too. Lean. Tanned. Such beautiful eyes. Dark, kind eyes—

She stopped herself there. Good God, she thought. She was like a teenager with a crush. The sooner Will got here, the better.

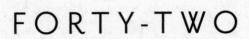

FORTY-TWO

It was Lindy who answered the phone call from Celia. They were all in the kitchen, apart from Angela, who was next door in the living room, watching TV. Several days earlier, she'd seen the shelf of box sets and started to look through them.

"I always meant to watch these," she said to Lindy. "I never seemed to have the time."

"You do now," Lindy had said.

Angela was currently working her way through a six-part adaptation of *Pride and Prejudice*. Ig was watching it with her, an episode or two every day after school.

Ig was spending more time with her than any of them. They had their own routine. Angela ate breakfast with him. She'd started helping make his school lunch. She helped him with his homework when he came home from school.

Lindy, Genevieve and Victoria were all taking turns driving him in to Hawker and back each day, rather than have him catch the bus. They thought he needed spoiling.

"Doesn't he take the bus to school anymore?" Angela asked one day.

An exchange of glances. None of them had mentioned the bus to her; they were sure of it.

In the kitchen now, the rest of them heard Lindy's side of the conversation with Celia.

"We're fine, Aunt Celia, thanks. Yes, she is too. A bit hard to say at the moment. Yes, that's right. You what? Oh, I'm so sorry to hear that. For six weeks? It must be hard, of course. Here? Tomorrow?" She gave them all a panicked look. "But you do know Dad's going to Ireland soon? Of course. Let me put him on."

She handed the phone to her father and hissed at her sisters, "She's sprained her wrist. Wants to know if she can come and stay here while she's recovering."

Five minutes later, Nick hung up.

"I gather you've explained already, Lindy? Celia's coming to stay. I know it's not ideal but I want you all to try to be nice to her. Please."

"Easy for you to say. You won't be here," Genevieve said under her breath.

"That's enough, Genevieve. Start setting a good example, would you?"

"Why do you always take Celia's side over ours? You care more about—"

As Nick and Genevieve continued to argue, Lindy started to get upset. Victoria tried to intervene, without success.

"Excuse me." Angela stood in the doorway, holding the remote control.

Nick stopped arguing. So did Genevieve.

"I was going to make tea. Would anyone else like some?"

"No, thanks," Nick said. He left the room.

Genevieve breathed out. "I'd love one. Thanks, Angela."

"Me too," Lindy said. Victoria said yes too.

"Just milk for me please," Ig called from his spot on the living room floor.

Nick was in the office. He was glad Angela had interrupted. It hadn't been serious—Genevieve and he had clashed like that for years—but it was better that they'd stopped when they had.

He picked up the itinerary beside him. He'd had an e-mail from Carol that morning with the final details. She was going to be away for a few days. A long-booked mini-break in Spain, but he wasn't to worry; everything was organized and she'd be at the airport in Dublin to meet him the following week.

It still felt wrong to be leaving. He'd had another conversation about it with Ruth, but she had assured him it was for the best. They all had to keep doing what Angela would be expecting to happen. Stay positive.

Yesterday, he had felt that way. Hopeful. Closer to her again. There had been moments when he had been overwhelmed with emotion. When he had heard Angela exclaiming over the landscape, or the color of one of the birds. It had taken him back in time. It was exactly how she'd been when he first gave her a tour of Errigal. So full of wonder. Had these reactions been New Angela's? Or his Angela's long-buried memories? When she came back, would she still have that sense of wonder?

Would she remember anything they had talked about?

Genevieve waited until just before nine o'clock that night to say sorry. To Angela, not to her father. He'd gone into the office, shut the door and not come out again.

Angela was sitting out on the veranda near her room, watching the evening sky. It was almost dark, with just the very last red trails of light visible.

"Do you mind if I join you?" Genevieve asked.

"Of course not," Angela said.

"Sorry about that fight before."

"Every family has arguments; don't worry. It's none of my business anyway."

Oh, yes it is, Genevieve thought. "We have another family member arriving soon too. Dad's aunt Celia. Our great-aunt. She was married to Dad's uncle. So she's not a real Gillespie but she thinks she is. Sorry. That sounded a bit rude."

Angela just smiled.

Genevieve felt an urge to keep adding detail, to try to spark a memory somehow. Perhaps also to warn New Angela? "She can be a bit tricky to be around, just to warn you. She's very critical. And Dad's going away soon. She'll be here the whole time he's away. It's his first trip overseas. He says he's looking forward to it but I think he's really nervous."

"Where is he going?" Angela asked.

Angela had been told about the trip several times. "Ireland. Just for a week. He's organizing his family reunion there next year. This is a reconnaissance trip. He's been working with a company of family tree experts in Dublin. A woman called Carol. They talk to each other nearly every day. We all think he's in love with her." Genevieve gave a merry, false laugh.

Angela's expression didn't change. She didn't say anything else either. Genevieve had seen this happen with her before. As if she wanted the conversation to end and to be left alone.

"Well, I'll leave you to the sunset," Genevieve said. "Good night."

"Good night," Angela said.

Angela didn't move from the veranda. She sat there, still, peaceful, watching the last of the color drain from the sky, the night and the stars appear.

What an interesting family these people were. In a funny way, she was glad Will and Lexie had been delayed. She wouldn't have had a chance to notice half of what she'd seen if they had been here with her. Angela was finding the Gillespies as fascinating as the scenery and the wildlife.

Genevieve was the real character, Angela had decided. Fun. Funny. All confidence on the outside. But there was more to her than that. A restlessness.

Victoria was definitely the less confident twin. Sweeter. More vulnerable. Preoccupied too. Angela had seen her lost in thought many times.

Angela liked Lindy very much too. She was very different from the other two, but she also seemed to be craving their approval, their attention. It probably was difficult to be a sister to twins. Especially for someone like Lindy, who still seemed to be finding her place in the world.

As for Ig . . . Angela smiled. She smiled whenever she thought of him. He was so solemn. So earnest. So interesting too, with his bird-watching, his friend Robbie, his expertise on the computer. He was so entertaining to be with. Easy. Over the past few days, though, she'd had to fight the oddest feeling. An overwhelming urge to hug him. To pull him close and plant a big kiss on his head. Yesterday she'd been on the verge of telling him she loved him, of all things.

And Nick? She was spending far too much time watching him too. It was his eyes, she realized. He didn't say a lot, but his eyes did. She also liked watching him with his children. The way he watched out for them all. Yes, he and Genevieve had been spiky with each other tonight, but usually he seemed entertained by her. He was always gentle with Victoria. They seemed to have a special bond. He was ever patient with Lindy. Amused by Ig. Who couldn't be amused by Ig?

Will was a good father too, of course. So patient and kind and loving to Lexie. Always giving her little surprises, like that tree house he'd built when she was little. He was handsome too. With his—

Angela stopped. She tried again, but nothing came to mind then either.

How odd.

She seemed to have completely forgotten what Will looked like.

The next morning, Victoria was in Port Pirie at the radio station. She had finished her first interviews with station families. She'd been glad of the distraction, glad of the excuse to drive out to their homesteads, spend time talking to the different family members. Anything to stop her mind from going over and over the fact of her pregnancy. She was still in shock, she realized. It hadn't sunk in properly. She didn't feel different enough yet, she'd said to Genevieve. It was almost a relief to switch back into interviewer mode. The station families' stories were fascinating, filled with memories of droughts, floods, isolation and adventure. She'd listened to them again back at home and made editing notes. She now just needed to put it all together in the studio, add some music and check her timings.

She'd been at work for an hour when she saw Keith outside. He mimed a coffee. She nodded and held up both hands to signify ten minutes.

He suggested they avoid the canteen and go out instead. They walked from the studio to the most popular coffee shop in town. It was bustling, as always. They got the last spare table. For fifteen minutes they talked about her interviews. Abruptly as ever, he switched topics.

"How's your mother doing?"

"She's well, thanks."

"So what does 'memory issues' actually mean?"

"She has issues with her memory."

"Very droll. Can you be more specific?"

"Yes, I could but no, I won't."

"She has amnesia, you mean?"

"Keith, how are you! Did you get that media release I e-mailed you?" It was one of the local councilors. Victoria was glad they'd been interrupted.

"Sorry about that," Keith said after the woman had gone. "You were saying?"

"I was saying thanks for being so concerned. And shouldn't we be getting back?"

"I'll ask you again next time we have coffee," he said, with a smile.

As they walked back inside the station, the receptionist handed Keith a bundle of phone messages. He glanced through them quickly as they walked down the corridor, already back in work mode.

At his office, they stopped. "You've nearly finished your editing, did you say? Well done. I'll have a listen. If it's all good, we'll air the first one next week. Have it to me by five, okay?"

"Sure," she said.

"Just one more thing."

She stopped.

"Is there any chance you'd like to have dinner with me on Saturday?"

"You said no?" Genevieve asked later that afternoon, back on Errigal.

Victoria nodded.

"There goes any chance of a full-time job," Genevieve said. She was only half joking.

"So be it," Victoria said. "One messy affair with a boss is enough for anyone, don't you think?" She lowered her voice even further. "I made a decision about Fred today too."

"You did? Those hormones have turned you into Super-woman."

"I rang him. I've asked him out for a date."

"You what? Without telling me? When? Tonight?"

Victoria shook her head. "He's going away on a stock-buying trip with his dad. When he gets back, in a week or so."

"And are you going to tell him—"

She nodded. "He needs to know. Even though it will change everything, I need to tell him."

FORTY-THREE

Ig was watching his father pack. The packing had been going on for a few days. Ig had been helping him.

He didn't usually get to spend this much time with his dad. When he was little, a few years ago, his dad used to take him out onto the station a lot, into the shearing shed, mustering the sheep, fixing the windmills or the fences, but they hadn't done that in ages, now that they didn't have any sheep. Ig had never really liked it that much anyway. He liked all the windmills and the weather instruments, and he loved driving the cars, but he wasn't really that interested in the sheep side of things, he'd decided. Robbie was the same. He thought sheep were boring.

It was always fun with his mum, though. He loved helping her on the computer, and going out with her visitors on those tours. It still was fun with her, even though she apparently wasn't his mum at the moment. He was calling her Angela like he'd been told to, but apart from that, it was pretty much the same as it always had been with her, except better, because she had more time to just muck around. Before all of this memory stuff, before her accident, she used to be cooking a lot, or rubbing her head with those headaches, or washing clothes, or sweeping. She didn't do any of that stuff now. She made cups of tea for everyone now and then, but mostly she liked to go for walks on her own or with him. She did heaps of reading. She took naps these days too. She'd also started watching DVDs. He liked watching them with her.

They talked about lots of different stuff on their walks. She talked about her childhood in London. On Google street view, they had even found the exact house she grew up in. She'd been amazed and had nearly cried. He couldn't think why they'd never done that before. Maybe because he'd never thought about doing it and she had never asked. He'd always known she was from London and he knew she sounded a bit different from other kids' mothers but it was also just her voice. Genevieve and Victoria and Lindy kept saying that she sounded much more English since she had the accident, now that she was New Angela, as they called her, but he couldn't really hear much difference.

He knew loads more about his mum now than he knew before. The suburb she had grown up in was called Forest Hill and her house was on a hill and there had been a few trees round it so it was a good name. It was near a famous museum called the Horniman Museum. He'd been able to show her that on Google street view too. She'd told him the museum had lots of very interesting exhibits of birds and bugs and beetles, and even a huge stuffed walrus, of all things. He'd gone straight to their Web site. Together they'd looked at everything in the museum, watched videos, taken a virtual tour, read all about the walrus. His mum had gotten all amazed again, pointing to the bird displays she remembered, the gardens she'd had picnics in. It looked like a really good place, Ig agreed. He'd like to see it in real life himself one day.

"Nearly there, Ig," Nick said now, putting another sweater in his case. "It's so hot here, I can't imagine wearing any of this cold-weather stuff."

"You'll need it, though. I looked it up on the Internet. It's going to be very wet and cold while you're there."

"I think it's very wet and cold in Ireland most of the time." Nick stopped packing and sat on the bed. "You doing okay, little mate? About your mum?"

Ig nodded.

"She's still your mum, you know. Deep down. She'll come good soon."

Ig nodded again. They were silent for a moment as Nick resumed his packing.

"If I had to make up a new life, I'd give myself super-powers," Ig said. "Not just another husband and another kid like mum has."

"Would you?" Nick said. "What kind of superpowers?"

"Wings. And being invisible. And maybe some kind of weapon that came out of my fingertips or my feet or something, that would take my attackers by surprise."

"That'd be handy at school, I guess. Being able to fly or be invisible."

Ig nodded.

"You okay being back at school here?"

Ig shrugged. "It's okay." He hopped off the bed. "See you later, Dad."

"See you, Ig."

He was at the door when his dad called him back.

"You'll look after your mum for me while I'm away, won't you?"

"Yep," Ig said.

As he walked outside to his cubby, he felt pretty good. He liked talking to his dad about grown-up things like that.

Celia's bus arrived on time. Genevieve and Nick collected her. Genevieve suggested they have a cup of tea in the café in Hawker before they drove out to Errigal.

"It might make it easier to know about the ground rules, Aunt Celia," she said as they took seats at a corner table. She was glad there was no one they knew here today. The other customers were all tourists.

"'Ground rules'?" Celia said. "That sounds a bit extreme."

"We're doing everything exactly as our neuropsychologist has advised us," Genevieve said. "We all call her Angela, not Mum. And we all go along with whatever she says about her life in London, about her husband, Will, and her daughter, Lexie."

Celia sniffed. "It all seems very self-indulgent. Nick, what do you think about it?"

"Angela has a temporary brain injury, Celia," he said.

"This is part of her treatment. You're welcome with us, you know that, but you do need to follow our lead."

Good for you, Dad, Genevieve thought.

"But will she ever recover?" Celia asked. "Or will we have to keep up this charade forever?"

Genevieve only just kept her temper. "It's a rare enough condition, but yes, other people who have had it have recovered their memories. Not always everything, but usually most of it."

"How long has it taken them?"

"Weeks. Months. In one case we read about, years. There's no set pattern to it. If you find it too tricky, perhaps it would be best if you didn't come and stay." Genevieve ignored the sharp look from her father. All her protective instincts were firing. "We'd hate Angela to have any kind of setback."

"You're not being very subtle, Genevieve," Celia said.

"I can be even more unsubtle, actually," Genevieve said. "Please don't do or say anything that might upset Angela, Celia. Because I'll be watching to make sure you don't."

"Are you going to let her speak to me like that, Nick?"

Genevieve answered for him. "Dad will be in Ireland soon, Celia. I'm in charge while he's gone."

"That's enough, both of you." Nick stood up. "Let's go home."

Angela didn't appear until Celia had been in the house for an hour. She'd stayed in her bedroom reading. When she did join them, Genevieve and Victoria both noticed she had her shirt buttoned up wrong.

Genevieve made the introductions, describing Angela as an overseas guest. "All the way from London."

Angela held out her hand, smiling. "It's nice to meet you, Celia."

"Nice to meet you too," Celia said.

With that, Angela left the room again.

"She looks just the same," Celia said, too loudly, once Angela was gone. "You wouldn't be able to tell there was anything wrong with her."

Genevieve tried to hush her. "What did you expect?"

"The way you were carrying on I was expecting a completely different person. But she seems perfectly normal."

"It shows itself gradually," Victoria said.

Celia took a delicate sip of tea. "I'll look forward to seeing it."

Nick's departure was now just one day away. He announced he was going to Port Augusta to get last-minute items of warm clothing, as well as some Australian souvenirs for Carol.

Lindy took the opportunity to take over the computer. Since they'd come home, she was in there whenever possible. If she wasn't updating her cushions Web site or checking for new orders, she was Skyping Richard in Melbourne. She'd been talking to him for only five minutes that afternoon when she came running up the hall to share the news.

"Richard wants to come and visit!"

"While Dad's away?" Genevieve asked.

"Dad won't mind, will he?"

"Richard knows all about Mum, doesn't he?" Victoria asked. "He'll be able to cope with it?"

"Of course he will. And of course he knows. He and I talk about everything, all the time. Last night he Skyped me just as I was about to Skype him. It's like we've got some kind of spiritual connection."

"Wow," Genevieve said. "Though I'd call it more of an Internet connection than a spiritual one."

"You're just jealous," Lindy said. "Because I've got a boyfriend and you haven't." She flounced out, back to the computer again.

Victoria put her hand on Genevieve's arm. "Don't. Just let it go. Let her go."

"How can I? All this happening with Mum, and it's as if Lindy hasn't even noticed."

"We're all coping in our own way. We all need a distraction. Maybe Richard's her distraction."

"And maybe getting annoyed with Lindy is mine," Genevieve said.

Genevieve waited until she'd heard Lindy finish her Skype call. She tried to remember Victoria's advice. Be kind. Be understanding.

She joined Lindy in the office. "How are you doing, Lindy? About Mum? Are you okay?"

"Fine," Lindy said. "Why? Has something happened to her today?"

Genevieve dug her nails into her hands. "It's just we're all finding it a bit hard. Her being her, but not her. I wanted to make sure you're doing fine with it."

Lindy seemed puzzled to be asked. "Well, sure. Everything's happening like Ruth said it would, isn't it? We just have to go along with it. Stay patient and positive. Keep busy ourselves. So that's what I'm doing. That's okay, isn't it?"

Genevieve wasn't sure whether she wanted to slap her sister or hug her. "Sure, Lindy. That's great."

Nick hadn't gone to Port Augusta to get clothes and souvenirs. He'd gone to see his psychologist once more before his trip. He told Jim all that had happened since his last visit. It took some time.

"Confabulation?" Jim said. "It's a fascinating condition. And Angela's in very good hands. I've heard of Ruth myself. I'm also sure she's right: your trip to Ireland is for the best, not just for the reunion but for you and for Angela. How has your relationship with her been affected?"

"There isn't one. It's like she's a stranger, a temporary guest on the station. We say good morning, good evening; we talk about the weather."

"Even so, do you feel any connection to her? Does she still feel like your wife?"

Nick gave that some thought. "Yes. She keeps reminding me of the old Angela. The Angela from years ago, I mean, not the Angela she was before the accident. She's relaxed. Happier. She laughs a lot. She goes for long walks. Reads. Watches TV."

"The old Angela didn't?"

"She was always too busy. She'd been getting bad headaches too. For months."

"Has there been any physical contact between the two of you?"

Nick shook his head. "There wasn't even before the accident. Not for a long time, anyway."

"Let me rephrase that. Do you still feel attracted to her? More or less than you did with the old Angela?"

"The old Angela was beautiful. The new Angela looks the same."

"You still find her attractive?"

He nodded.

"That's a good sign. How are you feeling?"

He told the truth. "I'm sad. I miss her. I'm scared she won't come back. That this is it. And that I wasn't a good husband to her before the accident. That if she has any memories of me, they're—" He stopped, his voice faltering. After a moment, he continued. "That they're not good ones. That it's over between us. That when she comes back she won't love me anymore."

Jim waited quietly until Nick had stopped talking. "Do you still love her?"

He nodded.

"Then hold on to that. Go away, have some time to yourself, away from Angela, away from your family. And in the meantime—"

"Please don't say be patient. Or positive."

Jim smiled. "I was actually going to say *bon voyage*."

At seven a.m. the next day, Genevieve and Nick were in Hawker, waiting for the bus to Adelaide. They knew some of the people who were also waiting. They'd had brief conversations, but they were practiced now at not saying much about Angela without appearing rude. Yes, she was coming along well. Yes, they were very lucky; it could have been so much more serious. Yes, it was great that Nick's trip was still going ahead.

"You're sure you've got everything?" Genevieve asked him once they were on their own again.

"Passport, ticket, euros. Yes, thanks."

"And Carol's definitely meeting you at Dublin airport? I haven't heard you talking to her lately."

"She's been away. But everything's organized."

"You won't have an affair with her, will you, Dad?"

"For the last time, Genevieve, I am not and I will not be having an affair with—"

Genevieve linked his arm. "I'm teasing. I promise. You know it's my job in the family to annoy you."

He smiled. "You're very good at your job."

The bus pulled up. The other passengers moved forward. The driver got out and started to load the baggage.

"I'm proud of you, you know," Genevieve said suddenly.

"Another joke?"

"I'm serious, Dad. I'm really proud. I know things are hard for everyone at the moment, but I think it's a big deal that you're doing this trip. I love that you're still doing it. And I love you, by the way. Even if I cleverly hide it sometimes."

He hugged her. A proper hug. "I love you too. Even when you're doing your best to drive me mad."

"Me? Surely not. Send us postcards, won't you?" she said.

"I'll be back home before you get them."

"Send one anyway. And remember, Ig wants a book about Irish birds."

"What should I bring you?"

"A leprechaun doll. And some rosary beads. I'm joking. I don't need anything. Just come back safely. And take care over there."

"And you take care of everyone here." He hugged her again. "Especially your mum."

"I will. I promise." Genevieve waited there, waving, until the bus went out of sight.

Back on Errigal, Angela was in her room. She was holding a digital camera, practicing how to use it. Ig had brought it in to her that morning. It belonged to his mum, he'd said. She hadn't used it in ages. Maybe Angela would like to give it a go?

She'd sat out on the veranda with it for a while, taking some shots, but the older lady, Celia, had come and sat beside her and started asking her dozens of questions. How old was she? Where had she grown up? What was her husband's name? What was her job? Before long, one of the girls had come out and interrupted. They often seemed to do that. Angela didn't mind. She'd caught Celia looking at her in an odd way once or twice. It made her feel uncomfortable.

The camera was easy to use. Out on the veranda, she practiced some more. She could look at her photos immediately too. No waiting for them to be developed. She could take hundreds to show Will and Lexie when they arrived.

They'd be here soon. She'd have to ask Genevieve or

perhaps Victoria to drive her to the airport to get them. Genevieve had taken Nick to the airport today. Or to somewhere to catch a bus to the airport. She hadn't heard all the details. She'd been outside as they were leaving, leaning against the fence, looking out over the paddocks, marveling again at how often the colors changed out here. He had come up to her and said good-bye.

He had looked at her and for a moment, she'd had the strangest, strangest urge to put her arms around him. To hold him tight. She'd almost been able to imagine the feel of his body. . . .

It was so odd. Perhaps it was just as well he'd gone to Ireland. And Will really had better get here soon.

FORTY-FOUR

Thirty-six hours of travel. Nick had counted them down. The bus from Hawker. Flights from Adelaide to Melbourne. Melbourne to Dubai. Dubai to Dublin. Hours waiting in what felt like overheated, overlit, overcrowded shopping centers rather than airports. More hours sitting in a cramped seat, too close to a complete stranger, with nothing to do but eat or watch movies on a screen the size of an envelope. More than once he'd felt the panic rising. He was trapped in this metal tube up in the sky, thousands of kilometers from his wife, his family, from Errigal. He had to get out of there. He couldn't get out of there.

But now here he was. In Ireland. In Dublin.

It was six o'clock in the morning. He was in the immigration line behind dozens of others, his passport ready.

Outside, Carol would be waiting for him. She'd be holding up a sign with his name on it, she'd told him. They were going to get moving right away, driving across to Mayo that day. The itinerary was tight, with so much to see and do in eight days. But she was confident they'd manage it.

He moved forward a place. Then another. Finally, he was called forward. He handed over his passport, waiting for the warm Irish welcome, the witty comment. Nothing. It was stamped and handed back to him, the next person beckoned forward.

He'd just stepped out into the baggage hall when he heard a buzzing noise. The buzzing turned into a tune. "Danny Boy." Genevieve or Ig must have changed the ringtone on his phone.

"Dad, are you there yet?" It was all four kids, on loudspeaker. "How was the plane?" "How are you feeling?" "What films did you watch?" "What's Carol like?"

"I'm not outside yet. I'm waiting for my bag. How's Angela?"

He heard Genevieve shush the others. "She's fine. No change. We're all fine. Just checking you're okay and that the phone is working."

"I'm fine too," he said. He briefly told them about the flights, the food, the films. His bag appeared. "I better go." He was about to say, "Give your mum my love," when he stopped himself.

"Say hi to Carol from us," Genevieve called before she hung up.

Nick had expected only a few people outside waiting with signs. There were more than thirty, many with large banners decorated in ribbons and paint, welcoming home emigrants. He saw reunions between parents and children, meetings with grandchildren. Chauffeurs in suits held up iPads bearing names, instead of handwritten signs. Carol had said she'd be right there waiting too. She must have been delayed. He double-checked, rereading the names on the other signs and iPads. No, nothing for Nick Gillespie. He checked his phone. No message. She had his number. His phone was working. She was probably driving. Trying to park the car. The plane might have been early. He'd just have to wait.

Thirty minutes later he was still waiting.

An hour later he was still waiting.

He'd called the mobile number she had given him several times. No answer. It was too early for anyone to be at her office, but he called there all the same. No answer, no voice mail either.

Ninety minutes after the plane had landed, he was still waiting. He couldn't get an answer on any of her numbers. He pulled out a printout of the last e-mail he'd sent her. She had the right arrival time, the right date. They had last spoken just before she went on holiday. She had been as bright and cheerful as ever, all organized and ready to go, she'd assured him. He'd sent through the latest payment, and the additional fee to cover their travel expenses. The final fee would be paid at the end of this week.

So where was she?

There was no point sitting in the airport any longer. He was starting to feel light-headed from lack of sleep. Even if there had been a rental car outside waiting for him, he knew he was in no condition to drive across the country to Mayo on his own.

He saw the tourist information desk. Fifteen minutes later, he was on his way to the taxi stand, with the name and address of a city center hotel.

It was freezing outside. The sky was gray. There was steady rain. The taxi driver smelled of cigarette smoke. He grunted when Nick gave the name of the hotel. The Gresham on O'Connell Street. As they drove, Nick waited for the witty chat, the stories. There was nothing. The driver turned up the radio. It was a pop station. The DJ sounded more American than Irish.

Nick hadn't expected green fields, whitewashed cottages and stone walls here in Dublin. But in the early-morning winter light, the suburbs in from the airport seemed gray and bleak. They got stuck in a traffic jam, in the middle of the morning rush hour. He looked out at rows of shops, at pubs, all with the Irish names he'd expected. Kavanagh. Fagan. Kennedy.

The hotel looked expensive, five stories high with a granite facade and flags flying out front. But what choice did he have? He hadn't researched hotels in Dublin. He'd expected to have only one day here, when he'd finished touring other parts of the country. He paid the taxi with an unfamiliar bill and carried his luggage in. He booked one of the cheapest rooms, trying to do the calculation from euro to Australian dollars. His room was in the back of the hotel, overlooking a garage. The rain was still pouring down. He had to turn on the bedroom light. If he hadn't seen the clock downstairs telling him it was ten a.m., he would have thought it was still before dawn.

If only Angela were here. He'd had the same thought on the plane. At each airport. At each step of the journey.

He meant to lie down and close his eyes for just a few minutes. He woke with a start three hours later. His phone had beeped. A text message. It must be from Carol, at last.

It was from his network provider, welcoming him to Ireland.

He took out his itinerary again. He called all the numbers he had for Carol. No answer.

He had the address of her office. He'd go there. Maybe there was a problem with her phone. He got directions from the hotel receptionist. It was close by, she said. Right on the river.

He found the building, three stories, red brick. It was dilapidated-looking. Three steps led up to the front door, a row of buttons on the side. He looked for her company name. It wasn't there. He pressed the top button. No answer. The next button. It took him five buttons to get any reply. He started to explain, talking into the intercom. The person at the other end didn't speak, just buzzed open the door.

The hallway was cold. The walls had peeling paint. There was a box of brochures on the ground, with a pile of letters on top. He quickly leafed through them. Nothing for Carol's company. He checked the box. The brochures were for an Irish cabaret night in a hotel farther along the river.

He knocked on the nearest door. No answer. He went up

the stairs. There were two doors. He knocked on both. One room was occupied. A man in his thirties, with a beard, heavy-rimmed glasses. No, he told Nick, he didn't know Carol. But he was new there. It was a short-term office-rental setup. "You could try upstairs," he said.

There were three doors upstairs. He tried all of them. The first opened as he knocked on it. An empty room, just a battered desk and a few discarded power leads on the floor. The window didn't look over the river, but onto an alleyway. He looked down. Litter blew along the ground. The second office was being used as a storeroom. The third office was occupied. A young woman, Indian he thought, working at a computer. No, she said, she didn't know anyone here called Carol. She'd been in the building for eight months. Was he sure he had the name right? The right address?

Nick showed her one of Carol's e-mails. Yes, the woman confirmed, it was definitely this address. But this was just a short-term rental place, she said, as the man downstairs had said. Tenants came and went all the time.

There were no more rooms to try. If Carol had ever been here, she wasn't any longer.

He stopped for a coffee and a sandwich on O'Connell Street. He had an urge to call home, to talk to—who? The only person he wanted to talk to about this was Angela. The one person he couldn't talk to about this was Angela.

On the way back to his hotel, he passed an Internet café. Five minutes later, he was at a terminal. He keyed in the Web site address of Carol's company. It wouldn't load. He retyped it. Still nothing. How long was it since he'd gone to this site? Months, he realized. He and Carol had always communicated by Skype or e-mail. He'd had no need to visit her Web site again after the first time.

He called her number again. No answer. About to log out, he sent a quick e-mail home and then went outside into the cold and the rain.

There was no denying it. He knew what had happened. He'd fallen for an Internet scam. He had been targeted by someone with an Irish accent, wit and charm, who had strung him along, step by step, euro by euro. Until the last minute. The last week, more accurately. The last time he'd sent her money.

But he still wanted to convince himself he was wrong. He had her bank account details. He'd track her down through that. If it was a Dublin-based bank account, he just needed to go to the head office, explain what had happened. Surely they'd be duty bound to give him some information?

He checked the e-mail. It wasn't a Dublin bank account. It was a UK one. On Jersey, the island. An offshore tax haven.

He went to the police instead.

Two hours later, he was on his way back to his hotel. He'd met a sympathetic policeman in the city center station. Not a policeman, a guard, he'd learned they were called here. A young man, in his late twenties. He'd listened as Nick explained the situation. He'd called the numbers on the e-mail from Carol. He'd googled the Web site.

Nick had saved him the bother of having to state the obvious. "I've been conned, haven't I?"

"I'm sorry, sir. I think you have. Was it a lot of money?"

"A bit," he said. More than he was ever going to admit.

"Does she have your credit card details? You might need to cancel them if she does."

That was one positive. She didn't. He had sent her all the money via electronic transfer. To Dublin, he'd thought. To a bright, cheery office full of genealogists in Dublin. Not a tax haven on some island. Had she ever even been in Dublin? There was no way of knowing. But he knew one thing for sure. She wasn't about to turn up.

All the bad thoughts came at him again. He was an idiot. A fool. How had he been so stupid? Why hadn't he realized? He'd been a stupid, sitting duck. How much money had he sent her? For nothing? What a—

Stop those thoughts.

He'd been taught how to. He had to remember the lesson now. They were just thoughts. He had to let them flow past. Yes, it was bad; yes, he'd been conned. But it wasn't the end of the world. He hadn't been hurt. It was only money. He concentrated on those rational thoughts instead, turned up their volume in his head. He began to feel calmer. He made himself imagine his psychologist talking to him. "Yes, Nick, you're in an unexpected situation. How are you going to react? Because you're in charge of your own reaction. You can decide how to feel about it. Yes, you can feel humiliated. Stupid. Embarrassed. Now, move on. What else can you feel? Relief that it wasn't worse? Even a small admission that somehow, deep down, you had always suspected Carol was too good to be true?" Or was that hindsight, trying to salvage some pride? Yes. But it was all helping him to feel better. It was only money. He was still here, wasn't he? In Ireland. The land of his ancestors.

But what the hell did he do now?

Back in his room, he was at a loss. He was tired, but he couldn't sleep yet. He was tempted to go downstairs to that big bar he'd seen opposite the reception desk, to take a seat, order a pint. The first pint of Guinness on Irish soil that he had been promising himself. But this wasn't the time.

He went downstairs and took a seat on the other side of the lobby. He ordered tea. He would read while he drank it. Not a newspaper, not a book. He took out his uncle's research notes. At the last moment, he'd packed them. He'd read through them all already, back in Australia, at Celia's, at the hospital, in those bad first days after Angela's accident. He'd needed all the distraction he could find then. He'd actually felt pity for his uncle as he read his notes. Everything in them was so different from the detailed information Carol had sent him. His poor uncle, getting it all so wrong.

The facts in here could still be wrong. All these addresses of Gillespie homelands, birth certificates, other documents. Who was to say his uncle hadn't been conned at some stage too? But they were better than nothing. And they were now all he had.

FORTY-FIVE

"That's it," Ig said, leaning back in the office chair. "You're all set up."

Genevieve shook her head. "How can you be ten years old and know how to set up a Web site?"

"Because it's easy. And I'm nearly eleven."

"It can't be easy or I would know how to do it too." The screen in front of them was full of color. The title was across the top: *The Hair Raiser*. Ig had found a cartoon of a woman under a hair dryer, wearing cat's-eye glasses and smoking a cigarette in a long holder. Under that, Genevieve had written: *Your secret is safe with me. Not!*

"I can't believe you're doing this," Victoria said. "You're asking for trouble. After everything that happened in New York and to me. Seriously, Genevieve. It's bad karma."

"It's not! It's just a bit of fun. I have to do something to stop my poor brain from atrophying. None of you lot will let me near your hair, not even Celia. I can't just sit around waiting for Angela's to grow again."

"Let's get started," Ig said, pulling his chair close to the computer again. "Tell me some secrets."

"Okay, let me think. One of the actors on that first series I worked on went through rehab three times. He broke out each time, literally knocked down the door and made a run for it. We were all sent out to try to find him. I think I looked in every bar in Greenwich Village."

"The poor man. Why should anyone but him and his family know that?" Victoria said. "He might still be going through treatment. You could set him back months."

"Fair enough. Too personal. What about that music video I worked on? That indie band from Seattle. The singer is gay. She's not married to the bass player at all."

"So what?" Victoria said. "That's her business."

Genevieve spun around. "Stop heckling, will you? I'm trying to launch my career as a controversial gossipmonger and you're making it very difficult."

"I don't approve—that's why."

"I think I liked you better when you were under my thumb." She winked as she said it. Victoria just rolled her eyes. "Okay, Ig. She wins. Forget the celebrity gossip. I'll start with hairdressing horror stories from my past instead. If this site becomes the go-to place for hairdressers to swap tales, I'll get loads of advertising from the big shampoo companies. Instant riches."

Ig waited. So did Victoria.

"Go on, then," Victoria said. "Give us some horror stories."

"I can't think of anything. Misbehaving film stars aside, I always really liked my clients." She took the mouse from Ig, googled a hairdresser's federation and found the chat room. "I'll ask other stylists to e-mail their tales anonymously. I'll get hundreds then." She typed quickly: *Any horror stories? Badly behaved clients? Bleach disasters? Get it off your chest and onto my Web site!*

"What are you all doing?"

Genevieve looked over her shoulder at Lindy. "Talking about you. Where's Angela? I thought you were supposed to be keeping an eye on her."

"She's outside with her camera. Mum never took all these photos before this, did she?"

"I don't think she ever even turned her camera on," Victoria said.

"Her photos are really good," Ig said.

"How do you know?" Genevieve asked.

"I uploaded them for her. I'll show you." He took the mouse back from her.

"How do you even know the word 'uploaded'?" she asked. "You're some sort of shrunken man in a kid's body, aren't you?"

Ig ignored her, clicking until he found a folder marked "Angela's photos." He showed his sisters. There were dozens. No big, sweeping landscapes but lots of tiny detail. The blue door of the pottery shed, with the red rosebush beside it. Sun shining on the metal bars of the sheep pens. The golden stone of the chapel. A pink galah feather on the ground.

"They're really good," Victoria said. "They'd make beautiful postcards."

"Any more word from Dad?" Lindy asked.

"Just that one e-mail," Genevieve said. "He's a bit jet-lagged but it's all going well."

"Can I have the computer now?" Lindy asked.

"You're Skyping Richard again? He'll be here soon enough, won't he?"

"He's had to delay his trip. He's still coming, but he's gone away for a few days to do some intensive study first. Down to Phillip Island. A friend of Jane's has a holiday house there."

"Do you mean Horrible Jane's gone with him? It's just the two of them away together?" At Lindy's nod, Genevieve gave a low whistle. "You're very trusting. Or do I mean very naïve?"

"Of course I trust him, Genevieve. Trust is the cornerstone of any good relationship. She's just his flatmate. He's my boyfriend. I actually need to check my Web site for new orders. I've finally finished the wisdom tooth one. It took ages."

Victoria pinched Genevieve. Ig smiled to himself.

"Well done," Genevieve said. "Want me to run it through spell-checker for you?"

"Very funny." Lindy took a seat and clicked onto her Web site. The others were just leaving when she stopped them. "This has to be a joke. Is it you, Genevieve? Because it's not funny if it is."

"Of course it's funny if it's me. What are you talking about?"

"This order for twenty cushions. Oh, my *God*. It's not for twenty. It's for two hundred cushions. Two *hundred*."

"It must be a typo."

"It's not a typo," another voice said.

They turned around. Celia was standing at the door. "I ordered them."

"But two hundred?" Lindy said. "Did you mean two?"

"No, I meant two hundred. It could even be more. I thought your cushion covers would make perfect souvenirs for everyone who comes to your father's Gillespie reunion. Something handmade, by a Gillespie herself. You can decide on the design, but I thought a few shamrocks might be nice. And simple wording. 'Gillespies Reunion, Ireland,' and the date should do it, don't you think?"

All their mouths were now open.

"But that will take me weeks. Months," Lindy said. "And it will cost you a fortune."

"You've got the time and I'm prepared to pay. It's my contribution to the reunion. I loathe flying, so I can't be there. This way I can play a small part. My husband would approve, I'm sure."

Lindy beamed. "I can't believe it! I'll be able to use up all my supplies. I might even have to order more!"

"No!" Victoria and Genevieve said as one.

Lindy sprang out of the chair and threw her arms around Celia. "Oh, Celia, thank you! You're a lifesaver. I'm going to get started right now."

Celia patted her hair down. "Careful, now. No need to be quite so boisterous." But she couldn't hide the fact she was pleased.

Later that morning, Genevieve set out with Victoria to drive to a station sixty kilometers to the west of Errigal.

They'd arranged the trip two days earlier. A joint mission, Genevieve had dubbed it. Victoria was going to interview all three generations of the station family, the Ryans. Genevieve was going to do their hair.

Genevieve was soon in her element. They set up a production line in the house. All seven members of the family, male and female, old and young, took turns talking to Victoria in one room. After they'd been interviewed, they went to the sunroom at the back of the house to have their hair cut or styled by Genevieve. She even managed to do a perm, using the laundry sink. It all took her back to her earliest days as an apprentice hairdresser in Port Augusta, the chat, the constant activity, moving from one person to the next so quickly. Each family member asked about Angela, of course, but the conversation had quickly widened to cover everything from sports, health issues, TV programs, weather, celebrity gossip, relationship problems.

"That was brilliant," Genevieve said as they waved goodbye five hours later. "Maybe we should go into business together."

Victoria raised an eyebrow. "Really? You'd last a month out here."

Genevieve shrugged. "Two months, maybe."

Shortly afterward, the turnoff to Hawker and Errigal appeared. They kept driving. At Genevieve's urging, Victoria had made an appointment with her former doctor in Port Augusta. She'd asked Genevieve to come with her.

In the car they could talk without any fear of being overheard. "Is it a wasted trip, though?" Victoria said. "Do I really need to do another test? I've done three. They've all been positive. How could they all be wrong? And I feel different, Genevieve. I'm sure I'm not imagining it. It feels like something is happening. Something inside me."

Genevieve reached across to squeeze her sister's hand. "You're going to need to see a doctor eventually. It may as well be now. Have you decided what you want to do?"

"I haven't been able to think about anything else. I've changed my mind a hundred times already. But I'm nearly thirty-three, Genevieve. This might be my only chance to have a baby."

"But it's—"

"I know it's his. I know what you think of him. What everyone thinks of him. But that's not the baby's fault. And he wasn't all bad. He was smart and he could be funny and he—"

"Was married. With kids," Genevieve interrupted.

"I knew that. I knew it was just an affair. I knew there was no future in it. I knew all that at the time. But it was my choice, Genevieve. I still wanted it. And I'm not a complete innocent, no matter what Mum said in her letter."

"And Fred? Have you thought about him? What you're going to tell him?"

"I can't stop thinking about Fred. It's all so complicated, isn't it? But he has to know. I have to tell him. As soon as he gets back." She hesitated. "Even if he decides afterward that he never wants to see me again."

Genevieve just squeezed her hand again.

"Yes, you're pregnant," Dr. Reynolds said.

This was the first time Dr. Reynolds had seen either of

the twins in nearly five years. Before she'd done the tests, Victoria had told her everything, all the circumstances. If she was expecting any sort of lecture, she didn't get it. The older woman was matter-of-fact as they worked out the dates since Victoria's last period. She was nearly eleven weeks pregnant.

"Have you given any thought to your options, Victoria?" Dr. Reynolds asked.

Victoria hesitated for only a moment. "I want to have it."

"And the father?"

"He won't be involved."

"Does he know you're pregnant?"

Victoria shook her head.

"He has a right to; you know that," Dr. Reynolds said.

"I'll be the father," Genevieve said. "I mean it, Victoria. We'll do it together."

"It'll be hard work," Dr. Reynolds said. "It's hard work for a couple. It's extremely hard work for a single woman."

"She's not a single woman," Genevieve said. "She's got me. I'll be—"

"Genevieve, are you still talking for your sister? I thought you'd have grown out of that by now."

Genevieve stopped talking.

"I know it'll be hard," Victoria said. "But I think I want to try."

Ten minutes later, they were on their way back to Errigal. Genevieve was now driving.

Victoria turned in her seat so she was facing her. "Am I crazy? I can't have a baby on my own, can I? I don't have a proper job. I live at home with my parents. I'm in serious debt. I'm not even a grown-up myself. How can I take care of a baby?"

"Because it's a baby. It's tiny. We can handle it. We've already practiced on Ig. Look how well he turned out. Our baby will be a cinch after him."

"Our baby?"

"Of course it's our baby. You think I'd let you do this on your own? You won't be able to keep me away. Except for when you're going through labor. Then he or she is all yours. I'll be outside with the cigars and the other dads."

Victoria's eyes filled with tears. "What would I do without you, Genevieve?"

"Wither and die?" Genevieve became serious. "Let's slow this all down, Victoria. Take it one step at a time. My advice is, we don't tell anyone anything yet. Not Fred, not anyone at home, anyone at all. Let's keep it between us for now, until you're completely used to the idea. You're beautifully womanly. You won't start to show for a while yet."

Victoria nodded. There was plenty of time to tell everyone, after all. She looked down and placed her hand on her belly. "There's a baby in there. Can you believe it?"

"No, I can't," Genevieve said. "It's incredible. I always thought the nuns were making it up."

While Genevieve and Lindy drove Ig into school the next morning, Victoria and Angela went out for a walk. Angela had her camera with her. At breakfast, she'd asked about a wildflower she'd seen, a small blue one. She wanted to photograph it but hadn't been able to find it again since her first sighting. Victoria remembered there was a clutch of them at the foot of the hill that was home to their swings. They were on their way there now.

It was a beautiful morning, clear and warm. A quartet of colorful birds was flitting around the trees nearby. Angela pointed them out, asking what they were. Native parrots of some kind, Victoria said.

"I'll ask Ig about them later," Angela said. "He knows a lot of birds. He should be a tour guide when he grows up."

"I think he wants to be a computer hacker, but that's not a bad second option," Victoria said.

There was a comfortable silence between them. Victoria tried to remember whether it had been like that when New Angela was Old Angela. She couldn't remember ever actually going on walks like this with Old Angela. Her mum was always doing something, planning something, getting ready for something or cleaning up after something. Was that just what life was like when you were a mother? You were so busy with your children you didn't have time for your children? She felt a lurch inside her. Not the baby kicking; it was too early for that. But the realization. She was going to be a mother. She was going to have a son or a daughter. By the end of the year.

"I'm pregnant, Angela."

She said it without thinking. She said it because she suddenly had to tell someone other than Genevieve. She said it because she wanted to say it to her mother, even if she was the new version, not the old one.

"Are you?" Angela said. "Is that good news or bad news?"

"I don't mind being pregnant. But I'm not in a relationship with the father. I mean, I was, but I'm not now."

"Have you told your parents?"

"Not yet. I don't want to spoil Dad's trip. And Mum's away."

"You should probably ring her."

"I thought I'd wait until I could tell her face-to-face," she said.

They kept walking. Angela asked more questions. How many weeks pregnant was she? What was her due date? How was she feeling? Normal questions, interested but not overly concerned. A stranger's questions, not a mother's. But still oddly comforting to answer.

"Have you had any nausea or morning sickness?" Angela asked.

"Not really. I've been lucky, I guess. But I feel different. Full up, if that makes sense. As if something is going on but I'm not sure yet quite what."

"You know to avoid soft cheeses? Pâté? And if you do get morning sickness, just—" Angela frowned. "Sorry; I've forgotten it right now. But I know it worked for me every time."

"Every time?"

"In all my pregnancies."

"How many pregnancies did you have?"

Again, that look of confusion. "One. Lexie's. That's odd. I nearly said three."

Three. Three pregnancies, one with twins, one for Lindy, one for Ig. Victoria was on the verge of saying something when Angela stopped and pointed. "That's it there, isn't it? The blue flower."

They didn't mention the pregnancy again until they were nearly home.

"Angela, what I told you before, my news—would you mind keeping that to yourself?"

"What did you tell me before?"

Victoria smiled. "It's fine. Don't worry."

Later that night, Genevieve was upset. "Forget about her remembering three pregnancies. I can't believe you told her you were pregnant."

"We were talking. It was so relaxed, she looked like Mum, and she sounded like Mum. I suddenly wanted to tell Mum."

"But she might tell everyone now. Before you're ready to tell."

"I asked her to keep it quiet. I trust her."

"I hope you're right."

The next day, a Saturday, they watched and waited for a sign that Angela had said anything to the others. There was nothing. It was Celia who was surprising them. Celia and Lindy. Since the reunion cushion order, they'd become a kind of team.

"Lindy's just sucking up to her now she knows she's got money to spare," Genevieve said.

"Don't be so cynical," Victoria said. "They actually get on. I think Celia's good for her. She's got Ig working too."

The three of them had taken over the woolshed. Celia

was getting them to sweep the floor and then spread tarpaulin everywhere. She was directing it all from a chair set up in the doorway.

"There's no point in having all the cushion material in boxes and having to send Ignatius out to dig around in them anytime you want a piece of thread," she said. "You need a system."

"How do you know about systems?" Lindy asked, putting the broom down for a moment and wiping her sweaty hair off her forehead.

"I worked in my husband's spare parts business for forty years, Rosalind. We supplied more than two hundred repair businesses around the state at one stage. There's nothing I don't know about supply and demand."

"I thought you were just his secretary."

"I ran it all. He was the figurehead. The unfortunate truth is that in a spare parts business the customers prefer to deal with a man than a woman. Sexist, but true. Let's get to work here. We're going to unpack all the boxes and set up a system with your colored threads, your cushion covers and your stuffing."

"What about my cubby?" Ig said.

"We just want the contents, Ignatius. You can still have the boxes. They'll be lighter to move around then too."

"A win-win situation," Ig said, continuing to sweep.

"Where's Angela?" Genevieve asked Victoria. "She's not on the veranda or in her room."

"She's out near the gum tree," Victoria said. She was at the kitchen table with her recording equipment, replaying her recent interviews. "Taking photographs of the leaves, I think."

"Can you keep an eye on her? I'm going to have a long bath. Use up all the water while Dad's away and can't tell me off."

"Sure," Victoria said.

Outside, Angela had stopped taking photographs. She was trying to decide whether to read or nap. It was so relaxing on Errigal. The weather was so good, day after day. It got a bit hot sometimes, but the house was cool, and the veranda caught any passing breeze.

She should be doing a bit more sightseeing, really, but she'd decided to wait until Will and Lexie arrived. That way they would see it all for the first time together. The area was so beautiful. There was so much to photograph. She'd decided to capture details rather than the sheer size of it. That would be impossible in a photo. The colors changed so much, the vastness of the sky—a photo would never do it justice. Perhaps she could even use some of these images when she got back to London. Re-create some of those incredible colors with some of her glazes.

She remembered all the ceramic birds she had done before Christmas in London. She thought of the pottery shed that little Ig had shown her. Why wait until she was home again? That would be a great surprise for Will and Lexie when they arrived, if she had already started work on a new project.

She walked across to the shed. It took her several attempts to open the old blue wooden door. As she tugged at the handle, a breeze blew a strand of the climbing rose near her. She reared back. It was as if she had been slapped. She put her hand to her cheek. Had it scratched her?

No, it was the smell of the rose that had startled her. She stood still for a moment. Something was just out of reach in her mind. Something about the rose. Had the Gillespies told her it was a special variety? It looked like an ordinary rose to her. They had roses in London too. A row of them in the back garden. Will looked after them.

She caught the stem and smelled the rose again, searching for that elusive memory. Was it about how difficult it had been to grow flowers out here? That must be it.

It was cool inside the shed. She turned on the light and shut the door again to keep out the heat. She picked up several pieces of work from the drying rack. She wondered what they were supposed to be. They were just odd shapes. There were so many of them too.

She couldn't wait to feel the clay in her hands again. What would she start with? One of the exotic Australian birds she and Ig had seen on their bird-watching trips? A blue wren? A parrot?

No, she'd do her favorite bird. A robin.

She cut off a piece of clay and rolled it in her hands, softening it. She pictured a robin, the little plump body, the chest that she would glaze in that distinct rusty orange. *Robin redbreast* really was a misnomer. She pictured the tilt of its head, the delicate shape of its tail feather. She'd need some wire too, to make the spindly legs. She'd ask Ig to help her find some.

She shaped and smoothed, loving the familiar feel of the

clay under her fingers. It was always so soothing. She opened her hand. It didn't look like a robin yet. She started again. Her second attempt was no better. She'd try a different way, she decided. Form the body first, then the head, then join them.

Once again, the finished product looked nothing like a robin. How odd. She'd been making a dozen of these every day before she left for this trip. Maybe she should do another sort of bird.

She tried. The wren looked like a squashed plum. The sparrow looked like a sausage. She had the pictures of them in her head, but they wouldn't translate to her hands.

It was so strange. It was as if she had forgotten how to do them.

FORTY-SIX

Nick was lost. In an unfamiliar rental car, on an unfamiliar Irish highway, trying to make sense of Irish signs and see the road ahead through the sheets of rain pelting against his windshield.

For the past two days he had stayed in Dublin, in the same hotel on O'Connell Street. He'd e-mailed home again, telling Genevieve once more that all was fine. If he told them what had happened, they would only worry. They had enough to worry about as it was. They'd had just one more brief phone call too. He had described green fields and stone walls, getting inspiration from the tourist brochures on the desk in front of him, as he looked out of his hotel window at the garage and the gray skies.

He'd reread all of his uncle's notes. They were more boring than Carol's notes, but they sounded more truthful. There was information about the original cousins who had come out to Australia from County Mayo and County Donegal. There was a sketch of the family tree, more place-names, more listings of different sets of husbands and wives, each with at least five children. The same names kept appearing: Joseph, Ignatius, Aloysius for the boys; Honora, Mary and Josephine for the girls. Some had more details written by hand beside them. His uncle Joe's writing? Perhaps. Joe had managed to gather a lot of information, especially considering he'd done it before the days of the Internet. Before unscrupulous con artists came along to take advantage of idiot outback farmers who hadn't realized they were being fleeced from day one.

No, he wouldn't let himself think like that. He had to accept it, deal with it, move on. Those three phrases were becoming his mantra.

He decided to try to verify his uncle's notes. It had to be easier to do here in Ireland than from the other side of the world. He asked for help at reception. The city was full of places to research family trees, he was told. He was given a list of addresses.

He made his way through the city, crossing the river, the wind and rain lashing at him. He walked along the crowded streets, hearing many different accents and languages. He looked up at the old stone buildings, down at the Liffey River, gray and muddy in the winter light. There seemed to be rubbish everywhere. There were so many poor homeless men and women too, begging on the streets, people walking past them, mostly ignoring them. Nick gave them all the change he had.

He queued at the family research office near Dublin Castle, and had a brief conversation with an official, giving all the names and dates he had. After a short wait, he was given a photocopy of a death certificate from the 1840s. It was definitely one of his ancestors. All the details tallied with his uncle's notes. It was like a shot of adrenaline. He *had* come from this place. He did have a history here in Ireland.

He got in line again, gave the extra information he'd found on the certificate and was given more photocopies. Again, he struck gold. Another ancestor's birth certificate, a great-great-aunt, with even more details: her religion (Catholic), her father's occupation (tailor). He felt like he was on an historical treasure hunt, trying to put together an intricate jigsaw puzzle stretching over generations. He was sure now that Carol's research had been faked. It didn't matter. He was the detective now.

That night he decided he would still go to County Mayo. He had a definite ancestral address now, outside the town of Westport, in a place called Liscarney. A different address from the one that Carol had given him. His ancestor's occupation was different too. Carol had told him the Gillespies were all farmers. "It was in your blood, Nick." But the certificates he'd seen today had described them as tailors and shopkeepers. No farming background at all. Which meant that the two cousins who had come to Australia, and had found themselves in the middle of nowhere, had probably been starting from scratch. Not just new to Australian conditions and climate, but to farming life altogether.

He'd been on the road for six hours. It had been dark by four p.m. It was nearly eight by the time he drove into Westport. After deciding to go off the highway, he'd gotten lost yet again. He'd driven through one small town after another. Perhaps they looked beautiful in the summer, with a blue sky above them and flowers in window boxes. In winter, in the pouring rain, they looked soulless and depressing. The only people he saw seemed to be running from their cars to shops, umbrellas aloft or hoods pulled up. He hadn't seen anything that resembled any of the photographs he'd spent the last year poring over or uploading onto the computer's screen saver. All he could think about was the big blue sky above Errigal. The space and the light there. How huge but also how full of promise it must have seemed to his ancestors, coming from a small, damp, cramped country like this. He passed what he assumed were farms, a collection of buildings, stone walls enclosing fields that were smaller than the yard at Errigal. He passed other fields holding fifteen black-faced sheep at most. That was it? That was their flock? At its peak, there had been ten thousand sheep on Errigal.

The rain kept falling. He'd expected it to be wet—it was winter, after all—but he hadn't expected the rain to fall constantly like this. There was no letup. The fields on either side of the road were flooded now, lakes of silver water covering what he presumed were once crops. The sky felt like it was just meters above his head. He'd had his headlights on since he left Dublin. Of course it was going to be different from Australia; he'd known that. But even discounting what had happened with Carol to sour his arrival, he'd expected more. A sudden kinship, a feeling of homecoming. He'd thought the land, the scenery, would speak to him, touch him somehow.

All it did was make him homesick for Australia.

He'd phoned home that morning before he set off. He kept up the charade that all was going as planned. Genevieve had assured him in turn that everything was fine on Errigal, that there was no change with Angela, no big news. He'd hoped she wasn't lying as much as he was.

Westport was hilly, with a series of one-way streets, a fast-flowing river. He pulled into the parking area of the first hotel he saw. He was drenched by the time he got his bag out of the car and found his way into reception. He checked in for two nights. His room had a better view this time than the one in Dublin, as far as he could tell at night-time. There was a tree to look at, at least. He was hungry. Thirsty. He'd have a hot shower first. His body was still aching from the flight. His muscles had tightened even more after the long drive.

As he walked past the hotel bar, he heard music. A traditional session of some sort. The first live music he'd heard. He decided to postpone the shower. Have something to eat and enjoy the music instead.

He found a table to the side of the room, near an open fire. There were three musicians, a guitarist, a fiddle player and an accordionist. There were only a few other people in the room. A waiter appeared. Nick ordered fish and chips.

"Anything to drink, sir?"

Nick looked across at the bar. The wooden counter was polished to a gleam. He'd been in Ireland for three days without so much as a sip of Guinness. It was time he had one.

As his meal and pint arrived, so did a busload of people. A group of American tourists, on a five-day guided tour of Ireland. They filled the seats around him. A couple sat beside him and introduced themselves as Ken and Patty from Cincinnati. "We know, it rhymes!" Patty said. They had Irish ancestry too; everyone on the tour was in search of their Irish roots.

There was a sing-along. He knew this wasn't an authentic music session, that it was staged for tourists just like him, but they played all the songs he loved: "Danny Boy," "The Rocky Road to Dublin," "Whiskey in the Jar." The Americans were in great spirits beside him, singing along. Several of them even attempted to do some Irish dancing. The mood was so happy, the conversation flowing, everyone having a wonderful time. This was exactly how he'd expected Ireland to be. As he'd imagined it.

Himself and Angela here together.

He got up and left before he finished his pint. He didn't want to be there without her.

FORTY-SEVEN

All was peaceful on Errigal. Angela was in the living room, watching a DVD. Celia was in her room, napping. Lindy was sewing. Genevieve and Victoria were in the kitchen, cooking and talking.

Ig appeared. Since he'd gotten home from school, he'd been in the office, at the computer. "You've got an e-mail, Genevieve."

"How do you know?"

"You left your e-mail open."

"No, I didn't."

"Then I must have seen you type in your password and remembered it," Ig said.

"You little brat. Who's it from? One of my gossipy hair-dressers?"

"Someone called Matt. He wants to know if you'll be here next week. He wants to visit you."

Genevieve nearly pushed Ig over on her way to the computer.

Twenty minutes later, Victoria and Genevieve were on their way up to Swing Hill. It was a hot and muggy afternoon, but it was the only place they could talk and definitely not be overheard.

"You're sure you're okay to walk this far?" Genevieve asked.

"It's not that far," Victoria said, smiling. "And I'm fine, I promise. You're the one I'm worried about. I thought you were going to hyperventilate when you got that e-mail. It's great news that Matt's coming, isn't it? Why are you looking so terrified?"

"Because I'm here. Living at home again. It would be great news if I was living in a New York apartment and could meet him in some cool bar for a drink. I'm not the person he met there. What if he doesn't like me anymore? I couldn't think up some witty repartee if you paid me."

"I'll help you write some lines before he gets here. Genevieve, relax, would you?"

"You're right. Anyway, as he said himself, it's just a flying visit. A last-minute decision. He might not even get here."

"No. He might get some terrible disease the day before he flies out and die. Stop it. Be happy."

"I am happy about it. I'm shocked how happy I am about it. I'm giddy as a goat. I'm worse than Lindy about Richard.

I need to calm down, don't I? He's just being nice. Polite. Dropping in to say hello."

"That's right. Dropping in to say hello. And flying across the world and then driving an extra three hundred kilometers to do it."

Genevieve wrote back to him that day. It took her five attempts before she was happy with her tone. *Great news! Would love to see you. I should warn you your phone won't work out here, so here are the directions now. I'll keep an eye out for you. Genevieve.* She hesitated and then added two kisses. *XX.* She pressed send and then logged out. She spoke without turning around.

"I know you're there, Ig. And keep your beady eye off my password. I'm changing it daily to keep it safe from you."

"I'll just wait till you leave your e-mail open like last time, then," he said, pulling over a chair beside her.

"So you didn't hack into it?"

"I'm good but not that good," he said. "How's your Web site going?"

"It's not. I haven't had a single e-mail from a single hairdresser with any horror stories. I lie. I had one, telling me off, saying there's enough negativity in the world and all her clients are lovely. What is it with all these positive people? Do I just have evil blood running in my veins, Ig?"

He nodded.

"All right. Let's try again. Can you help me do another site? A sickeningly positive one? I read an article once that said apparently all people really want to do is look at celebrities and cats. So let's do one like that instead."

Ig took over the computer. Once again, it didn't take him long to set up a basic site.

"What do you want to call it?" he asked.

"Let's tell it like it is. Call it 'Photos of Lots of Lovely Celebrities with Nice Hair and Cats that Look a Bit Like Them.' Is that too long?"

"I'll make it fit," Ig said.

An hour later, it was ready. Ig had turned out to be as fast at finding digital images as he was at Web site setup. Genevieve sat back and called out names of celebrities from one of Lindy's gossip magazines. Ig swiftly found photos of them. Together they scrolled through the hundreds of photos of cats online until they found one that looked even vaguely similar. Genevieve didn't bother with a caption, simply getting Ig to post the two images side by side. She started laughing six pairs of photos in.

"I don't care if no one but us sees these," she said, laughing again as Ig matched a photo of a fully wigged Dolly Parton with a groomed white Burmese. "I want this to be my job forever."

"Now what?" Ig said, after they'd posted twenty pairs. "Do you want to go live now?"

"You even know that term? You're spooky. Yes, go for it."

With great ceremony, Ig pressed a key. They both sat and looked at the screen.

Nothing happened.

"How will anyone know it's there?" Ig said.

"Good question," Genevieve said. She gave it some thought. She'd learned a few social media tricks while in

New York. A friend there had worked in marketing for a drinks company and knew ways to spread the word quickly, leaving links and catchphrases on other Web sites and blogs across the Internet. Genevieve activated a Twitter account she hadn't used in months and sent out a message on that. She jumped from blog to blog, chat room to chat room, leaving a link to the new site on each, with the same tagline each time. *Cats! Celebrities!* She did it fifty times.

"What are you two doing?" It was Lindy.

"Nothing," they said, spinning in their chairs so the screen was hidden.

Lindy rolled her eyes. "You're more childish than Ig, Genevieve. And he is a child. Dinner's ready."

"You've actually cooked for once?" Genevieve said. "I'm impressed. What are we having?"

"Toasted cheese sandwiches. You have to make them yourself."

In the kitchen, Lindy, Victoria, Genevieve, Ig and even Celia took turns with the ingredients and the grill. Angela hadn't joined them yet. She was outside with her camera again, taking what looked like close-up shots of the stonework on the woolshed.

They were all still sitting around the table talking when she finally came in. She was smiling.

"Victoria, I've remembered," she said. "The best cure for morning sickness is dry toast."

FORTY-EIGHT

Nick was in the dining room of the Westport hotel. He'd just finished a full Irish breakfast and was now on his third cup of coffee. He'd slept badly. Not because of any jet lag. His own thoughts had kept him awake. Thoughts of home. Of the kids. Of Angela.

He reached into his pocket and took out her Christmas letter. It had lost the power to hurt him. He was reading it for a different reason now: because she had written it. The old Angela. He still didn't like what she'd had to say but reading it somehow kept her close. This was what she had been thinking about, for all those weeks he'd been trying hard not to worry her. She'd been worrying anyway. About him, about the kids. She should have been able to talk to him about all of this. But he had been too preoccupied with his own worries, distracting himself with the family research—

"More coffee?" It was the young waitress. No thanks, he said. He wanted to get on the road again.

In the middle of the night, he'd made some decisions. He would stay in Mayo one more night, drive out to the area his uncle had said was the Gillespies' homeland. Take some photos. And then tomorrow he would head south to Cork. Not north to Donegal. He hadn't been able to find any definite address for his Gillespie ancestors up there. He did still want to see Errigal, the Donegal mountain the station was named after. But not on his own. For now, he'd go to Cobh, where he knew his ancestors had sailed from.

Before he left, he checked his e-mails on the hotel computer. There was one from Genevieve.

Hope all still going great with Carol. All fine here. We're thinking of you. Lindy still sewing up a storm with her reunion cushions. Was that your idea? Genius if so!

He had no idea what she was talking about. He still hadn't decided what he was going to do about the reunion. He hoped being in Cobh would help him decide. It was time to phone home again. Time to tell them what had happened with Carol too.

Outside in the car, he took out his phone and dialed the Errigal home number. It rang and rang. They must all be out somewhere. He'd try again later.

In the kitchen at Errigal, the phone finally stopped ringing. No one had answered it.

At first, Victoria had thought she'd gotten away with it.

"Thanks," she was about to say to Angela. "I'll let my interviewee know about that dry toast tip." But then Angela sat down beside her and continued talking.

"What did you say you were, Victoria? Nearly three months pregnant? You might be lucky and not get any morning sickness at all."

Across the table, Lindy was openmouthed. Celia looked equally shocked.

"I knew it!" Lindy said, recovering. "You kept denying it, but I knew. Are you pregnant too, Genevieve?"

"No!" Genevieve said.

"Well, if it doesn't rain around here, it pours," Celia said.

Angela looked around. "I'm so sorry; didn't everyone know?"

"Don't worry," Victoria said. "It's fine."

"I'm sorry. I didn't realize it was a secret."

"But who's the father?" Lindy asked. "It's not that radio guy, is it? The married one? Or is it Fred Lawson? Oh, Victoria!"

"It's neither of them," Genevieve answered for Victoria. "It's someone else."

Victoria nodded. "I'd just started going out with someone before I left Sydney. It's his."

"You were having an affair with Mr. Radio and another guy?" Lindy said. "God, you were busy."

Victoria started to cry and ran out of the room.

"Oh, well done, Lindy. Thanks for that," Genevieve said.

"I was joking. How come you're the only one around here who is allowed to joke?" She stalked out, slamming the back door behind her.

———

Genevieve found Victoria in her bedroom. She was sitting on her bed, still crying.

Genevieve held her close, rubbing her back, waiting for the tears to stop.

"It'll all be fine," she said. "It will be. Don't worry. And maybe it's better everyone knows now."

"It's not better. Genevieve, what am I going to do? You heard what Lindy said. About the father. Everyone will be asking me that."

"And we'll tell everyone else about your other boyfriend. It'll be fine. I promise. I'll help you."

Victoria just sobbed again. Genevieve held her tighter.

There was a quiet knock at the door.

"If it's Lindy, I don't want to see her," Victoria said. "Ever again."

It wasn't Lindy. It was Angela. "May I come in?"

Victoria and Genevieve exchanged a glance. This was the first time Angela had sought them out. The first time she had come into any of their bedrooms. They watched as she took a seat on the antique chair beside the dressing table. It was where their mother always used to sit whenever she came in for a chat.

She apologized again. Victoria and Genevieve assured her again that it didn't matter. That they would have told the rest of the family soon in any case.

"Please tell me if this is none of my business," Angela said. "But I think you should tell your mother. I know that if my daughter was pregnant, I'd want to know, to help her in some way."

"I'll phone her tomorrow," Victoria said.

"What would you say to Lexie if she did get pregnant?" Genevieve asked. "In circumstances like Victoria's?"

"I don't think it's for me to say."

"Please, Angela," Victoria said. "You're a mother. It'd be really helpful to hear what you think."

Angela was quiet for a moment. "I suppose I'd want to know how she felt. Was she sure there was no prospect of a relationship with the father? Was she truly aware of what lay ahead, what it would mean to have sole care of a child?" She stopped there. "And then I would say you have to do what is best for you. I know I didn't have a clue when I got pregnant for the first time. Then I found out I was having twins."

"Twins?" Genevieve said.

Angela frowned. "Not twins. Just one. Lexie."

The sudden tension in the room dissipated.

"You're an adult," Angela said to Victoria. "It's your life, your body, your baby now. But you also have a family around you. That will help. I didn't. If it hadn't been for Joan—" She stopped again.

"Joan?" Victoria prompted.

"Not Joan. I'm getting confused. If it hadn't been for my next-door neighbor in London. She was wonderful. She was there nearly every day. Will was a wonderful father—he still is a wonderful father—but at times like that you really do want women around you."

Standing up, she made one of her usual abrupt departures.

She was barely out the door before Victoria started talking.

"She *is* coming back. She is," she said. "You heard her. First about twins. Then Joan. It's like Ruth said: her memory will come back in fragments. I think it's started."

"But why now?" Genevieve said. "Because we were talking to her about personal things? About being pregnant? Being a mother? Maybe that's where we've been going wrong, treating her like Angela the tourist. Maybe we do need to talk to her as if she still is Angela our mother."

"Ruth said we shouldn't. She said we need to go along with what she says to us, let her take her time, just be pati—"

"Don't say it. We've tried that. And nothing's happened. Why don't we try a different approach? Ruth said herself that it's a constantly changing science, that no one knows what the brain is capable of doing. So let's do our own experiment."

"I'm not sure. Lindy might say the wrong thing. And Ig is just a kid."

"Not them. Us. We try it, whenever we're alone with her. And keep it to ourselves for now too."

Victoria chewed her lip. "I don't know."

"We can't wait forever, Victoria. Your baby is going to need a grandmother."

After his second night in Westport, Nick was on the road again, halfway between Westport and Cobh. Two hours down, two to go. The rain had finally stopped. The sun started to show itself for the first time since he'd arrived in Ireland. Nick had to pull off the main highway and drive several hundred meters up a quiet, country lane. Not because he was lost.

Because it was so beautiful.

This was the Ireland he had expected. On both sides green fields stretched out. There were mountains in the distance, the glint of water from either a real lake or a newly formed flood lake. The light was so different from what he was used to. Softer, muted: everything blurred but still full of colors. It wasn't just gray now. There were countless other shades, green, orange, yellow. A shaft of sunlight hit the side of the mountain, illuminating a whitewashed building.

The morning before, he had visited the area near Westport where his ancestors had come from. He'd seen small, rocky fields surrounded by stone walls. The low gray sky. Alongside the modern houses there had also been the ruins of several buildings, either sheds or houses; he couldn't tell. There was a soft, misty beauty there. The sound of the wind through the trees. Silver lakes surrounded by reeds. In the distance, the steep slope of Croagh Patrick. He knew it was called Ireland's holy mountain. He saw a small flock of bedraggled sheep, several cows in a corner field. He climbed over a stone wall and walked to the top of the nearest hill. The ground was muddy underfoot. He kept thinking about his Gillespie ancestors. How it must have felt to leave this land, where every field, every bend in the road, must have been so familiar. How it must have felt to find themselves on the other side of the world, battling new weather, huge distances, under the vast Australian sky. Knowing they would never see these fields, their families, their homeland again.

He took out his phone now and dialed home. It was early evening there. This time Genevieve answered. He asked about Angela first. All was fine, Genevieve told him. Everyone was home, except for Victoria. She'd gone into Hawker. "Any big news?" he asked.

"None at all," she said. "What about you?"

"A bit of news," he said. He told her about Carol. Two minutes later, he was regretting it.

Genevieve wouldn't stop laughing.

"It's not that funny," he said.

"Oh, Dad, it is. It's terrible, but it's funny. I'm so sorry. So what on earth have you been doing if you haven't been driving around with her? And why didn't you tell us when it first happened?"

He told her the truth. That he hadn't wanted to worry them. He told her what he'd been doing in Dublin. The few genuine facts he had uncovered about the Gillespies. And that he was now on his way to Cobh. Not because of the reunion. It would probably be canceled. But he still wanted to see what his ancestors would have seen more than one hundred and thirty years earlier, as their ship sailed out to Australia.

"You might cancel the reunion? Why? You found all those Gillespies around the world yourself, didn't you? Not Carol? We're bound to be related in some way, even if they're only our twentieth cousins five times removed. Don't cancel it yet, Dad, please. I can't begin to imagine what Lindy will do about her cushions if you do." She told him all about them. All two hundred of them.

He agreed to postpone the decision for now. "I'd better go," he said. "You're sure Angela's okay? That you're all okay? You'd tell me if there was any news, wouldn't you?"

"Of course I would," Genevieve lied.

She had her fingers crossed as she said it.

After she hung up, she joined the others in the lounge room. Everyone except Victoria was there, watching the final episode of *Pride and Prejudice*. Over recent days, one by one, they'd all started watching it with Angela.

Genevieve leaned against the door. "Would it spoil the ending if I told you they—"

"Shut up, Genevieve," Lindy said from her spot on the sofa. "Don't spoil it."

"Do you mean you haven't guessed what's going to happen? Have a look at the cover of the DVD, Lindy. Is that a giveaway who might be ending up with who?"

"You are so cynical. No wonder you're still single."

"And you're not? You're having a Skype affair, Lindy. You've seen Richard in real life for what—four hours in total? So don't pretend you are the queen of love's young dream to me."

"That's enough, you two." It was Angela. "Stop teasing her, Genevieve. We're trying to watch this."

Lindy was wide-eyed. Even Ig turned around.

In shock at hearing what had definitely sounded like Old Angela, Genevieve did as she was told.

It was only after Mr. Darcy and Lizzy had driven away in their carriage, and the image was freeze-framed on their kiss, that she dared to speak again.

"I talked to Dad, if anyone cares. You know, that man who is normally here? Who is traveling around Ireland on his own?"

"How is he getting on?"

It was Angela speaking, again.

"He's good," Genevieve said. She tried to keep her voice calm, to hide another sudden dart of hope. "He's great. It's all going well. He's on his way to Cobh now."

"Did you tell him about the cushions?" Lindy asked.

"I sure did," Genevieve said. "He thought it was a great idea."

She wouldn't mention the Carol disaster. Not yet, at least.

"I'll be in the office if anyone's looking for me," Genevieve said.

She sat at the computer, drumming her fingers on the desk. What a night for Victoria to be out on her date with Fred. Genevieve was tempted to pick up the phone and call her anyway to tell her about Carol. After being apart for so long, juggling time zones every time they wanted to talk, she relished every minute of being in the same place as her sister.

Victoria had been so sweet earlier. Nervous, excited. Genevieve had done her hair and makeup. She'd also helped her choose her outfit. They'd decided on a pretty summer dress, in daisy-printed cotton. Genevieve had pulled out two pairs of sandals. "Either of these would look great," she said.

"No, thanks. I'm wearing the lucky boots."

"It's eighty-two degrees."

"I'm wearing them," Victoria said.

Genevieve had been secretly delighted. She'd given them to Victoria two years earlier, when her twin first moved to Sydney and was trying to find work. Genevieve was in New York, but they'd still been talking daily on the phone.

Victoria had applied for three jobs, and was down to the final stage in one. "Send me lucky thoughts, will you?" she'd said to Genevieve.

Genevieve had misheard. "Lucky boots?"

Victoria had corrected her, laughing. "Thoughts, not boots."

The next day, Genevieve saw a beautiful pair of boots in a shop on Mott Street. It cost her three times as much as the boots cost to get them couriered to Sydney. They arrived the morning of the final interview, with her note tucked inside: *I can't be there but these lucky boots can.* Victoria wore the boots. She also got the job.

Were they working tonight? Genevieve wondered. Victoria was meeting Fred for a drink and a meal in the Hawker pub. She wondered what was even possible between Victoria and Fred now. She was having another man's baby. How would any man cope with news like that?

Genevieve hated the idea of Victoria being hurt. She decided to think about Matt instead. They'd e-mailed several times since his surprise message. He'd explained that he was in Australia location scouting for a new film, a horror story that would take full advantage of the wildness of the scenery. He was flying into Maree, three hundred kilometers north of Errigal. After he'd finished his work there, he was going to drive down to see her. He wasn't put off by the distance. He might find an even better stretch of lonely road for his film, he'd said. *See how diligent I am?*

Diligent or deluded? You might get chased and attacked by a demented outback killer, she'd e-mailed back.

Even more points for my diligence if I am, he'd e-mailed.

Restless, Genevieve decided to check her new Web site. Maybe there had been a visitor or two already. But first, a cup of tea.

As she passed the living room, she peeked in. Ig and Lindy had gone, but Celia and Angela were still there, watching television. A gardening program, by the look of it. At least that meant Genevieve didn't have to protect Angela from Celia. She'd been polite with Angela so far, but Genevieve still didn't trust her.

In the kitchen, she'd just put on the kettle when she heard it. The sound of someone sobbing. Where was it coming from? The television? No, it sounded different from that. More real.

It was Angela.

Genevieve went straight in to her. "Angela? What is it? What's wrong?"

Angela just kept crying, her hands over her face.

"What happened?" Genevieve asked Celia. "What did you say to her?"

"Nothing," Celia said. She looked as stunned as Genevieve. "We were just watching a gardening show I'd recorded and she suddenly started to cry."

Genevieve crouched beside her chair. "Angela, what is it? What's wrong?"

"I miss him. Could I ring him? Please?"

"Miss who, Angela? Ring who?"

"My husband. Where is he? Could I ring him?"

Genevieve didn't know what to do. Was this another memory breaking through? Was she thinking of Nick in

Ireland? She tried to remember Ruth's advice. Should she go along with it?

"It's a bit late now, but you can ring him tomorrow," she said.

Angela kept sobbing.

Genevieve had never seen her mother cry like this. It was heartbreaking. She also didn't want Celia to see her like this.

She touched her mother on the shoulder. "Angela, would you like to come and sit outside with me?"

As Genevieve guided her outside, Angela kept sobbing.

"Please don't cry. We'll ring him in the morning," Genevieve repeated.

"But I can't remember his phone number. How can we ring him?"

Genevieve still didn't know whether she was thinking of Will or Nick. "If you give me his full name, I'll look it up for you, if you like." She held her breath. *Please, Angela. Please say Nick Gillespie. . . .*

"His name is William Somers," Angela said. "He lives in Islington." She gave Genevieve his full address.

Half an hour later, Genevieve went in search of Celia. Angela was now in her room. As abruptly as she had started crying, she had stopped. She had been quite calm by the time she went to bed.

"What was it that sparked the tears?" Genevieve asked Celia. "It had to be something on the TV."

"I told you, it was just a gardening program. A segment

about roses. She was fine until they played a song. That's when she started crying."

"What song?"

Celia couldn't remember.

Genevieve rewound the gardening program until it was at the rose segment. She turned up the volume, expecting the song to be Bette Midler's "The Rose," or the one by Seal. It was a song she'd never heard before. A male singer, a deep, haunting male voice, singing about a rose for his darling. She fast-fowarded to the end. The credits said the song was "Only a Rose" by Geraint Watkins. She went into the office and googled him. He was a Welsh singer. She'd never heard of him, but their mother obviously had.

Genevieve started googling something else then. A William Somers or Summers. Architect. Islington. London.

Moments later, there was a long list on the screen. She scrolled down. Ten entries in, she saw it. WSA. William Somers Architects. An office address on Upper Street, Islington, and a home address nearby. The same street that Angela had named.

"Found you," Genevieve said.

She was still awake at one a.m. when she heard the sound of Victoria's car outside. She was sitting up in bed when she came in. "Well? How was it?"

"It was great. Really great."

They'd talked all night, Victoria said. About Canada. About Sydney. His plans for the future. Her documentary series. It had been so easy. So great. Like the old days, but even better.

"And what did he say about, you know. . . ."

"His letter? Just that he was so happy I'd met him and would I meet him again."

"I don't mean that. Did you tell him?"

"That I'm pregnant? No."

"No?"

Victoria went bright red. "I was too busy kissing him."

FORTY-NINE

Cobh was everything Carol had promised Nick. The sun was shining as he drove into the town along the coast road, with its view of a narrow harbor lined with colored houses. The town itself was dominated by a cathedral up on a hill. It also had the steepest streets he'd ever seen. He drove up one, the car engine straining. At the top, he parked. He had a perfect view over the town and harbor, the open sea beyond. The street was almost at 90 degrees, the houses built at what looked like impossible angles. They were also painted different colors, reds, greens, yellows. Most had window boxes too, empty of flowers now, but he could picture them in the summer, how bright the street would look, how bright the whole town would look.

Carol had mentioned a hotel on the waterfront, not only

for their accommodation but also for the Gillespie reunion. He saw now that it existed, but had she ever been here? he wondered. She had sent receipts, he remembered. He now suspected she'd never made the trip, just kept the money he'd paid and sent him falsified receipts and information off the Internet.

He drove back down to the waterfront, parked the car and walked the length of the harbor. It was a busy, bustling town geared toward tourists. There was a museum devoted to the *Titanic*, another to all the emigrants who had left Ireland for a new life in America, Canada, Australia.

He booked into the waterfront hotel and went up to his room on the third floor. Had he somehow been given the best room? It looked out over the water, across to a small green island, farther beyond to the sea. Down below was a bandstand, old-style lamps. To his left, an art gallery and the dilapidated wooden wharf used by the *Titanic* passengers. This hotel dated back to the 1800s. Perhaps his own ancestors had even stayed here the night before they left for Australia.

He realized he no longer cared that he had been conned, that Carol and her company had turned out to be fakes. His ancestors had definitely sailed from Cobh. He had all the information about their journeys in the files at Errigal. He'd had that even before Carol became involved. His uncle's files had confirmed it. The two Gillespie cousins had been in this town. His connection here was real.

All he wished, again, was that Angela were with him.

An hour later, he was being taken on a personally guided tour of the hotel's facilities by the young manager, Fintan.

"And you could have the welcome night party here," Fintan said, as they stood in the large dining room at the front of the hotel, the bank of windows looking out over the harbor. "We could arrange for musicians, Irish dancers, storytellers. Dining-wise, you could have a full sit-down meal or buffet style, seafood, oysters, whatever you like. How many did you say you're expecting?"

"Around two hundred."

Nick imagined Fintan hearing the sound of a cash register. But he was being very helpful. He'd also confirmed Nick's suspicions. He'd had no contact at all with Carol.

Fintan finished his sales pitch, talking about menus, prices per head, accommodation offers. It was all white noise to Nick. He didn't know the first thing about organizing gatherings like this. It was why he had been so happy to pass it all over to Carol. At home, it had always been Angela who took care of any parties or celebrations.

Fintan was still talking. "It really is the perfect venue, as you can see. I'm sure your guests would find it very moving, in fact, to stand in this room and look out at the same view their ancestors would have seen, so many years ago."

He didn't need to lay it on quite so thick, but Nick could picture it. Picture himself, standing here in this room, surrounded by Gillespies from all over the world: America, England, Australia, Canada. There had even been interest from Gillespies in Argentina.

If he did go ahead with it, would the kids make the journey too?

Would Angela?

He spent the next two hours walking through the town. He climbed the steep hill he had driven up earlier, with the houses at the impossible angles. He thought how much Ig would love to see this. How much he would like Ig to see this. Back down on the waterfront, he leaned against the barrier. The sun was going down, a soft light spreading across the water, turning the sea a silver color. There was rain coming; he could see the dark clouds building to the west, but there was still sunlight. Everything looked polished.

He heard a text come in on his phone. It was Genevieve. *Have some news. Can you talk?*

He called her. She was in Port Augusta, in mobile phone signal range. She told him what had happened with Angela the night before. The tears. The song.

No, Nick confirmed. He didn't know that Welsh singer either.

"I still think it's a good sign, Dad; don't you? It had to be the lyrics that made her cry. It's all about someone giving their darling a rose. And that's not all. She talked about Will again. I know his surname now. It's Somers." She spelled it for him. "I looked him up. He really is an architect. In London. In a place called Islington."

"Has she asked to phone him again?"

"She hasn't mentioned him since. Once she stopped crying, it was as if she forgot all about him. That's why I'm sure it was you, Dad, not him that she was thinking about. You and the rose. And that's not all. She told us off last night too. Me and Lindy. We were fighting. And she sounded like Old Angela, not New Angela. I'm going to ring Ruth about it tomorrow. These have to be good signs, don't you think?"

He agreed. He told her to call him immediately if there were any more moments like that. They spoke for a few more minutes. He briefly described Cobh. He told her he was still deciding what to do about the reunion. He sent everyone his love, then said good-bye.

Sitting on a nearby bench, he took out Angela's letter again. He usually avoided one particular section, but he read it all now—about Will, Lexie, their house in Islington, their life in London. Will wasn't just Angela's fantasy figure. He was a real man.

What was it about Will that Angela had once loved? How was she able to remember him so clearly all these years later? What kind of a man was he? Nick hated himself for thinking it, but the suspicion wouldn't go away. Had there been some contact between them recently?

Back at the hotel, he asked about an Internet café. The hotel had a computer he could use, the staff said. It didn't take him long to find what he needed to know. Afterward, he phoned Genevieve again.

That night, he ate dinner in the hotel bar. A group of Australians had gathered there, men and women about his age, all a little merry. He could have joined them. Stood beside them at the bar on the pretext of getting another drink. Asked where they were from, what they were doing in Ireland. They would have invited him to join them; he was sure of it. They could have swapped travel and Irish ancestry stories.

Not tonight. He had an early start in the morning. He had to be at the Cork airport before nine a.m. He was catching a flight to London.

FIFTY

In the kitchen of the homestead on Errigal, Celia was making tea. Angela sat at the table reading a novel.

"So, we have the house to ourselves today, Angela," Celia said. "Peace and quiet at last."

"I'm still here," Ig called from his position on the living room sofa, where he was reading a computer magazine. He had a day off from school. "And Joan's coming over later."

"Of course," Celia said. "And Robbie's here too, I suppose?"

"No," Ig said. "He's away at the moment. On holiday."

"Oh, really?" Celia said, looking across at Angela and rolling her eyes.

Angela didn't respond.

Genevieve and Victoria had gone to Port Augusta to do some grocery shopping. At the last minute, Lindy had decided to go with them. She hadn't been off the station in days. She was going stir-crazy, she'd said. She had cabin fever. She hadn't even been able to Skype Richard. He was still on Phillip Island with Jane.

"Cabin fever? On a huge outback station?" Genevieve said. "Only you could find it claustrophobic."

"Don't be mean," Angela said.

Again, they had exchanged glances. That was definitely Old Angela speaking again. She didn't seem aware of it. She simply said her piece, then returned to her book. She was working through all the books in the living room bookcase. All of which she had read before.

Now Ig climbed off the sofa and came into the kitchen. "Do you want to go on another bird-watching walk, Angela?" he asked.

She put down her book. "I'd love that, thank you."

"I'd like to come too," Celia said. "Unless I'd be in the way?"

"No, of course not," Ig said. It was obvious he was lying.

Celia smiled. "Before we go walking, Ignatius, I need to check my e-mail. You're the computer wiz, I believe. Can you please turn it on for me? My book club is meeting again next month. I really should find out what the book will be."

She followed him down to the office and watched as he turned on the computer and opened it to a search engine for her. He did it all without speaking.

As she sat down she turned to him. "Now, I wonder, would you do me another favor? I promised my next-door neighbor's grandson that I'd bring him back some real sheep's wool from a real sheep station. There are still little bits and pieces out in the woolshed, I noticed. Could you please run out there and get me as much as you can find?"

"But we swept it all up. When we were unpacking all the cushion stuff."

"Not all of it. I'm sure I saw some caught in the floorboards. It doesn't have to be a bale full. Just as much as you can get. As quickly as you can."

"Why? Are you going home soon?"

"Not yet, no. But I'd like you to get it for me now, please. While I'm thinking of it."

She waited until she was sure he'd gone. She knew that Angela was still in the kitchen.

After the drama with that rose song the evening before, she'd decided that this had all gone on long enough. If Angela's brain damage was as bad as they kept saying, then how could she read? How could she watch DVDs? Make conversation? Not only that: If the neurologist was right, and this was a temporary state of mind, then surely Angela should be starting to regain her own memories by now.

Celia knew she wasn't the only one thinking that way. She'd heard Genevieve and Victoria talking about it too. They seemed to have forgotten how voices carried here at nighttime, in the still air, from one open window to the next. They believed their mother was starting to come back to them too. They'd noticed that pieces of information from her real life had been prompting strong memories and reactions. Yet they'd decided to keep that observation to themselves. Manage it their way. Despite the fact that Nick had asked Celia to keep an eye on them all in his absence. He hadn't said it in so many words, but that was what he wanted, Celia was sure.

She knew that what she was looking for had to be here in the office somewhere. She'd heard Angela joking about it once with Joan, one Christmas, several years earlier. Joan had been teasing her about her latest Christmas letter, saying Angela had just cut and pasted it from earlier letters. "I did not," Angela had said, laughing. "They're all one hundred percent originals. I've got a file of them if you ever want to refresh your memory. They're historical documents. I might even donate them to the state library."

"Really?" Joan had said. "Which section? Fiction or nonfiction?"

Celia started to look through the filing cabinet. She'd have to be quick. Ig had looked suspicious. He was a smart boy. Didn't miss a trick.

She found it in the third drawer. A big folder in an upright file marked in Angela's neat handwriting. *Christmas letters*. More than three decades of them. There wasn't time to read through them now. She didn't need to, anyway. She'd received and read all of them over the years already.

She wondered whether Angela realized that the only time she had ever mentioned Celia was this year. In the letter that had caused all the trouble, the one that Nick had accidentally sent out. In more than thirty years of writing about her family. Year after year, Celia had looked for even a passing mention of herself. It was never there. The written— the unwritten—proof of how little regard Angela had for her.

It took her only a few minutes to write a note, attach it to the folder and make her way to Angela's bedroom. She placed it on the bedside table. There'd be no missing it. If reading these letters didn't spark Angela's memory, then nothing would.

She was back in front of the computer when Ig returned, holding a handful of dirty pieces of wool.

"This was all I could find," he said.

She took them. "Perfect, thank you."

"You didn't even look at them."

"I have seen wool before, Ignatius." She pretended to log off from her already-logged-off e-mail account. "Ready for our walk?"

Ig now wished his sisters hadn't gone away. When Genevieve had asked him whether he minded being left in charge for a few hours until Joan arrived, he'd been pretty happy. He and Angela had already talked about taking another walk. He'd thought Celia would stay behind, like she usually did. But then she invited herself. And when she'd sent him off to get wool, he'd had a feeling it was only because she wanted to do something in the office. Now she was bossing him around about where they should go for their walk, when he and Angela already knew where they wanted to go. The weather looked bad, Celia said. A summer storm was forecast. They needed to stay close to the station. No, they didn't, in Ig's opinion. He liked rain. Especially because he didn't see it much. Also, storms were really good in summer, after it was hot, when they came with thunder and lightning, and sometimes there were even floods.

He also wanted to get started on The Plan. His and Angela's plan. They hadn't told the others yet, but it was coming together. He had given Genevieve a shopping list today for the things he needed. He hoped she could read his writing okay.

He was packing all the picnic stuff in his schoolbag when the phone rang. Angela never answered it. Celia was in her room. He'd have to get it. It was Joan.

"Ig, I'm so sorry. I can't get over today. I've come down with a stomach bug. You wouldn't want me around, let me tell you. Can you all manage there without me?"

"Sure," he said. "Get better soon." He hung up.

It rang again. It was Joan, laughing. "Nothing like getting straight to the point, Ig. You're sure everything is okay there?"

"Great," he said. He wanted to get going, not stand around all day talking.

"Okay, then. I do like a man of few words. Say hi to everyone. I'll be there tomorrow, I hope."

"See you," he said.

He really was in charge now. He wished he could call down the hall, "Hurry up!" to Celia, like Genevieve did to him sometimes. He looked out onto the veranda. Angela was waiting, sitting in the chair. They could always just sneak off, he supposed.

Celia appeared. "I was right. These shoes are better for walking. I'm ready now."

The three of them walked around the property looking for birds, but it just wasn't the same with Celia there. Usually he was the one who pointed out the birds to Angela, the corellas and the galahs and even a kookaburra now and then. He had also been waiting to show her a wedge-tailed eagle. They'd looked for one every day and hadn't had any luck. Today, finally, he saw one. Just as he was about to point it out, Celia got there first. "Look, Angela! An eagle!" she said. They all stopped, staring up at it. Celia went on and on about it, how they often came in pairs, how incredible their eyesight was, how high they flew. All the things Ig had wanted to tell Angela. He was really cross she was there now. She'd ruined everything. He wanted to go back to the homestead.

"I feel sick," he said.

Angela stopped. "Do you? What's wrong?"

"Joan rang before. She's got a stomach bug. I might have it too. I need to go home."

"But we've just come out," Celia said.

Angela put her hand on his forehead. Just like she used to when she was his mum. "You are a bit hot, Ig," she said.

"I want to go home," he said again.

Celia sighed.

"Come on, then, Ig," Angela said. "The weather's changing anyway. It might be for the best."

Back home, Celia took up her usual position in the living room. Ig knew that if his sisters were here, they would offer to make her a cup of tea. He supposed he'd better do it. He was happy when she said no. He thought Angela might go into her room for a lie-down. She often did after their walk, but then, this had only been a short one. She didn't. She was outside again with her camera. Taking photos of the sky. It was filling up with big black clouds now. There was definitely going to be a storm.

He joined her, not saying anything, just following her around.

"I never get tired of this," she said to him. "All that space and sky. It's beautiful, isn't it?"

He nodded. He remembered going up to one of the lookout points on the station with his dad once, just before a storm. That had been pretty amazing, up high enough to see the clouds actually coming across the Chace Range at them. They had just gotten home in time before all the thunder started, then the lightning, then the rain for nearly an hour, solid. The creeks on the station had flooded that day. They'd lost their power for a few hours too. Ig had loved every minute of it.

Celia called out from the back door. "I'm going to watch a film. Angela, would you like to watch it with me? Ignatius?"

"No," Ig said.

"No, thank you, Celia," Angela corrected him.

"No, thank you, Celia," he said. His mum always liked to correct his manners like that too.

He had the idea after Celia went back inside and shut the door. He and Angela could go to the lookout now. She would like it there. She could take even better photos of the storm too. He didn't want to go in and tell Celia what they were doing, but he knew he wasn't allowed to go anywhere without letting someone know where he was.

He went inside. The living room door was shut, but he could still hear the TV blaring.

Gone to the lookout with Angela, he wrote on a scrap of paper. He left it in the middle of the kitchen table, picked up the car keys from the hook by the door and went out to Angela again.

"I've got a great surprise," he said. "Come with me."

She followed him to the shed. He pointed at the car and handed her the keys. "Here, you drive."

She laughed. "Where to?"

"The lookout," Ig said. "It isn't far. There's never any other cars."

"I don't think so, Ig."

"Okay. I will."

She laughed again. "Ig, you're ten years old."

"Nearly eleven. And I've been driving since I was nine. It's only five minutes away. I'm a good driver."

She looked at him for a moment and then she smiled. "Oh, why not," she said. "Come on, then."

They got in. He pulled the driver's seat in as close to the wheel as he could. He had to stretch to reach the pedals and it took him two attempts to start the engine, but he did it. Moments later, they were on the dirt road.

That part was easy. Driving up the narrow track to the top of the lookout wasn't quite so easy but he managed it.

He was right. Angela loved it up there. She kept taking photos: not of birds, though. They had all disappeared, hiding from the storm, Ig figured. She was taking photos of the sky again, the huge clouds that were now heading toward them, getting closer and closer.

They were still up there, on the other side of the lookout from their car, when the storm hit. It was very sudden. There was sunlight one minute and then it went dark, and there was a crash of thunder and it started to rain. They both made a run for the car. This time Angela got in the driver's seat.

"I don't think we should drive in that, Ig. Let's just wait till it passes. What do you think?"

He nodded.

The rain battered down on the roof of the car. It sounded like the thunder was just outside. There was a flash of lightning. It looked like it was very close. What if the lightning did hit the car? It would explode and they would be burned alive. He couldn't help himself. He started to cry.

Angela turned to him right away. "Oh, Ig, don't worry. It's just a storm. We'll be fine."

There was another huge crash of thunder. A flash of light. So close.

"Mum!" he cried out, burrowing across the seat to her.

She pulled back from him. "Did you just call me Mum?"

He stared at her. "I didn't mean to," he said.

There was more thunder. The rain sounded like stones on the car roof now. The sky kept filling with flashes of light. He'd never been so scared. He was going to be in big trouble too when Genevieve found out he'd taken the car. And that he'd called Angela *Mum*. He started to cry again. She pulled him closer.

"It's okay, Ig. We'll be fine. The tires are rubber. They'll keep us safe."

He didn't say anything. He just held on tightly to her.

An hour later, they were parking the muddy car back in the shed. The worst of the storm had passed. Ig was happy again now. Angela had driven back. The roads had started to get slippery—they had even skidded a little bit a couple of times—but she had held the car steady.

"You'd think I'd been doing this for years, wouldn't you?" she'd said to him.

She had. Ig didn't say anything. He'd also decided not to tell the others about any of this. Especially the calling her *Mum* bit.

Celia hadn't even noticed they were gone, Ig realized, as they came inside. She had the volume on the TV turned up so high they could hear it even over the sound of the rain on the tin roof.

"Okay, kiddo," Angela said. "Have a shower and get into some dry clothes."

"Okay," he said.

He smiled to himself as he went into the bathroom. He'd always liked it when she called him *kiddo*.

Genevieve, Victoria and Lindy weren't home until after dark. They were full of talk about the storm. They'd had to wait at two of the creek crossings for the levels to go down enough for them to pass through. What Genevieve called *idiot tourists* had kept driving across in their rented 4WDs, filming themselves whooping and shouting as the water reached past their tires.

"That'd be great on YouTube, wouldn't it?" she said. "'Here's what we looked like just before we drowned.'"

"Any news here?" Victoria asked Ig. "What did you get up to while we were gone?"

"Not much," Ig said.

FIFTY-ONE

If Nick had ever imagined a London architect's office—not that he'd ever had cause to before today—it wouldn't have looked like this. He'd expected a glossy, sleek building, floor-to-ceiling windows, minimal furniture. Intimidating staff. Classical music. He double-checked the address. Upper Street, Islington. It was the right place. The right name on the door too. WSA. Will Somers Architects.

It was on the first floor, above a dry cleaner's, in the middle of a row of clothing and gift shops. The taxi driver from Paddington station had told him Islington was a pretty exclusive kind of suburb these days. There was also a Tube strike on, apparently, which was why the roads were so crowded. Sitting in the back of the taxi, Nick could hardly believe that he was in London. In a black cab. That he'd just

traveled from Cork to Heathrow. From the airport to Paddington. He'd gone straight to the Islington Hilton, where
his room had been ready. It was incredible, he thought
again. His daughter able to organize all these travel arrangements from a sheep station in outback South Australia.

Genevieve had e-mailed him the night before, after
they'd spoken the second time. When he'd told her what
he'd decided to do, she insisted on taking care of all his
bookings. Her e-mail was businesslike.

> All organized, Dad. Your flight details at-
> tached. Get the Heathrow Express (ticket also
> attached), then a taxi from Paddington sta-
> tion to Islington. You're booked into the Is-
> lington Hilton. It's on the same street as
> Will's office. I rang and made you an appoint-
> ment with Will. I didn't go into detail about
> who you are, I just gave him your name. I've
> been thinking about other things Mum has said
> to us. Ig says she's talked a lot to him about
> her old house. Can you go there too, to Forest
> Hill? There's also a museum nearby called the
> Horniman. Ig said she talked about that to
> him too. There's an old walrus there appar-
> ently. Loads of birds. They all matter to her
> in some way. I'll e-mail you directions. Could
> you please get lots of photos of it all, and
> of yourself there too? So we can show them to
> her when you get back? We all think this is a

great idea of yours to go there. Love from
everyone. G xxxx

His appointment with Will was for one p.m. Still an hour away. He walked the length of Upper Street and back. Past restaurants, clothes shops, cafés, gift shops, an Irish pub.

In the taxi on the way to Islington, he'd seen places he recognized from films, books. Baker Street, a statue of Sherlock Holmes out front. Once again, he thought how different this trip would have been if Angela had been beside him. This was her home city and he was here without her.

After his walk, there was just time to go back to the hotel and change into a fresh shirt. He didn't need to reread Angela's letter. He already knew what he wanted to ask Will.

He pressed the buzzer beside the door right at one p.m. He thought of the Will she had written about, so successful, so sought-after. The Will who lived in the big London house, who—

A man's voice sounded from the intercom. Nick had expected a secretary or receptionist. He gave his name.

"Come on up," the voice answered.

The stairs were narrow. The walls needed painting. Nick could smell food cooking, something with spices, from a nearby restaurant kitchen, he guessed. One flight of stairs, and then another door with the same WSA logo painted on it. He pushed it open.

There was paper everywhere. Cardboard tubes, with architectural drawings sticking out, leaning against walls. Two desks close together, one covered in more folders and paper. The other with an old computer on it. Behind that a man in his mid–fifties, standing up, talking on the phone. He looked over, held up a finger to say he'd be with him soon.

Nick took a seat.

He imagined Genevieve firing questions at him. "But what did he look like, Dad?"

He was shorter than Nick. Five-ten, maybe. He was wearing a suit, the jacket unbuttoned. It was hard to tell what color hair he'd had, because there wasn't much left of it. Brown? Dark brown?

Genevieve's questions kept coming. "But was he hand-some? Thin? Fat? Come on, Dad!"

Handsome? No. He looked kind of . . . What was the word? Puffy. Red faced. But also pale. Blotchy. That was it. He was blotchy. Like a man who spent too much time in-doors. Or a man who drank too much.

Was that what Nick himself looked like these days? No. He'd been the same weight for years. He was still fit, tanned too. And he still had his own hair.

Was he actually comparing himself to this man? Yes, he was.

Will seemed to be having an argument with his caller. Something about an attic extension, the staircase being faulty. He kept switching between being soothing and being defensive. "I'll be over tomorrow. Yes, I know I recom-mended those builders. I've never had any complaints about them before. Two p.m. Right. Bye." He put down the phone and rolled his eyes. "Sorry about that." He held out his hand. Nick took it.

"Nick Gillespie," Nick said.

"Will Somers. How can I help you, Mr. Gillespie?"

It was half past eleven on Errigal. Everyone was in bed. Angela was awake, reading a magazine. It was still raining outside, but it was a soft, steady fall now, not the tumultuous downpour of before.

She heard a sound at the door. A tiny knock. "Come in," she said.

It was Ig.

"I can't sleep," he said.

"Oh, Ig, I'm sorry," she said. "But it's very late. You should try."

"Will you come and tuck me in?"

"Of course."

She followed him down the hall to his room. It was the first time she'd been in here since she'd come to stay on Errigal. He clambered back into his bed. She tucked the covers in tightly around him. "There you go. Snug as a bug."

He smiled at her, and shut his eyes.

Back in her room again, she took a seat on the side of her bed. Why had that felt so familiar? Why did this seem to keep happening to her? Doing something and feeling like she'd done it before. Not just tucking Ig in, but also the line about being snug as a bug. Other moments. In the woolshed earlier, when she was taking photographs, she'd had a flash of memory of a party. But there hadn't been a party since she was here. Had they told her about one? Perhaps that was it. She was hearing so many stories from the family all the time, they were getting mixed up in her own mind.

It would be different when Will and Lexie were here. They'd be off doing trips on their own. She wouldn't be spending so much time with the Gillespies.

Angela took off her slippers again and got into bed. As she reached for her book, she saw something on the bedside table. She hadn't noticed it before. It was a thick folder with lots of paper inside it. A note was attached to the front. *I think you will find this most illuminating.*

The note was unsigned. She opened the folder. It looked like a letter. Lots of letters.

She put on her glasses and started to read.

Nick had tried three times to explain to Will who he was and why he was there. Each time they were interrupted by the phone ringing. Will apologized. "My secretary's only part-time. Day off today, as you can see."

"Could you take the phone off the hook?"

"And lose a possible client?"

"It's important," Nick said.

"Everyone thinks their renovations are important. And everyone wants it done now. You're Australian, are you? Been living in London long? How you can handle this climate is beyond me. I'd prefer sunshine twelve months a year."

"Have you ever been there?"

"Not yet. One day. When Concorde's flying again and I win the lottery and can get there in five hours instead of . . . What is it, thirty-five hours nonstop?"

"Not quite," Nick said. He had to ask now, while the phones were quiet. "I don't live here. I'm visiting. My wife's from London. Her name is Angela Richardson."

Will just looked at him.

"Angela Richardson," Nick repeated.

"Right," Will said. "So she's showing you around, is she? Great. And so who wants the work done, her family?"

"She's an old friend of yours. From years ago."

"Of mine? Your wife is an old friend of mine? Where is she?"

"Still in Australia."

"She asked you to drop in and say hello? She's got a better memory than me."

"You used to go out together. About thirty-four years ago."

"We did? Angela, did you say?" He frowned. "Dark curly hair? Great eyes?"

"That's her."

"God, I haven't thought about her in years. How is she?"

"Good. We've been married thirty-three years. Four kids."

"Good for you. In Australia? In sunny Sydney?"

"You don't know where she is? You haven't been in touch with her?"

"In touch with her? Why would I? Listen, Rick—"

"Nick."

"Sorry, Nick. Look, I don't know what—" The phone rang. "Excuse me." He answered. "That's right. Attic conversions, bathroom extensions. Yes. Sure, I can. Tomorrow. Today? Sure. See you then. Yes, I know the street. I'm a local myself." He hung up. "Sorry, Nick. I'm caught up here today, as you can see. What can I do for you?"

"I want to talk to you about Angela."

"It was a long time ago. I can't see—"

"She's had an accident. Her memory's been affected. I

happened to be here in London. She's mentioned you a couple of times. I was hoping you'd tell me what you remembered about her. It might help spark more memories for her."

"She has amnesia or something? Sorry to hear that. Look, now's not the time. Are you staying nearby? We could meet later. Talk over a pint or something."

They agreed on a time. Eight p.m. Nick suggested the Irish pub on Upper Street.

"Fine," Will said. "I'm not barred from there yet. Joking. See you then."

He'd picked up the phone to make a call before Nick had even left the room.

Outside, Nick checked the time. It was too late to phone home. He passed an Internet café, went in and sent a quick e-mail instead.

    It's the right Will. Meeting again later to-
    night. Dad x

Once again, he followed Genevieve's instructions. He took the Tube from Angel station up the road. Got off at London Bridge. Took the train to Forest Hill.

It was nearly two thirty as he came out of the station. He stood on the footpath and looked around. Why hadn't he made this trip with Angela before? In all their years of marriage, she'd only ever been back here twice, when her parents died. It had been chaos while she was gone. Joan had nearly moved in full-time to help out.

Had he ever asked Angela about her childhood here? He

must have, in the beginning. He was sure he had. But then so much had happened so quickly for them. Meeting in that pub in Sydney, getting engaged, not just a first-year-of-marriage baby but twins. He knew she was from South London, from a council estate, but had he ever even seen photos of her house?

He followed Genevieve's directions. Walked along the main road, turned left at a small grassed area, walked up a hill and there he was. On the street Angela had grown up on. There was a row of terraced houses, all identical in design, two windows downstairs, two windows upstairs. Each with a patch of front garden. That was it. She'd grown up in the end house, according to Genevieve. It had a geranium in a pot at the door, but beyond that, it looked like the others. A little shabbier, if anything.

He did as Genevieve had asked and took some photos, feeling self-conscious. "Take one of you in front of it too," she'd asked. There was no one to take it. He wasn't going to do one of those selfie things the kids laughed about. The other photos would have to be the proof he'd been here.

Just as he was about to leave, a middle-aged woman came up the hill, carrying shopping bags.

"Excuse me," he said.

She looked suspicious. He explained why he was there, that this was his wife's childhood home. Maybe she even knew her.

"Richardson? No, must have been before I moved in. No one of that name here now."

She reluctantly agreed to take a photo. Just as reluctantly,

Nick stood in front of the house and smiled. It was only when he looked at it when he got back to the bottom of the hill that he realized her thumb had been over the viewfinder.

It was raining again, heavily, as he crossed the road to the Horniman Museum. No wonder this had been a big part of Angela's childhood. It was a grand mansion with a huge clock tower, in the middle of what looked like ordinary suburban houses. It was already starting to get dark, but he could see cultivated gardens around it, open spaces, and far off, a view of the London skyline. He came inside out of the rain. What was here that Genevieve had wanted him to see? Stuffed birds? A walrus?

At the reception desk, he asked for directions.

The woman pointed. "Just down there. You can't miss it," she said.

She was right. It was the first thing he saw as he walked into the large display room. A huge walrus, perched on a fake iceberg. It was the size of a baby elephant. It was also strangely smooth. He walked over to the security man sitting nearby. "That walrus? What's funny about it?"

"Everything, if you ask me." The man explained the background, that it had been stuffed in the last century by a taxidermist who'd never seen a real one and so filled up every inch of the skin. "But he's the star of our show now," he said. "People travel for miles to have a photo taken with him."

Nick held out his camera. "Would you mind?"

The guard took several. Nick checked. No thumbs. "Thanks."

He did a quick circuit of the rest of the large room. It

was crammed with cases of stuffed birds, skeletons, animals, reptiles. He was glad to be outside again ten minutes later.

Ig woke up before dawn. He lay there and looked out the window. The birds were noisier than ever. They always were after lots of rain. His dad had explained it. The ground got churned up; insects and worms rose closer to the surface. It was a feeding frenzy for the birds. Ig had liked the words *feeding frenzy.*

Angela should see it too. It would be good for her photos and for their Plan. Genevieve had bought everything he had asked. Pots of paint, green, red, blue. "What are you up to now?" she'd said the night before as she handed them over. "I was expecting your list to say ten bottles of Coke and eight bags of chips, not half the contents of a paint shop."

"It's a surprise," he told her.

"You and Robbie?" she said.

"Not exactly," he said.

He and Angela were doing a mural. A mural of a bird aviary on the side of the shearing shed. It was a big blank wall at the moment. He was going to paint it white first, and then with Angela's help he was going to draw all the birds around the station. He'd been practicing his drawings and he had them just about right now. And Angela said if he made a mistake, it didn't matter, that birds came in all shapes and sizes and if he really wasn't happy with any of his drawings, then they could just paint it white again and start a new one.

He knocked on the door of Angela's room. There was no answer. He knocked again and called her name. Still nothing. He opened the door and stepped in. "Angela?"

She was asleep. There was paper all over the floor. He stepped closer. They were his mum's letters. The Christmas letters. The ones they had all read through for their Boxing Day play that didn't happen.

She opened her eyes, sat up and reached for her glasses. "Ig? Is everything all right?"

"Yes," Ig said. "The birds are really good after the rain. I thought you might want to see them."

She sat up straighter and looked around at all the paper.

"Do you want me to pick them up?" he said.

"Thanks, Ig. They must have slipped off the bed after I read them last night."

He gathered them, all out of order, but he didn't think it mattered. He put the folder back on the end of her bed.

"I'll wait on the veranda," he said.

He was about to step outside when she spoke again. "Ig? Can I ask you something?"

He nodded.

"Could you shut the door first?"

He did.

"I'm sorry if this sounds a bit strange," she said.

He waited.

"Ig, am I your mother?"

FIFTY-TWO

"I don't believe it!" Genevieve's voice carried around the whole house. She was in the office, at the computer. "Ig? Ig, are you there?"

"What is it?" Lindy called back from the kitchen.

Genevieve appeared in the doorway. "It was a joke. A silly joke, and I've had two thousand hits already. It's madness! A few photos of cats. What's the world coming to? I need to do more, immediately. Where's Ig?"

Victoria looked up from her breakfast. She shrugged.

"Lindy?"

Lindy was at the other end of the table, sewing. Celia was opposite her, also sewing.

"Nothing from Dad?" Victoria asked.

"Nothing," Genevieve said. "Not since that last e-mail.

Infuriating in its brevity." She calculated the time. It was eight a.m. in South Australia. Still the previous night in London. "They're obviously getting on like a house on fire." She heard voices outside and peered out the window. "Speaking of best friends, here they come, Master and Mrs. Thick as Thieves."

"We're doing something at the back of the woolshed and none of you can look until it's finished, okay?" Ig said as they came in.

"Does it involve weapons? Chemicals? Warcraft of any type? Or let me guess—it involves paint," Genevieve said.

"I'm sworn to secrecy," Angela said.

"Can I please have the computer?" Lindy asked, putting down her cushion. "I think my e-mail must be down. I haven't heard anything from Richard for three days now."

"You can have five minutes," Genevieve said. "Then I need it for more of my groundbreaking work linking cats with celebrities. Ig, wait till you see. We've gone viral."

"I need ten minutes," Lindy said. "That computer belongs to all of us, not just you. And I can't believe you're calling putting cat photos on a Web site your 'work.'"

"You're right, Lindy, thank you. It's more of a life's passion than work."

In London, Nick now had a long list of words he could use to describe Will to Genevieve.

A bore. A pain. The most tedious, self-absorbed man it had ever been his misfortune to meet.

He'd been in his company for two hours now. They'd met at the bar in the Irish pub as arranged, found a table, ordered meals and drinks. Guinness for Will. A pint of Coke for Nick. "On the wagon?" Will said. "I'll have a pint later," Nick answered. As they sat down, Nick waited for him to start asking questions about Angela. Nothing.

Once Will had confirmed this was Nick's first trip to London, he hadn't drawn breath. Nick heard all about Will's family history in Islington, going back four generations. How his grandparents had bought a three-story house when it was almost a slum area. He detailed all the landmarks in the area, including the Angel Clock Tower and the Islington Town Hall. He told Nick about the old Roman roads. The antique traders who had once lived and worked in Camden Passage. "All overpriced vintage hat shops and middle-class gift shops there now, if you ask me."

Nick eventually interrupted him, trying to bring it back to personal matters, back to Angela. "Did you ever get married yourself?"

"Twice. Worst two mistakes I ever made."

Because he hadn't married Angela? Was that what he meant? "How long did you and Angela go out?"

Will looked uncertain. "How old were we? Nineteen? Twenty? I can't really remember how long. A few months, maybe?"

"Angela remembers it being a couple of years."

"She's got a better memory than me, then. It was the seventies, remember. If we did go out that long, we weren't exactly 'exclusive.'" He made quote signs with his fingers as he said the word *exclusive*. "I went traveling too. Spent six months in India. Went for the architecture, stayed for the drugs." He laughed, too loudly.

Nick said nothing. Not that Will seemed to care.

"I met my first wife there. A free spirit like me, I thought. Let me tell you, by the time she'd finished dragging me through the divorce courts, the last thing I'd call her was free."

Nick had a feeling he'd used that line before. "Any kids?"

"Two boys with her. Both in their thirties now. Living with their girlfriends. No grandkids yet. They don't have much to do with me. She turned them against me, after I had an affair with my secretary. Biggest mistake I ever made."

"Your current secretary?"

"I wish. Lazy as sin, this one, but a looker. No, a different woman. Good thing I moved to the office above the laundry, because she took me to the cleaners too." Another too-loud laugh. There had been a stepson from that marriage too, he said. He didn't see much of him either. He and that former wife weren't on speaking terms. "The kids always take the mother's side, don't they?"

"All sons? You don't have any daughters?" Nick asked.

"No. Shame. They might have looked after me in my old age." He gave that laugh again.

Nick couldn't picture Angela with this man for five minutes, let alone two years. "So, do you have any photos of Angela?"

"I wouldn't have a clue. Place is a bit of a mess. Bachelor living and all that. But I'm only two streets away, if you want me to take a look. I have some good whisky too. You must be sick of that Coke by now." Nick had stuck to it. Meanwhile, Will had drunk three pints of Guinness.

It was less than five minutes' walk to his house. They

passed more terraced houses, much bigger than the ones on Angela's childhood street. Steps led up to front doors, all with fanlights. The houses were three stories high. The curtains were drawn back in one. Nick was able to see into the front room. A dinner party was in progress, eight or so people sitting around a long table, a chandelier overhead. BMWs and Saabs were parked in the street outside.

"Here we are," Will said. "Home sweet home."

Nick tried to ignore the cold wind as Will stood out front and pointed out architectural features. "The windows get smaller as they go higher. Those rooms were for the servants and no one cared whether they had enough light. Now this street is full of New Labor people. Sold us all up the river, if you ask me. I don't have time for politics anymore. They're all as bad as each other."

Nick expected Will to go up the stairs to the grand front door. Instead, he opened a gate in the iron railing and headed down to the basement.

"Sorry; you'll have to slum it down here. I had to sell the rest of the house to pay the second lot of alimony. Good thing my parents are dead. They don't know this is all that's left of the family jewels."

Will's basement flat made his office seem tidy. It looked like there'd been a break-in. Papers, books and CDs were strewn everywhere. There was a musty smell. A dead plant in the corner. It looked like a teenager's haunt.

"Take a seat," Will said.

It was hard to find one. Nick moved a pile of newspapers and sat on the sofa, by the dead plant. Will went into the kitchen down a narrow hall. Nick could see it was as cramped and dirty as the living room. He heard the clink of glasses.

"Scotch or Irish?" Will called.

A question, at last. The first one Will had asked him. "Irish. From Donegal and Mayo. My ancestors left in—"

That laugh again. "Not you. What whisky? Scotch or Irish? Prefer the Scotch myself."

"Scotch is fine," Nick said.

Will came in with two glasses filled to halfway and the bottle tucked under his arm.

"So, a photo of Angela?" Nick asked.

"Somewhere. Probably. It's all coming back to me now. She used to like to go to that museum out near her house for picnics. The dead zoo place." Another laugh.

"I was there today. The Horniman Museum."

"That's right. Place gave me the creeps."

"But you might have a photo of her there?"

"Maybe. I met her through my cousin, I think. There's probably a group one of us somewhere." He went across to the bookcase and shifted a pile of soccer magazines. He picked one up. "I'm an Arsenal man, through and through. Their ground's just up the road. Shame it's not the weekend. I'd take you to a match. Hell of a team. I was at a match last . . ."

As Will kept talking, Nick realized there was little possibility of a photo of Angela here. Or of Will being able to find it if there was. Genevieve had asked him to get a photo of Will too. Sorry, Genevieve, but no, he decided. He tipped the whisky into the already-dead plant and stood up.

"I need to go. Any message for Angela?"

"You're leaving already? Tell her hello. Hope her life turned out better than mine."

Back on Errigal, Genevieve hadn't had a chance to call her father. A new drama had blown up. Lindy had been in tears now for nearly half an hour. They'd started when she was in the office.

Genevieve, Victoria and Celia had been in the kitchen. Genevieve was washing up. Victoria was cooking. Celia was sewing. Angela and Ig were still outside. At first, none of them reacted. Lindy's sobs continued.

Celia eventually looked up from her sewing. "Shouldn't one of you go and check on her?"

"She's probably just broken a nail," Genevieve said from the sink.

Lindy appeared, holding a piece of paper, her eyes filled with tears. "I hate her so much. I *hate* her. She did it deliberately. I know she did. It's not about him. She doesn't even want him. It's about ruining things for me." Then she spun around to Genevieve. "You didn't write it, did you? You and Ig? Somehow send this pretending to be from Richard?"

"We're too busy finding photos of cats. Sorry," Genevieve said. "Why? What does it say?"

"You tell her, Victoria," Lindy said, handing her the e-mail. "I never want to see it again."

Victoria read it quickly, then summarized. "It seems that while Richard and Horrible Jane were away on Phillip Island, they—how shall I put it?—got together. Afterward, Jane told him that she was in love with him, that she'd been in love with him for months. And he realized he had strong feelings for her too. He's very apologetic but feels he owes it to Jane to explore the possibilities of this new relationship. So regrettably he won't be coming to visit after all." She turned to her sister. "Oh, Lindy. I'm so sorry."

Lindy gave another sob and ran down the hall to her room.

"On the bright side, I suppose that's one less bed to make up," Genevieve said.

Out at the woolshed, Ig and Angela had finished the first coat of paint. The wall gleamed white, the surface uneven in parts, but it had the makings of a good canvas, they agreed. They were sitting on upturned crates eating their snack. Ig had brought it out in his schoolbag again. Biscuits and juice.

They hadn't spoken much during the painting, or since their conversation that morning. When Angela had asked him, "Ig, am I your mother?" he had waited and thought about what he should say. His sisters and his dad had told him to go along with the idea of her being from London, that she had a husband called Will and a daughter called Lexie.

But she had asked him a direct question. And it was true. So he had nodded.

"Am I the others' mother as well? The twins? Lindy?"

Another nod.

"And Nick is my husband." She said it just like that. It wasn't a question. She picked up the folder of Christmas letters. "This is all about my life, isn't it? I wrote all of these."

"Yes," he said. "You send one of those letters out every year. On December first. I help you send them."

"Did I do one last Christmas?"

"Yes," Ig said.

"But it's not here?"

"Not yet," Ig said.

She looked at him for a long time. Then she smiled. A big smile. He smiled back. She opened her arms. He stepped forward and she gave him a great big hug.

He'd missed her hugs.

"Can I tell everyone you've remembered?" he asked.

She looked serious again, as she shook her head. "Ig, would you please keep this between us for now? A kind of secret? I need to do some more thinking about everything. I need just a bit more peace and quiet first."

He nodded. That made good sense to him. If he did tell the others, he was pretty sure there'd be a big fuss. And his mum wanted peace and quiet, not a big fuss. "Do you still want to go and see the birds?"

"Yes. Yes, I do."

"I'll wait outside."

She joined him five minutes later, still in her dressing gown, wearing sneakers instead of slippers, carrying her camera. They walked around the yard, out almost as far as the old chapel. There were birds everywhere. She took lots of photographs. The sun was coming up, everything turning golden around them, the slopes of the Chace Range changing from darkness to a glowing red. As they started to walk back to the homestead, there was the sound of a kookaburra, the cackling filling the air around them. It made Ig laugh. It always did.

"Is that your favorite bird?" she asked him.

Ig nodded. "Sorry we don't have robins," he said. "They're your favorite, aren't they?"

She nodded. "But kookaburras are pretty good too; don't worry," she said.

Ig passed her another biscuit now. She was looking at him again in that kind of funny way, like she was really concentrating on something.

"Are you remembering some more things?" he asked.

"I'm trying, Ig. I'm trying as hard as I can."

"That's good." He took another bite from his biscuit.

In the kitchen, Genevieve hung up from talking to her father in London. He had called before she'd had a chance to call him. He hadn't gone into detail about the meeting with Will. "Your mother had a lucky escape," was all he'd said. He confirmed there had been no contact between Will and Angela. He also had other news. He'd changed his flights. He was on his way home.

"But what about the rest of his trip?" Victoria said. "He didn't see much of Ireland, did he?"

"He said he saw all he needed to."

Twelve hours later, Nick was in a plane taxiing down the runway at Heathrow Airport. It had cost him almost as much as the original fare to change his flights. But it was worth every cent. He sat back in his seat and shut his eyes as the plane took off.

FIFTY-THREE

ust after one a.m., Genevieve was woken by Victoria's urgent whispers beside her.

"Genevieve, wake up. Please, wake up."

"What is it?"

"I need you. Something's happening."

They went into the bathroom together. Victoria spoke in a low voice, then showed her. Blood.

"Does it mean something's wrong? Am I having a miscarriage? What can I do? Can I stop it?"

"I don't know. Victoria, I'm so sorry. I don't know."

"Can you look it up on the computer for me? Please? I don't want to go into the Hawker hospital. I'll know too many people there. There must be something I can do; lie down or something? Please, Genevieve, quickly."

"Come back to bed. Lie down. I'll find out what I can."

As she helped her sister back to their bedroom, they saw there was a light in the guest room.

They didn't need to ask each other. Genevieve tapped on the door.

"Come in," a voice called.

Angela was sitting up in bed, holding her camera, looking through her photos. "Girls? Is everything all right?"

"No," Genevieve said. "Angela, we need you."

Angela and Genevieve stayed with Victoria throughout the night, urging her to hang on, urging the baby to hang on. But it didn't help. The blood kept coming. They called Joan as the sun was coming up. She was there before eight a.m. She was not just a former nurse. She'd had two miscarriages, she told them. She was so sorry, but yes, it looked like that was what had happened.

Victoria couldn't stop crying. "Don't say it's for the best. Don't say it, please," she cried into Genevieve's shoulder. "I wanted it. I really wanted it."

"I know you did." Genevieve held her sister tight. "I know. I did too."

There were whispered conversations between them all. Lindy and Celia were told the truth. Ig was simply told that Victoria wasn't well. They decided they would explain it to him more fully when there was more time. Other plans were made. Victoria had been due to go to Adelaide to collect Nick from the airport that day. His flight was due in at four p.m. Joan was now going to drive, but would bring Victoria with her. The bleeding had stopped but she needed to see a doctor. Joan knew a good women's clinic in Adelaide. They could go straight there, before the airport. Genevieve wanted to go with them. She'd heard from Matt that he was coming today but she'd e-mail him, she told Victoria. Or try to get him on his phone. Tell him she was sorry, but she wouldn't be on Errigal today after all.

Victoria wouldn't let her. "Joan will take care of me. Please stay here. I want you to see him."

Angela wanted to go with them to Adelaide too. She had been so attentive to Victoria all night long. She'd even held her in her arms as Victoria cried.

Genevieve had only had a brief opportunity to fill Joan in on Angela's condition, about the snippets of memory that seemed to be returning. But she didn't think it was a good idea for Angela to be at the airport to meet Nick. Or to leave Errigal yet. She shook her head. Joan took her cue.

"I don't think so, Angela," Joan said. "Not this trip. Next time."

Angela accepted the decision, they were relieved to see.

By ten o'clock, Joan and Victoria were ready to leave. Genevieve held her twin close. She didn't need to say anything. Victoria knew how she felt and what she wanted to say.

Angela had just returned to her room and was straightening her bedcovers when there was a knock at her door. It was Celia.

"Poor Victoria," Celia said. "It's probably for the best, but of course she won't see it like that yet."

"No," Angela said, continuing to make her bed.

"They woke you in the night, I believe."

"Yes, they did."

Celia stayed, as if she was waiting for Angela to say something else.

Angela stayed silent.

"Did you get the folder I left you?" Celia said. "The letters?"

"I did, thank you," Angela said.

Again, Celia waited. Angela continued tidying her room, hanging up a dress in the wardrobe.

"Interesting reading, I hope?" Celia said.

"Very interesting, thank you. If you'll excuse me, I need to go and find Ig."

"Of course." Celia stepped aside.

Angela made a point of closing the door tightly.

Lindy was following Genevieve around the house. She had stopped crying about Richard. She had asked dozens of questions about Victoria. She was now asking about Nick.

"He must have said something else about the Gillespie reunion," she said. "Is it definitely going ahead or not? I'm not going to keep sewing two hundred cushions if it's not, I'll tell you that for nothing."

"Why not? If Dad decides not to hold it, you'll still have handy Christmas presents for the rest of us. For the next fifty years."

"You're no help. And thanks for all the sympathy about Richard, by the way. Not. If it was Victoria that had happened to, you'd be all over her, wouldn't you? But not me—"

Genevieve lost her temper. "Victoria just had a miscarriage, Lindy. Have you happened to forget that? She lost her baby. I think that might be a little bit more important than your alleged boyfriend jumping into bed with your evil nemesis, don't you? And if you don't mind me saying, I never liked him anyway. He was spineless. Anyone could see he was terrified of Horrible Jane. Who wants a boyfriend like that?"

"He was not! He told me she was really bossy and that she was jealous of all of us, and of me."

"So he was a gossip as well as spineless. You're better off without him. You're too good for him."

Lindy hesitated, as if trying to decide whether she was being insulted or praised. "Do you mean that?"

"Of course I mean it. You're a catch, Lindy. When you're not feeling sorry for yourself, you're smart and funny. You're cute. I'd get rid of the ponytails myself, but what do I know? I've only been a hairdresser for fourteen years."

Lindy tugged at one of the ponytails. "Do you really think so? I read an article that said lots of women use a breakup as the chance to give themselves a new look. Should I do that? Would you cut my hair now?"

Genevieve briefly closed her eyes and prayed for patience.

An hour later, she had turned Lindy's long straight locks into a very becoming bob. Lindy was thrilled. She got Genevieve to take photos of it from all angles to e-mail to her friends in Melbourne.

"Should I e-mail it to Horrible Jane and Richard too?" she said. "Show them that I've moved on?"

"It has only been a day since you found out about them," Genevieve said. "Maybe wait a bit."

Ig came in from the shed. He had green paint on his cheek and white paint on his hands. He stopped and looked at Lindy.

"That looks great. You look really pretty."

She gave him a suspicious glance. "Do you mean that? Because I think Genevieve bribed you to say that last time."

"She did last time. I did it for free this time. You look good."

Lindy kissed him and Genevieve and then nearly skipped down the hall to the office.

Genevieve started sweeping up the hair and putting her scissors and combs away in her bag. Ig washed his hands and then started getting the makings of a sandwich out of the fridge.

"It's only eleven o'clock, Ig. A bit early for lunch, isn't it?"

"We've already eaten our morning tea. We're hungry again."

"You and Angela are getting on pretty well out there, are you?"

He nodded.

"Does Robbie like her too?"

"Yep," he said.

"You okay, Ig?"

"Yes, thanks."

"Can I come and see the shed yet?"

"No."

"Not even a peek?"

"No."

"What do you and Angela talk about all the time?"

"Stuff."

"Ig, has she said anything to you that might make you think she is starting to remember things?"

He stopped midway through buttering the bread. "Why?"

"Last night, with Victoria, when she wasn't well—" She stopped. "I just wondered. There were a few times when it felt like she was Old Angela, not New Angela. You haven't noticed anything, have you?"

"No," he said. He didn't turn around, just kept putting the cheese on the bread.

An hour later, he was back again for more biscuits. It was afternoon teatime, he said.

"Are you two doing anything out there except eating?" Genevieve asked from her spot at the table. She was going through recipe books, trying to find something she could actually cook.

"We're working hard. It's giving us appetites." He pulled the chair over to the pantry, climbed up, got the biscuit barrel that was supposed to be out of his reach, took a handful and climbed down.

"Are you nervous about your friend coming today?" he asked, as he pushed the chair back.

"Of course not."

"Then why do you keep walking out to the gate? Every five minutes. We've been timing you."

"Exercise," Genevieve said.

"Do you love this guy? Are you going to marry him?"

"Don't be cheeky. And if you say anything like that in front of him, I'll kill you."

"I'm being curious, not cheeky. You told me it's good to be curious."

"It's a thin line."

"So are you in love with him?"

"I hardly know him. But yes, I like him a lot. Why? What's with all the questions?"

"Because he's nearly here. There's a car coming."

"What?" She ran to the window. There was a dust cloud moving up the road toward them. Less than seven minutes away. "Why didn't you tell me?"

Genevieve ran from the kitchen to the bathroom. She checked her hair. Her makeup. Her clothes. Checked her teeth for spinach, even though she hadn't had any spinach. She sprayed some perfume on her wrists and under her ears, then thought that was too much for this time of the day and tried to scrub it off. She now had four red marks instead. She tried to cover them with foundation, and only managed to smear it everywhere. She washed it all off and ran back to the kitchen, just as his 4WD pulled up in front of the homestead.

It was actually him. Coffee Guy. Matt. The man she had been e-mailing. The man she had last seen in her tiny flat in New York, after a night of the best sex and laughs she'd had in years. He was now getting out of his car and standing in front of her family house in outback South Australia.

She wanted to run out to him. Then she thought that looked too eager and she slowed to a walk. Then she remembered he had just driven three hundred kilometers to see her. That deserved a run.

She hadn't thought about how she would greet him. Whether they would shake hands. Whether she would play it cool. In the end, she did neither. She saw him there, smiling at her, and she hugged him. He hugged her back. He smelled of aftershave and coffee and sweat, and if she hadn't known for a fact that Angela and Ig were peeking out from behind the woolshed, she would have kissed him right there and then. Possibly taken him straight into her bedroom.

"Hi," she said. "Fancy seeing you here."

"Hi," he said. "I was just passing by and thought I'd drop in."

It was as easy as that between them, as instant as that. She brought him inside, made him coffee. They took it out onto the veranda. There was so much to talk about, questions back and forth, quick jokes, tales from his film set. Even a mention of his brother. A joke from Genevieve back about that.

One by one, her family appeared. First Lindy, who too obviously gave Genevieve a big thumbs-up. Celia greeted him as if she were the lady of the manor, welcoming him to Errigal and then returning inside again. Angela was friendly but distracted. Genevieve had told Matt in her e-mails about her mother's situation. Just in time, she stopped herself from introducing Angela as her mother. Instead, she described her as a guest.

"A paint-covered guest at that," Angela said, holding up whitewash-covered hands. "Excuse me, won't you?"

Ig was last to appear. Genevieve made the introductions. He and Matt solemnly shook hands.

"Are you really from America?" Ig asked.

"I really am," Matt said.

"Are you really making a film up here?"

"I don't know yet," Matt said. "I'm having a look around first."

"It's not another horrible film, is it?" Ig said.

Matt glanced at Genevieve.

"He means horror film," she said. "Ig was an extra in one that was filmed up here a couple of years ago. They paid him ten dollars."

"All I had to do was walk past the camera a few times. Like this." Ig demonstrated, walking back and forth in front of Genevieve and Matt.

"Wow," Matt said. "I can see why they hired you. That's some walk."

Ig gave his little smile. "So is yours a murder film too?"

"Not this time, no. It's about zombie rabbits taking over the world."

"Seriously?" Genevieve said. "It's the one you were telling me about in New York?"

He grinned. "Farewell, teenage vampires; hello, dystopian zombie rabbits. More to the point, hello lots of zombie rabbit merchandise."

Matt told them he'd been scouting locations farther north. He was flying to Western Australia on Saturday, in two days' time, to visit possible locations there too. Meeting with government officials to discuss tax incentives. A film like this was worth a lot to the local economy.

"Why don't you film it here?" Ig asked. "You could stay with us for free."

Matt laughed. "Thanks, Ig. It's not just me. There'll be about a hundred of us."

"We've got sleeping bags," Ig said. "Are you going to take him to Swing Hill, Genevieve? If I was a zombie rabbit, that's where I'd live."

"Swing Hill?" Matt said.

Genevieve explained.

"There are only three swings there, though," Ig said. "Dad said he'd build me one too, but he hasn't yet."

"I'll leave you mine in my will, Ig," Genevieve said.

Matt said he'd like to go there. Ig was invited to join them but declined. He was busy, he told Matt.

"But I can't tell you what I'm doing because it's a secret. So please don't even ask."

"I won't, I promise," Matt said, just as seriously.

"Great kid," Matt said, as he and Genevieve walked through the gates, in the direction of Swing Hill. "Great family."

"Nice, but not a sane one among them," Genevieve said. "Apart from me, of course."

As they walked, they talked. He asked more about Angela, how her recovery was going. He listened, asked more questions. His grandmother had dementia, he told her. Was it something like that? A bit, but this was temporary, Genevieve said. They hoped so, at least.

They kept walking. She pointed out the landmarks, feeling like a tour guide, showing him the Chace Range, Elder Range, Wilpena Pound and Rawnsley Bluff. She told him the statistics she knew too. That the Flinders was Australia's second-largest mountain range. That Wilpena Pound was so big it could hold Uluru ten times over. She pointed out galahs screeching in a nearby gum tree, a wedge-tailed eagle hovering to their right. They saw a goanna, long-tailed and prehistoric-looking, on the path in front of them.

"It's incredible," he said, shading his eyes, looking around. "No wonder you came back here."

"It's my Hotel California," she said. "I keep trying to leave. I just never can."

They started climbing the track to Swing Hill. She let him go first, so he'd get the full impact of the view.

"Wow," he said, as he reached the top. There was a magnificent 360-degree view around them. It was their station, as far as they could see, she told him. After a few seconds of taking it in, he turned toward her.

"It's really good to see you again, Genevieve," he said.

"It's kind of incredible to see you again, Matt," she said.

"It's so beautiful up here. I can't take my eyes off it." He was looking at her, not the view. "So, where were we? I remember. Ready? Guess the film. 'Here's looking at you, kid.'"

She smiled. "*Star Wars*," she said.

"'You had me at hello.'"

"*The Amityville Horror.*"

"You really are good at this," he said. "I'll make it harder. 'I've a feeling we're not in Kansas anymore.'"

"Easy," she said. "*The Muppet Movie.*"

He didn't ask her any more.

He kissed her instead.

FIFTY-FOUR

In Adelaide, Victoria and Joan were in the waiting room of the clinic. Victoria's name was called. She turned to Joan. "Will you please come in with me?"

The doctor listened as Victoria told her what had happened, gave her all the details, all her dates. She did another test. The doctor examined her. Then she confirmed what Victoria already knew. She had lost the baby. "It doesn't mean you won't be able to conceive again. It just means it wasn't—"

The right time for this baby. She had heard it from Joan, from Genevieve, even from Angela. In her head, she knew it was true. In her heart, it still hurt. She'd wept the whole journey down in the car. Joan had stayed quiet beside her, reaching over now and again to hold her hand.

She needed to know more, what had happened, why it had happened. When it had happened. The doctor was kind, gentle. She gave her all the information. Victoria's cervix was closed, she said. That meant that the pregnancy had been over for some time, even though the bleeding had only happened in the past day or two. The fetus had—

Victoria couldn't hear the word *died*. Not out loud. Not yet. But she needed to know what might have made it happen.

"We can never know for certain," the doctor said. "In the first three months, it happens so often. Have you been sick at all? Sometimes it can be that."

Victoria shook her head. Apart from the food poisoning at Christmas time. The doctor asked lots of questions about that. Victoria told her about the contaminated prawns, how sick they had all been. She began to recall what else they'd had for Christmas lunch. Parma ham. Soft cheeses. All the food she'd since learned a pregnant woman should avoid. She began to cry again. "I made it happen, didn't I? I did it. It's my fault."

"It's not your fault." Joan was fierce about it. "It happened for its own reason. I won't let you blame yourself, Victoria. I won't."

The doctor let her cry again. She offered her brochures, details of counselors. At the door, she touched Victoria's shoulder in sympathy. "Let yourself be sad about it. Grieve all you need to."

Outside in the car, Victoria cried again. Joan took her in her arms.

"I want my mum," Victoria sobbed.

"I know, darling. I know."

Joan let her say all she needed to say, listened as

Victoria cried and tried to speak. Victoria had known it would be hard to be a single mother. That she'd have to get in touch with Mr. Radio eventually, that he had a right to know he was the father. She knew that it wouldn't have been easy, any of it. But she'd been ready. Once she'd known for sure she was pregnant, she'd felt ready for anything. Ready to be a mother. It didn't make sense; she knew that. She'd been less than three months pregnant. But once she'd made the decision to have it— She started crying again. It had been her baby. And now it was gone.

Joan suggested a walk. They drove to a spot beside the river. Together, they walked along the pathway. Victoria's tears began to ease. She asked Joan to tell her how it had been for her, with two miscarriages. Joan didn't cry as she shared her story. But she had cried for a long time when they happened, she told Victoria. Even now, sometimes, she thought about those two babies. She knew what ages they would have been. When their birthdays might have been. Back then, miscarriages weren't talked about as much. Women were expected to keep quiet about them, get on with things. But she had never forgotten.

Back at the car, Victoria glanced at herself in the mirror. Her eyes were red-rimmed, her makeup smudged. Joan offered to collect Nick on her own, to leave Victoria in a café, or by the river, for time alone. Victoria shook her head. She wanted solitude but she also wanted to see her dad.

They were at the airport just a few minutes before his flight landed. Victoria hadn't decided how much to tell her father. All of it, or perhaps none; she didn't know yet. It seemed impossible all this had happened while he was away.

Impossible that he had been to Ireland and England in the past seven days.

The passengers from his flight started to appear. She saw him and waved. He stood out, tall, so tanned. She'd expected him to be exhausted, but he looked well. Purposeful. That was the word. He looked better than he had a week ago. She threw her arms around him as if she were a little kid again.

"Any news?" he said. "How's Angela? Is everyone okay?"

"We're all fine," she said.

Together they walked over to where Joan was waiting.

Genevieve was trying to find Ig. On the way back from Swing Hill, Matt had remembered he had some merchandise in his car from a previous film he'd worked on. He thought Ig might like it. Genevieve had already looked outside, calling his name. No reply. She checked all around the house. She walked into the living room. Celia and Angela were there, watching *Downton Abbey*.

She waited until the end of a heated exchange between a butler and a housekeeper. "I'm sorry to interrupt, but have either of you seen Ig?" she asked.

"No, not for a while. Sorry," Angela said.

Celia pressed pause with a sigh. "He's out in his cubby, I suppose."

"No, he's not. I can't find him anywhere."

Angela offered to help look. Thanks, but no need, Genevieve said. She was sure he wasn't far away. She walked into the kitchen. Matt was standing by the window, holding his phone in the air.

"You can try standing on the roof," Genevieve said, "but I'm sorry to say it still won't help."

"You've seriously survived out here for this long without a cell phone?"

"We've only just got running water. Sorry about this, but I seem to have temporarily lost my little brother."

"Can I help look?"

"No, I'd probably lose you as well. I'm going to check the buildings outside again. I'll be right back, I promise."

She gave him a quick kiss. Then another, slightly longer one.

On Swing Hill, after kissing for a long time and only just stopping themselves from doing a lot more than kissing, she'd made a suggestion. She would take him for a drive around the station, to all the lookout points, and to the Aboriginal paintings. Errigal mightn't be ideal for his zombie rabbits, but who knew what other film he might be scouting for in the future? And after that, she would take him into Hawker for a drink in a proper outback pub. If they got moving, there was time for all of that, and to be back before Joan, Victoria and her dad returned. She wanted Matt to meet everyone. Especially Victoria.

"Do they rent rooms in that pub by the hour?" he'd asked, as they walked down Swing Hill together. He had his arm around her. His fingers were stroking her bare shoulder. She was finding it hard to stay upright. All she wanted to do was keep kissing him. Do more than kiss him. As soon as possible.

"By the hour?" Then she got it. "That's as long as you could last?"

"I'm out of practice. I haven't been with anyone since you."

"You haven't?"

He shook his head. "Have you?"

"Dozens. Out here, I'm spoiled for choice." She shook her head. "No."

That time, she followed up on her urge to kiss him. It was another ten minutes before they were walking again. Again, she was surprised by how good she felt around him. How easy it was. There was no playing games, no pretending. He'd made it clear and she'd made it clear that they were very glad to see each other and the sooner they got into bed, the better all round. The Hawker hotel was certainly an option, she told him solemnly. But she usually knew a lot of people there. It could be awkward.

"There's always the great outdoors," she said. "A blanket under the stars. A campfire. Wine. Marshmallows on sticks. Or if we can't wait that long, a blanket under the sun. No campfire, because there's a fire ban anyway. No wine either, because I'm driving. And I don't like marshmallows."

"Me neither. Let's skip the marshmallows. And the campfire. I'm just about ready to skip the blanket."

"We'll need the blanket," she said. She leaned in and whispered in his ear.

"You're right," he said. "We'll need the blanket. Could we go and get that blanket now?"

That had been the plan. Come back to Errigal, give Ig the film merchandise, pick up some picnic things, a bundle of blankets and go for a drive together. She'd even decided where she was going to take him. A secluded, shady spot by the creek about twenty minutes' drive away, which only the Gillespies and a few other people in the area knew about.

After the recent storm, there might even be a trickle of water flowing. Either way, it would be private. She was finding it hard to keep her hands off him, even in the kitchen. As soon as she knew for sure where Ig was, they could go.

She found Lindy in the office, watching YouTube videos about sewing techniques. No, she hadn't seen Ig for ages either, she said. "I think Matt's gorgeous, by the way," she whispered. "So sexy. I love the accent too."

Matt was standing right behind Genevieve. "Thanks," he said.

Lindy went red.

Matt joined the search. They tried the buildings outside again. The pottery shed. The woolshed. There was no sign of Ig, but they caught a glimpse of what he and Angela were working on. A mural. It wasn't finished yet. There was just the whitewashed background and outlines of several different birds so far, with a big gum tree in the center, half-painted.

They checked the cubby. The car shed. No Ig, but both cars were there. That was a good sign, at least, she told Matt. "It means he can't have gone far."

"Someone might have taken him?"

"No, he might have driven himself."

"But he's just a kid."

"An outback kid. Matt, I'm sorry, but I'm really worried now."

By six o'clock, there was still no sign of him. Genevieve had radioed around to the neighboring stations. They'd called the Hawker police station. It was only staffed part-time. Today wasn't one of those times. They'd keep looking on their own.

On her third search of the buildings, Genevieve found Angela leaning against the fence. She looked pale. Worried.

"Angela? Are you okay?"

"I'm just trying to think where he might have gone. Where he might be."

"We'll find him; don't worry."

"Wherever he is, he'd be sticking close to the tracks," Angela said. "He's scared of snakes, remember. Terrified."

Genevieve went still. There was no way New Angela would know that. "How do you know?"

"He always has been, since he was a little kid. We were outside once, and one went past, near the fence. A King Brown. I shot it in time. It didn't come anywhere near him, he was never in any danger, but he was so terrified. Screaming. He cried for hours afterward."

Genevieve wanted to call out to Lindy to come and hear this. She wanted to keep Angela talking. This was important. This was a definite memory. A real memory. Angela hadn't seen any snakes since her accident. She hadn't been near a gun. But Genevieve wasn't sure Angela had even noticed what she'd said.

"I'm going to go and look in all the buildings again," Angela said. "Just in case he's fallen asleep or is hiding somewhere."

Genevieve watched her go. She wasn't imagining it. Angela wasn't reacting like a guest. She was beginning to react like a mother.

She and Matt met in the yard, after searching in different directions.

"Genevieve, I'm sorry to say this, but could someone have taken him? Someone driving past—"

"You've seen too many films."

"I have. But should you contact the police again, in case—"

He didn't have to say it. In case Ig was now hundreds of kilometers from here.

She called the police in Port Augusta. And in Port Pirie. Just in case.

By eight p.m. they were all still looking. They met in the kitchen to swap notes. Celia was still convinced they'd find him nearby. "Of course no one's taken him. We would have heard a car."

"How? You and Angela were watching TV. Lindy was on the computer. Matt and I were at Swing Hill." Genevieve spoke her thoughts aloud. "Think, Genevieve, *think*. Where would he go?"

Lindy came in. She'd just driven out to the Pugilist Hill lookout and had also followed the nearest creek for as long as she could. Nothing, she reported. There was no water running either. One less thing to worry about.

"What about Swing Hill?" she asked. "Has anyone looked up there?"

"We'd just been there when I noticed him missing," Genevieve said. "We would have passed each other if he was going there."

Outside, a car arrived. Then a 4WD. Their neighbors. Kevin Lawson. Fred Lawson. Word was spreading. An hour later, Joan, Victoria and Nick arrived from Adelaide. Genevieve rapidly filled them in. Nick joined the search right away. Victoria stayed inside by the UHF radio, while Joan helped search the station buildings again, all of them hoping fresh eyes might find fresh clues. They checked inside every room in the homestead again too, in case he happened to be hiding. Nothing.

More neighbors arrived, more 4WDs. The house was filling with people. Outside the UHF radios were crackling with information being exchanged.

"Can you stay close to Angela?" Genevieve whispered to Joan. "There are too many people around. They'll start asking her questions, thinking she's the old Angela. It could confuse her."

She was too late. Angela was already outside, talking to some of the station hands. They weren't asking her any questions. All anyone was doing was talking about Ig. They were starting to fear the worst. That Ig had wandered along a creek bed, fallen, was lying injured somewhere. Or worse. That a car or a truck had passed by without any of them noticing, and he was now far away.

Nick had taken over the search organization. Those with 4WDs were going to drive along the farthermost tracks that ran out into the middle of the saltbush-covered paddocks. Joan and Celia had taken over the kitchen. The kettle was on constant boil. They produced plate after plate of sandwiches, even scones. Victoria was staying by the radio. Angela and Lindy had joined in the 4WD search crews.

The sun went down, after a spectacular sunset. It was as sudden as always, a sunlit sky one minute, ten minutes later, darkness.

It was Matt who saw it. While the Gillespies were busy

searching elsewhere and getting updates from their neighbors, he'd walked out to the fence farthest from the homestead. He noticed a light flashing in the direction of where he had been with Genevieve earlier that day. A faint light, but it was flashing at regular intervals.

Genevieve was in the kitchen with Victoria, talking on the UHF radio. He interrupted her. "I think I saw something."

She came outside with him. He was right. It was a signal of some kind. She shouted out to her father and then she started running, Nick behind her, Matt closely following, across the paddocks, all of them stumbling on the track in the dark.

Genevieve started calling as they drew closer. "Ig? Is that you? Ig!"

He was on top of Swing Hill, curled tight in the middle swing, trembling. Trembling so hard the swing was shaking. He was crying his eyes out.

It took all three of them to get him off the swing. He'd been there for so many hours his muscles had stiffened. The shock and the night air had made it worse. Nick carried him down the hill. Genevieve ran ahead, shouting, "We've found him. We've found him. He's okay."

Angela was first to the back door. The neighbors wouldn't have noticed anything strange in her behavior. Only the Gillespies could see the difference. She had taken charge.

She ran a bath, filling it with lukewarm water. They lowered him into it. He was still trembling. He hadn't spoken yet.

"Do you need the Flying Doctor?" Joan asked. "I can radio. They'd be here in an hour."

"I think he'll be fine," Angela said.

As Ig sat in the warm water, the worst of the trembling stopped. Angela kept talking to him, her voice soft. Genevieve stood at the door, ready to help. Lindy and Victoria were in the kitchen, serving sandwiches and tea to all the people who had helped in the search. One by one, their neighbors started to leave. Genevieve saw Fred talk to Victoria. A whispered conversation. A brief, close embrace. Before long, it was only the Gillepsies, Joan, Celia and Matt left.

Genevieve joined the others in the kitchen. "Dad, I'm sorry. What a welcome home."

"It's fine. I'm fine. The main thing is Ig's all right." He gestured toward the bathroom. "What's happened? Has she remembered? She's different. Is her memory coming back?"

"Something's happening," Genevieve said. "There have been flashes over the last couple of days. This is the longest. We don't know if she realizes it, though. She hasn't said anything and we don't want to pressure her, just in case."

"But the way she's been tonight . . . Does she know Ig's her son?"

"I don't know. But she's not letting anyone else in there to look after him."

Soon after, they heard her calling for Nick. She had coaxed Ig out of the bath, dried him and dressed him in pajamas. Joan had prepared his bed with his favorite blanket. He'd started to walk and then begun to tremble again.

"Can you carry him?" Angela asked Nick.

Ig looked up. "Hi again, Dad."

"Hi, little mate," Nick said. He picked him up in one easy motion. "Gave us a bit of a scare there."

"Sorry," Ig said. He was shivering again. "But I . . . I was up there and I saw—",

"Tomorrow, matey. Tell us tomorrow."

Nick carried Ig into his bedroom. Angela tucked him into his bed.

"Snug as a bug?" she said.

Ig smiled. Nick kissed him good night. Angela stayed with him until he fell asleep.

Afterward, in the kitchen, they heard the whole story. Angela had gathered it in bits and pieces from Ig as she bathed him.

"He wanted to go up to Swing Hill with you, Genevieve. He wanted to show Matt the eagles. They'd been around this morning. He followed you, but then he saw you both—" She hesitated.

"Kissing," Genevieve said.

Angela nodded. "And he got shy. So he hid until he saw you coming back. Then he decided to go up there anyway. He had the camera. He wanted to take some photos of the eagles for me, as well as for Matt. He was standing there when he saw it. A King Brown."

Genevieve explained to Matt. It was one of the most poisonous snakes in Australia. It could grow to six feet long, two inches thick. It could swallow a rabbit whole.

Angela continued. "He ran over to the swings and jumped up into the middle one. He said he curled up as small as he could so it wouldn't get him. It disappeared, but he thought he'd seen it go under the base of the swings. That it was waiting for him to get down. Then it started getting dark. He didn't know if it was still there. He was there for hours, terrified—" She faltered.

"And no one checked up there again, did they?" Genevieve said. "Because I kept telling everyone Matt and I had been there."

"But then Ig remembered the camera," Angela continued. "He kept turning the flash on and off. That's what you saw, Matt."

Genevieve squeezed his hand.

Nick seemed to notice him then for the first time. "Sorry. Who are you?"

"Matt," he said. "Matt from New York."

"Genevieve's boyfriend?"

"Dad!" Genevieve said.

"Yes," Matt said. "Her boyfriend."

Soon after, Angela made another of her abrupt departures, announcing she was going to bed. She left the room. Joan was staying the night. She'd had a long enough drive that day already. Lindy made up the last spare room for her. It was too late for Matt to go anywhere. They made up a bed for him in the living room.

"I can sleep there," Victoria whispered to Genevieve. "You and Matt can have my double—"

Nick heard. "Not under my roof."

"Dad, please. I'm thirty-two years old. I'm an independent adult."

"Not here, you're not. No offense, Matt."

"None taken, Nick," Matt said.

One by one, they all went to bed until only Victoria, Matt and Genevieve were up.

While Matt went out to his car to get his bag, Genevieve had her first opportunity to talk privately to Victoria, to hug her. She just wanted to sleep, Victoria told her. Sleep and cry.

"Please, Genevieve, go to Matt. Don't worry about me now."

"I'll always worry about you. That's my job."

"Go and show him the stars. I bet he'd like to see them."

Genevieve and Matt were gone for a long time. There were a lot of stars out there to see. And the best way to see them was lying down. On a blanket.

FIFTY-FIVE

oan was first up the next morning. She always woke at five thirty. She was in the kitchen making a cup of tea when she heard someone behind her. It was Angela.

"Good morning."

"Good morning," Joan replied with a smile. "Have you checked on Ig?"

"He's fast asleep. No temperature. He'll be fine."

"Did you sleep?"

"Off and on."

"That was some night."

Angela nodded. "Joan, will you please come for a walk with me?"

"Later? Sure."

"Not later. Now. Just the two of us. Before everyone else wakes up."

Angela's tone was different, Joan noticed. "Of course," she said.

It was still dark. Joan borrowed a jacket from the coat-rack by the door. Angela was already fully dressed.

"Do you mind if we walk out to the old chapel?" Angela asked.

"That'd be great," Joan said.

They took their mugs of tea with them. They had done this walk together often. Talked in the old chapel many times. As the years had passed, they'd shared all the ups and downs of parenting and married life. Joan had been grateful for Angela's advice many times too.

The sun started to appear as they were halfway there, a slow glow on the horizon. They were both quiet as they walked. The paddocks on either side of the track were covered in saltbush, the leaves turning from black to silver gray. They reached the chapel. The stone looked dark orange in the dawn light. A windmill two paddocks away was creaking. There was a flock of galahs somewhere near, their squawks coarse in the quiet of the morning.

It wasn't until they were sitting on the last remaining pew that Angela spoke.

"I know who I am, Joan."

Joan was cautious. "You do?"

"I'm Angela. Angela Gillespie, aren't I?"

"Yes," Joan said.

"Nick's wife. Mother to four children."

Another nod.

"What happened to me? My mind feels all—"

Joan waited.

"Strange. Confused. I was awake all night. I couldn't seem to work out what was real and what wasn't. Now I think I know. But I'm not completely sure. I need you to tell me."

"Angela, I don't know if it should be me. It might be better if you hear it from your family. Or your doctor."

"Please, Joan. I need to know everything you know."

Joan told her. All that had happened since the night of the accident. The operation. The coma. The loss of memory. The diagnosis of confabulation. Angela's stay on Errigal as a guest, not as herself. Angela listened but didn't say anything.

Joan finally came to an end. "Do you remember any of that?"

"It's all jumbled. I know I had an accident, an operation, but I don't remember any of it. I remember some of the time in the hospital. I know I've been here on Errigal, but it's felt so different. That I was doing everything differently."

"When did you start to realize?"

"It's been coming slowly. In flashes, off and on. It's been very confusing."

There was another silence; then Angela turned to Joan again. "What happened between me and Nick?"

"What do you mean?"

"Something went wrong, didn't it? I know he's my husband. I know I love him and he loves me, but something is wrong and I can't remember everything about it. Did we have a fight?"

"A bit of one."

"What about?"

Joan shifted in her seat. "Angela, it's not my business."

"Please, Joan. I only have pieces of it in my head. I know you're my oldest friend. I need you to tell me everything."

By the time they came back to the homestead more than an hour later, there was still no one else up. Joan decided it was time for her to go home.

"Thank you," Angela said. "For everything."

"I'll be thinking of you. All of you. I'm only ever a phone call away."

"I know that."

They hugged each other tightly.

Angela went into the office. She sat down at the chair. This all felt more familiar too. The view from the window. The desk. The filing cabinet beside it. She had a sudden memory of a folder of letters in there. The folder that was now under her bed in the guestroom. She'd read the Christmas letters several times. She was uncertain of Celia's reasons for giving them to her, but they had helped. They'd been like signposts through the fog of her memory, snapshots of her family life over the past three decades. Even through her memory confusion, she'd had questions about them. Surely things couldn't have been that good, all the time. Surely they must have had some fights over the years. The letters read as if the Gillespies were some kind of cross between the Waltons and the von Trapps. But she was grateful she'd read them. Even if she didn't quite remember writing them all yet.

She turned on the computer. It felt like a long time since she'd done that. Joan had said they'd all treated her as a special guest in the homestead over the past weeks. She could remember reading, sleeping, watching films, listening to music, walking, taking photos. . . . Feeling good. Peaceful.

She automatically typed the words that would open her e-mail account. She was asked for her password. Once again, her fingers seemed to find the right letters and numbers. "Errigal" and her year of birth. Too obvious, probably. She was glad of it now.

Forty-five new e-mails were waiting for her, dating back weeks. The earliest were from people thanking her for the most recent Christmas letter. *That's what I call honest!! Bring it on!!* The letter they were writing about hadn't been in the folder Celia had given her.

Angela found it in her Sent folder. She didn't remember e-mailing it out. Halfway through reading it, she had to stop. How could she have sent this? Her most personal, private thoughts.

Another memory flash. She hadn't sent it. Nick had. The night of Ig's accident. While she was at the hospital with Ig. It had caused trouble between them.

She looked through her in-box again. The e-mails about the Christmas letter had stopped in early January. After she'd had her accident. Other e-mails had come in after that. Several junk ones. Inquiries about their station stay program, from America, Germany, Scotland. Memories of that came rippling into her mind.

There was another e-mail. From Nick. The date on it

meant something to her. She frowned. It was the day she'd gone to see the specialist in Adelaide. Why had Nick e-mailed her?

She clicked on it and started to read.

Dear Angela

I'm sorry about this morning. About so many things. That I'm not the husband you want me to be. That things have gone so bad between us. I'm sorry I'm not coming with you while you have those tests. I know how scared you are, but I didn't even say good-bye to you properly today.

Everything you wrote in that Christmas letter is true. I should have talked to you about everything and I'm sorry I didn't. I'm sorry this is so late, but I'm going to try to tell you now.

I had to make that deal with the mining com-pany, Angela. I had no choice. I owed so much money. Nearly a million dollars. It's hard even to write the amount. It felt impossible to say it out loud to you. Year after year it kept building. I couldn't see any way out. All I could think about was how much I had let you down. Not just you, my parents, my grandpar-ents. What kind of inheritance I'd be leaving the kids. When the mining company made the offer, it felt like a lifeline. I took it.

I was able to pay off the debt, but I still couldn't sleep, couldn't think straight. I felt like I was drowning in my own thoughts, in worry. Until I eventually went to the doctor, and he told me what I think I knew myself. It was depression. I have depression. I've been seeing him about it for months now. Seeing a psychologist too. I should have told you. But I couldn't talk about it. It was hard enough admitting it to myself, let alone telling you. I was too ashamed. Embarrassed. I thought it was better to say nothing at all than to even try to explain.

When I read your Christmas letter, all I felt was more guilt. There it was in your own words. How unhappy you were. How you wanted to change your life. I knew it was my fault. I was jealous too. Of someone you had known years ago. Someone you still thought about. I couldn't talk to you about him either. I didn't want to hear what you might say.

You said in your letter that you wanted things to be different. I feel the same way. I have for a long time. That was something else I

wanted to talk to you about while we were in
Ireland together. I was going to suggest we
change everything. Change our lives. Leave
Errigal. You, me, Ig. The girls too if they're
still living with us. A fresh start. A city,
so that Ig can have a chance to go to a bigger
school, but still have us nearby. I thought
about Perth. Melbourne. Then Adelaide. I always thought it would be good to live near
the sea. I even looked at seaside houses for
rent in Adelaide. Do you remember those great
holidays we had down there when the girls
were little? And again after Ig came along?

I didn't know if it would be possible financially. Until the night of the party, when
Kevin Lawson approached me. Said he wished I'd
come to him before I'd accepted the offer from
the mining company. I always knew their station was in better shape than ours, that
they'd come through the drought better. They've
got big expansion plans, he told me. He and
his son Fred. They want to try new ways of
station management, methods Fred learned in
Canada. Try new breeds. They're looking for a
new property. He wanted to know if we were
interested in either selling the remainder of
Errigal or leasing it out on a long-term ba-
sis. He e-mailed some costings to me after the
party. If we were careful, the lease money

would be enough for us to live on each year. Enough to help us start again, somewhere else. Try a different kind of life together. I told him I needed to think about it.

What I really want to do is talk to you about it. About all of this. When you get back from Adelaide, when you've had a chance to read this, I want us to go away. Just the two of us, for a few days.

Because I still want to try to convince you to come overseas with me. Not just so we can talk about the Lawsons' offer. Not just because you've been a Gillespie for thirty-three years. Or because I want to brainwash you into thinking a family tree is the most exciting thing in the world. Or because I want you to see Ireland, or go back to London again.

I want you to come with me because my life is always better when you're around. Even if I don't always say it. But I'm saying it now and I mean it. I'm sorry for hurting you. I'll try harder to be the husband you want me to be, I promise. I love you, Angela Gillespie. And I always will.

Nick

She read it twice. She didn't cry. She just read it slowly, letting every sentence settle inside her.

Ten minutes later, she'd logged out of her e-mail account and was on a different Web site. She heard footsteps in the hall and turned, expecting it to be Ig.

It was Nick.

She was taken by surprise at the sudden thump of her heart.

"Good morning," he said.

"Good morning," she said.

"Did you sleep?" he asked.

"A little. You?"

"Not bad. I've just checked on Ig. Still fast asleep. I'm making coffee. Can I get you one?"

"That'd be lovely, thanks."

He brought it in several minutes later, placing it on the desk beside her. Outside, the sky was already a vivid blue. It was going to be a hot day.

"You're up early," he said.

"Just looking at something on the computer," she said. "Do you need to use it?"

"No, thanks," he said.

"I didn't ask you last night. How was your trip?"

"Full of surprises," he said. He glanced at the screen. "What are you looking at?"

"Real estate Web sites." She paused. "I'm trying to find houses to rent by the sea in Adelaide."

A moment passed, then he put down his cup. "You read my e-mail?"

"Just now," she said. "For the first time."

He was staring at her as if she were an apparition. "Are you—? Is it—?"

She stood up. She smiled at him. A big, beautiful smile. "It's me, Nick," she said. "I'm back."

Ig could hear voices in the office. It sounded like his mum and dad talking. And talking. He stretched in the bed. He noticed his favorite blue blanket. Why was that in here in summer? Then he remembered. Yesterday. Last night. Swing Hill. The snake. Being scared. Being found. The bath. His mum. His dad. He stretched again.

"Robbie?" he said out loud.

Nothing.

"Robbie?"

Still nothing.

Robbie hadn't been there on Swing Hill either. If he had been, maybe Ig wouldn't have been so scared. Maybe the snake would have sensed there were two of them and gone away. Maybe it had gone away anyway. It was just that Ig hadn't seen it go.

He said Robbie's name once more. Still nothing. It didn't matter. It was always like this with Robbie. He came and went as it suited him. But he'd be back. Ig was pretty sure about that.

He did another stretch. His stomach rumbled. He was suddenly really hungry. He heard his mum and dad's voices again. They were definitely in the office. He'd go in there and see them.

As he got to the office door, he saw they were hugging.

Not talking anymore, just holding each other tight. Really tight. That was okay. Hugging he could handle. It was the other stuff he didn't like so much. The stuff Genevieve and Matt had been doing.

He stood at the door and gave a cough like he'd seen done in films.

They turned.

"Ig!" Angela said. She gave him a big smile. "You're awake! Come here."

She pulled him in close between them. He smiled. He'd always liked it when they did this, ever since he was a little kid. It was what he thought of as an Ig sandwich. His dad on one side of him, his mum on the other.

She looked down at him. Her eyes were all sparkly, as if they had tears or something in them. "How are you feeling?" she asked.

His dad was looking down at him too. He had those sparkly eyes as well.

Ig thought about it for a moment.

"Hungry," he said.

FIFTY-SIX

Yes, Ruth said, when Genevieve phoned her. She would most certainly like to see Angela. They made an appointment, in six days' time. The news was great, she said. Wonderful.

She told them what to expect. That Angela's "old" memory would keep coming back. That there would be overlaps of her memories from the past month too. That she might have lots of questions. They should answer what they could. She advised that there might still be occasional moments of confusion, but they didn't need to be concerned. It was part of the recovery process. All they needed to do was be patient with her. Of course, Genevieve said to Ruth. And yes, they were feeling very positive now too. It felt good to joke about it.

Over the next few days, there was almost a party atmosphere in the house. Joan visited every day. Even her husband,

Glenn, dropped over, bringing their kids and grandchildren. They were visiting from interstate.

Fred Lawson visited twice too. To check up on Ig, he said. But they could tell it was mostly to see Victoria.

Celia was now sleeping in the guestroom. Angela was back in her room with Nick.

"I hope you don't have a relapse," Genevieve said. "You'd get a hell of a fright waking up next to the man of the house."

They ignored her.

Matt had been able to stay for only one more day. They'd all liked him. Most important, he met with Victoria's approval.

She, Lindy and Ig watched from the kitchen window as he and Genevieve said farewell.

"Are they going for some kind of kissing record?" Lindy asked. "Ig, don't look."

Ig was glad not to.

"This is the real thing for Genevieve," Victoria said. "It's serious. He's the one."

Lindy raised an eyebrow. "Is that your super-ESP twin-sense at work again?" she said.

"No," Victoria said. "She told me this morning."

Genevieve had come into Victoria's bedroom for a long chat. Matt was outside talking to Nick. While Genevieve held her, Victoria had wept again. In public, in front of her family, she was managing to stay strong. Alone or with Genevieve, she allowed her real feelings to show. She was so sad. Heartbroken.

The night Ig was found on Swing Hill, she'd told Fred

about the miscarriage. They'd managed to find some quiet time together, after everyone had left.

"What did he say?" Genevieve asked.

"That he was really sorry," Victoria said.

"That's all?"

"It was all I needed him to say."

After that, Victoria asked Genevieve to change the subject, to talk to her about Matt, to please try to make her laugh, even a little. There'd never been anyone who could cheer her up better than Genevieve.

When Genevieve came in after Matt drove away, they all pretended they'd been doing anything except looking out the window.

"Don't even try," she said. "I could hear you all sniggering through the glass."

"We were swooning and sighing, not sniggering," Victoria said, smiling.

Genevieve looked around. "Where are Mum and Dad?"

"Where they always are now," Lindy said. "Over at the chapel."

"Again? If it hadn't been deconsecrated, I'd start to think they'd gone all religious on us."

Angela and Nick had been at the chapel most of the morning. After months of not being able to talk to each other, they now couldn't find enough time together.

Angela had already heard from Joan about everything that had happened since her accident. She needed to hear it all again from Nick. Not just the facts. She needed to know how he had felt.

He took it slowly. He told her how scared he had been the night of her accident. The bad days afterward. How hard it had been when she hadn't recognized him as her husband. His fear that she might never get better.

They talked about his e-mail. He told her more about the debt. His depression. About his visits to the doctor. About the psychologist.

When she asked him why he hadn't told her any of this before, while it was happening, when she might have been able to help him, he fell briefly silent.

"I was embarrassed."

"About what?"

"About feeling so weak. Lost. Everything I thought you wouldn't want in your husband."

"But you've always been everything I want in my husband. I thought you knew that."

"In your Christmas letter—"

"Nick, if I'd known anything about how you were feeling, I'd never have written that. I wouldn't have needed to. I would have understood. Like I understand now. I just needed you to tell me. To talk to me."

He took her hand. "I know that now. I'm sorry."

"Are you still seeing the psychologist?"

Yes, he told her. It was helping him. She was glad, she said. He asked her about the headaches. She had to think for a minute. She couldn't remember getting any. Not for ages. The doctor and the specialist had said they could have been stress related, she told him. And when the stress had gone from her life, it seemed so had the headaches.

She needed to say something else to him. About her Christmas letter.

"Nick, I should never have said I wanted a break from you all. Or that I wanted to press a pause button. Because it happened, didn't it?"

"You didn't make it happen, Angela. It was an accident."

"I know. But it made me realize something. I had it all wrong. I don't want to be a different person. What I want to do is stay being me, but do things differently." She tried to explain more. "I always thought I had to be in charge of everything, of everyone, the house, the family, my visitors. That if I didn't keep everyone organized, then everything would fall apart. But I was wrong about that too, wasn't I? You all got along fine without me being in charge."

"It wasn't fine. We didn't like it. None of us liked it."

"But you managed, didn't you? Everyone played a part and you got through it. The more I think about it, the more I remember enjoying it. It was fun. Relaxing. I feel like I got to know everyone in a different way. Maybe I needed to learn to step back now and again."

He smiled at her. "Maybe you didn't have to go to such drastic measures, though."

She smiled back, lifted his hand in hers and kissed it.

"I've been thinking about the Lawsons' offer," she said.

"So have I," he said.

They talked more about it. It was starting to feel exciting. There was a lot they'd have to do to make it happen.

Meet with the Lawsons, first and foremost. But it was definitely possible.

So much seemed possible now.

Four days later, Nick drove Angela to Adelaide for her appointment with Ruth.

Once again, Genevieve made the hotel booking. She chose the same hotel Angela had stayed in all those weeks earlier.

"If you can't remember it from the last time, Mum, it will be like the first time all over again."

"Genevieve, please," Nick said.

Angela just smiled.

She and Nick started talking even before they'd driven out of the Errigal gate. She had already heard a lot about his trip to Ireland. About what had happened with Carol. His visit to Angela's old street in Forest Hill, to the museum. Over the past few days, they had talked about much more too. Old and new memories. Their visit to the lookout in the Adelaide Hills before they were married. Was that why she had gone there the night of her accident? They'd never know for sure. Her memory of that night still hadn't returned. They talked about the tour of Errigal he'd taken her on recently. She remembered loving it. She remembered flashes of their conversation that day too.

Now, as they drove, Nick told her about meeting Will.

He shared every detail he could remember. The shambles of an office. The shambles of a flat. The soccer magazines. The bad jokes. The double alimony. Perhaps he exaggerated a little. Perhaps he made Will sound shorter than he was. Fatter. Balder. Sweatier. He also described a smell of cats in the basement flat that he didn't remember being there. But he did want to give her as much detail as he could.

"He was that awful? Really?"

He nodded. "Really."

"He could be a bit of a know-it-all, but I always thought he'd turn out better than that."

"So I gathered," Nick said.

She laughed and then abruptly, she stopped. "You did that. For me. Flew to London, tracked him down."

"Genevieve found him. I just did the legwork. I needed to see him for myself. Know what my competition was."

"And?"

"No competition."

"You're right." She reached across for his hand. "Thank you."

He gave her hand an answering squeeze. "Anytime."

It was a cheerful meeting with Ruth. She had invited several colleagues to meet Angela. A confabulation case was rare. Ruth ran a series of tests, saying she'd have the results in a week or so. But she believed there was nothing to be concerned about. It was clear to her that Angela was making a great recovery.

After they said good-bye to Ruth, they drove down to the sea. Not to look at possible houses. There was plenty of time for that. They wanted to sit on the beach for a while. Look out at the water together. Talk.

They had decided to accept the Lawsons' offer. They were going to leave Errigal and move to the city. But not immediately. There was something else they were going to do first.

"Are we too old for this kind of thing?" Angela said.

"Speak for yourself. I still feel thirty years old."

"I mean it, Nick. Are we mad to be thinking about changing everything? Upending our lives?"

"I think we'd be mad if we didn't."

They drove back into the city center and checked into their hotel. They'd asked for a double room. They were given a suite.

"Your children arranged it," the receptionist said. She read out the note Genevieve had dictated over the phone. "'Happy second honeymoon. Hope you don't mind, but we'll need to borrow the money from you to pay for it. Have fun! Love, Genevieve, Victoria, Lindy and Ig.'"

Angela still had incomplete memories of her time in Adelaide before and after the accident. Ruth had warned her there would always be blank spots. A memory of the view from this hotel had stayed with Angela, though. The suite they were given was even higher than the one she'd had before. The bed was as large. The linen was as crisp and white.

They were also alone. Not in their bedroom in the homestead, where there was always a good chance that someone would knock on the door at an inopportune moment.

They lay on the bed. Nick took her in his arms and smiled down at her, tucking a lock of her hair behind her ear.

"You've defied nature. Do you know that?" he said.

"I have? With my wonderful memory tricks?"

"There's that, yes. But not just that. You've gotten more beautiful the older you've got."

He leaned down and kissed her. She kissed him back,

holding him close. She knew every inch of this man. Knew the feel and the smell and the warmth and the kindness and the love of him. She had forgotten some of it for a while. But now she remembered everything about him.

Some time after, Angela's mobile phone rang. They ignored it. Nick's phone rang. They ignored that too. They also ignored the bedside phone when it rang. They had better things to be doing than answering phones.

Later, Angela lay in bed as Nick returned the calls. They had planned to go out to dinner. But it was so nice here in the suite. The room service menu sounded delicious. The view of the skyline outside was beautiful, the sun going down, the lights of the city starting to flicker on.

Yes, Angela's tests had all gone well, Nick was telling Genevieve. "Ruth's very pleased. But unfortunately we ran out of time. We need to stay down for another day of tests."

"Another two days of tests," Angela whispered to him.

"Another two days of tests," Nick said. "Maybe even three."

Angela couldn't hear what Genevieve was saying. But she could guess.

Nick hung up. "She said we are a pair of liars and we don't deserve to be their parents."

Angela smiled. "She's right," she said. "We don't."

He lay down beside her. "She also said we now have to do our best to forget all about them. She seemed to think that was very funny."

"It's a bit funny," Angela said.

They were facing each other. She gazed at him, at his

beautiful, handsome, familiar face, into his kind, dark eyes. She was about to speak when he beat her to it.

"Welcome back, Angela Gillespie," he said. "I missed you."

"I'm glad," she said, just before she kissed him. "Because I missed you too."

FIFTY-SEVEN

Four months later

The Gillespies were all gathering behind the woolshed. All except for Genevieve. She'd instructed Victoria to take dozens of photos of the grand unveiling and e-mail them to her in Canada immediately.

It was the beginning of July, a cold winter's day. There had been frost on the ground that morning. They were all dressed in warm clothes, boots, thick socks and coats, stamping their feet to keep the chill away, keen to get started.

Joan had done the catering again. Sausage rolls, as usual. Lindy had helped her ice two dozen cupcakes. The celebratory meal was set up in the kitchen. Celia wasn't there, but they would be drinking tea out of her very fine teacups and eating off her even finer crockery set. Six weeks earlier, Celia had sold her house in North Adelaide and moved into an upmarket elderly residential complex nearby. She should have done it years before, she'd told Nick. She now had lots of company around her. Lots of support if and when she needed it. Her enjoyable stay in the Hawker hospital after Christmas had put the idea into her head.

Lindy had helped her pack up and move. To everyone's surprise, she and Celia had grown close since they'd started working on Lindy's cushion business together. Lindy had started referring to her not as her great-aunt, but as her mentor. Celia had gone quite pink-cheeked when she heard that. She'd given Lindy the china as a "thank you for helping me move" gift.

Today's big event should have come sooner. But so much had kept getting in the way of the mural being finished. Ig had refused to work on it unless Angela was helping him. He also wouldn't let anyone else near it. Angela had been up and down to Adelaide for appointments often since she'd "come back." It was how they all referred to the return of her memories. Ruth had been up to the station too, staying overnight. She was almost a family friend now. She'd asked Angela if she could write up her case and submit it to medical journals. Angela was very happy for her to do so. She looked forward to reading it herself, she said.

"Lindy, come on!" Victoria called, rubbing her hands together to keep warm. "We're freezing out here."

Lindy poked her head out of the office window. "Hold on. Don't start without me."

"What's she doing in there?" Nick asked.

"Skyping Ireland, I guess," Victoria said. "Or e-mailing Ireland."

"She's in love with Ireland," Ig said.

It had been that way since Lindy had taken charge of organizing the Gillespie reunion. After returning from Ireland, Nick had sent a group e-mail to the international Gillespies. He'd chosen his words carefully, not mentioning Carol but explaining that there had been some discrepancies in the genealogy information he'd received from Ireland. That the information he'd sent them about the Gillespie homelands might not be accurate. No one cared. They all still wanted to go to Ireland. They liked the idea of staying in Cobh. Nick didn't need to organize a whole week of touring Gillespie homelands, they said. They could do that for themselves. But wouldn't it be fun to all meet up in Cobh even for a couple of nights together?

Lindy had come into the office one morning to find her father looking through the latest e-mail from Fintan in the Cobh hotel, asking about the reunion plans. She'd finished another Gillespie cushion—her tenth—and wanted to know whether there was any point in doing more.

She'd asked what he was doing. He showed her all of Fintan's e-mails. In his latest one Fintan had attached information about the heritage walks in the town, as well as a list of museums, restaurants and craft shops.

"That looks like fun. Let me e-mail him back for you," she said. So she had. Fintan had e-mailed her back. They'd spoken on the phone. Then started Skyping. Nick and the others were now lucky if they managed to get onto the computer at all.

Lindy had also started playing a lot of Irish music around the house. Not folk songs. Fintan and his girlfriend played part-time in a band. An indie one, not a traditional one. It also turned out his parents owned the waterfront hotel. He was only working there until he'd earned enough money to give their band a go full-time, he'd told Lindy. Luckily, there was always work in the hotel, especially in the summer, when Cobh was jammed with tourists. She should think about coming over sometime, he said. Not just to help organize the Gillespie reunion. His parents would definitely give her work. She wouldn't even need a visa, with her mother being English. She could apply for a UK passport. Fintan was full of good ideas, it seemed. They'd all heard a lot about them.

Closer to home, there was still no sign of mining machinery moving onto Errigal. The Gillespies had, however, finalized their lease arrangement with the Lawsons. It would begin in the new year. Nick had also met with the mining company's lawyers regarding the caretaker clause he'd signed. He would stay on until the end of December. The role would then be taken over by Fred Lawson.

Fred had big plans for new breeding programs on Errigal. While he was setting those up, he could easily manage the caretaking role on the acres leased to the mining company. It would also make sense for him to live on-site. The Errigal homestead was large. There was plenty of room for him to live there. And, as Genevieve said, Fred would be spending so much time on Errigal visiting Victoria, he may as well move in permanently.

Victoria was continuing to work part-time at the radio station, but she'd also taken on a new role. She wasn't just helping Angela with her station stay business. She'd virtually taken it over. She'd already updated the Web site, with

Ig's help. She'd hosted four different couples, from the US, Germany, Sweden and Italy. She'd also announced ideas to expand it over the next year or two. She and Fred were going to do up the shearers' quarters, turn them into what they were calling "boutique rustic accommodation." She had ideas to expand their tours too, to include more information about the birdlife, the geology, the Aboriginal history. Offer gourmet dinners each night. Fred seemed to be closely involved in all her ideas.

Nick hadn't been happy about the two of them living together without being married. Angela had talked him around. It was clear to everyone that it was serious between Victoria and Fred. And just as clear that they would get married one day. But not yet. When it suited them.

And as Victoria said, it meant there would still be a Gillespie on Errigal.

"One of us has to stay living up here, or Joan will pine," she said.

Joan wasn't going anywhere, she'd told Angela. "Glenn says he'll only be carried off here. I feel the same. But rent a house with a big spare room, won't you? And put my name on the door."

Everyone now knew about their plans to leave Errigal after Christmas. With the help of the Lawsons' lease money, Nick, Angela and Ig were going to rent a house in Adelaide as close to the sea as they could afford. Nick was thinking about studying again. A history degree, he hoped. Angela had looked into photography courses. They'd also had early discussions with a school in Adelaide known for its excellence in computer education. It ran a scholarship program for children showing exceptional IT ability. Ig had already been assessed and invited to apply.

They would be applying. But not yet.

They were having an adventure first. Nick, Angela and Ig. They were hiring a camper van and taking off on a three-month trip around Australia, leaving in early January. They'd already cleared the time off school with Ig's teachers. They didn't have a set itinerary. They were going to make it up as they went along. See as much as they could. Ig couldn't wait. He'd already set up a Web site. He was going to write a weekly blog about their travels, so Joan, Celia and his sisters could see what they were doing. His mum was going to take the photos for it.

He didn't know yet whether Robbie would be coming with them. His friend still hadn't returned, but Ig was confident he would.

"Do you miss him?" Genevieve had asked when they'd been walking up to Swing Hill, a few days before she flew to Toronto to start working on Matt's new film.

"No," Ig said. "I think about him instead. That's nearly as good as having him here."

They were carrying a pot of paint with them. Genevieve had decided not to wait until she died to bequeath her swing to Ig. They were adding his name underneath hers on the middle one.

Matt hadn't set his film in South Australia or Western Australia. The Canadian government had given him much better tax exemptions and the landscape was just as empty. It wasn't a film about zombie rabbits. He'd been sworn to secrecy while he was doing the location scouting. It was a big-budget historical drama starring two Oscar-winning actors. The director was his Emmy Award–winning brother. There was a cast of dozens and a crew of hundreds, including five makeup artists and four hairdressers. Megan was one of the makeup artists. Genevieve was one of the hairdressers. It would have been difficult for her to get work in the USA, but Canada was a different story. Especially when she was being sponsored by a large film company whose production manager happened to be her boyfriend. Matt's brother had also forgiven her. Matt had told him he had no choice.

Lindy finally emerged from the office. They were right. She had been Skyping Ireland.

It was time for the grand unveiling. A green tarpaulin had been stretched across the wall of the shed. Ig stood on one side, Angela on the other. On the count of three, they pulled at the ropes. The tarpaulin fell down in a heap.

"Ta-da!" Ig said.

The mural was revealed in all its bird and gum-tree glory. Ig had done all the drawings. Angela had helped him color them in. There was an almost-recognizable blue wren. A not very recognizable galah, kookaburra and cockatoo. An odd-shaped emu and a wedge-tailed eagle with oversized wings that looked more like a pterodactyl. Everyone still showered Ig with praise. They already knew he was better on the computer than he was at drawing birds. In the right-hand corner, so small they nearly missed it, was a robin. Underneath it, Ig and Angela had signed their names.

It's FANTASTIC! Genevieve e-mailed back when Victoria sent her the photos. *But tell Ig from me—he still REALLY needs a haircut.*

EPILOGUE

It was December first.

Nick was in the office on Errigal. He typed the last sentence and then called out to his son. "Ready when you are, Ig."

It was now less than five weeks until they left on their big trip around Australia. He and Angela were going to start packing soon. Ig had finished weeks before. His bag was already by the front door.

They would all be packing again in eight months' time. For their trip to Ireland for the Gillespie reunion. Two weeks earlier, they'd been given a surprise. While Nick was in Adelaide visiting Celia in her new home, she'd presented him with a check. A big check. Enough to cover their travel costs to Ireland. More than that. Enough for Nick, Angela and Ig to go traveling for a month or two afterward. To London. To France. To Italy. Wherever they decided to go together.

"I can't take this," Nick had said. "You've already been generous enough to Lindy."

"You can take it and you will," Celia had said. "You've always been kind to me, Nick. You and your family. I want you to have it."

As Nick waited for Ig and Angela to join him in the office, he keyed in the final address. His e-mail would be going to the two hundred Gillespies attending the reunion. It was the draft plan for their three-day gathering, with a link to the Cobh hotel's Web site. It was the last e-mail Nick would be sending them. Lindy would be the contact person from now on. It made sense. She was there on the ground in Cobh, after all.

She'd flown to Ireland in late July, her ticket paid for by Celia. Her cushion material had followed by ship. They still heard from her nearly every day. She was having the time of her life, she said. Fintan, his family, his girlfriend and their friends were so great, so welcoming, so creative. She'd already fallen in love twice. Irishmen were gorgeous, she said. She'd found her calling in hotel work, it seemed. She did a bit of everything, waitressing, cleaning, bartending, reception. No two days were the same. She was in regular contact with Celia as well. Before she left, she'd helped Celia buy an iPad. They played online Scrabble with each other every day. Lindy often Skyped her for business advice too.

Ig came into the office. Angela was with him. She stayed at the door.

Nick turned and smiled at her. "You sure you don't want to take over? You know what date it is?"

"I'm staying right back here," Angela said. She'd already announced several weeks earlier that she wouldn't be sending any more Christmas letters.

Ig cut and pasted the link to the Cobh hotel, tested it and declared the e-mail ready to go.

"What do you want to put in the subject line?" he asked his dad. "'Plans for the reunion'?"

"I was thinking of something different," Nick said. He told them what it was. "If you don't mind my borrowing it?" he asked Angela.

"It's all yours," she said with a smile.

Nick keyed it into the subject line. *Hello from the Gillespies.*

"Ready?" he asked Ig.

"Ready," Ig said.

They pressed the send button together.

ACKNOWLEDGMENTS

My warmest thanks to the many people who helped my research for *Hello from the Gillespies*:

Keryn Hilder and Henry Hilder for all the detail about station life in the Flinders Ranges.

My brother Paul McInerney for his on-the-ground tour guiding and research help, and my research assistant and niece, Ruby Clements, and my mother, Mary McInerney, for accompanying me on my research trip.

Dublin-based neurologist Siobhan Hutchinson for the information about confabulation and brain injury and for reading my early chapters, and Dr. Deirdre Coyle in Dublin for answering my many other medical research questions.

Louise Ní Chríodáin for background on radio stations, and also the team at LM FM in Drogheda, County Louth:

Gerry Kelly, Louise Ferriter, Deirdre Hurley, Brian Curran and Aaron McNicholas.

Noreen Murphy and Catherine O'Connor for their insights into life as a twin. Tom Walsh and Deirdre Mac Giolla Rí for their insights into being the parents of twins-plus-one.

Robyn Bramich in Latrobe, Tasmania; Deborah Costello in Dublin; and once again, Keryn Hilder, for their hairdresser tales.

My brother Rob McInerney for the loan of his imaginary friend from childhood.

Rachel Crawford for sharing details of being an Australian in New York.

Hello from the Gillespies is a work of fiction. Any errors of fact are mine, and not the fault of any of the people above, who helped me so generously.

For their help in all sorts of other ways, thank you to Austin O'Neill, Sinéad Moriarty, Noëlle Harrison, Murray Sheehan, Sarah Duffy, Clare Forster, Susan Owens, Margie and Mark Arnold of Meg's Bookshop in Port Pirie, John Neville, Stephanie Dickenson, Maria Dickenson, Sarah Conroy, Brona Looby, Sabine Brasseler, Karen O'Connor, Bart Meldau, Frances Brennan, Ashley Miller, Frances Whaley, Kristin Gill, James Williams and Justin Tabari.

My three publishers: Everyone at Penguin Australia, especially Ali Watts, Arwen Summers, Saskia Adams, Gabrielle Coyne, Ben Ball, Peter Blake, Lou Ryan, Sally Bateman, Chantelle Sturt and Greg Cormack. At Penguin UK: Maxine Hitchcock, Clare Bowron, Lydia Good, Katie Sheldrake and Joe Yule. At Penguin US/New American Library: Kara

Welsh, Craig Burke, Ellen Edwards, Daniel Walsh and
Diana Kirkland.

My agents: Fiona Inglis of Curtis Brown Australia, Jonathan Lloyd of Curtis Brown UK and Gráinne Fox at Fletcher &
Co. in New York.

My two families: the McInerneys in Australia and the
Drislanes in Ireland and Germany.

And, as always, my love and thanks to my husband,
John, and my sister Maura for everything they do to help
me write each novel.

Photo by Ashley Miller

International bestselling writer **Monica McInerney** is the award-winning author of ten previous novels, one short-story collection, and numerous stories and articles. She grew up in Australia, one of seven children, and has split her time between Australia and Ireland for more than twenty years. Monica and her Irish husband currently live in Dublin, Ireland.

CONNECT ONLINE

monicamcinerney.com
facebook.com/monicamcinerneyauthor

Learn more about Monica McInerney
and
enjoy a behind-the-scenes peek
at the inspiration for

HELLO FROM THE GILLESPIES

in the
Readers Guide,
including
A Conversation with Monica McInerney
and
Questions for Discussion,
available at
monicamcinerney.com and penguin.com.